HERO'S MIND

Hero Academy Series Book 2

P.E. PADILLA

Cover by Joolz & Jarling

❀ Created with Vellum

PARTIAL MAP OF DIZHELIM

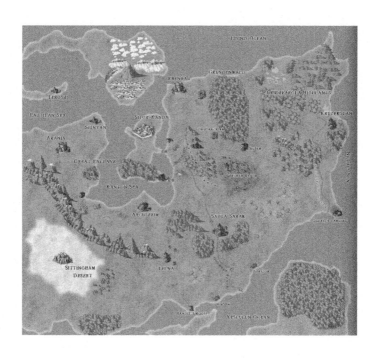

"It is true that one can be trained physically to perform the actions required of a hero, but it is the mind, one's ability to reason, to learn, to decide that truly transforms one from a simple warrior into something quite heroic."

Vulmer Liadin, first headmaster at the Academy at Sitor-Kanda, Year 28 AOD.

PROLOGUE

"Tell me a story," the girl said to her brother.

"What?" he said. "I told you one yesterday, *Lilianor*." She hated it when he used her full first name.

She ignored the jibe. "I know, but I want another one. With excitement and danger." She spun around, swinging her arm as if it held a sword. "Oh, tell me about Zejo Troufal, the Hunter of Rogue Wizards. He's your favorite anyway."

That was true. He loved stories of Zejo. The man wasn't just *a* hero, he was the boy's hero, idolized since the first story he had heard of him.

He guessed his sister wasn't all that bad. She was younger than him, by nearly three years, but they did enjoy doing things together. Not many twelve-year-old boys felt that way, he knew, but maybe his sister was just better than other boys' sisters.

"Hmm," he said. "I might know a few stories. Do I have any that I haven't told you already?"

She looked at him like he was simple. "How would I know

that? Maybe you should tell me all of them and then I can answer you."

The boy smiled. She had him there. She was quick. For a girl, and a young one at that.

"How about the Power Twins of Drachvorden?"

"I've heard it, but that's fine. I love that one."

"Okay. That one it is. Let me see, how does it start...?"

She rolled her eyes at him. "The city of Drachvorden happened to have visitors one day, less than two years after the War of Magic ended. They weren't just any visitors, though..." She made a rolling motion with her hand and smirked at him.

"Right, right. So, they weren't just any visitors. No, it was Gamore Nabavian and Xadorn Deleer, also called the Power Twins. They weren't really twins at all, but two rogue wizards who traveled together, taking what they wanted and using their magic to destroy any who tried to stop them.

"Of course, at that time, right after the War ended, there were still some who had magic left, though not nearly as strong as before the War used it all up. Some used their abilities for good, to help rebuild what had been destroyed in the War or to search for ways to bring back the magic that was fast leaving the world.

"Others, though, decided they were better than other people, that their magic gave them the right to do whatever they wanted. The rogue wizards were a problem because normal people couldn't fight them. Or wouldn't, anyway.

"Then there was Zejo Troufal, the greatest hero ever to live. He was a boy at the end of the War, too young to have been called up to service. As the War was ending, a group of soldiers who had deserted their army attacked the village in which Zejo lived. He fought, devising ingenious ways to trap or kill the attackers. When he was done, the attackers were defeated and the village was saved, but Zejo's parents had been killed.

"With nothing left for him, the young man, only seventeen at the time, began to travel. The world was large and he had nothing holding him back, so he decided to explore everywhere his feet could take him. The only problem was that everywhere he went, there seemed to be trouble.

"He carried a pair of curved swords his father, a blacksmith, had made him from the blades of some old scythes. Before his village was attacked, Zejo Troufal used them to harvest wheat, and he had come to be very skilled with them. Only those two swords, a waterskin, and a small pack went with him when he left his home village to explore the greater world.

"It seemed that each time he stopped at a town or village, there was trouble from former soldiers or, even worse, from a rogue wizard. So it was that in only the fourth village he stopped at, he met a problem that would increase his reputation drastically.

"The Power Twins.

"Zejo had heard of them, of course. The two had been wizards in the War of Magic and had been luckier than most when it ended. They kept their sanity, and some of their power. Enough that they could do as they liked unopposed, for the most part.

"They were not really twins at all, as I said. In fact, they weren't related and didn't even resemble each other. Gamore had hair the color of straw. Xadorn had dark brown hair and was nearly half a foot taller than his companion. Rumor had it that the name started as a joke, one that cost the teller his life. The twins adopted it to spite any who would laugh at them.

"Xadorn was a fire wizard and Gamore specialized in ice

spells. After a time, they became lazy and hired a group of minions to do most of their dirty work, reserving their own time and energies for the most difficult opponents. Bored with staying in one place, they traveled, sometimes passing through a village peacefully and at other times burning it to the ground.

"The small village of Drachvorden seemed to be heading toward the second type. It had been a fair-sized city during the War, but much of it had been destroyed and most of its citizens had been killed or had fled years before. It was a shadow of what it had been.

"Zejo had himself been going from place to place, helping wherever he could. He was only one town over when he heard about the twins, that they had just arrived at Drachvorden and were causing trouble.

"He decided to do something about it.

"The first thing the hero did was to visit the area around Drachvorden when it was dark. He had always paid close attention to tales of any rogue wizard, and he had come to understand their personalities better than most. He knew the twins would be confident in their power and that, though they had thugs and soldiers working for them, they wouldn't put out sentries.

"He was right and was able to sneak to the edge of the village without being seen. There, he watched and listened. Most of the men were with the twins in a tavern, but others had scattered around, visiting brothels or occupying themselves in other ways. They had done terrible things in the town, including murder, rape, and torture for no other reason than for entertainment. Zejo learned some other things that would be helpful, and then he returned to his room in the neighboring town to rest.

"The next evening, the hero went back to Drachvorden, but this time his mission was different. He started with the twins' minions who weren't in the tavern. Wherever he found them—terrorizing citizens, assaulting townswomen, taking the brothel's services by force—he stopped the men. Most he killed, but some he left unconscious and in the care of those they had been accosting. Those Zejo killed probably had an evening less painful than the others.

"Finally, he was ready. Making sure there were no innocents around, Zejo Troufal lit several bales of hay on fire in the center of the main street, just outside the tavern. He threw a rock half as big as his hand through the tavern window to get attention.

"The laughter and shouts in the tavern quieted and Zejo imagined those inside trying to figure out what had happened. He didn't leave them wondering long.

"'The twins are truly siblings,' he shouted. 'No two people so ugly could be anything but true brothers.'

"It seemed a silly thing to say, but Zejo knew the pride of wizards. He wasn't surprised when men rushed through the tavern doors, drawing swords and readying other weapons, no doubt with orders from the twins to kill whoever they found.

"The street was empty except for the burning hay, Zejo nowhere in sight. The twins' men began to search for him, but before they went more than a few steps, the flame in the bales reached the pockets of dirty, grease-covered straw Zejo had created. Billows of black smoke poured from the fires, blanketing the area around the tavern.

"'Find who did this,' Gamore said. 'A gold piece for their heads.' The men rushed to search for the culprit.

"Zejo went into action. He cut through the men, some literally. Others he was able to knock out or incapacitate in other ways. Soon, only a few of them were left. Those, and the twins themselves.

"'Leave this town,' he shouted from his hiding place. 'Leave now and you will continue to live.'

"Of course, the twins only laughed. The smoke was

clearing and there was no way for the firestarter to hide any longer.

"Or so the twins thought.

"Zejo had put on the clothes of one of the men that seemed to be a leader among the twins' minions. As the few remaining men returned to the twins, he did so also, keeping to where the smoke was thickest. When he got close enough to Xadorn, he stumbled and acted as if he would fall. He let his momentum carry him into a somersault, adjusting the swords he had hidden behind his back out of the way as he had practiced often. He rolled gracefully to his feet, slashed into Xadorn with both of his curved swords, and then rolled back into the smoke.

"Xadorn Deleer dropped to the ground, already dead. Gamore looked at his companion in surprise and stepped toward him to see what was wrong. As he did, he brought up his hands, already beginning to cast a spell. A curved sword came around from behind and slashed his throat.

"The rest of the men were stopped within minutes. Altogether, there were fourteen dead, including the twins. That left seven left alive and in the custody of the town. For their crimes, they were all hanged the next day.

"Word spread of the defeat of the Power Twins, and the town of Drachvorden erected a monument to Zejo Troufal. From there, his legend only grew."

"Yay!" the girl said.

The boy bent at the waist into a sweeping bow. "It's too bad people get old and slow. Zejo was still pretty young when he beat the twins. It got harder later on because he didn't have magic, and as he got older he wasn't able to do the things he did when he was young."

"That's not true," Lilianor said. "He was always a hero, even when he got old. Sure, he couldn't move as fast or fight as well, but that didn't matter because he used his greatest weapon—his mind—and he beat all the bad guys by outthinking them. A hero doesn't make excuses for not having powers. He uses the skills he has and continues to protect and save people."

The boy thought about it, and about the stories he knew of his idol. "Huh. I guess you're right. For him, it was how smart he was and how he always prepared for what might happen to him. Some of the stories are when he's really, really old. Like forty, or a hundred."

She nodded emphatically. "You remember that. Don't ever forget that a hero is a hero as long as he—or she—uses whatever skill or ability they have to protect even one person. Don't you forget that, Erent Caahs."

Aeden Tannoch had never fought with anyone like Master Yxna Hagenai, the Master of the School of Edged Weapons at vaunted Sitor-Kanda, commonly called the Hero Academy. Nor had he ever crossed his swords with the weapon she used. It was a completely new experience for him.

Yxna was an older woman. At least, so he had been told. Her long hair—plaited into a braid that reached the bottom of her back—was totally grey. The problem was that her face was devoid of all wrinkles, and though she didn't smile often, she was strikingly pretty. Aeden would have put her in her mid-twenties with that smooth skin and lovely, pouting lips. Her piercing hazel eyes only added to the allure, the light brown with green lightning flashing through them giving off a sense of crackling power.

But Aeden wasn't there to stare into those eyes or to wonder at her age. He was there to fight.

And fought he did. As much good as it did him.

He fought with his normal swords. In some places in Dizhelim, they would be called cutlasses, though he didn't really think that fit. In a few places, like Shinyan, they would be called broadswords—the name he used for them. They were slightly curved, with a wider blade than most swords people carried in the parts of Dizhelim he'd been to, and were single edged. He'd had them made especially for him when he was still traveling with his adopted Gypta family. They were part of his body.

He had been told by several people he could do things with the weapons that defied belief, that he was the most skilled fighter they had ever seen.

All that, and the grey-haired woman with a single straight, double-edged sword made of flexible steel ran him up and down the training yard, never allowing him to strike her. To be fair, she had not struck him yet, either, but then again, he didn't think she was trying that hard.

The woman was simply amazing.

Aeden charged again, interweaving his swords to strike at his opponent from many different angles, striking out time after time in a flurry that he knew was nearly impossible to see because of its speed.

Yxna's sword somehow parried them all. She barely moved more than an inch or two at a time, mainly angling the blade, and somehow his weapons clanged off hers. It was all he could do to keep his own swords from straying too far from the centerline and making him vulnerable to a counter-attack. Which she rarely did anyway.

They danced across the training field as he tried to break through her guard, or to confuse her with feints, or to over-whelm her with speed. None of it worked.

Then she began to flow. There was no other word for it. The movements were so graceful, they almost brought tears to his eyes. She twisted and spun, her sword slashing one moment and then darting out to bite at him with a straight thrust the next. In an eyeblink, she had gone from defense to offense, not allowing him the slightest chance to strike back.

Still, her face was calm, her breathing nearly soundless. Even that braid seemed to obey her unconscious demands, only moving the slightest bit.

It was breathtaking.

Her sword came out of nowhere, somehow slipping through his guard. At the last moment, she turned her blade. And slapped him on his cheek so hard it made his eyes water.

She had frozen, standing in what he could only call a soft stance, weight distributed perfectly on her feet, lightly placed on the training ground, right foot forward, knee slightly bent, back leg almost straight. The sword in her right hand still quivered where it had slapped his cheek.

Aeden blinked. Twice.

He crossed his swords in front of his chest and bowed to her. "Master Yxna," he said.

A small smile graced her lips and all he could do was stare. Who *was* this woman? *What* was this woman?

She snapped to attention, left hand wrapped around her right, which still held her sword, and made a slight bow. "You are very skilled. Thank you for obliging me."

"I…" he said. "No. Thank you. I've never seen—or felt—anything like that." He rubbed his cheek as he said it. There had to be a welt there in the shape of the sword. It stung too badly for it to be otherwise.

"Yes," she said. "Sorry about that. Bad habit. Often students will argue about a strike if you touch them softly. I have learned to touch…less softly."

"She's right about that," Marla Shrike said, bringing cups of water and handing one first to Master Yxna and then to Aeden. "I've had welts that…oh. Ouch. Maybe I've never had one that bad."

"Marla," the master said.

Marla ducked her head as if the master had slapped the top of it. Aeden got the feeling that she had. On numerous occasions.

"Oh, okay. I've had some bad ones, but that's why I'm your best student." She smiled widely, showing all of her teeth. The beautiful redhead somehow transformed herself into a jester at that moment, and Aeden stifled a laugh.

Master Yxna gave Aeden's sister another smile. This one looked to him like the one his mother used to give him, the one that said, *You are a silly child, but I still love you.*

"I'm being truthful, though, Aeden," the master said. "Your skill is remarkable. I can't remember the last time I was pressed so sorely. Are all in your clan as skilled as you?"

Aeden looked into his cup. "I'm the last of my clan, aside from a childhood friend I just discovered was alive. The animaru killed them. But before, I was accounted a fair hand with my weapons. My father was a great warrior, as skilled as any. I only wanted to be like him." He suddenly wanted to be somewhere else.

"I have heard that Sartan Tannoch was a masterful warrior. A little wild when he was younger, but always a man of honor and skill."

Aeden's head snapped up. "You knew my father?"

Master Yxna shook her head. "I did not have that privilege, but I have spoken with those who had witnessed his skill or who had fought him. Ah, I misspeak. Not those who had fought against him personally, but against the clan. I have been assured that if they had fought him, they would not have been there to tell the tale. I hear he had the clan magic as well."

"Aye. All warriors of the clan do." Aeden held his arms up and showed her the tattoos on his wrists marking his completion of the trial of combat and the trial of magic.

"I see," she said. "Why didn't you use your magic against me?"

"I would never," he said. "You asked me to spar with you so you could gauge my skills. It would not be honorable to bring in magic."

"Yet, when fighting for real, you would use these abilities."

"In fighting the animaru, I would, yes. I would not use them against another human, unless that person attacked me in a dishonorable way or with magic or trickery."

"Ah," the master said. "I see that you share your father's sense of honor, or at least his rules to govern the code he lived by. Others, perhaps, do not share your viewpoint, however. Some might use magic as an unfair advantage though their opponent did not." She swung her expressionless face slowly to Marla, then back to Aeden.

Marla blushed furiously.

Master Yxna's lips curved ever so slightly upward.

"But matters of honor and actions fitting or unbefitting warriors makes a long and tempestuous discussion. There is something to be said for using every ability to your advantage, especially when the safety of the entire world rests in your hands. It may be something to think on further."

"I can see your point, Master," Aeden said. "The world is a lot more complex now than I ever thought it would be. Thank you for your guidance."

Master Yxna bowed her head slightly. "Marla tells me you rise before dawn every day and train, without fail. Even injured, on your way back from defeating Izhrod Benzal, you insisted on slowly performing some of your exercises each day."

Heat traveled up Aeden's neck to his cheeks. It was probably just the welt her sword had put there. "Aye. I have worked too hard to develop my combat fitness. I'd not like to lose it when it will be so important in the near future."

"Aeden Tannoch, you would make a wonderful student. I admire your work ethic, and it has obviously paid off. You are the hardest working person I have met since..." She tapped her index finger on her lips, tilting her head and looking skyward. "Oh, since my beautiful Marla here. I tease her, but she is very nearly an ideal student."

"Very nearly," Marla said spitefully.

"Yes, very nearly. If only she could repair that dysfunctional attitude, she would be a dream come true."

Marla broke out in a laugh and Master Yxna chuckled with her.

"Perhaps you will teach her a thing or two, as her long-lost brother," the master said.

"I'll surely try," Aeden said, "but I think her head is as hard as highland rock. Just like her brother."

Master Yxna sighed exaggeratedly. "Well, one can only expect so much. Come, some of the masters wanted to speak with you, Aeden, and Marla as well. I will accompany you, if that is acceptable."

"Of course," he said. He not only liked the master and was in awe of her skills, but he enjoyed watching her interaction with Marla. It was obvious the two of them had a special relationship, almost like mother and daughter, though Master Yxna's appearance made it hard to accept an age gap that wide. He was happy his sister had such relationships and was happy. It made him feel good. "I really appreciate your help, Master Yxna. Maybe we can spar again and you can help me improve."

"It would be my honor and privilege, Aeden. It surely would."

eden Tannoch, Marla Shrike, and Master Yxna
Hagenai strolled to the administration area of the
Academy, which was a fifteen-minute walk from the
mundane combat training ground. It was surreal to Aeden
how beautiful the place was. Huge trees, manicured but wild
at the same time. Paths of flagstones or simple gravel passed
through verdant lawns and around shrubs and flowering
plants.

A pair of deer grazing on one section of the grass lifted
their heads and watched the trio pass with interest. They
held no fear in their eyes at all.

Marla noticed her brother looking at the animals. "There's
no hunting on the Academy grounds. The animals have come
to rely on not being molested in any way as long as they're
within the outer walls."

"That's remarkable," Aeden said. "I imagine many come
here specifically so they're not targets of hunters."

"Not so much," Master Hagenai said. "The areas
surrounding the Academy are vast, and then there's the
Verlisaru Forest to the south. With so much land to roam,

even if hunters do stalk some of them, it isn't a big concern. There are predators, of course, but they are allowed to roam freely and act according to their nature within the confines of the Academy also. With plenty of game, they keep clear of people but not of their prey."

"I see," he said. "You allow nature to make its way without too much interference from humans."

"Exactly," Marla said. "A great deal of magic is balance and cooperating with the way the world works. When people try to go against the natural way of things, that's when balances get upset and bad things happen."

"Bad things like the War of Magic?" he asked.

"Yes, precisely like that."

It was interesting, and Aeden was glad to hear it. For the most part, his clan had respected the natural order, preferring to work with it rather than to try to force it to their will. He had been afraid that the magical activities at the Academy would be a classic war against what was natural and right.

"You will learn all about it, if you decide to allow the Academy to teach you," Master Yxna said.

Aeden watched the deer move off at a slow walk to taste vegetation farther away from them. "Hmmm." He still wasn't sure what he'd do. Here he was, walking along on a peaceful path, chatting with a sister he had never known he had and one of the masters of the famed Hero Academy, yet the world drew closer to plunging into everlasting darkness.

"What's on your mind?" Marla asked him.

"What? Oh, I was just thinking. Everything seems to have slowed down, nearly stopped. I mean, granted, we needed some time to heal after dealing with Benzal and you dealing with Quentin, but..."

Master Yxna stopped and her companions stopped with her. She turned to face Aeden. "But you're concerned about the state of things, that there are still animaru out there, that your job is not complete."

"Yes," he said. "There must be something else I should be doing."

"*We* should be doing," Marla stressed. "We."

Aeden smiled at her. "Yes, my dear sister. *We* should be doing. There are other enemies out there, maybe ones who can open portals like Benzal and bring more animaru here. We know that there are definitely more animaru out there, even if only the ones that were brought over before. And yet, here I stand, looking at these beautiful grounds, not doing anything about people who may be dying by tooth and claw and magic even as I speak."

"Peace, Aeden," Master Yxna said. "Let's meet with the masters, then we may be able to figure out a path to tread. Don't be too anxious. This defense of our world, it is not a short-term project. It may very well be years or even decades. A day or two to recover from your trials and perhaps learn things that may help you in the future should not be scorned."

He sighed. "I know you're right, but having missed being able to help my clan, my father and mother, by no more than half a day, I'm anxious to do what I can and as soon as I can."

The master patted his shoulder and began walking again. "I completely understand. Let's go and see what our meeting will tell us. The time for action may be closer than you think."

Marla led the other two to the meeting room outside of the headmaster's office. His clerk, Aletris Meslar, let them in immediately, giving Marla a little wave. "The headmaster is waiting for you," she said, motioning toward the closed door off to her right and shifting her eyes back to the stack of papers in front of her.

Aeden had been in meeting rooms before, but he had not

seen the headmaster's office or the large area outside of it. Paintings of distinguished-looking men and women adorned the walls in elegant frames, no doubt the headmaster's predecessors.

The largest of the pictures was just above the woman who had waved them toward the room. It was of a man, bald on top with only fringes of hair around the sides. As if to make up for his mostly bald pate, his grey hair was long and his white beard even longer, splaying out wildly as if he had been struck by lightning. The amber eyes seemed to drill into Aeden and he marveled at the skill of the painter. If the man's eyes were half that intense in real life, he must have been intimidating indeed.

Marla noticed Aeden studying the painting. "That's the Great Prophet himself, Tsosin Ruus. The founder of the Sitor-Kanda Academy."

"He looks...focused," Aeden said.

"He looks scary is what he looks," she replied. "When students come to the headmaster for discipline, they are made to sit in front of it to wait. Many of them break down before the headmaster even gets hold of them." She laughed.

"You didn't think it so funny the first time you experienced it," Master Yxna said, "if I recall correctly."

Marla shivered. "Like I said, scary."

They entered the room, which was larger than Aeden thought it would be. There were six people already seated at a table that was more than large enough for the three newcomers and several others besides.

"Ah," the headmaster said. "Aeden, Marla. Come in. Please sit down. We can start immediately. Good morning, Yxna." The Master of Edged Weapons nodded in greeting.

Aeden took a seat between Master Yxna and Marla, eyes on the headmaster. He had met with Master Qydus Okvius before, but his appearance still put Aeden ill at ease. His sharply pointed head and ears, long thin face, and the white beard and mustache that seemed only to stretch out his features more gave him an appearance of which Aeden had never seen the like—as if he weren't entirely human, but partly bird of prey. The way he scowled didn't help. It was not a stretch of the imagination to believe the man woke up in the morning with that stern look on his face.

"Good morning, Headmaster," Aeden said. "Masters."

Marla smiled widely at Master Qydus, apparently unbothered by his glaring. She had told Aeden not to worry about how he looked. He rarely showed emotions, she said, and his stern visage didn't reflect his feelings.

"I would like to introduce everyone first, if I may," the headmaster said. "Pardon me if it is not necessary in one instance or another, but I feel it is only right. My fellow masters, you know Marla Shrike, a longtime student of this Academy. This young man is her long-lost twin brother, Aeden of Clan Tannoch, of the Croagh aet Brech in the Cridheargla highlands."

Aeden bowed his head to the other masters, and most of them returned the gesture.

"Master Yxna Hagenai, Master of the School of Edged Weapons, needs no introduction to any here, I believe, as you have acquainted yourself with Aeden already." His gaze seemed to linger on Aeden's cheek, but then he continued. "To my left is Master Isegrith Palus, Master of the School of General Magic."

Aeden nodded to the master. He had met her already as well, and she wore the same robes as the last time he made her acquaintance. She was a handsome woman, grey streaking through her long hair. Her robes were mostly green, fringed in white fur, her cloak held at her neck with a golden brooch in the form of some type of creature, perhaps a dragon. She sat straight with chin raised, every bit the distinguished master Aeden had always imagined teaching at the Academy. Her curt nod was a marvel of efficacy, adequate yet sparing in its energy.

"Next to her, may I introduce Master Saelihn Valdove, Master of Life Magic. She is especially interested in your reports of the power of life magic when combatting the animaru."

Master Saelihn was moon-pale with long, silvery-white hair. Some kind of tiara or diadem on her forehead gave her an exotic look, though her beautiful oval face and high cheekbones would not look out of place in any kingdom Aeden had been to. Aeden's eyes locked on her own, the most peculiarly light blue he'd ever seen. Only the movement of her arm to wave, the sleeve of her blouse trailing gossamer silk, let him blink and look away. He bowed his head to her as well, an inadequate gesture for such a majestic creature.

"Master Marn Tiscomb, the Master of the School of Prophecy, is beside her," the headmaster said.

Aeden had met this man before. He was bald as well, dark hair on the sides of his head, and he had a wispy beard and mustache. His bland face looked to Aeden as if it were melting, and his deep-seated, too-small dark eyes peered out above dark circles that suggested the man didn't get enough rest.

The Croagh nodded politely to Master Marn as well, though he had to focus on not showing his distaste. The master had scolded Aeden for coming to the Academy the first time and told him in no uncertain terms that not only was he not the Malatirsay, but that he would call the Academy guards if Aeden ever showed his face on campus again. The master didn't greet Aeden in any way, only stared at him blankly.

"And finally, Master Goren Adnan, Master of the School of Military Strategy."

Master Adnan looked as a seasoned general should. He had a mane of white hair and a beard that was reasonably under control, all of it surrounding a face that had small scars in several places, and one large scar traveling from the top of his right eyebrow, down the bridge of his nose, and to his left cheek. The slash that caused that scar could have cost the man one or both of his eyes, but instead, it gave the rugged face a look like chipped stone; indestructible and unyielding.

Aeden bowed his head even more deeply for Master Goren than for the others and the master snapped his right fist to his chest in salute and smiled. Aeden liked him immediately, even if he was a little in awe of a man who actually taught an entire Academy full of warriors in ways to conduct battles. He would definitely be talking to the master whenever he could arrange it.

"So, now we are all acquainted," the headmaster said. "Let us get on with why I have asked you here." He turned to face Aeden and Marla directly. "I have discussed the things you have told me with these masters and a few others. We have also taken the liberty of discussing matters with Evon Desconse, the *assector pruma*, First Student, of the School of Prophecy. It was he, I believe, who first discovered our misunderstanding of the Song all these years."

Master Marn fidgeted in his seat, his eyes darting from the headmaster, to Aeden, to his own hands, which he was wringing on the table.

"It is our corrected understanding that the Malatirsay, the one for whom we have been waiting for these last three thousand years, is indeed not one, but two. Further, it is the belief of those present, as well as a few other masters who could not attend this meeting, that you, Marla, and you, Aeden, are in fact those two. It is the consensus of these masters that you, together, are the Malatirsay, long-awaited heroes who will lead us to defeat the animaru threat to our world."

Aeden found his breath being sucked away. It wasn't news to him, not after Marla and Evon had explained everything, but it was still a shock to hear it from the leader of the Hero Academy himself.

"As such, we pledge to grant you any aid we can provide to the end of performing the necessary tasks to prevent the darkness from engulfing Dizhelim. We are speaking with the other masters individually, to apprise them of the facts and of our conclusion. We cannot make a formal announcement at this time, not until we have discussed it with all forty-nine of the masters. We hope you understand."

The room went silent, all the masters looking toward him. Why weren't they looking at Marla? Was he supposed to say something?

No one spoke for nearly a minute. Aeden felt beads of sweat along his back, dampening his shirt. Why wasn't anyone saying anything? They were all just looking at him.

"Uh," he finally got out. "Thank you?"

Master Qydus's eyes crinkled and Aeden thought he spotted a smile under all that beard.

"Who is to determine what aid and what tasks are necessary?" Master Marn asked. For a master, Aeden would have thought he'd be able to control the sneer on his face a little better. Then he remembered that the man had become a master only recently because of the previous master being murdered.

"Who?" the headmaster asked. "Well, Aeden and Marla, of course."

"We would pledge our service and our resources to these two...children, allowing them essentially anything they want?"

Any trace of humor left Master Qydus's face and voice. "You would argue otherwise? You, the Master of Prophecy? The one, of all the Academy, who should champion and hold dear the Bhavisyaganant, the Song of Prophecy, the definitive document foretelling the dark times and the need for the Malatirsay to save the world?"

"I...that is...they are young?" The way he said it sounded to Aeden like it was a question.

"They are. They are also the heroes we have been promised for three millennia. Is Marla not far and above the finest student the Academy now has, possibly has ever had? These *young* people have already done more in the cause against the darkness than any in this room has done in a lifetime. They are the chosen of prophecy. If there is doubt in any discussion, it will be my recommendation to act on what these two suggest. Or do you not believe that the Song grants power to its chosen?"

"It's not that," Master Marn said. "I was simply making an observation."

"Perhaps we will speak about your observations at a later time. We will not do so now." The headmaster let out a short breath and then addressed Aeden again. "Aeden, your sister is already a student here, but you are from the outside. I have assured you of our pledge of service. Let me now give you another assurance, one I am capable of making within my authority as headmaster. As of this time, you are considered accepted to the Academy at Sitor-Kanda as a student. Please avail yourself of any training, information, or other aid we would provide to any other student. I know there are several masters already who would like to speak with you, both to give information and to accept it." He tilted his head toward Master Saelihn and winked at her. She rolled her eyes slightly and smiled.

"I thank you, Master Qydus, and all of the masters. I look forward to learning from each of you. And thank you for your pledge of support. The animaru invading our world are no joke. If we can't control them, I'm afraid they will destroy all life on Dizhelim."

"As was prophesied," Master Qydus said. "We will adjourn and speak with you individually. Do not hesitate to come to me or any of the masters here if you need something. If you wouldn't mind, Master Saelihn would like to speak with you about using life magic against the animaru, and Master Goren would like to question you on the capabilities of our foes so he can begin to prepare plans for what will no doubt be a major military encounter."

"It will be my pleasure, but I would suggest that my friend Khrazhti be included in the discussion with Master Goren. She led animaru troops for almost three thousand years and was the dark god S'ru's high priestess before she realized that he meant to destroy all life here and she changed sides to join us."

"It's true, then?" Master Goren said. "You truly have one of them, a commander no less?"

"It is. She's half human, but we can discuss that later. The important thing is that she is our ally and she has lived a long time, learning and fighting and gaining experience. We would be stupid not to consider what she says."

"I agree wholeheartedly," Master Qydus said. "Besides which, she is a delightful person. Any who cause her problems"—he glared even harder at Master Marn—"will be spoken to very harshly, or possibly something more."

Aeden kept his composure, but he was smiling on the inside. The headmaster's support of Khrazhti would go a long way in making her feel welcome. She was already self-conscious enough about her heritage. The master's statement would help smooth things out.

"Thank you, Master Qydus," Aeden said.

"Very well. You may stay in here and speak with the masters if you'd like, or you can choose another location. I will leave it to you, unless you would like me to remain."

Aeden traded a glance with Marla. She gave him a small nod.

"Here is fine. We would welcome your involvement if you are interested, but I understand if you're too busy."

The headmaster looked into Aeden's eyes, and this time there was no doubt about a smile. "My boy, you are the reason this Academy and all of us exist. There is no other task more important. I would like to know as much as I can. I will remain."

Master Marn was the first one out the door, almost seeming to flee. Marla looked after him and shook her head. The other masters were studiously neutral in their expressions. Master Isegrith also left, apologizing that she had a class to teach, but the rest remained.

"Marla, do not forget that we must also schedule a meeting to discuss your transgressions during the investigation of Master Aeid's murder. Your actions, and your punishment. I would think tomorrow at fourth bell would be an ideal time."

"Yes, Master Qydus."

Master Qydus asked his assistant to have food brought in, and Marla seemed only too happy to leave to fetch Khrazhti. It seemed they were going to be there for a while, but at least they were finally working toward something. It wasn't as much action as Aeden had desired, but it was a start.

✵ 3 ✵

Marla jogged to the rooms where Aeden's friends were housed. It was a student dormitory that had not been used for some time, at least not for students. Occasionally, visitors were allowed to use the space as if it were an inn, but essentially, those who traveled with Aeden now had the entire thing to themselves, including a dining room that they were using like a common room. She had no doubt she would find Khrazhti there, along with everyone else in her new circle of friends.

She pushed through the entry and saw exactly what she had thought she would. The entire group of them, sitting on chairs near a blazing fire and drinking out of cups or mugs. It seemed to her like what a family gathering would be. She smiled, feeling a connection to these people she'd never experienced with so large a group before.

She hadn't known them for a long time, but they had faced danger together, bled together, and done something heroic and important. They were a kind of family, and not only by extension from her brother, who had been associated with them for a longer time.

Fahtin jumped to her feet and rushed to hug Marla. Marla wasn't sure if she'd ever get used to that, but she hoped she did. She tentatively wrapped her arms around the beautiful Gypta girl and patted her back before releasing her.

"Marla!" Fahtin said. "You're just in time. Tere was going to tell us a story."

"No, he wasn't," the archer said, white eyes glinting in the firelight. "They're trying to force me into it. Like always."

Lily Fisher tossed her red hair and rolled her eyes. "He'll tell the story. He just wants to complain about it first." Tere glared at her, but she only smiled more widely at him.

As expected, Evon was here as well. He always seemed to find a reason to be around the others, especially Fahtin. But then, why wouldn't he? She was delightful, likely the kindest and most caring person Marla had ever met, and of course she was breathtakingly gorgeous. Evon's feet didn't even touch the ground when he was around her.

Jia and Aila were off to the side, the dark-haired women chatting softly. They both waved at Marla as she neared the circle of tables where everyone was. Where was Raki...ah, there. She spotted him, sitting in plain sight near Tere, excitement on his face, no doubt for the story. Marla's eyes always skipped off the boy when she wasn't specifically searching for him. Uncanny. It reminded her that she needed to introduce him to the masters. It had to be magic, what he did—even though she couldn't sense it. What else could it be? People didn't just disappear like that naturally.

"Sorry," Marla said. "I can't stay. I only came to fetch Khrazhti. Aeden wants her to meet Master Goren. He's the Master of the School of Military Strategy, and he really wants to meet her."

Fahtin sat back down in the chair right next to Khrazhti. It still seemed unreal to Marla that the animaru woman had lived three thousand years. Her pale blue skin was as smooth as any teenager, and it was easy to see since the animaru didn't wear much in the way of clothing. The Academy student didn't blame her, though. If Marla had Khrazhti's sleek, toned body, as human-looking as any in the room—except the color, of course—she'd probably show off her physique as Khrazhti did.

The only thing besides her color—and maybe her abnormally tall stature—that really gave her lineage away was her large, glowing blue eyes. They had no pupils, so it was a shock at first, but Marla had found that Khrazhti was as expressive in her own way as anyone else, once you spent enough time with her. Her hair was strange, too, growing only on the very top her head and not coming anywhere near her long, pointed ears. It reminded Marla of old pictures of the astridae, a fae race that died out or left around the time of the War of Magic. Not because their hair was like that, but it just seemed sort of magical. She really couldn't explain it.

"He wants to meet with me?" Khrazhti asked. Her Ruthrin had improved even more since Marla had known her, though she still had a slight accent, a little like those from Arania. Aeden had told Marla that Khrazhti had learned the common tongue in just a few weeks. It was impressive.

"Yes. He's actually pretty excited. It's not often he gets to meet a military commander who had lived for thousands of years."

The blue woman smiled slightly, another thing she was doing more naturally just since Marla had met her. She got up from her chair, ready to leave.

"You wanna come?" Marla asked Evon. "Marn fled when Master Qydus slapped him down for being an idiot."

"Marla, please," Evon said. "He's a master."

"Yeah, well, he probably shouldn't be. Anyway, we might need someone in there who actually knows something about prophecy."

Evon's eyes darted from Marla to Fahtin—who was whispering something to Aila at the time and missed it completely —and then back to Marla. He pushed his fingers through his blond hair, making the curl he somehow kept in the front bounce. She could see in his eyes that he wanted to go to the meeting, but he also wanted to stay where Fahtin was. She chuckled.

He finally sighed and nodded.

The three waved goodbye to the others and headed out the door. There was no reason to hurry, so they walked at a normal pace toward the administration building.

"Master Qydus wants to meet at fourth bell tomorrow about my punishment. You know, for going to Fyrefall and all that."

"Oh," Evon said. "That means they'll deal with me next."

"Yeah, or he may tell you tonight to be there with me tomorrow."

He turned his head back toward where they had left the others. Marla thought he might bolt, but he only sighed again, apparently resigned that it would happen whether he ran or not.

"Any luck on the letters you found in Ren Kenata's robes?" he asked, changing the subject.

"Grrr. No. Damn thing is frustrating. I've tried every technique I know to figure out the key, or keys. I can't seem to do it. I've never had a code I couldn't break within a few days."

"I'm sure you'll get it."

Marla looked to Khrazhti, paying close attention to what they were saying, but not speaking herself. "Do the animaru use codes, Khrazhti?"

"Aeden explained it to me," she said. "We have no such thing in Aruzhelim, and no such word in our language. It is curious to me, this making a secret language. We do not work so hard to communicate with fear of being overheard."

"Consider yourself lucky, then," Marla said. "This is driving me to distraction. It's completely unintelligible. I can't figure it out."

Evon laughed. "It's good for you to struggle. Maybe it'll make you see how the rest of us feel when you learn everything so easily and we can't begin to comprehend it. It's like when we were studying Eutychus Naevius's work. Math and logic. Ugh. Why anyone would try to reduce a beautiful thing like magic to something as horrid as numbers, I don't know. Do you remember when you tried to explain Naevius's theorems to me and—"

"Oh, gods," Marla said.

"What? What's wrong?"

"I...you just...give me some paper. Quick, I know you brought some so you could take notes. Paper and a pen." She snapped her fingers in front of him.

Evon slung the satchel he typically carried everywhere from his shoulder and fished out a piece of paper and a pen.

Marla stepped up to a pole lantern lighting the path and dropped to the ground with legs crossed. She unstoppered the bottle of ink Evon handed her and began scribbling on the paper. "Yes, yes. If the series holds true, then it would shift like this..." she mumbled.

"Marla?"

She threw her hands up and whooped. "Evon, you are a genius. That's it. I've got it. Using Naevius's third theorem of alternating magical series and applying a standard two-character shift, I think I've got it. I'll have to go through each of the letters later, but I'm confident that's it. Someone from the Academy must have created this. Either that, or a scholar during the Age of Magic. Oh, I can't wait to translate those letters."

She shoved the pen and ink bottle back at Evon and folded her paper, placing it in her pocket, then she began strolling toward the administration area, whistling as she went. After a few steps, she turned and looked back at Khrazhti and Evon, both with mouths hanging open and staring.

"You coming?" Marla asked, then started whistling again. And walking.

They scrambled to catch up.

When they arrived, Marla opened the door for her two companions and then followed them in, closing the door behind her.

"Ah. Welcome, welcome," the headmaster said in that archaic Alaqotim that was apparently the same version of the language the animaru used. Whenever she heard the dialect of the language, Marla could pick out words that were almost like the Alaqotim she knew. She was usually able to get the gist of what was being said. "Please, sit. We would like to discuss with you some of your experience and expertise."

Khrazhti's eyes scanned the room. When they found Aeden, she smiled and immediately seemed to become more comfortable. Aeden smiled back, stood, and gestured toward the chair next to him, the one Marla had been sitting in earlier. The animaru sat down and addressed the headmaster in Ruthrin.

"Thank you, Master. I appreciate greatly that you are speaking my language, but we can use Ruthrin in case there is someone present who does not understand the pure—pardon me—my version of the Alaqotim language."

"Of course, my dear," he said. "Just let me say that I find it remarkable that you learned to speak our common tongue in so short a time."

She dipped her head to Master Qydus. "I seem to have a certain facility for languages. A fortunate trait, I believe."

"Master Qydus," Marla inserted into the pause. "I asked Evon to come with us. I hope that's all right."

"That's fine, and good thinking. Evon is well-versed in the Song and will likely be a valuable resource in our discussions. Welcome, Evon. Please sit where you'd like."

The headmaster quickly introduced Masters Goren and Saelihn, the former saluting Khrazhti and the latter staring wide-eyed at her, though with the smile she wore, it wasn't threatening. Khrazhti nodded to the masters, poised and confident. If Marla was in her place, an animaru facing a master of life magic, she would be as nervous as a new whore at an army camp.

Master Goren started off, his anticipation evident. Honestly, Marla hadn't ever seen the rock-solid man so...she couldn't think of the word. Jittery? Anxious? It was something she never thought she'd witness.

"Khrazhti, Aeden tells us that you are three thousand years old, and that for much of that time, you have been engaged in combat and leading forces that battled with other large forces."

"Yes, Master. That is correct."

"Please, please, call me Goren. As an experienced and respected military commander, it would make me uncomfortable for you to use a title. It would be like a general referring to a sergeant as "Sir.""

"Very well, M...ah, Goren. Thank you."

"I would like to know something of the forces you commanded, if you would share with me. If I ask something of you that you are not comfortable speaking about, just say so and that will be the end of it."

Khrazhti nodded. "I have nothing to hide. My honor requires me to help my friends, as does my desire. Any information I can provide to help protect this world I will contribute."

"Wonderful. Thank you. To start, how many animaru are there, how many are in Dizhelim, and what number of troops did you command?"

"There were originally three hundred fifty-two thousand one hundred twenty-seven animaru. That increased by one almost three thousand years ago when I became the first animaru ever born and not created. The last I knew, there were three thousand animaru in Dizhelim, but that was before Aeden destroyed some of them and before Izhrod Benzal opened a portal and brought more. I do not know if Quentin Duzen also transported animaru here from Aruzhelim. My rough guess is that there are between five and eight thousand animaru in this world at this time."

Master Goren's mouth dropped open and he stared into Khrazhti's glowing blue eyes. "Did you say there are over three hundred fifty *thousand* animaru?"

"That is correct, though I estimate that Aeden and his allies—including myself—have dispensed final destruction to several hundred of those, with others being transported back to Aruzhelim through the twinkling."

"I see. The...twinkling?"

"Yes. For a reason unknown to me, and to any animaru I have asked about it, some animaru do not simply go dormant when they are damaged severely. For most, devastating injury will cause them to drop to the ground as if destroyed, unless true destruction from life magic is involved. They regenerate, eventually coming back to full strength, the time required depending upon the damage.

"For those with the twinkling, however, when a certain damage threshold is achieved—even through life magic, which does not exist in our world—they disappear, as if they wink out of existence. They immediately appear at their home, though weakened. For those with this attribute, they will disappear from this world and appear back on Aruzhelim, so the total number of animaru will not change because of them."

"I didn't know about that. Thank you for explaining it."

"As for the forces under my command," she continued, "the numbers varied depending on directions from S'ru. At times, I commanded up to forty thousand troops. I was the supreme commander, in addition to being S'ru's high priestess, of all the animaru here in Dizhelim as well."

"Forty..." Master Goren swallowed. "Thousand."

"Yes. I had generals underneath me, of course. My chain of command was very detailed and effective. One cannot control that many troops by oneself, especially if you considered most of them were seren, and a good number of forgren were also included." Aeden chuckled at that and Khrazhti smiled, seemingly proud that she had made a joke.

"Uh," Aeden said, "you'd have to know what forgren are for it to be funny. Sorry."

Master Goren seemed to be trying desperately to regain his balance. Marla didn't blame him. He'd just found out that they might be waging war with an army larger than any five kingdoms could even hope to put together. Maybe any ten.

"The purpose of these animaru coming to our world is..." Master Goren said, though Marla was sure he already knew the answer.

"To destroy life and light and prepare the way for the god S'ru to make this world his own," Khrazhti said.

"Why then, have they not attacked any of the nations? With thousands of soldiers that cannot be killed by most methods, why do they wait?"

Khrazhti looked to Aeden, tilting her head as if confused. "They are focusing on the *Gneisprumay*."

"Wait," the headmaster said. "*Gneisprumay*? First enemies?"

"First *enemy*," Khrazhti corrected. "Or possibly most

important enemy. It is a title, the plural form indicating respect."

"What is this *Gneisprumay?*" Master Goren asked.

Khrazhti looked even more confused. "It is Aeden, of course. He was the one I was sent here to kill."

Master Saelihn raised a hand to get the others' attention. "Do you mean to tell us that there are thousands of animaru in our world right now, and their primary task is to kill Aeden Tannoch?"

"Yes. I thought that was made clear. I am sorry if I did not communicate that effectively."

Aeden examined his hands. He seemed to be trying his hardest to disappear.

"We're sorry, Khrazhti," the headmaster said. "You are blameless for our confusion. It's just something that we were ignorant of."

"I see. He is named clearly in S'ru's prophecy and the god himself commanded me to see first to his defeat."

"Prophecy?" Evon sat up straighter. He had managed to be invisible so far during the discussion, but the mention of a prophecy he hadn't heard of before would get him interested, of course.

Khrazhti turned to him. "Yes. It is the only prophecy the animaru have, given to us by S'ru five thousand years ago."

"But, but," Evon sputtered, "that predates the Song."

"It is not a song," Khrazhti said. "Animaru have no songs and no pretty writing. It is straightforward, just like speaking."

"Fascinating," Master Qydus said. "Can you tell us this prophecy? Is it written somewhere?"

"Written? I do not know. It may have been written, but I have no need of that. I memorized it more than two thousand years ago. As I said, it is not pretty speech, and it is not long."

"Can you repeat it for us?" Evon said, taking out his pen, paper, and ink.

"Of course, Evon. Would you like me to tell you in my language or translate it into Ruthrin?"

Evon was fumbling with his pen, his hand shaking so hard in excitement, Marla thought he might spill the ink all over himself. She reached over and took the ink bottle, removing the stopper and setting it on the table to keep him from doing so.

"For now, the translation would be great," the young blond-haired man said. "But if you can tell me the original later, I'd like to write that down, too. An animaru prophecy. I never would have thought it possible..."

Khrazhti watched Evon for a moment, allowing him time to get settled. When he looked up to her, pen in hand with ink in the tip and hovering over his paper, she nodded and recited it in simple speech.

"Here is the prophecy S'ru gave to the animaru:

AGES PASS, ISOLATION IN THE DARKNESS, CENTURY AFTER century
    In the end time, the door will open
    A world of light, but of plenty, open for conquest
    The fessani will unlock the portal, to their dismay
    Animaru shall flood forth, preparing the way
    The weak will succor, seeking favor of the dark
    And will be subjugated
    Darkness, unlife, all will be changed
    For the glory of S'ru
    The enemy will stand forth, Gneisprumay
    Wielding light, animaru will fall
    Destroy the Gneisprumay they must, or face eternal isolation

S'ru will empower them, to his own glory
As at the first, so will it be again
Balance for time unending
An earned reward"

EVON MADLY SCRIBBLED AS SHE SPOKE, HANGING ON EVERY word. Marla had no doubt he would be analyzing the entire thing as soon as he got back to his room.

After Khrazhti finished her recitation, the conversation was subdued. A few questions were asked about the prophecy, but Khrazhti told them the animaru didn't analyze it like the humans did. They simply accepted it as being what it sounded like and that was the end of it.

Master Saelihn questioned Khrazhti about the effect of life magic on the animaru, but that, too, was simple. It hurt them, and could destroy them. Since the animaru were un-alive, the only thing that could permanently harm them was life itself.

It all made Marla wonder why a Malatirsay was necessary to begin with. She—and Aeden—could use life magic, but so could many others. Master Saelihn herself wielded it more expertly than either of the twins. So what were she and Aeden for? Why the prophecy and all the secrets if nearly anyone with some magical talent could do as good a job? There had to be more. She hoped they figured out what sooner rather than later. All the unknowns were driving her crazy.

Master Qydus finally called an end to the meeting. "We appreciate you making yourself available, Khrazhti, but we will not take too much of your time. I'm sure we will request the privilege of speaking with you again, but for now, accept our thanks and carry on with your evening. Feel free to come and see me or any of these other masters if you have questions or concerns."

"Thank you, Master Qydus," she said. "I will do so."

As everyone rose to leave, the headmaster said, "Don't forget our meeting tomorrow, Marla. Evon, you might as well come with her so we can take care of both of you at the same time."

"Yes, Master Qydus," Marla and Evon said at the same time.

Conversation was at a minimum as Marla and Evon walked Khrazhti and Aeden back to the common room where the others no doubt were still chatting. Marla had Ren Kenata's letters on her mind and Evon was certainly thinking about the prophecy as he absently stroked his satchel. Aeden seemed distant, too.

Once they arrived at the dormitory, Marla bid Khrazhti and the others goodnight and hurried back to her room to start on her project. She wasn't going to sleep until she had deciphered all the letters and figured out what was going on. Maybe she'd finally get some answers.

4

The next morning, Marla got up early and headed over to meet the others for breakfast. She had only gotten a few hours of sleep because she was up so late with her decoding work, but she was too excited to be tired. It would hit her later, but that was fine. She had things to tell everyone.

Only Aeden and Fahtin were in the common room when Marla got there. Aeden had, no doubt, been up for hours and had already performed his daily exercises. Something was definitely wrong with the man. How could one not want to sleep at least until dawn?

"Good morning, Marla," Fahtin said, smiling as always.

"Morning," Aeden said after swallowing a gulp of milk.

"Good morning," Marla answered. "Where is everyone?"

"They'll be down in a few minutes," Fahtin said. "Master Qydus has assigned a few of the kitchen staff from the administration area to serve us food here. There's a small kitchen and they can make food fresh. It's like having our own inn."

Marla smiled at the woman. She found she did that a lot around Fahtin. How could one not?

As the Gypta had said, within a half hour, everyone was sitting around, eating bread and waiting for more food to arrive. Evon had shown up, too, which was no surprise. He was as much part of this family as Marla was.

"While we're all here," Marla said, "I wanted to tell everyone I succeeded in translating the letters I found in Ren Kenata's robes, thanks to Evon nudging me in the right direction last night."

"Anything interesting in them?" Tere asked.

"Actually, yes. I have them here. Do you want me to read them?"

Overwhelmingly, the others indicated that they did. Well, all except Urun. He sat quietly in the corner of the room, considering a piece of bread on the plate before him.

"Okay. They're short, not so much letters as notes, and they don't say much, but maybe some of it is valuable." She picked up the first and held it up so her voice would carry. "There are no dates on them, by the way, or any greetings or closings, so I'll just read them in the order they're stacked:

THE COUNCIL IS WAITING FOR THE REPORT ON YOUR MISSION. DO NOT DELAY IN SENDING IT THROUGH THE USUAL CHANNELS.

CONTINUE TO INTERACT WITH THE ACADEMY CHILDREN. WE MUST KNOW WHAT THEIR PLANS ARE SO WE CAN ACT ACCORDINGLY. DO NOT LET THEM DISCOVER YOU ARE OF THE COUNCIL.

TRY TO FIND INFORMATION FROM THE OTHERS ON ANYONE TAKING UP THE MANTLE OF THE MALATIRSAY, NO MATTER HOW RIDICULOUS THE CLAIM SEEMS. EVENTS ARE

PROGRESSING AS PER THE PROPHECY. WE MUST BE READY TO ACT.

FIND OUT EXACTLY HOW THE ACADEMY CHILDREN ARE BRINGING THE ANIMARU TO DIZHELIM. CAN WE USE THIS PROCESS TO OUR BENEFIT?

BE SURE TO NOTIFY US IMMEDIATELY IF THERE IS ANY MENTION OF THE COUNCIL OR OF THE DARK PROPHECY. THE TIME IS NOT RIGHT YET FOR US TO EMERGE FROM THE SHADOWS.

THERE HAS BEEN A CONCENTRATION OF STRANGE MAGICAL ENERGY DETECTED. OUR OPERATIVES ARE INVESTIGATING, BUT TRY TO OBTAIN INFORMATION FROM YOUR SUPPOSED ALLIES ABOUT ANYTHING THAT MIGHT BE CAUSING IT.

"AND THAT'S IT. THERE ARE A FEW THINGS IN THERE THAT pique my interest, but what do you think about them?"

"Dark Prophecy?" Evon said. Marla knew he would focus on that one. "Are they talking about the animaru prophecy?"

"I don't think so," Marla said. "From the other notes, it seems they're not completely familiar with the animaru. It seems they're talking about yet another prophecy. Have you ever heard the Dark Prophecy before, Evon? From the context, it's not just any dark prophecy but *the* dark prophecy."

"No."

"Too bad. Anything else?"

"What's this with the Academy children?" Aeden asked.

"I wondered about that, too," Marla said. "I'm thinking they were talking about Quentin and his group. It seems they didn't know Ren was working with someone else, this Council."

"It sounds to me," Tere said, "they're not on friendly terms with the ones who were bringing the animaru over. So, what does that mean? Are they on our side or are they against both us *and* the animaru? What's their angle, their goal?"

Marla tapped the paper with her finger. "Also excellent questions. I got the same sense of it as what you say, but I can't answer your questions. For now, I think we have to assume they're against us; otherwise they probably wouldn't be concerned about the Malatirsay."

"You could take that to mean they want to know when someone claims to be the Malatirsay so they can become allies," Aila said. "I'm not saying I take it that way, but it's a reasonable assumption."

Marla considered the woman's point. She read over the notes again silently. "Yes, you're right. It all depends on your viewpoint going in, I guess. Good observation."

Aeden raised a finger in the air. "*The time is not right to emerge from the shadows*, it said. What would make it the right time and why are they hiding in the shadows to begin with?"

"What about that magical energy thing," Fahtin asked. "Is that like what happened with Tere when he lost his ability to see the magical matrix? Where do you suppose they're investigating and what will they find?"

"All great points," Marla said. "We have a lot to think about, or to learn. Anything else anyone can pick out?"

No one spoke.

"Okay, then. I'll make note of those things and keep thinking about it. Maybe you can, too. Let me know if you come up with anything. Ren Kenata is out there somewhere, and he's no doubt back with his Council working on their plans. We need to find out what those are, and if they're in support of ours or against us. Then we need to act accordingly. I think things just got more complicated."

For the rest of breakfast, Marla engaged in innocuous chatting with the others, relaxing and enjoying the company. Too soon, it was time to go with Evon meet with the masters. Aeden and Fahtin wished them good luck. Marla hadn't told the others about it, only her brother and the Gypta woman. They'd find out eventually, but it was actually sort of embarrassing, so Marla kept quiet about it for the time being.

"Ready?" she said to Evon.

"No, but let's go anyway. Maybe you can try to get a few points in our favor by telling Master Qydus about the letters."

Marla chuckled. "Way ahead of you. I already wrote out copies to give him. Anything we can do to distract him from us breaking the rules is a good thing."

They walked slowly to the headmaster's office and arrived exactly on time.

"Go on in," Aletris said, her expression sympathetic. "He's expecting you."

Marla put on her best penitent expression and stepped into the headmaster's office. He looked up from the papers he had been reading and motioned for them to enter in and sit down in front of his desk.

"Close the door, if you please, Evon."

Marla's nerves hummed, the familiar squirming in her stomach going frantic, as they always did when she was called to this office for something she did wrong. It wasn't fear of punishment, but rather the sinking feeling that she had disappointed Master Qydus.

She hated that feeling.

"Before we start, Master Qydus, there is something I need to tell you. I was able to decipher the letters we found in Ren Kenata's robes, the ones that have been giving me so much trouble since I found them. I made copies of them in Ruthrin for you. I believe they have important information within them."

The headmaster took the proffered sheets of paper and skimmed them with his eyes. One white eyebrow rose. "I see. Thank you, Marla. We will discuss this later. You weren't by any chance waiting for this meeting to give me these, hoping to mitigate your punishment, were you?"

"I...no, Master. I just translated them last night. Evon helped me to realize that the main part of the key for the code was based on Naevius's third theorem of alternating magical series."

"But...?" he said.

"But I did hope they would mitigate my punishment, even slightly. I hoped that you would see the importance of what has been happening, and of the actions I have taken."

"Yes, I believe I understand your motivations. I thank you for your honesty." He set the papers down and folded his hands on the desk. "Shall we begin, then?"

Marla nodded, then studied her hands interlaced in her lap.

"You were given a rare opportunity of freedom to act in the investigation of Master Aeid's murder. All in all, you did an adequate job in carrying out your responsibilities. However, it was made clear at the start of the investigation that you were not to enter into restricted areas. Did you not understand this rule?"

"We understood it," Marla said.

"Evon?"

"Yes, Master," her blond friend said. "I understood the rules."

"Yet you broke them," the headmaster said. "You entered into a clearly defined restricted area, into Fyrefall. Is that correct?"

"It is," Marla said.

"I would have your reasons."

Marla looked up to the master's face, but couldn't meet his eyes. "Quentin Duzen killed Skril. We found his body, cast to the ground like carrion. Quentin's trail was clear and so we followed. It led into Fyrefall and we were faced with a decision. We could travel all the way back to the Academy and ask permission, most likely losing the trail forever, or we could follow it, knowing we would face punishment."

"It was essentially the same choice faced by your colleagues," Master Qydus said. "They chose to return."

"They did. Since they were returning, we charged them with reporting on what happened, so that the masters would know about Quentin—though we knew him only as an unidentified murderer at that point—and about those dark creatures we had fought. Even if we fell in trying to get to the murderer, the knowledge would not be lost."

"And when you went into the restricted area?" the master prodded.

"We were almost killed," she said. "But not by any creature or magic, but by a group of humans that had to have been sent after us. I believe they would have found us even if we hadn't gone into Fyrefall. They were obviously sent by Quentin."

"So, since you were fortunate in escaping not only the men but also any of the special dangers of the place—dangers which the masters are aware of and so marked the area as restricted—it was acceptable to break the rules and enter?"

"No. I didn't mean it that way. Master Qydus, I am sorry we had to disobey. For what it's worth, I pressured Evon into coming with me. He argued against it, but in the end, he accompanied me because he wanted to help protect me. I'm also sorry I dragged him into it.

"I do want to make it clear, though, that I understand the

reason for the restrictions. They are to keep us from extreme danger. I also know that if given the chance, I would make the same choice. I—"

"You would choose to disobey again?" the headmaster interrupted. "You are telling me that you haven't learned you were in error and you would do the same again? You realize this is not helping your case, do you not?"

"What I'm trying to say..." Marla found that her hands were clenched in fists and she consciously relaxed them. "Is that I understood my choices. I could follow a rule designed to keep myself safe or I could risk myself to capture someone who had already murdered at least two people, one of them a master and the other my best friend. Comparing my life with how many others Quentin might have murdered, I chose those others. I cannot idly stand by and allow people to be killed, or as we found, the entire human race to be sold to those dark monsters.

"When I say I would make the same choice again, I am being truthful. It would assault my conscience, as it already has, but in the end, I see the matter as a choice between my safety and that of many others. I will always choose to sacrifice myself for the greater good. It is really the only thing I'm completely sure of in this life. I would choose to do the same if in the same situation, given one small change. I'd make sure Evon didn't follow me."

"Master Qydus," Evon said. "For the record, whatever it may do to my punishment, I would also make the same choice. I'd never let my friend go into danger alone. I lost one already for that reason. I'll never let that happen again."

Master Qydus blew out a breath, making his bushy mustache flap with the force of it. "You two don't really understand the disciplinary process, do you? Marla, with how many times you've been involved in it, you would think you'd know by now that you're supposed to say things that *help* your cause, not make you look like a chronic and unrepentant rule-breaker."

"I know, Master. I'm sorry I'm such a problem for you and the Academy."

"Yes. Quite." He let out a sigh, not nearly as forceful as the previous breath. "I do appreciate your honesty and your selfless mentality, but the fact remains that you have disobeyed a rule given to you specifically to keep you from harm. As such, you will need to be punished.

"The two of you will receive similar punishments because you both made choices, regardless of pressure or duress. Marla, I am requiring you to teach classes in those subjects for which you are qualified. Essentially, those are the schools you have mastered. Especially you will be helping Master Yxna with her edged weapons students and Master Esiyae with her air magic students. You will fit these activities in with your already busy schedule."

Marla moaned inwardly at that, but didn't respond outwardly. She noticed the headmaster's eyes drilling into her, waiting for an outburst. A moment passed and he nodded.

"Evon, you receive the same punishment, though the bulk of your work will be with the School of Prophecy. As *assector pruma*, you already have these responsibilities, but you will have added to them whatever Master Marn sees fit, as well as the master of the other school you have mastered. In addition, you will be on call at a moment's notice by any of the masters working with the Bhagant and the new animaru prophecy."

"Yes, Master," Evon said. Marla was proud of the way he made his voice sound like he was receiving a punishment though his eyes twinkled like he'd just received a reward.

"Further," the master continued, "I charge both of you with aiding Aeden Tannoch with any activity he performs or with any help he might need in the service of his calling as one half of the Malatirsay. You both claim that you will sacrifice yourself for others, for your friends? You will prove this. Sitor-Kanda was built for our time, for that young man—and Marla, of course—and you will dedicate all your energies, even your lives, to make sure he succeeds. Am I clear?"

Marla couldn't help letting the smile out that had been building as the headmaster said that last part. "Yes, Headmaster. I understand completely."

Evon echoed her thought, a smile on his face as well.

"Begone. I have work to do. I will speak with you later after I've had a chance to look these notes over, Marla."

Both of the students shot to their feet so they could leave before the headmaster changed his mind. Before they got to the door, though, Master Qydus spoke again.

"Oh, and Evon, I would like you to extend that protection and your aid to Fahtin Achaya. Not as part of your punishment, but as a request."

The smile on Evon's face doubled. "Yes, Master. I absolutely will."

Master Qydus made a sweeping motion with his hand and turned his attention to the papers on his desk.

Marla and Evon scrambled out of the office, nearly tripping on each other as they rushed past the clerk and out into the sunshine.

❧ 5 ❧

Time passed quickly for Marla Shrike. With her normal class load, the new teaching responsibilities the masters had assigned her, and trying to complete her testing for the mastery of two more schools, she barely had time to think, let alone dwell on what she and the others needed to do to protect Dizhelim.

The truth was, she didn't even really have time to converse with her brother and her new friends. But she made time for that, shaving off an hour or two of sleep here or there to be with them.

"You look tired, Marla," Aeden told her one evening in the common room of their dormitory building. To make things easier for her, she had taken to sleeping in one of the unused rooms in the building. She'd even moved half her stuff over from her normal room.

"I've got a lot going on," she said.

"Yes, I know. You're maybe pushing yourself too hard."

She smiled at him and he returned it. She knew him well enough now to know he'd said that to sound reasonable. No way in Percipius's realm would he slack off. If anyone worked harder than she did, it was her twin brother.

"Seriously, though," he said, "I wonder what we should be doing. I am enjoying learning what I can and working with the masters, but aren't there things we need to do? The animaru are out there. What are they doing? Shouldn't we go out and search them out, destroy them?"

She nodded. "I'm anxious about that, too. I don't like all this waiting. I think about it a lot. What can we do?"

"I don't know, but sitting still here when people might be dying out there doesn't seem like the right thing."

Fahtin came and sat next to Aeden. "It may be that the best thing we can do is to learn more about our skills and abilities. Then, when there is clear direction as to where we need to go, we'll be better able to handle what comes at us."

"Spoken like someone who has been talking to the masters about her own special abilities," Aeden teased.

"I'm just curious what these visions mean," she said defensively. "Also, I still don't have a good explanation as to how I was struck by lightning and didn't die, or even get injured."

"She's right, Aeden," Marla said. "Magic has been strange for the last few months. No one is really sure why. Are Fahtin and Raki demonstrating seeming magical abilities because of the changes, or are they maybe causing the changes themselves?"

"Okay, okay," he said. "I wish these strange magical power surges would help me to figure out how to enhance my spells. It doesn't seem fair that it helped you cast that spell you'd never managed before to help you escape from Quentin, but it does nothing but frazzle my nerves whenever a surge comes through."

"Don't worry," Fahtin said. "You'll figure them out. You've already figured a few of them out. Stuff takes time."

"I guess." He put his head in his hands and pulled on his hair.

Marla patted him on the head. "I'm sure we'll figure something out soon. We've got people scouting around in many areas. When they come back with information, we'll speak with the masters and decide what the next step is. Take advantage of whatever you can learn now. You may be sorry later if you don't take advantage of the opportunity.

"Oh, speaking of which, I need to get going. I need to teach another edged weapons class. Wanna join me?"

"I'll have to pass this time," Aeden said. "I'm supposed to meet with Master Saelihn in a little while. She's helping me work on the spells of the Raibrech and also trying to teach me some other life spells."

"No problem. Have fun. I'll probably be back in a few hours."

Marla waved farewell to the others in the room and headed for the training grounds.

On the way, she thought about what Aeden and Fahtin said. They were right, of course. The Malatirsay should be out stopping the animaru, not carrying on a normal existence in the Academy. It was important to gain new skills, but she felt so helpless. She didn't like that feeling at all.

As she walked, Marla mentally went over some of the advanced techniques from her unarmed combat classes and her long weapons classes. She had recently finished the written and verbal parts of her final tests, but she had yet to take the practicals. She was close to mastering both of those schools. Finishing two at a time like that was rare...for others. For her, it seemed a matter of course. Sooner rather than later, she would add mastery of those schools to her list.

She smiled at that, but then realized that she would have less and less time in the future to master the other schools she was training in. She would miss that, the sense of accomplishment and the joy of learning and developing. Why couldn't those damn animaru wait until she was finished? In the entire history of the Academy, she was the only one to have a chance at mastering all forty-nine schools. She would have liked to have done it.

That was the wrong attitude, of course. The sole purpose of her existence was to save the world from the animaru. Whether with the mastery of one school or all of them under her belt, the most important thing was to use what she had learned to do the job she—and her brother—had been prophesied to do.

She arrived at the training grounds and blinked. That seemed fast. Her mind shifted to what she would be working on with her students as she stepped up to them. Another teaching session, and then she'd move on from there.

৩৩৩

Tere Chizzit dove through the air, turning a tight somersault and landing lightly with a slight forward momentum. He pulled an arrow from his quiver, nocked, drew, and released it smoothly, then dropped his shoulder and rolled to dissipate some energy. Without a pause, he changed directions, shifting to his left while releasing another arrow to his right.

Three translucent objects, blobs really, struck the ground where he had just been. Another two had been broken up by the shafts he had launched at them.

This seems to take a lot more effort than it used to, the old archer said to himself. *What am I doing here?*

As he zipped by, he noticed a flash of red off to the side.

Lily was watching. Of course she was.

Tere moved erratically so the blobs streaking toward him wouldn't make contact. They seemed to come from everywhere, and not just in straight lines. They were getting harder and harder to dodge.

He shot two more out of the air and shifted his center of gravity to roll out of the way of another when something came flying in from his right. He barely saw it as it struck his shoulder, spinning him.

Right into the path of two more.

His body jerked as they slammed into him, upsetting his balance even more. He tried to target the others with his bow, but he lost their position completely and ended up covering his face with his hands so as not to get pelted in that sensitive area.

He waited for a few seconds and realized there were no other strikes to his body. Putting his hands down, he looked toward the area near Lily.

Two of the masters stood there, considering him.

He slammed the arrow he had in his hand back into his quiver and walked toward them.

Master Esiyae Yellyn, the Academy's air magic expert, was a tall, slender woman with stark white hair, much like his own —what little he had—but brighter. He looked as if a hard life had earned him the lack of color, but hers, well, hers looked like it had been bleached. With magic. It was the color of snow and was held back with a black headband. Her pretty face watched him as he came toward them.

She wore a long dress, snug around her ample chest and thin waist and falling a bit wider under that. The top of the dress had no shoulders, but had long sleeves, leaving a patch of pale skin visible, all of it spotless and perfect. Like many of the masters, Tere had noticed, she looked far too young to have the experience he knew she had. Must have had something to do with using all that magic.

The other master was Ailred Kelzumin, Master of the School of Water Magic. He was a solidly built man with a close-cropped beard, short hair peppered with grey, and another too-young face. His blue tunic was belted over a darker undershirt and matched with midnight blue trousers. Very fashionable, Tere thought. No standard uniforms for the masters of the Academy, it seemed. Each wore what they liked, and their clothing often revealed something of their personalities, just like with normal folks.

"You failed to track the projectiles again," Master Esiyae said, her voice smooth and soothing.

"Yes," he said. "I told you, I lost my ability to track things in the magical matrix of the world."

"Yet you were able to dodge seven of them and shoot another five from around you," Master Ailred said. His voice was a bit scratchy, and deeper than the other master, of course.

"I've had a bit of practice dodging things," Tere said. "There's always someone trying to shoot me with something. It must be my wonderful personality."

Lily laughed, a husky sound—but still remarkably smooth —that threatened to make him smile. At least she got his sarcasm.

"It is extraordinary, really," Master Esiyae said, "that you can do as well as you do. I say this not in reference to your blindness, of course, but that you can do such things without any magical aid."

"I couldn't have done half as well," Lily said, "and I'm not just saying that. If you can do this without your magical sight, I believe every story I've ever heard of you. I always thought they had been embellished."

"Oh, come on," Tere said. "I told you, I'm not that man anymore. Besides, the stories *are* embellished. Exaggerated. Hells, most of the ones I've heard are downright lies."

"I truly doubt that, Tere Chizzit," Master Esiyae said with a soft smile that would have made Tere stop and stare at her if he weren't so old and worn out. Damn it, he liked the woman, despite his best intention not to.

"Well, the fact remains that I can't pass your little test, something I could have done with my eyes closed—and I'm not trying to make a joke—back when I was in my prime."

Master Ailred chuckled. "How I would have loved to have seen you in action back then. Your abilities amaze me now, but as a young man, Erent Caahs, hero of the people...it must have been spectacular to see. I remember back then, hearing of your exploits. I have always wanted to meet you, to be honest."

Tere would have blinked, if his eyes did that sort of thing. "Just how old are you, Master Ailred?"

"It's of small consequence. What's not is your description of how your abilities used to work. It fascinates me, not only the mechanics of it, but how your powers suddenly disappeared. I would very much like to help you regain them, thus our inviting you to take these little tests."

"I'd like them back myself, along with my youth, but some things only come once. I'm afraid I'm as useless as an animaru with..." He remembered that two of his listeners were women and aborted what he was about to say, "Well, anyway, I'm not of much use."

"That's not true, Tere," Lily said. "You're the leader of our group, the one who always knows what to do, and the one who usually bails us out of a sticky situation. If you don't believe me, come and talk to every other one of your friends. In some ways, you're the most important of the whole group."

Tere started to sputter, but changed the subject instead, turning toward Master Esiyae. "Have you had enough of pelting me with magic for one day? I'm a bit tired and could use a nice chair and some ale."

She flashed that smile again. "Yes, Tere, I believe we have

done enough for today. Thank you for your assistance. I will think on the matter and perhaps speak to some of the other masters. If there is a way to regain your abilities, we will find it."

"I appreciate that, but don't bother yourself over it. Like I keep telling everyone, Erent Caahs is no more. All that's left is this worn-out old husk called Tere Chizzit. Good day to you both."

Tere headed toward the dormitory where they had been staying, Lily on his heels. She sped up to match his stride. It probably wasn't difficult, the damn woman was as tall as he was.

"Do you really feel like you're worn out and useless?" she asked him.

"I am."

She pulled on his shoulder, spinning him to face her. "Do you think I'm useless?"

"You? No, of course not. You've got serious skills, kid. Finest archer I've ever seen. You're not half bad with the blades, either."

"Really?" she asked, her cheeks flushing prettily as if trying to match her hair. She blinked and shook her head. "I mean, really?" The second time didn't sound nearly as excited.

"Yeah. You're good."

"So if I'm not useless, then what does that make you? You took on me, Jia, and four other Falxen all at the same time."

"Not alone."

"Okay, not alone, but you did more than half the work by yourself. And that was *after* you had lost your magical sight. So if I'm not useless and you beat me, Jia, and at least one or two of the others, then you aren't useless either. Don't let me hear you saying it again."

"Or what?" he said.

"Or I'll spank you, or something. Just don't. You are the same hero I have idolized since I was a little girl."

"Great, now you make me feel even older."

"Grrrr. You are such a crotchety—"

"—old coot? Yep, I am. Thank you for making my point."

Lily's face lit up with a smile that made Tere's heart hurt. "You are such a pain in the ass. Come on, let's get you that ale." She took his arm and circled it with hers and started him moving toward their common room.

6

"*Kavach!*" Aeden said as he finished the casting of the enhanced version of Saving Force. The glimmer of a shield rippled around him, then disappeared.

Missiles of fire, air, water, and what seemed like pure magic taking solid form slammed against the barrier, flashing brightly and then dissipating harmlessly. Aeden felt each strike. He also felt the shield weaken with each hit.

The barrage stopped.

"You may dispel the shield, Aeden," Master Isegrith Palus said. "That will be sufficient for our purposes."

Aeden did as directed, simply switching the magic off mentally. He wasn't sure when he had learned that little trick, but it was more helpful than he had thought it would be, the ability to just let go of an active spell to end it.

"That was remarkable," Master Saelihn Valdove told him. "It is one of the more powerful shield magics I've seen." Her voice, contrasting with Master Isegrith's stern and commanding tone, was soft and comforting, almost a whisper. Aeden found that when she spoke, he focused intently on her, not wanting to miss anything she said. It helped that she was the master of the School of Life Magic, the single most important type of casting for his purposes. It was the only way to permanently destroy the animaru.

"Please tell us again," Master Isegrith said, "how you learned this magic you do." She was the Master of the School of General Magic, probably the most popular, or at least populous, college at the Academy.

"It's my clan magic. In the Cridheargla, nearly all the clans have their own system. There are similarities and differences. I think originally, long ago, there was one set of spells, but as time went on and the clans separated, things changed. It's called the Raibrech, a series of twenty spells that, I have found, are mostly based on the Bhavisyaganant."

"When you say they are based on the Song of Prophecy, what do you mean by that?" Master Saelihn asked.

"I'm still learning about my magic, trying to squeeze out more power, but I know now that sixteen of the spells correspond to the sixteen quatrains of the Song. The words of power for each is a trio of words taken directly from the Song's verses, in Dantogyptain."

"And you speak Dantogyptain?" Master Isegrith asked.

"No, Master, not really. I have the Song memorized, and I can say a few things, but otherwise, no."

"You have the Song memorized?" Master Saelihn asked.

"I do."

"Would you recite it for us?"

"I...I suppose I could. Possibly," Aeden said. "I find it difficult to speak it. It naturally wants to come out as a song."

A slow smile crept across Master Saelihn's face. "I asked the wrong question. Would you sing it for us?"

Aeden felt his face flush, though the master's smile did make him feel more comfortable. He'd sung in front of others many times, but it still made him nervous. What if he forgot the verses? What if his voice cracked? He'd make a fool of himself.

"Aye," he said anyway. "I could do that."

"Please do," Master Isegrith said.

Aeden cleared his throat and began. As he sang, he closed his eyes and enjoyed the feeling of the magic swirling around him. It also helped him to concentrate on not acting out the movements of the spells that came so naturally to him now. He'd found throwing magic about willy nilly was rarely a good thing. So, instead, he let the power suffuse him and energize him, and sang until the Song ended.

When he opened his eyes, both masters were staring at him, Master Saelihn's light blue eyes almost glowing and Master Isegrith's hazel eyes, unblinking, drilling into his own.

"That," Master Saelihn said breathlessly, "was a very great concentration of magical power. I could feel the *qozhel* building as you sang."

"Marla told me about the qozhel. I don't know much more than the name. Most of what I know about magic is just the Raibrech."

"How did you learn this Raibrech of yours?"

"When I was a child, I was trained the forms—the movements. My trainer would watch and correct our form and then we would pair the words to the gestures."

"'Our?'" Master Saelihn said. "There were more trainees than just you?"

"Oh yes. All young people in the clan were trained in combat and in the Raibrech. We spent our lives up until we were fourteen years of age training."

Master Isegrith put her hand to her forehead. "Your clan had groups of children running about casting magic they did not understand?"

"No, Master. It wasn't exactly like that. The elders

suppressed our magic so we could train. They only removed the block when we took the Trial of Magic."

"Ah," Master Saelihn said. "So the first time you actually felt the qozhel flow through you was during your trial."

"Aye. The first time we could actually do magic was during the trial."

"That seems an odd way of doing it," Master Isegrith said. "It surprises me anyone at all passed the trial. How did it feel, using the magic after training for so long without it?"

"I...uh, I don't really know. I couldn't call up the magic and I failed my trial. My clan beat me nearly to death and that's how I came to live with the Gypta."

Master Isegrith's eyes softened and she laid a hand on Aeden's shoulder. "Of course. I forgot. You told us your story before. I am sorry."

"Perhaps we should explain some things about the way magic works," Master Saelihn said, a sad smile on her face. "We will start with a review of the qozhel.

"The world is full of magic, though it may not seem to be so. In the Age of Magic, there was more of it, and there were many more people who could take advantage of it, but to this day, there is some power for those who know how to find it. This power is the qozhel. Think of it as the quantifiable unit of magic. For any spell, any magical ability, the qozhel is what fuels it.

"The way each caster gets the qozhel, however, may be different. For some, the power may come from the surroundings, from life around them or sunlight or even from the ground itself. There are more ways than one to extract the power and make it useful as well."

Aeden listened intently, but he was already starting to get lost. The masters must have seen his expression, because Master Isegrith took over.

"We mustn't confuse the source of the power with its

effects. While it is true that qozhel can be borrowed from the wind, it does not necessarily mean it will be utilized for air magic. The caster designates what the magical energy is used for. Thus, using power from a river may be used to fuel fire magic, though there are affinities and impedances that must be accounted for.

"The ways of extracting Master Saelihn alluded to are things such as gestures, verbal components, material components, and mental components. Theoretically, a master of a particular spell or type of magic could use any number of these to cast the spell, tailoring the way they use the magic to what they desire to do. For some types of magic—schools of magical thought, as it were—a caster may never have to use a verbal component at all, for example, but could conjure the magic through mental focus alone, perhaps with a slight gesture.

"The reason we are discussing this is that the way you use your magic, it appears you are extracting qozhel from the sound of the Song itself. You are using gestures—complex ones at that—and you are focusing your mind, but for now, the verbal components are the most powerful and they make a connection between the caster—you—and the effects you create. Does this make sense to you so far?"

Aeden blinked. He'd been concentrating so hard on what the master was saying, he didn't realize for a moment that she had asked him a question.

"Oh. Yes, it makes sense. Does it make a difference how synchronized or how synergistic the different components are?"

Both masters stared at him, wide-eyed. *Oh, great*, he thought. *I've made an idiot of myself.*

"Has someone explained this to you before?" Master Saelihn asked in her smooth, soft voice.

"No, Master."

Master Isegrith put her hand up to forestall the other master from speaking again. "Then why would you ask that?"

Aeden swallowed. "It seems to me that as I try to refine the way I cast the spells of the Raibrech, meshing the different components makes a difference. In the ones I've managed to enhance, it was because I finally got a sense of the cadence of the Song and where each word coincided with a particular movement."

The two masters smiled at each other.

"You are truly Marla's twin brother," Master Isegrith said.

"What Isegrith is saying," Master Saelihn said, "is that you are correct. The ideal situation for all casters to achieve is a perfect synchronization of all the components and the extraction of qozhel for use in carrying out the spell. In short, if you find the perfect combination of components and use them effectively, you may wield power unknown since the Age of Magic. Depending upon how much qozhel is available, of course. That's one of the problems with our current age: there is less power available, less qozhel in the world."

"I see," Aeden said. "I'm glad I was on the right track. It's frustrating that I can't more quickly figure out how to enhance my spells. I'll need all the help I can get with what we're facing."

Master Isegrith shook her head. "Don't you see, Aeden? That's what we're saying. You don't have issues with not enough *qozhel* being available. Your spells seem to take power from the Song itself. It shouldn't be possible."

"Oh," he said. "Well, I was told that Dantogyptain is even more the language of magic than Alaqotim. I guess it's true."

"No, no, no," she said. "You misunderstand me. Others have studied and experimented with the language, even with the Song, but none were able to channel the qozhel as you do. I would be interested to know if Marla could do so as well, given the opportunity to study the Song in Dantogyptain, that is. Aside from that, I believe you are unique in being able to do what you do."

"Ah," he said. "I have wondered what was special about me...and Marla. I've seen others use life magic to kill animaru, so it couldn't only be that. If there's something only she and I can do, especially something so significant, that would explain why the Malatirsay is needed."

"Indeed," Master Saelihn said.

"So," Aeden said, "there's no easier way you can show me that I can enhance my spells and become more powerful?"

"I'm afraid not. It seems clear that you will need to discover how to fit the pieces together to increase the efficacy of each spell. I'm not even sure that once you figure it out, and can use the enhanced spell, that the same process or gestures would work for Marla. If she can even do what you do."

Aeden deflated. Well, it had been worth a try.

Master Saelihn's eyebrows rose. "There is something I am curious about, however. You are obviously intelligent, like your sister, but do you have her affinities? She is a natural student, learning at a much more rapid rate than others. Would you like to try to learn some other magic? Perhaps a life spell or two, or even fire, stone, or water?"

Aeden's mood lifted immediately and he smiled at the master. "Absolutely."

"Good. Now, I will start with a few exercises and we will see if you have an aptitude for a particular type of magic. Stand here and face me. I will..."

By the time Aeden finished with the two masters, his brain was sore. He'd never felt anything like it. It couldn't dent his smile, though. He jogged toward the common room of the dormitory, hoping someone was there. He simply had to show off the new spell he'd learned.

7

Raki tried to stand up straight, but his body wanted to curl up on itself, to disappear from the scrutiny of the two masters in front of him. Master Roneus Lomos was the head of the School of Stealth at the Academy. He was a tall man, and slender. His dark brown hair was a little long, just brushing his shoulders, but Raki wasn't one to find fault with that, not with the mess of brown curls that covered his own head. Unlike Raki, however, the master had a neatly trimmed beard and mustache. He also had a kind face, or at least a calm one. Master Roneus wasn't scary at all, so far as people went. But he *was* a master. That was pretty daunting.

Beside him, like a shadow made flesh, loomed Beldroth Zinrora, the Master of the School of Dark Magic. She definitely *was* intimidating. Master Beldroth was the perfect picture of what Raki had always imagined a dark sorceress would look like: tall, with purple-limned white hair and skin darker than almost anyone else Raki had ever met. The most extraordinary thing about the master was her eyes, which glowed faintly, matching the strange tattoo or glyph on her forehead. Whatever the glowing writing symbolized, it must have been magical. The Gypta boy strained against his body's desire to fade from view and escape.

At least Jia had come with him. He liked the woman, and if there was any comfort at all in this situation, it was in her presence. Raki looked over to her, only a little taller than he was, and her eyes held sympathy. She smiled brightly at him, which made him feel marginally better, but he'd still rather be invisible.

"We have been told that you have a certain affinity for stealth," Master Roneus said.

"And that you seem to embrace darkness to manifest it," Master Beldroth added. "It may be you have an aptitude for dark magic."

Raki shuddered. Evon had arranged for him to meet the masters for a few tips to improve the skills he'd been developing. The Academy student also suggested that Jia accompany him because she was somewhat of an expert in stealth, being a former assassin and all.

The boy had asked her about it and if her Falxen name had really been Shadeglide. She smiled—as she almost always did—and told him it was the truth, but she liked the simple name her parents gave her better. Still, Raki thought her Falxen name was fantastic. When he thought about her, he referred to her as Shadeglide, but never aloud.

"We have also heard that you, Jia, are something of an expert in stealth," Master Roneus said.

"Oh, I don't know about expert," the blue-haired woman said, "but my skills were adequate to complete the missions I was assigned."

"I'm sorry," the master said. "Missions?"

"Yes," she said smiling. "Missions."

The masters looked at each other and then back to Jia. "I still don't understand. Missions for whom?"

"For those who assigned them to me. In many of my missions, I needed to infiltrate fortresses or castles."

"What exactly did you do in these missions? May I ask?"

"Sure. They were normally assassination missions, though sometimes I had to abduct a target or provide information by spying on someone. You know, whatever the leader of my brace gave me."

Master Roneus paled and swallowed hard. "I'm sorry. Did you say *brace*?"

Jia looked from master to master. "Did no one tell you my background?"

"No," Master Beldroth said. "I'm afraid not."

"Oh. Ooh, that's embarrassing. Yeah. Um, so I was one of the Falxen."

"You were a Blade?" the Master of the School of Stealth asked.

"I was. Does that make you not like me?" She put a single index finger up to her lips and cast her eyes downward as she said it.

He blinked at her. "I...uh...no. I simply wasn't aware."

"Don't worry, though," she said, perking up with her eyes going wide. "I'm not one anymore. Lily and I are done with that. The others in the brace, they were working for someone who wanted to sell out the whole human race. We decided to join Aeden and fight the animaru. I feel much better about that than what I used to do."

"I see," he said.

The masters seemed at a loss for words, which made Raki feel much better. Jia, without even trying, had flummoxed both of them.

Jia tilted her head so the masters couldn't see her and

winked at Raki, the goofy face she made clearly communicating the humor of the situation. She had done it on purpose. The former assassin was quickly becoming his favorite person.

Master Roneus finally regained his composure. "Raki, we would like to observe you moving stealthily. Please come with us. We have a sizeable area set up with different zones, custom-made for practicing moving quietly and without trace. We shall set you loose and then evaluate your skills."

Raki's heart doubled its rate. He began to feel sick to his stomach. He didn't know he was going to have to perform for the masters. What if they laughed at him? More than ever, he felt like disappearing and running as far away as he could.

A warm hand closed around his. He spun his head to see who had grabbed him.

Jia's warm, pretty face was inches from his. Not grabbed. She had only laid her hand on his to get his attention. She was smiling at him, of course, her blue eyes locked on his as if searching him.

"Masters," she said, not taking her eyes from him. "Could I run through the area first? Raki is still a little tired from the last few days' events. Maybe he could rest and see what the area is about while I give it a try. I think he might be more comfortable that way."

"Oh, of course," Master Roneus said. "We hadn't anticipated evaluating your performance, but yes, that would be fine."

"Great," she said, squeezing Raki's hand and quirking an eyebrow at him.

They arrived at the training area and stepped up to a little rise, perfect for watching those within the practice space.

To Raki, it looked like a playground. There were trees off to one side, from sparse to heavy forest. Butted up against that area were other zones with different types of structures, some of wood and others of stone. There were complete buildings, no doubt meant for scaling, walls to get over and around, and even a tower that rose up into the sky above the surrounding trees. In short, it was a place that would allow someone to practice the art of stealth and infiltration in a variety of ways.

He stood with his mouth open staring at it.

"Very well," Master Roneus said. "The introductory course is through those trees, there." He pointed off to the left. "The task is simple. Make it through the area, avoiding the traps to obtain the flag at the end. Attempt to leave no trace, for the judgment of how well the course was mastered is based upon not leaving evidence of your passing. The traps, while simulating actual harmful or fatal mechanisms, will not do serious damage if tripped."

"Hmm," Jia said. "Is that all? What about those other areas, the ones with the walls and buildings?"

"Those are more advanced. There are four flags total, and advanced students are to obtain one or more without triggering traps and without being seen by the observers, but we will focus on just the first area for today."

"Okay," she said. "Sounds great. Is this timed?"

"What? Oh...umm...for competitions held between students of the upper rank, yes, we time how long it takes to complete the tasks. But we'll not be doing that today. Even if we wanted to, I did not bring the timing glass."

"Hmm," she said, then shrugged. "Do you want me to start now?"

"You may start when you like. Perhaps you'd like to prepa..."

Jia took off at a jog, heading straight into the forested area. Within a few seconds, she was swallowed up by the shadows of the trees.

Master Roneus huffed but that was all. Raki looked over

at him as he and the other master scanned the trees, looking for Jia. He had a smirk on his face and looked to be anticipating the sound of a trap activating.

There was nothing but silence.

As Raki waited, he felt more than saw something off to his right, in the area where the buildings were. He caught the flash of a shadow that he swore put its finger up to its mouth in a shushing motion. The Gypta boy smiled and looked up into the sky to keep from laughing out loud.

A few minutes later, Jia appeared next to the masters, only slightly behind them. Raki saw her before they did and she winked at him.

"Did she make it?" she asked innocently, looking past them toward where they had been focusing.

Both masters jumped and spun toward her.

"How did you get over there?" Master Beldroth asked.

"It was the fastest way back from the tower," she said.

"The tower?" Master Roneus said. "Impossible."

Jia pulled out a flag and handed it to him.

"Yes, that's the flag from the forest."

She pulled another from her pocket.

"And the fortress."

Another.

"The barracks."

Finally, she brought another flag from her other pocket.

Master Roneus blinked at her. "That's the flag from the tower."

"I know," she said cheerily. "That one was a tough one. Those simulated deadfall traps were very tricky. Good job."

Raki managed to keep from bursting into laughter, but just barely.

After composing themselves, the masters walked the areas with Raki and Jia in tow. They were unable to find any tracks that proved she had been there. Jia walked along silently, pulling off leaves from trees and tearing them as she went. She also dropped them to the ground, which seemed to irritate the Master of Stealth a bit.

By the time Raki had his turn, he was in such a good mood that his nerves had disappeared. He only did the first area, the one with the forest, but he captured the flag and left very little in the way of tracks. Master Roneus only found two instances of what he claimed to be marks Raki left, but the boy recognized them as things planted purposely by Jia when the four of them went through together.

Master Beldroth performed a few diagnostic spells on Raki and found he had an affinity for dark magic. She was unsure if the boy would actually be able to learn to cast dark magic spells, but she offered instruction if Raki wanted to learn. He agreed to learn about dark magic as well as stealth from Master Roneus. Both masters seemed satisfied as they parted company, and Raki headed back to the dormitory common room with Jia.

He was glad that he seemed to have some magic, but he was even more excited at what he'd seen Jia do.

"That was fantastic," he told her. "You amazed and irritated them at the same time."

"I didn't do it to be mean, but to make them think about how they'd been acting. They are masters at the Academy, but there's no reason to look down on others. I wanted them to see that there's more out there than their own schools."

Raki's mind spun. How had Jia gotten so good? She had completely befuddled the masters and their training course.

"Do you think you could help me out, maybe show me how to get better?" he asked her.

She flashed that smile at him again. "I thought you'd never ask. You and I are going to be good friends, Raki Sinde.

I've got a lot of stuff to show you, and I know you'll be a natural at it."

He swiped his long hair out of his face and matched her smile tooth for tooth. This was the kind of training he had only dreamed about.

❧ 8 ❧

"**W**ho told you that you had any talent for scrying or prophecy, girl?" Master Marn Tiscomb asked Fahtin.

She winced at the question. Maybe she was simply out of sorts, but the master's words almost seemed rude to her. "No one, Master," she said, trying to maintain a smile. "Only, these visions seem like more than simple dreams."

"They're *dreams*," he said. "I don't know what it is with you young people, that you must have delusions of grandeur. Every one of you think you are special in some way. First the boy who thinks he's the Malatirsay and now this." Those last parts were more mumbled under his breath than said outright, but Fahtin heard every word clearly.

Evon looked at her, shrugging slightly and looking embarrassed. "The headmaster suggested that Fahtin come and speak with you," he said to the master.

The older man huffed. "Oh, very well. Evon, fetch paper and ink. Write down these visions the girl here—"

"Fahtin," Fahtin said.

Master Marn gave her a level look. "The visions the girl

here thinks she's had. We can file them along with the rest of the supposed visions the other dreamers have had."

Evon lifted his finger, a flash of anger coming to his face. Fahtin shook her head at him. The master was entitled to his opinion. She would dictate her visions and then leave.

Evon sighed. "Yes, Master Marn."

Fahtin spent the better part of an hour retelling visions as Evon dutifully jotted them down. He was only doing it for show anyway. The Academy student had already written detailed accounts of what Fahtin had seen, and with much more interest than Master Marn showed.

When she had finished, she stopped speaking and Evon put his pen down. The master had been fiddling with a pen of his own, and Fahtin caught a glimpse of doodles on a piece of scrap parchment before the master covered them over with a book.

"If that is all..." Master Marn said.

Fahtin stood up. "Yes. Thank you for your help. Good day to you, Master."

"Yes, yes. Good day." He had already turned his attention back to the papers on his desk before Fahtin could even make it through the door.

Outside the office, Evon led her toward the front entrance of the School of Prophecy.

"I'm really sorry about that," he said. "I...don't know what to say."

Fahtin smiled at him. It was easy. She had grown very fond of Evon Desconse. "It's not your fault. Marla did tell me that it would be a waste of time talking to him. I thought she just didn't like him, but apparently her accusation as to what type of person he is and the way he interacts with others was correct."

"He's a little rough around the edges, maybe a bit arrogant, but he's a new master. He was just raised up, and I don't think he's settled in yet."

"Really, Evon?" she said. "Are you really going to defend him?"

He swung his blond head back and forth, scanning for anyone else in the area, then narrowed his blue eyes at her. "No, not really. He was a disagreeable man even before Master Aeid's death. He never liked me because I was *Assector Pruma*, the school's First Student. He liked to call me 'First Ass.'"

Fahtin gasped.

Evon put his hands up. "Not anymore, though. I'm *his* First Student now, so he at least has stopped calling me that. In my presence, anyway. Besides, it's a common enough joke among the students. Marla calls me that."

"Well, I think he's very rude, and I will not be talking to him about any of my visions from now on. Marla is right about another thing, too: you are a much better person to confide in and to explain what I see."

His face colored slightly. "Thank you. I do believe you have some scrying abilities, at a minimum, and possibly some talent for prophecy. We'll figure it out, Fahtin. I know more than most in the Academy about these subjects. It's the primary focus in my education so far."

"I know. Marla told me that, too. Come on, let's get back to the others. Aeden and Raki were supposed to meet with the masters today, too. I want to find out how it went. I'm sure they're excited about it. And you know, I think when Marla calls you that, it's a joke. I can tell you two are best friends."

"I know. We've always joked around that way. I ignore her when she calls me that."

It was a pleasant ten-minute walk to the dormitory common room. To Fahtin, it seemed like they were all becoming closer, almost like a family. She smiled at the thought.

As Evon opened the dormitory door for her, though, her thoughts turned to another family. Her real family. The smile slid off her face.

"What's wrong?" Evon asked. "What did you just think about? You went from happy to sad in less than a second."

"Oh," she said, "I'm sorry. I thought of my family. I don't know where they are or if they're safe. When we left them, we had just been attacked by the animaru."

"I remember," Evon said. "Aeden told us about it. I'm sure they're fine. They said they were going to leave and go west, right?"

"They did say that, yes."

"The animaru wouldn't have attacked them if they sensed Aeden had left."

"I guess."

"I'll tell you what, Fahtin. I'll ask around, see if I can find out anything. If I was more familiar with them or had objects that belonged to them, we could try to make a locator. In a few days, I could have the materials together and we might be able to look for them magically."

Her heart quickened. "Really? That would be wonderful, Evon."

He nodded emphatically as he gestured for her to step inside the common room. "Then that's what we'll do. I won't rest until we find out how your family is and where they are."

Fahtin clapped. "Thank you. It would mean a lot to me."

"What about the family?" Raki asked. Somehow, he was standing next to Fahtin. She hadn't even seen him step up to her.

"Evon says he's going to help us get news of the family. He might even be able to find their location magically, but it'll take a few days to get the materials. Whatever that means."

Raki swiped some hair from his face. "That would be great. You're the best, Evon."

"I'll do what I can," Evon said. "You are like family to me now. It's the least I can do."

Fahtin noticed his cheeks reddening again. With his pale skin, he really did color at the slightest little thing.

"Good," Marla said from across the room. "Everyone's here. Who's going to be first to tell us how their appointments went with the masters?"

MARLA WATCHED FAHTIN, RAKI, AND TERE, NOTING THEIR facial expressions when she asked who was going to tell about their day first. She'd been with Aeden for his meeting, so she wasn't as interested in hearing him tell it. What she wondered was how the others fared.

Fahtin started by telling Marla she had been right about Master Marn. Her tale made Marla laugh because she could see the so-called master saying and doing the things the Gypta girl described. In mid-thought, Master Qydus's scowling face appeared in her mind and the red-haired student realized she needed to correct her attitude a bit. Sure, Marn Tiscomb was a poor master, but he had been given the position by the other masters, so she needed to be careful and at least try to pretend he deserved some respect. She didn't want to be known for saying unkind things about a master. It set a bad example. She had been taught to be better than that.

She'd have to keep most of her thoughts to herself.

Tere reluctantly told his account of meeting with the masters. He didn't seem in a good mood, grumbling about how he was old and used up. Lily smiled at him and told him he was being too critical of himself, but he wasn't having any of it. By all accounts, his meeting had figuratively dumped a bucket full of cold water onto his head.

Marla delighted in Raki's account of Jia breaking the stealth test wide open, but she was also surprised. Marla had performed some of the tests in the School of Stealth and they were no joke. To do what Jia did, quickly and without being noticed at all, let alone leaving no traces of her passing, was barely short of miraculous. Raki seemed to have done a good job, too, and Jia praised his performance with no formal instruction.

When Jia said she'd be helping Raki to learn the subtleties of stealth and bladework, the boy grew as wide a smile as Marla had ever seen on him.

Aeden explained his experience with the masters as he typically did: like a military briefing. It wasn't that he couldn't tell an exciting tale. He did so when he was recounting stories or experiences of others. She had noticed, though, that when it was his own achievements he spoke about, he downplayed much of it. She helped him, describing his experience with the masters and how he had astounded Master Yxna with his sword skill.

She had also spoken with Master Isegrith and Master Saelihn and had a pretty good idea of how things went with them. She inserted what she had been told and Aeden fidgeted and wore a forlorn look as if he had been set upon. He had impressed the masters at every turn, and she'd be damned if she wouldn't show a little pride in her twin and let everyone know how amazing he was.

The stories finished, pockets of conversation broke out. Little groups chatted together, increasing the overall noise in the room quite a bit. Marla took the opportunity to search out Lily.

She stepped up to the red-haired archer. Lily was taller than Marla and seemed to have twice as much hair, though the color almost a match to the shade of Marla's, perhaps a bit more vibrant, a deeper red. With her skin-tight and skimpy clothing, the archer cut quite a figure. She wasn't arrogant about it, though, which Marla appreciated. She'd never liked beautiful women who made it obvious they knew how they looked. Lily seemed almost embarrassed about it at times, and the Academy student could easily believe the other woman actually dressed that way for ease of movement.

"Lily," Marla said. "I'd like to show you something, if I can."

"Sure, Marla. What is it?"

Marla looked around the room, then jerked her head toward the door. "How about outside. Bring your bow."

Lily raised an eyebrow but picked up her bow, slung her quiver over her shoulder, and headed for the door. Tere noticed and followed, a quizzical look on his face. Marla picked up a wrapped bundle and followed her. Before she reached the door, though, she beckoned to Evon as well.

The others seemed to think something exciting was happening, because conversations stopped as first Lily, then Marla, then Tere and Evon went by. By the time Marla stepped out through the doorway, there was a line of the others right on her heels. Even Urun, usually the quiet loner of the group, came along.

So much for being discreet.

She and Evon joined Lily while most of the others stayed back to watch.

"Evon, if you would please," Marla said. "Create a pillar of water about...there." She pointed to an area thirty feet or so away, across a grass area in front of some trees bordering the dormitory.

He tilted his head at her, but then shrugged and did as she asked. A pillar about six feet high and two feet around appeared where she had pointed. Marla projected an ice spell

—a combination of air and water spells, actually—and froze the pillar solid.

With a human-sized ice pillar in front of them, Marla picked up her wrapped package and handed it to Lily.

"A colleague and I have been working on some things in the School of Artifice. One of them seemed like it would be useful to you. I mixed it with another project I had completed in the School of Alchemy. Go ahead and unwrap it."

Lily did so, unlacing the cloth bundle and peeling back the flaps. She dropped the covering to the ground and held up a quiver full of arrows.

"Ooh," she cooed. "It's beautiful."

Marla had modified her original design, guessing at the taller woman's dimensions. The quiver was designed to lay flatter against the back than a common container, and a bit wider. It held more arrows than the one Lily always wore, which seemed like it would be a welcome feature. But that wasn't really the gift.

"I hope you like the quiver," Marla said. "It's my own design. That's not really the thing I wanted to show you, though. It's a little extra thing. Here, let me help you with a demonstration."

Marla put her hand out and Lily handed the quiver over to her.

"Now, I'm going to hold the quiver. Pick up your bow and pull out one of these arrows." A score or so of the arrows had red fletching on the shafts. She had seen Lily's eyes when they first landed on the arrows. They were very distinctive and, if Marla said so herself, quite striking to look at.

"Um," Lily said. "Okay. Do you want me to shoot that icicle over there?"

"Yep, that's the general idea."

Lily nodded and grasped her bow in her left hand.

Selecting one of the red arrows, she pulled it smoothly out of the quiver and nocked it onto her string in a graceful motion. It was plain she had performed the action countless thousands of times.

Marla internally counted. One...

Two...

The tip of the arrow burst into flames, making most of those around them jump. Lily's eyes went wide, then she drew and loosed the shaft. It sped toward the target, striking it exactly where the head would be if the imaginary opponent was as tall as Lily herself.

Three.

The top of the pillar blew out like it had been struck with explosives.

Lily turned toward Marla, her eyes twinkling. "How...?"

"I coated the red arrows with a special substance. Inside the quiver, it is relatively inert. As the tip is pulled out of the quiver, it scrapes a little deposit of another compound. Within a second or two, the mixture reacts with air and ignites. I put a little extra kick in there so it packs a real punch on impact. If you get into the rhythm I've seen you and Tere achieve—pumping out more than one arrow per second—it's not a problem. They'll ignite on the way, the rush of air speeding the process so it'll flame up just in time to strike the target."

Lily's mouth moved but no sound came out. Marla leaned toward her and cupped her ear with her hand.

The archer pushed her bow at Tere and swept Marla up into a hug. She found her voice. "Oh, Marla, they're fantastic. Thank you so much."

"Yeah, well," Marla said into the other woman's shoulder. "I heard you liked fire arrows. The whole phoenix thing. It seemed like you might like them. We redheads need to stick together."

The larger woman released Marla and stepped back, smiling so widely Marla didn't think she'd have an unhappy thought for a week. "Thank you, thank you."

"You're very welcome. I made a hundred arrows...for now. The special part of the quiver can hold maybe thirty, with the rest being normal quiver space. With a little life magic thrown in—oh, did I mention I put a compound that carries life magic in the mix—those damn animaru don't stand a chance." Wincing, she called over her shoulder, "I'm sorry Khrazhti. No offense intended."

Tere handed Lily her bow back, shifting his face from her to the rapidly melting ice pillar. "Phoenixarrow, indeed," he said, patting the woman's shoulder.

"Marla," a voice said. "I finally found you." It was Lucas Stewart, the young student the masters often used as a messenger. "The masters have news and they want you to come see them. I was told that if you wanted to bring your brother, you could do so. Your brother?"

"I'll tell you later. Thanks, Lucas." Marla turned to find Aeden. He was already next to her.

"Let's go," he said.

Marla started toward the administration area but stopped before taking two steps. "Aww hells, come on. You all deserve to hear any news regarding the animaru invasion. It'll be easier to ask forgiveness than to get permission." Saying that sent a spike through her belly so soon after having a punishment meeting with Master Qydus, but it was true.

As one, all of them started toward the headmaster's office, leaving Lucas blinking and no doubt wondering if he'd get blamed.

Aletris Meslar, the headmaster's assistant, pointed toward the large meeting room near the headmaster's office. Marla quirked an eyebrow but led the others through the open doorway.

Master Qydus already sat at the head of the table. He gave a cocky look and a nod to Master Yxna, sitting two seats away from him. She looked to the table and shook her head.

"I assumed," the headmaster said, "that when I specified to Lucas that you were to come but Aeden was also welcome, that you would take it upon yourself to invite your other friends. Some of the masters didn't agree, not wanting to believe you would be so presumptuous."

"I'm sorry, Master Qydus," Marla said. "All of them have risked their lives in fighting the animaru threat. I believed you wouldn't begrudge them wanting to be involved."

Master Qydus smirked under his mustache and waved toward the seats. "We chose this room because it is sufficient to hold everyone. Please, be seated."

Master Yxna gave Marla a half smile, the kind that said, "You are a spoiled rotten child," and then patted the seat next to her. Marla obediently went over and sat there.

Master Isegrith, Master Goren, and Master Nasir Kelqen, the head of the School of Research and Investigation, were seated at the end of the table.

Once everyone was sitting, Master Qydus waved his hand and the door closed by itself. "We have just received reports of strange, dark figures skulking about and causing trouble in the kingdom of Telna. We would send our agents to investigate, but wanted to notify you first. Though you don't have the approval and acknowledgement of the entire Academy yet, I have decided that any activity related to the responsibilities of the Malatirsay will be shared with you before any actions are taken.

"Do you have any objections to sending an adept or two to investigate? We are of the mind that those operatives we employ who do not have the benefit of Academy training would be too vulnerable."

Marla looked at Aeden. He seemed content to sit silently.

She guessed she would be the one who would have to discuss it. Jia, of all people, beat her to it.

"Master Qydus," the blue-haired woman said. "I have spent a fair amount of time in Telna and am familiar with the area. I would be happy to investigate this report for you. I have fought the animaru. I am also more than capable of avoiding them."

"Hmm," the headmaster said. "I have heard of your skill. That would be a more favorable plan. I hesitate to send even adepts into battle with the animaru at this time. You believe you could do this safely?"

"I do, Master."

The headmaster glanced at the other masters, all of whom nodded.

"Very well," he said. "You have my leave to do so. Any—"

"I'll go with her," Aila said. Marla blinked at the woman. "I've fought animaru before, and I would not have Jia go alone. She might need someone to watch her back."

Jia smiled at her friend.

"Yes, quite," Master Qydus said. "Evon, please accompany them. You would do well to imbue their weapons with life magic in case it comes to battle with the animaru. You can also compile the report for us. We must begin documenting all our activities. These historical documents will be important after we have survived the animaru invasion."

Marla smiled inwardly at the master's words. He was correct, of course. They had the chance of recording history as it happened. His faith that they would be victorious made her feel a little better about what they faced.

"Yes, Master," Evon said, glancing at Fahtin. He sighed softly, but everyone else's attention had already moved on.

"Any other resources you might need are yours, Jia," Master Qydus said." Simply ask them of us and we will gather them. It is probably best that you leave tomorrow morning at the latest. It is unclear how old the news we received is."

Jia met eyes with Aila and Evon. "If possible, we will leave immediately. We can rest on the road, but I'd not like to delay half a day."

"So be it," the headmaster said. "Good fortune to you, and safe travels."

The three got packs together in short order and Evon filled out the paperwork for using horses from the stables. Within two hours, they were ready to depart.

Marla gathered with the rest of the small party's friends to see them off.

"Be careful," Aeden told them. "Make sure Evon casts life spells on your weapons before you get into battle with any of the animaru or you won't be able to hurt them permanently. Don't put yourself at risk. You're only to gather information, not to try to take on a whole army of animaru."

Aila bobbed her head and rolled her eyes, but only when Aeden wasn't looking right at her. When Marla's twin shifted his gaze to the small woman, she stopped her antics and met his eyes. Then she blew him a kiss.

Evon had his eyes locked on Fahtin, but she was listening to Aeden. Only when he finished speaking did she look over and see Evon staring at her. She smiled at him. His eyes went wide and then went to his hands, fiddling with his horse's reins.

The trio said their goodbyes and accepted those from their friends who wouldn't be going. Marla felt a pang of loss as Evon rode off with the other two. She didn't like to see her friend go off into danger. Like Skril did.

She cast the thought from her mind immediately. Evon would be fine. He could take care of himself and so could the two with him. *Come back safe*, she mentally sent to him.

It wasn't late yet, the sun just sinking into the horizon,

but Marla didn't really feel like sitting and chatting as had become her custom. She felt like eating a quiet dinner and then going to bed. Her eyes were gritty and her lids seemed to weigh pounds.

The others seemed as subdued as she felt, so after a quick meal, they all broke off singly or into small groups and that was that. As Marla headed to bed, she noticed some of the others heading to their rooms, too. Well, it was an eventful day; there was nothing wrong with trying to sneak in some extra sleep.

9

Aeden had gone to bed early the night before. He wasn't the only one. Many of his friends did so as well. He got up early, before dawn, to do his daily training. When he closed his door softly—so as not to bother anyone else—he turned and almost ran into Khrazhti.

"Good morning," she said as if it was normal to meet someone in the hallway in the dark of the morning.

"Good morning," he answered. "Why are you not in your room?"

"I would like to train beside you, if you will allow me."

"Of course," he said. "You're always welcome to join me. I just didn't expect anyone else to be awake."

"I do not require sleep."

"Oh, right. Let's go outside. Talking in the hallway may wake someone up."

She followed him out the door and onto the large grass area in front of the building. He set his swords down and began the stretching and warm-up exercises he started each day with. Khrazhti fell in step beside him, matching his movements perfectly. She had practiced with him several times, but she must have also performed the movements by herself, for she moved smoothly, transitioning between each action elegantly and gracefully.

They continued as mirrors of each other, flowing through unarmed practice sets and then more complex drills with swords. By the time the sun poked above the sliver of the horizon visible through the trees, a nice, glistening layer of perspiration coated his body.

Khrazhti wasn't sweating or breathing heavy at all.

He raised an eyebrow at her. "Do animaru sweat? Perspire?"

"No. Such a thing is unknown to us. In fact, the only reason I understand your words is because I asked Raki the first time I saw you training outside Satta Sarak. He explained this *sweat*. It is very strange."

"You don't do it either?" he asked. "You're half human."

"One time, after I had taken food and drink with you and the others, I found my skin damp when I exerted myself a few hours later. I believe I would do this thing, if I drank enough so that my body could leak the fluid out."

"Hmm," Aeden said. "I take it your body doesn't overheat when you exert yourself?"

"I do not believe so. It would be logical for my body to want to cool itself if it retained too much heat, but in all my time in existence, I have never been too hot."

Aeden's eyes widened, but he decided it was better not to comment.

"Are you ready to go back inside?" he asked her instead. "Maybe get some breakfast?"

"Yes."

They had just sat down with food when Raki, Tere, Fahtin, and Lily came down the stairs. The four newcomers joined Aeden and Khrazhti at the table.

Aeden noticed right away that Fahtin's eyes darted about and her breaths were quicker than they should have been.

"Fahtin," he said. "Are you okay?"

"I—" She brought a cup to her mouth, but her hand shook so hard, she nearly spilled the water. "I..."

Aeden put his hand on hers to steady it, then to set the cup on the table. "What is it?"

"I had some more visions last night."

"What were they?" Marla asked from the stairs. "Can you remember them?"

"Yes," Fahtin said. "I always remember them. They're not like dreams. It's like I was actually experiencing what I saw. I remember them as if they were memories of things I actually did and witnessed last night."

Marla sat down next to Fahtin and took her hands in her own. "Tell us about them. Do you want me to get paper and pen now to write it down or would you like to repeat them for me again later?"

"I don't know. I..."

Aeden put his finger under Fahtin's chin and gently moved her head toward him so he could look into her eyes. "Just tell us. I think it'll make you feel better. We can always record it later. Right now, I want you to relax. Can you do that?"

"I...yes. I can do that. They're just so real. I'm sorry, I'm being silly."

"No, girl," Tere said. "New things are scary. It'd be different if you had grown up having visions, but for them to start all of a sudden, that'd scare anyone. Just close your eyes and breathe, then tell us when you're ready. We're all your friends here."

Fahtin nodded and patted Lily's hand. It seemed to calm the Gypta woman.

"Okay," Fahtin said. "It started with a dark figure, or maybe more than one. It blended into the shadows of the place. I got the sense of a tunnel, or a series of tunnels. The darkened person was searching for something, some kind of prize. I don't know how I know that, but I do. I also felt like this shadowy person or persons may have been of the group of thirteen I saw in my other vision, or at least related to those thirteen in some way.

"It was about that time that I felt eyes on me. While I observed, someone or something else was observing me. Stalking me. I wanted to run, but was afraid I'd catch the attention of the shadows I had seen. I didn't want either to take notice of me.

"Then there was a flash of dull color, brown or grey, across my vision, too fast for me to focus on it. All I saw were teeth so large, they could easily tear a person apart. The other shadows had disappeared, but this new threat blocked the way forward, the path to whatever prize the shadows had been searching for. I didn't know what to do but to stay perfectly still and hope I didn't catch the thing's attention. I had no doubt it could kill me easily.

"A flare of light resolved itself into a room, with a city outside the window. Tere was there, pondering something. He didn't seem to see me. Another flicker and Tere was in a tunnel, moving along slowly as if expecting some danger. Again, the picture changed and I could see Tere looking out over a city. He was with some others, but I couldn't see any of them. I did recognize the city, though. It was Ebenrau. The buildings were distinctive, ones I've seen as we passed through Rhaltzheim before.

"A symbol of some kind, looking like it was drawn in fire, appeared before me. It had swirling lines and circular patterns. It was very pretty, but it made no sense to me. It disappeared after a few seconds, leaving an afterimage in front of my eyes for a time, but then everything faded to darkness.

"A final flare of light blinded me for a moment, and when I opened my eyes, I was in my bed and it was morning."

"What does it mean?" Raki asked.

"I don't know," Fahtin answered. "It could be a lot of nonsense. I didn't understand any of it."

Marla was rubbing her chin absently, Aeden noticed.

"Marla?" he said.

"Huh? Oh, it's interesting. Your feelings and sensations, they're common in accounts of those who are beginning to show scrying powers and the closely related powers of prophecy. I haven't ever interviewed any of these people, of course. Those talents are all but nonexistent for the last dozen centuries, at least. Except for Master Aeid. He had a shred of talent in seeing."

"Wait," Fahtin said. "They can't be extinct. There is a whole school in the Academy about scrying and prophecy."

"True, but what students and masters can do is based on spells. They're a pale imitation of natural magical ability. Mostly, they just study things that have been recorded from hundreds or thousands of years ago. There hasn't been anyone with legitimate prophecy or scrying powers for so long, it's not too much of an exaggeration to say we wouldn't even know what to do if we came across one." Marla looked Fahtin in the eyes. "When we came across one."

"Are you saying you think they really mean something?"

"You bet. Evon believes so, and anything he says about prophecy and scrying is something I take as plain truth. What we need to figure out is what they mean and what we need to do about it."

The room fell silent. Aeden studied Fahtin, then Marla. Both women were thinking furiously, but about what?

"You said there were tunnels, shadows, a beast, Tere, and Ebenrau, right?" Aeden asked Fahtin.

"Yes, that's right."

"I think it's clear, then. Some of us will go to Ebenrau and look around, see if we can find anything."

"Who will go?" Raki asked.

"Well, Tere seems to be required," Aeden said, shrugging while he shifted his attention to the archer.

"Wonderful," Tere said.

"As for who else, I don't know. We probably don't need all of us, but I suppose we could all go. Anyone *not* want to go?"

The others looked at those around them, all but Urun, who was examining his feet. Aeden thought if someone else had said they didn't want to go, Urun would have spoken up as well, but though he waited for a full minute, no one said a word. He'd have to have a talk with the nature priest. It seemed he was sinking into a funk again.

"Fine," Aeden said. "Fahtin, please come with me. Marla, do you think we would annoy Master Qydus if we went to talk to him about this right now?"

Marla had been watching Urun, too. She blinked, then turned to Aeden. "No. He rises and goes to his office early. Now would be a good time, I think. Do you want me to come with you?"

"Yes, please," he said.

The three went immediately to the headmaster's office and found him already seated at his desk, as Marla had predicted. His clerk was nowhere to be seen. Marla knocked on the half-open office door.

"Come in Marla, Aeden, Fahtin," Master Qydus said.

Aeden tilted his head. Marla met his eyes and shrugged, then entered the office.

It didn't take long to describe Fahtin's visions. She had calmed down some, for which Aeden was thankful.

"Yes," the master said. "Better to investigate these things. The sooner we can determine how accurate Fahtin's powers are, the better, I'd say."

"You...believe they're not just dreams?" Fahtin asked.

"Didn't you say they were not regular dreams?"

"Yes, but..."

The master's eyes crinkled. Aeden figured that meant there was a smile somewhere under the hair on his face.

"Fahtin, I have been at this Academy for a long time. I have spent most of my life studying magic and other related fields to prepare for the Malatirsay's arrival. One thing I have found is that when magic manifests, especially natural magic that comes upon one suddenly, the person already knows it is something special. If you say they are not normal dreams, then I believe it is the power within you making itself known. You will learn to be confident in your abilities in time. I already am."

Fahtin's eyes shone in the lamplight and Aeden half expected her to rush over and hug the headmaster. He smiled at what Master Qydus said, though. That simple statement meant more to Aeden's adopted sister than he knew. Or *did* the master know?

"Thank you," Fahtin said.

"Of course, of course. The important thing now, however, is to carry out your plans to investigate what you have seen. Only then can we determine how important the visions are in this case. I am assuming you will go with her, Aeden?"

"Yes, Master. I would not allow her to go toward danger without protection."

"Very well. Am I also to assume that those of your friends who still remain here will accompany you as well?"

"Yes, Master."

"Good. Marla, please make the arrangements. Mounts, supplies, funds, whatever is needed. You will be joining them."

Marla beamed at Fahtin. "Yes, Headmaster."

"If there is nothing further," the master said.

"No, sir," Fahtin said. "Thank you. We will be sure to let you know what we find."

"I would expect nothing less. Good travels, then. Keep safe."

As they left the office, they passed Aletris as she settled into her desk and arranged a small stack of papers that were slightly askew. She smiled at them, and they smiled in return, though no words were traded.

On the way down the steps, Aeden felt energized. Finally, they would be doing something other than waiting around for things to happen. It was fine learning with the masters and preparing for what was to come, but he craved action, doing something important. He should act like the Malatirsay. Whatever that meant.

Marla looked at him quizzically as he started whistling. Yes, it would be good to be on the move again, even if it did mean they might be jumping into danger with both feet.

❧ 10 ❧

It had taken less than two hours to gather the supplies and have the horses saddled and ready. The group ate an early lunch in their adopted common room and set out immediately after. Tere was impressed with how quickly they pulled it all together with so many little details.

For a change, they would be traveling in a more civilized manner. The headmaster had allocated funds so they could travel during the day and stay at inns each night. Tere had gotten so used to making camp off the road, so accustomed to being chased constantly, the thought of it seemed strange to him.

He shrugged and resigned himself to taking advantage of it while he could. The archer had a feeling they would be back to hiding soon enough, unfortunately.

The first day, they barely traveled the distance to Dartford due to their late start. They arrived in town well after dark. They dropped off their belongings in the rooms Josef had for them—one for Aeden and Raki, one for Tere and Urun, one for Marla and Lily, and one for Fahtin and Khrazhti—and sat down for a meal.

"We need to get back into the habit of telling stories each night," Raki said. "I miss that."

Tere watched Aeden's eyes light up with excitement. The Croagh wasn't all that much older than the Gypta boy, so he must remember having the same enthusiasm for tales.

"That sounds like a good tradition," Marla said. "The Gypta love telling stories, don't they?"

"We do," Fahtin said, "and we've heard some good ones while traveling the last few months. We can all take turns."

Tere nodded but had a sinking feeling he knew where the conversation was going.

"Who will go first? What will the first story be about?" Marla asked.

"Ooh," Raki said. "How about another story about Erent Ca—" The boy's head snapped to Tere and he immediately blushed bright red. "Oh, sorry."

"No more damn Erent Caahs stories," Tere said. "Most of them are pure lies anyway. Please, don't make me sit through the telling of any more of those. I beg you."

Lily sniffed. "Well, there goes my entire stock of tales I'd tell. I'm not sure I know any others."

"You've had a sad, sad life, Lily Fisher," Tere said with a smirk.

The red-haired woman swatted playfully at his shoulder. "Fine, if you won't let anyone tell stories about you, then you come up with one to tell us."

Tere thought for a moment as he took a sip out of his mug. "A story. Why does it always seem like I'm telling stories, and then when others' turns arrive, something happens and we start all over again with me?" He looked right at Urun as he said it.

The young nature priest had the decency to sink in his seat.

"Fine. I'll tell one, but after this one, I'm not going to tell another until everyone else gets a turn. Is that clear?"

Aeden, Fahtin, and Raki nodded, all three with wide eyes as if they were anticipating a grand song from a master bard. Urun sat motionless, his eyes glinting from his shadowed face. Marla laughed at how excited the Gypta were about the whole thing, but also nodded. Lily tsked.

"Such a grouch," she said, barely loud enough for him to hear.

"Okay. Since some of you"—he drilled his white eyes into Raki's—"seem like you'll die without stories about heroes, I have a good one for you. Who knows of the hero Zejo Troufal?"

Everyone looked at each other, shaking heads or looking confused. Not Lily, though.

"He was a hero right after the War of Magic. Zejo was also Erent Caahs's—I mean your—idol when you were a child."

Tere's mouth dropped open. "How? Who even knows that stuff?"

Lily smiled then pursed her lips. "I do. I know everything there is to know about Er—about you. Everything up to twenty years or so ago."

"Uh, okay. Anyway, you're right. Zejo Troufal was a hero when magic was failing, the gods were abandoning Dizhelim, and there were rogue mages getting into all kinds of trouble. He didn't have magic, or any special weapon. He was a normal man, with one difference. He had intelligence, creativity, and believed in preparing for everything to the full extent of his abilities.

"The story I'll tell is called Zejo Troufal and the Collector. Anyone heard it before?" He looked at Lily when he asked it. She lifted her chin prettily but shook her head. Good, he didn't want to disappoint someone by telling a tale they already knew.

He started. "Yeva Chernysh was one of the most feared mages in the armies of the Souveni Empire. His mastery of magic and his creativity in designing new spells was unmatched in the forces of Salamus and Gentason. When the War came to an abrupt halt, he was unable to acclimate to a normal lifestyle. After decades of battle, life without combat was too dull for him.

"During that time, the magic of the world was in flux. The last few battles of the War took a great toll on how stable magical power was as well as the physical geography of Dizhelim. Men and women who had used too much power sometimes burned themselves out or had their minds destroyed. Some had physical injuries, backlash from the battlefields where great amounts of power were used, and others were affected mentally by the horror of the whole thing. It was a dangerous time to live.

"Yeva Chernysh became known as the Collector. He got the name because of his habit of collecting something of every champion he ever slew. It might be a weapon—or part of one—or a piece of the person, even some memento such as a locket, ring, or other type of jewelry. Wherever he traveled, he took with him a wagon full of the trophies of his battles.

"He had started long before the war ended, but because of his skills, the strange habit was overlooked by the Souveni emperor. In fact, tales of his brutal battles were often passed from area to area, striking fear into the hearts of those who stood against the empire.

"After the War, the Collector traveled across the whole of Dizhelim with a small army of personal soldiers, servants, and of course, his wagon of souvenirs. In fact, the word *souvenir,* meaning tokens kept as a reminder, comes from his collection when he was in the Souveni military force.

"As I said, he would travel from place to place. He was always looking for his next challenge, a hero or champion he could battle to the death and add some little thing to his collection. He didn't always face them one-on-one, of course. At times, when the mood struck him, he would hunt down an opponent and simply throw his men at the enemy until he was dead, at which point he would harvest his memento. But a great majority of his victories *were* tests of combat between himself and the opponent.

"As his reputation grew, he found fewer and fewer champions to fight, so he began to challenge villages and small towns, often slaughtering the entire population.

"Yeva was always experimenting with magic, and over his long career, he had created a few spells that nearly assured his victory regardless of who he was fighting. Of these unique spells, the most often used was a shield spell that was superior to any other similar spell. It blocked magic, physical attacks, projectiles, explosions, basically anything that might hurt the mage. Unlike many types of shields, he could also cast his magic through it. With no chance of being hurt, he would often sit back behind his protection and pelt the enemy with spells until they succumbed.

"Now, all of this was common knowledge in a world where news of any type of duel or battle was passed from person to person and consumed hungrily by listeners.

"After hearing accounts of what the Collector's men had done to some villages, Zejo Troufal got it into his head to eliminate the mage for the good of all people of Dizhelim. He studied the man, gathering information for several months. Word spread that the Collector would be passing through the area where the small town of Krasca was located when Zejo Troufal happened to be nearby. He took that as good luck and planned to see what he could do about stopping the rogue mage.

"He had less than a week before Yeva would be in Krasca. He sped there from a neighboring town and explained to the town elders what he wanted to do. They were hesitant at first, afraid that they would rile the anger of the mage and ensure their destruction, but he eventually won them over after describing what he had in mind. With their blessing, he got started.

"Zejo directed the townfolk to dig a series of trenches in which they would lay traps. They built fences, something like normal corrals for livestock but specifically designed to channel a human force into a certain area. Additionally, he oversaw the building of places to hide—cubbies and closets where archers or crossbowmen could wait to attack, protected.

"The town worked for several days, finishing only hours before the cloud of dust indicating the Collector's caravan appeared.

"During the time of building, Zejo also had men ride to all the neighboring communities spreading word of a great champion in Krasca. He had no doubt the Collector would hear of this hero and come to do combat with him. The rumors called the champion Troujo, a mix of Zejo's first and last names.

"The Collector's forces arrived as the sun was going down. As was his custom—Zejo had researched it and found the man was consistent in this—Yeva had his men set up camp so he could challenge the town in the morning.

"That wouldn't do, though. Zejo knew the chance of his plan working was much better at night. He had already worked out what to do.

"'Yeva Chernysh, the one they call the Collector,' Zejo shouted from the darkness outside of town. 'I hear you have come looking for the hero Troujo. Come then. Meet your doom.'

"Yeva's troops gathered, the front line with torches. As

per Zejo's prediction, the mage sent his soldiers toward the town to prepare the way for their master.

"The first group fell into pits the townfolk had laid reeds across, covered by blankets, with dirt and sand sprinkled over them to hide their nature. The pits were deep, but that was not their hazard. As the first riders fell, the ones behind them backed up, not chancing that they would slip into the pits as well. At Zejo's command, several fiery brands were shot with arrows into the pits, lighting the oil puddled there.

"The soldiers went up in flames, screaming but not able to climb out. This irritated the Collector, but few of his men had fallen, so he commanded the others to continue.

"They did so, carefully skirting the pits the first soldiers had fallen prey to. They advanced more slowly than they had at first, watching for more trenches. Despite this, groups at the edges of the formation fell into pits like the first and were burned to death as well.

"Now the remaining soldiers advanced at a snail's pace, throwing rocks or torches ahead of them. They succeeded in uncovering a few more pits without falling prey to them.

"Then they reached the fences. Zejo watched and saw in their own torchlight how confused they were. These were not the rows of stakes used in warfare, but simple fences, some six feet tall but others only two or three feet high. Over the shorter ones, some of the mounted soldiers jumped. Half of them fell into pits on the other side of the obstructions. They burned as well.

"The other soldiers followed the fences, being careful to check for pits or for other traps. They found none. The line twisted around, and as the soldiers were spread out, their commanders halted the entire column. After several minutes, a group of foot soldiers was called up to tear up the fences and move them.

"During this time, Zejo and the townspeople did nothing

except shoot fire arrows at the pits. They quietly waited for the next phase of their plan.

"The town was still farther than an arrow could be launched. Only the few archers assigned to fire the pits were close enough, hiding in small pits obscured by dark cloth covers. Because of this, the soldiers didn't seem too concerned with being in the open.

"After the fourth obstruction was moved, though, things changed. There were still nearly two hundred soldiers making their way toward Krasca. They entered an area that was clear of the fences they'd been moving. The entire column halted, not quite knowing what to do.

"That's when the hidden archers uncovered their embers, lit their arrows, and shot toward where the column waited.

"Oil-soaked ropes, dusted with sand, burst into flames inside trenches. The fire raced alongside the soldiers, causing them to spin as the light flared around them. When it got to the middle, the light disappeared with a *ffft*. Nothing happened for a few seconds. The soldiers started to relax, a few of them laughing.

"Then the barrels of oil and sulphur buried in the ground exploded.

"Great craters opened up, and human and horseflesh alike were tossed into the air, much of it in smaller pieces than only a few seconds before.

"Not all of the soldiers were caught in the detonation, but many were. The others had all they could do to keep their horses under control. It was then that the men with bows, who had snuck up to a large, fence-like barricade draped in black cloth, started firing at the remaining soldiers.

"In minutes, the remaining troops were charging back toward their camp, some so quickly they didn't watch for traps. These ended up in more pits, which were set alight by the archers stationed for that purpose.

"'Enough!' the Collector shouted as he shot a fireball into the sky, lighting the entire area in a dull, red light. 'I come to challenge your hero and this is what you do? Your treachery will be rewarded. I need no army for the likes of you.'

"A glowing bubble appeared around Yeva and he began to cast flame about, burning fences, pits, and anyone in the way. He walked calmly toward the archers, leaving destruction as he passed.

"By the time he got close to the barricade where the town's archers had hidden, they had retreated back to the village. It was Zejo's turn now. He had prepared as best he could. With a little luck, some skill, and his plan, he could end the Collector.

"Zejo appeared in front of the mage, standing tall, sword in hand. 'I am Troujo,' he said. 'Come meet me, if you dare.'

"Without a second thought, Yeva shot a blast of power from his hand, crashing into Zejo, completely consuming him.

"Except, it didn't. The mirror that held Zejo's dim reflection shattered as the spell hit it. Another image popped up, fifteen feet from the first. 'Is that all you can do?' he shouted.

"A fireball slammed into the second image, destroying the mirror. The Collector growled, eyes darting to find his opponent.

"One more mirror reflected Zejo's image. The hero had practiced with the reflections each night since he had arrived at the town. By carefully considering where the mage would go—at the gentle goading from Zejo, of course—he was able to place the mirrors at the correct angle and have the cloth covering removed so that the flame from the burning barricades would lighten one image after another. With the third, his plan would nearly be complete.

"The mage turned and saw the third image. He raised his hand to throw his magic, but then stopped. He tilted his head and looked at the mirror, considering. Zejo tried to mentally force the caster to finish, to destroy the mirror, but Yeva hesitated. Why was he hesitating?

"The Collector turned from the image and faced the town. He began to walk toward it. Zejo had to do something fast. If the mage made it to the town, he would destroy the entire population. Thinking quickly, he picked up a burning piece of wood and ran toward the mage.

"'Hey,' he said. 'I'm here. Come get me.' He ran off to Yeva's left as if to circle the mage.

"The Collector's hand glowed and he followed the running man, sighting for the magic he would throw. He took one step toward Zejo, a glowing ball of power forming on his hand.

"That one step was all Zejo needed.

"The Collector stepped onto a trigger buried in the sand. It activated a device much like a crossbow, which released the tension, triggering six other like devices. All of them were attached to glass bottles of paint. They were flung at the target and all of them shattered against Yeva's shield.

"Covering the entire thing in black paint.

"The bubble surrounding the Collector was as good as a solid stone wall for seeing out of. The mage could cast through it—and he did—but without aiming, it did little good. Any paint that burned away was replaced by more dripping down from above. It would only last for a few seconds, but Zejo hoped it was enough.

"With curses and threats, the Collector fired off another blast of power and then dropped his shield, already casting the spell anew to protect himself again.

"He was too late. Zejo was standing just behind Yeva when the shield went down. Before he cast a new one, the hero slashed and tore out the mage's throat. The Collector's magic fizzled in his hands and he dropped to the ground, the liquid of his life pooling on the ground.

"When he brought the mage's body back to the town so they could hang it as a trophy, the gaping elders asked how Zejo had done it. He hadn't confided his entire plan in the town for fear they'd balk at it all being based on his ability to outthink his opponent.

"'I researched it, spoke with those who had been in the Souveni army with Yeva or those who had seen him use his magic,' he explained. 'Most who had seen him cast his shield spell told me it took at least two seconds to bring the magic up. I watched when he first cast it tonight, and that information seemed to be accurate. It only took me one second to cut his throat. That left me a second to spare before he burned me to a cinder.'

"The elders stared at him with their mouths open as he picked up his pack and headed out toward the west."

Tere took another drink from his mug, eyes on Lily. Her green eyes blazed, excitement dancing in them, nearly as bright as Raki's. Funny, he hadn't figured her for a big fan of stories. At least not ones that didn't involve Erent Caahs. He'd have to remember that. He had others she'd appreciate. Reactions like that might make him actually like telling tales.

❦ I I ❦

The next day was a full day of travel. After breakfast, the party saddled up and continued their journey north. It was a pleasant day for it, the sun shining, a few scattered fluffy clouds breaking up the blue of the sky. It was enough to make a man forget all the horrible things going on in the world and stop to take a breath.

Tere did so, sucking in a lungful of air and releasing it slowly.

Lily rode next to him, watching him. What, did she think he was going to do something miraculous and heroic right there on the road? Fool girl.

"...and so we took care of Quentin Duzen," Marla said, "but that didn't really close up all the little details about the murder of Master Aeid." She was talking to Fahtin, and ostensibly Urun, though the priest seemed to be paying as little attention as was normal recently.

Tere wasn't sure what was going on with the nature priest. When he had first brought Aeden and the two Gypta to Urun's home in the forest, he fell over himself at Fahtin's beauty. Now, he had the opportunity to converse with not only her but with Marla as well. Both women were striking—though if one were to choose a redhead, Tere would have chosen Lily—but Urun seemed uninterested in them.

"I'm certain Quentin was the actual one to murder the master. He told me as much," Marla continued. "But what else is there? He said the master had to die because he was about to announce that I was the Malatirsay. That hardly seems worth murder.

"Then there's his connection with the animaru and with Izhrod, though that one is easy because they were both Academy Adepts. Still, what are we missing?"

"Does there have to be anything missing?" Aeden asked. "Maybe that was it. The master planned to give evidence that you were the Malatirsay. That would be dangerous to their cause. You could have rallied the Academy to fight the animaru alongside you. All their planning would have been ruined. From what I've seen, the animaru, Benzal, Quentin—they all seemed to be relying on the Academy not finding out about them until it was too late."

"Sure," Marla said. "The problem with that is that I never would have found out about the dark creatures if I hadn't gone outside the Academy to investigate the murder. And what about Ren Kenata and his letters, the mysterious Council? I think there's still a lot we don't know."

"Aye, I have to agree with that part of it. Maybe we'll find out there was something more to Quentin or the master's death, but I think there are more important things for us to focus on right now."

"Things like what?" Raki asked.

"Many things," Aeden said. "There are still others out there who can bring animaru over from Aruzhelim. The ones with Quentin weren't from Benzal's lot. More importantly, we need to start thinking long-term. How are the animaru getting here now, and what are their plans? Is it still to kill me or have they given that up and moved on with their main invasion strategies? We can add in the uncertainty of how the different kingdoms and nations will react, too. Will they join us or try to bargain with the animaru?"

"Damn," Marla said. "You're right. On a good day, half the kingdoms out there would rather be at war with each other or some of the other half. Sutania and Rhaltzheim have been fighting for decades over land they believe belongs to them. It rarely ends up coming to physical battles, though that does happen, but you get ambassadors from those nations together in a room and you can feel the air heating up. There are similar situations with other kingdoms."

Fahtin leaned forward in her saddle. "Won't they put aside their squabbles when it comes to the possible destruction of all people in Dizhelim?"

Marla laughed. "Not likely. The only thing they'd probably be concerned with is if their enemies were destroyed first. I could see any number of nations joining the side of the animaru just to get a chance to destroy their neighbors. And to survive the coming invasion, of course."

"They will not," Khrazhti said softly.

"What was that?" Marla asked.

The blue woman spoke a little louder. "They will not survive. Any who join the animaru will spend their lives and power fighting their fellow humans, but in the end, the animaru will destroy them as well. There is no halfway for the god S'ru. He will cause this world to become like Aruzhelim: lifeless. It is the only way he will accept it as his new domain. All light and life will be eliminated. I believed once he would allow humans to remain. I was mistaken. It is a mistake to join with him."

"I don't know S'ru," Aeden said, "but I agree—joining your enemy and hoping for consideration when the war is done is a silly way of carrying on a war whose sole purpose is the annihilation of all life. Once humanity is devastated, what will there be left to resist the animaru?"

"You bring up a good point," Marla said. "We should probably start approaching rulers and gaining allies. With more animaru coming over, things will quickly get out of hand."

Tere listened to it all, agreeing completely. He had never wanted to involve himself in the politics of the world. It was bad enough dealing with a single ruler. Hells, interacting with one noble had, at times, made him want to jump into a fire. He was glad he wasn't the one in charge. He would fight or brave danger, but he wouldn't be talking with any of the rulers anytime soon.

The conversation shifted away from politics to less weighty topics. Aeden and Khrazhti slowed and drifted back to where Tere and Lily rode at the back of the group.

"So, Lily," the young warrior said. "I haven't heard your story."

"My story?" the archer asked.

"Yes. The tale of how you learned to be so good with the bow and the knives and how you found your way to the Falxen and then finally to us. Would you tell us?"

The woman actually looked flustered. She stammered to spit out words that made sense. "It's not a very interesting story. You don't want to hear it."

"Come, Lily," Khrazhti said. "You have heard my story, as well as Aeden's, Marla's, and others. Nearly all your companions have told their story. We would like to learn about you and how you became the great warrior you are."

Lily mouthed the words *great warrior*, her eyes focused far away.

"I guess I could tell it," she said, "but I'm being serious. It's not very interesting."

"Please tell us anyway," Khrazhti said, smiling at the woman. The animaru was really getting the hang of the whole smiling thing. Without thinking, Tere found himself responding to the expression and smiling back at her.

"Okay, but it's kind of embarrassing." Her cheeks reddened as she said it.

"Come on, Lily," Fahtin said. "We're all friends here. There's no need to be embarrassed."

"That's fine for me, but someone else might be embarrassed by it." She took a breath. "I'll just tell it and get it over with.

"I was born Lily Fisher in the town of Drusca, in Sutania. The town is famous for its firearms; several master smiths and alchemists work there to create the magnificent weapons. Of course, only the richest people can afford them, but that's another story.

"When I was four years old, my family moved to Arcusheim, similar to others I've heard of." She cast a glance toward Tere, but he did his best to ignore those green orbs.

"Of course, the most famous son of Arcusheim is Erent Caahs, the famous hero who, though he wasn't born there, was raised in the city. From the first tale I heard, I couldn't get enough stories about him. I idolized him, imagining he would come to town and sweep me up, choosing me as his apprentice and wife, making me the happiest girl in all of Dizhelim. You have to understand I was only five years old or so at the time."

She was staring at Tere again and he was regretting his desire to hear Lily's story, or at least hear it with everyone else listening. The sun seemed to be beating down on him more fiercely than it did earlier.

"I did say it might be embarrassing," Lily continued. "Anyway, my father supported my whims wholeheartedly. I told him constantly I wanted to be just like Erent Caahs. I would learn to fight as he did, and I would be a famous hero, defeating evil people and saving good ones. To that end, he got a child-sized bow for me and carved two knives from pieces of firewood. Even though I was a sickly child, he humored my dreams and listened to me endlessly chatter on about them.

"I practiced with the weapons constantly, asking everyone for tips to help me become better. The hunters and soldiers for miles around were at risk of being cornered and questioned, even asked to watch me perform mock battles to help me improve. But I was a little girl and they were always kind to me, even if I most likely was a horrible annoyance."

"Awww," Fahtin said. "I'm sure you were very sweet and extremely cute. Those men probably loved you like their own daughters."

Lily cleared her throat. "It could be. They were helpful. I remember when I was seven years old, I cut most of my hair off because I believed it made me look more like Erent Caahs. Of course, when I found out he always had long hair, I was disappointed, but not nearly as disappointed as my parents were that I had cut it.

"The point is, in every way I knew how, I worked toward being like my hero. The bow, the long knives, tracking, hunting, reading everything I could get my hands on, all of it. I taught myself to read because I heard tales of how he voraciously devoured every book he could find. It was a good childhood, if awkward and difficult.

"As I entered my teenage years, my obsession lost some of its shine with my parents. A child's infatuation with being a hero is one thing, but a young woman? Not so much. I saw the looks they gave me and, more importantly, those they gave each other. I was just waiting for them to talk to me about it all, and most likely take my weapons away. My fake weapons, that is. I still hadn't convinced my father to give me real knives, though my arrows were serviceable since I had learned how to make them myself.

"Then, toward the end of my thirteenth year, my family headed out toward the Great Enclave. My father had temporary work there and we would be staying for two months. I was so excited. On the road, however, bandits from the mountains attacked our caravan, much as had happened with the encali caravan when Erent Caahs had left Arcusheim to hunt for the man who killed his family.

"The men fought valiantly and the bandits were repelled. I helped, killing four myself with the arrows I had made. Unfortunately, as I drew back an arrow, another bandit lunged at me with a sword. I froze, scared to my core. At the last minute, my father jumped in front of me and was himself run through. I put an arrow in the bandit's eye.

"After the remaining highwaymen fled, I found my mother slumped against our wagon, a deep slash in her throat. Both of my parents had been killed. I was alone. I know, it seems like all the hero stories start with a child's parents getting killed, but sometimes stories are clichés because they're true.

"When we got to the Great Enclave, I didn't know what to do. I was a young girl with hardly any money and who knew no one. The money I had from my parents ran out quickly, and I needed to decide what to do. That's when I saw the announcement.

"There was to be a tournament in Metrovial, and included in the contests was an archery match. I used my last few coppers to enter, hoping I could get one of the prizes. As it turned out, I won the competition and received enough gold to last me for a while longer.

"With nowhere else to go, I stayed in the capital city, doing what jobs I could and living on the streets. It was a dangerous place for a young girl and I had to defend myself constantly. That became significantly easier when I was able to trade for two real long knives. They weren't high quality, but they had a decent edge. It only took twice defending myself with them to get a reputation for knowing how to use them.

"I lived on the streets for a few years, constantly practicing my skills and doing my best to gain new ones. I had found that hunting and tracking paid better than doing odd jobs in the city, so I settled into a routine. It was a harsh life, but I was making do.

"Then one day, a woman approached me. She moved gracefully. I had learned how to pick out those who were most dangerous, and she most certainly fit the bill. I was on guard, my hands on my knives as she explained to me that she was of the Falxen.

"She was a recruiter, and she had observed me over the course of a few weeks. She offered to bring me into the organization, where I could use my skills and never have to worry about going hungry again.

"I told her I would join on one condition. The Falxen would help me find the bandits who had killed my parents and they would let me kill them myself. She agreed and I traveled to their headquarters.

"They made special accommodation for me, since I already had the skills they wanted. I didn't have to train at their facility, only go through an orientation to familiarize myself with their procedures and methods. Several weeks later, accompanied by two Falxen and the information I desired, I found the bandit camp that had been responsible for the attack.

"I slaughtered every last man and woman in the bandit camp. Thirty-two people died receiving my arrows over the course of a week, all while my two Falxen companions stood back and watched in fascination. Half of those I killed I did so with fire arrows. I had grown fond of them, fancying that the shafts looked like little effigies of my own form, red flame dancing on their tips. I don't even know if the specific bandits I killed were the same who attacked my caravan, though the bandit group was the same. It had been a few years. Still, it gave some finality to the girl I had been before the attack.

"After that, I began work with the assassins. Every Falxen gives up their name and is given a new one, a one-word moniker that indicates something about the assassin. My new name was Phoenixarrow—all one word—for obvious reasons.

"During my tenure with the Blades, I successfully completed forty-eight missions. Each time, my conscience twisted my insides. All I could think was, 'what would my hero Erent Caahs think of me?' The answer was simple. He would kill me. I was the type of person he, in his heroism, always strove to destroy. I went from day to day, numb, trying not to think. Existing.

"Until my brace sided with the dark monsters that were here to eliminate all humans. I may have been a pathetic, murdering monster myself, but I had my limits. When I got the opportunity, I cast off my assassin cloak and begged an older, blind archer to spare me. Even as I did it, I knew, somehow, who he was, though I dared not speak of it. He, in his kindness, showed me mercy, as all great heroes do."

Lily blew out a breath and looked down at her saddle. The air was silent save for the clip-clop of the horses and the buzzing of a few flies.

For the first time since he had been blinded, Tere Chizzit wished his ruined eyes could shed tears.

❧ 12 ❧

The next day's ride consisted of harmless banter, a mood that was artificially light, and multiple extended conversations about when the party would arrive in Ebenrau. It was everything that made Tere hate being around people.

Except Lily. She didn't show any ill effects from emptying her heart the day before. In fact, she seemed in fine spirits. Tere, on the other hand, felt awful. This beautiful young woman, marvelous warrior that she was, saw him in a light that was not only unreasonable, but just plain false.

How could he tell her that her image of the man he used to be was wrong? Would it help her to reconcile him with the current old man riding nearby or would it shatter her very core, the thing that made her who she was? She had abandoned the life of a paid killer to become the hero she had always wanted. Would the truth of Erent Caahs—Tere Chizzit—kill that dream?

It was a tough call. He didn't want her to believe he was something he wasn't, but he didn't want to hurt her any more than she already had been. He decided he'd leave it alone for now. If she continued to travel with him, she'd find out what a petty, irritable son of a bitch he really was. If she came to it slowly, it might not even affect her. After all, she was surrounded by real heroes. Hells, the party had both halves of the Malatirsay, the greatest heroes in all of history, or at least the ones bearing the greatest expectations.

Yeah, he'd let her realize her adoration was misplaced and he'd help to gently nudge her toward Aeden and Marla. She had the potential to be one of the great heroes herself, if she'd just let go of her fixation with one washed-up archer.

He glanced at her again. *Oh Lili*, he thought, thinking of his sister Lilianor. *How I miss you. You would have loved this woman. Feisty, smart, and honorable. You would have been great friends. If only...*

He stopped that thought process abruptly. Nothing but pain down that road. It was unfortunate the red-haired woman shared the name of his long-dead sister, but coincidences happened. Tere had learned long ago to take the world as it was. The horrible, ruined, pile of animal feces that it was.

He sighed.

In the corner of his vision, Fahtin lurched in her saddle, leaning too far. Tere kicked his horse into quicker motion and pulled up next to the Gypta girl just as she was falling off her horse. He grabbed her, hugging her to himself and supporting her weight completely when her horse, spooked by the sudden movement, moved away.

Aeden and Marla seemed to be having a reaction to something as well, though they handled it more ably than Fahtin had. Raki had hunched into a ball, but remained on his horse.

"Lily, come help me," Tere said. He could feel Fahtin slipping from his grasp through he was squeezing her hard.

Lily jumped from her saddle and reached up to put her

hands around Fahtin's waist. Tere let the girl down slowly and Lily hugged her, lowering the Gypta to the ground.

"Are you okay, Fahtin?" Lily asked.

"What? Oh, what was that?" Fahtin shook her head and blinked several times. "It seemed like the world flip-flopped. I got really dizzy and felt like I was blacking out."

"I felt it, too." Aeden dismounted and came close to check on Fahtin.

"Me too," Marla said.

"And me," Raki wheezed. He still seemed under the effects of whatever happened.

Tere scanned the area and saw Khrazhti, her eyes tight as if she was in pain.

"Khrazhti?" he said.

"I am fine. There was a magical surge I had not antici-pated. It was...painful."

"What's going on, Marla?" Aeden asked.

"It's like before," Urun said. "I thought it was localized then, but perhaps not." He didn't look any worse for wear, but if something happened with magic, the priest would have felt it, too. Tere and Urun had felt magic do something strange when they were traveling north toward the Academy.

"I've felt something like it before as well," Aeden said.

Marla rubbed her temples. "Yeah, I felt a strange shift before, too. Just before I cast the spell Hurricane and did more damage than I thought possible. It's obvious: magic in the world is shifting. It has to have something to do with the animaru coming over from Aruzhelim."

"It has something to do with our quest," Fahtin said.

"What?" Marla asked.

"It's the same feeling I had when I was in my visions. Magic is...swirling. It's tumultuous. I think it's changing."

"I don't like the sound of that," Aeden said. "Is everyone all right? Before, there was only one occurrence, not a series of them. I'm assuming it's the same this time. I guess it's more important than ever to get to Ebenrau and figure out what's going on."

None of the party seemed to have lingering effects, so they mounted up and continued on their way. They made it to the city an hour before sundown.

The slanted rays of the setting sun washed over the walls of Ebenrau, one of the great cities of the world. It sat majestically in the northwestern corner of the eastern section of the main continent of Promistala, touching the shore of the sea on both the north and west sides.

Khrazhti drew in a huge breath when she saw it, significant because she didn't normally breathe. Tere wasn't sure what kinds of structures or communities they had in Aruzhelim, but from what she had said, they had no grand collections of buildings like a normal city of Dizhelim, let alone the one before them. She'd seen Satta Sarak, but the southern city wasn't the same type of spectacle as Ebenrau.

"What is the purpose of that structure there?" Khrazhti pointed to the gate made up of flat, heavy steel bars that overlapped and ended in sharpened points at the bottom.

"That's a portcullis," Aeden said. It was raised so only the bottom few feet showed in the mouth of the gateway. "It provides extra protection, along with the gates, for when the city is attacked. With it lowered, invaders not only have to get through the gates and crossbars, but the portcullis as well. Since it's all one piece, it is strong against battering rams."

Khrazhti's eyes followed the outline of the gate to the portcullis. She nodded. "How is it lowered?"

Aeden pointed through the gate to a small building nestled against the wall, just barely visible from their distance and angle of vision. "In that building, there is a control with a simple machine, a winch. The ropes go from the winch to the portcullis along the wall and through pulleys. Do you have machines like winches in Aruzhelim?"

"Yes, we have simple machines, but no fortifications like this. Most battle is done in the open, not with one side hiding behind rocks."

Aeden laughed and the two moved ahead to get a better look as they approached the gate.

Tere scanned the silhouette of the entire city through the gate. Ebenrau had always seemed...sharp to Tere. The spires, the slender but tall buildings, even the windows seemed to bleed toward the heavens, almost as if some force were stretching them skyward. The walls were high and sturdy, but even they seemed graceful, with sharp crenels on top and massive doors that, though wide, were much taller than their girth.

A pit of nausea attacked him as he watched the dying sunlight dance on the city's walls. He frowned, working his jaw to try to reduce the taste of bile in his mouth, and leaned over to spit, but found Lily staring at him. He swallowed instead. The taste nearly made him vomit.

"Are you all right, Tere?" the woman asked.

"Yeah. No. I just don't really care for this city, is all. It's... it's nothing."

"Are you sure? You want some water or something?"

"No, damn it," he said. "It's nothing, I said. I just...it's that...oh, let's just get inside and get this fool trip done and over with. Maybe it's my lucky day and someone will kill me."

He yanked his reins and started his horse moving toward the gate.

You're some piece of work, he told himself. *Yelling at the girl. What's wrong with you? She's never been anything but kind to you, except when she was trying to kill you, but you can't blame her for that, her not knowing who I was. She's just trying to be nice.*

The others had taken his lead, following a few horse

lengths behind him. Aeden was quietly talking to Khrazhti, no doubt explaining more wonders of the city. The others were more subdued than normal.

Lily rode alone, just behind and to the side of Tere.

"I'm sorry, girl," he called over his shoulder to her. "Bad memories are being churned up, making me churlish. It's not your fault. I'm an ornery old man, is all."

She moved up next to him, her eyes sad. He wished she didn't do that. He didn't deserve her sympathy.

"You want to talk about it?"

"No," he said too quickly. She flinched as if struck. "That's the problem with living, the memories sort of bunch up, waiting to spring on you. They seem to know when the right time is to do it, too. When they can knock the legs out from under you."

The girl didn't say anything, only kept pace with him, her horse next to his. After a few more minutes, he couldn't tolerate it anymore.

"Lela," he said.

Her eyes lit up and she nodded, realizing the problem from that one word. She was a smart one, this girl. There was no need for him to explain who Lela Ganeva was to her. She knew all the stories, probably knew backward and forward how he met Lela and fell in love with her.

He knew she'd heard the story of how Lela had been killed in front of him. Tere himself had told that story, mostly to stop the others from asking for more stories about the man he used to be.

"She made me promise her I'd take her here one day, show her the city, maybe catch a riverboat to see the scenery. She was so excited when I told her I'd do it. She reminded me whenever I'd visit her, told me about how great it would be.

"I never did get around to keeping that promise. There was always another crisis, some other thing for Erent damnable Caahs to go and do. Up to when that bastard took her away from me, away from everyone. It would have been better if I'd left it alone and let him keep her captive. At least she'd be alive."

Lily had moved her horse up closer to him as he was looking toward the city walls. He hadn't even noticed until she put her hand on his arm. "I'm so sorry," she said, her eyes watery.

"Yeah, me too." He patted her hand with his. "So, anyway, seeing the city doesn't really bring back good memories, though I had some of the place, once. I'm sorry if I'm in a foul mood. It's just that…"

"I know," she said softly. "I know. So many stories about her. I wish I could have met her."

"She would have liked you. She always did know how to see into the heart of people. Lili was like that, too. My sister. Even young, she was the best of people. Sometimes I wonder what the gods have against the world, that people like them are taken away and old, bitter bastards like me are still here, plodding away."

A few tears fell down Lily's cheek, but she smiled. Gods, how it hurt to see that sad smile. "You old, bitter bastards have prevented so many other good people from being taken away. It doesn't make up for it, but it should mean something."

He couldn't answer for the lump in his throat. Instead, he put his head down and guided his horse to the gates of the city.

❦ 13 ❦

"**C**ome to order," said Alloria Yurgen, Vituma of the Dark Council. "We have much to discuss."

It was a formality. The other twelve members of the Council were already in their seats and—for the most part—quiet. They had simply been waiting for the meeting to start.

"Things will begin moving more quickly," she said. "The time for hiding and watching is nearly at an end. The signs point toward this being the end of the age, the era that all Council members have been awaiting for the last three millennia."

Chin raised, she swiveled her head slowly to make eye contact with each of the others. Their expressions ranged from stoically waiting for her next words to excitement dancing in their eyes. What she didn't see was any sign of inattention. Good. They realized this was not just a meeting for the sake of gathering. They had real matters to discuss.

"Ren Kenata," she said suddenly in the silence. Yoniko Takesi jumped. She had been focusing on Gareth Briggs, across the table and over one place from her. The man was handsome, if older, but Yoniko should know better than to stare at him like that.

"Yes, Vituma," the Teroshimi man said. He was good-looking as well, though Yoniko wouldn't allow herself to stare at *him*. He was of an upper class, higher than the woman's family, and she wouldn't risk dishonoring him or herself.

"When last we met, you revealed to us that Quentin Duzen had most likely been killed by this Marla Shrike and her friends. Have you been in contact with your spies at Sitor-Kanda?"

"I was able to contact one of them. The only information I obtained was that indeed Quentin was killed."

"And the matter of the letters in your robes that fell into the hands of the Academy?"

Ren dropped his eyes to the table. He didn't blush, but Alloria knew he was feeling his shame keenly. Teroshimi were more prickly about that than most. "I haven't heard anything about them. As we discussed, all but one were encoded. That one was from Quentin and shouldn't cause any problems. For the others, it may be that it won't be worth the work necessary to decode them."

"It may be?"

"Yes. If they make it a priority, they'll eventually be able to crack the code and read them. They were notes from the Council to me. They wouldn't reveal much information about us, but they would indicate that we exist as a group."

"You will contact your spies and have them notify you immediately if the notes are decoded," Alloria said. "You will then notify us."

"Yes, Vituma."

Alloria swept her long hair back over her shoulder. It was pale blonde, almost white, and stood out in stark contrast to her black clothing.

"It is unfortunate we no longer have suitable allies within

any of the groups of Academy graduates. We must remedy that. Izhrod Benzal is dead and Quentin Duzen is dead, along with their close associates. Who is left that can open portals to Aruzhelim and continue the migration of the animaru to our world?"

None of the Council members answered.

"Sirak Isayu, Thomlyn Byrch, you will make this your priority. Find out which humans are working with the animaru and to what extent. We must keep track of what is happening. We must *control* what is happening."

"Yes, Vituma," Sirak said, bowing his dark head. His accent from the far south of the continent of Promistala was unusual, as was the man. Only through a strange chance was he part of the Council at all. He had proven his worth, though, which was all that mattered.

"I'll get it done," Thomlyn told her. The man appeared to be a joke, one not suitable for the Council's work, but his jovial demeanor and bushy white beard hid a shrewd man who could get results when assigned a task.

"Ren, you will continue trying to find suitable Academy graduates who might be able to make the portals. Do not recruit them, but identify them and bring your information to the Council. We must decide if we want to work with the dark creatures or against them. Having the ability to reach their world will strengthen our bargaining position, should we choose the former."

"Yes, Vituma," Ren said.

"Until we get more information, we will not be able to act outside of what we have been doing and the preparations we have been making. I will not fail in the task that has been handed down for over a hundred generations. Now, if there is nothing—"

"I've got something," Thalia Fendove said.

Of course she did. Alloria focused on the other woman.

Of all the Council, Thalia was nearly the complete opposite of Alloria. Whereas the Vituma was tall—taller than most on the Council—and had straight blonde hair and very pale skin, with blue eyes so light they were nearly colorless, Thalia was more than half a foot shorter, with wavy dark hair, dark eyes, and olive skin. Alloria's face was long and slender while Thalia's was rounder, with fuller lips. The Vituma sometimes felt like a twig standing next to the curvier woman.

Their personalities did not mesh, either. The darker woman was a schemer and selfishly pursued her own objectives, whereas Alloria acted only in the interests of the Council. To be fair, all of the other members had their own agendas and acted in their own interests, but Thalia seemed to have taken the process and made it an art form. Pursuing personal projects was fine, but the Council needed to be the most important thing. Alloria didn't believe for a moment that it was that way for Thalia Fendove.

"What is it?" Alloria asked.

"There has been some kind of power spike near Ebenrau."

"Power spike? What do you mean?"

"I don't know exactly what it is, but one of my associates felt some strange magical energies near that city. I sent a team to try to find it and see what it is. It could be some sort of magical weapon or a group of casters working together for some purpose."

"I see," Alloria said. "If it's important, why aren't you there sniffing it out? I would think that if it's significant, you would want to go find it yourself."

The dark-haired woman's lips curved into a predatory smile. "I may go check on it, once my team finds out what it is. I have many other things occupying my time. I can't go running off at every little thing."

"Meaning that you think it's important enough to tell the Council about it, but not enough for you to risk any type of danger investigating it. Do us all a favor, Thalia, and keep these things to yourself until you have more information."

"As you wish. I thought you might like to know. I will keep any further discoveries to myself."

"Amatia," the leader said, "Do you sense anything similar to what Thalia describes?"

The seeress raised her brown eyes from where they had rested on the table and shook out her long, dark hair. "Things have been difficult lately. I am sensing some...interference in my visions. I cannot support or deny what Thalia has reported. I'm sorry. I will inform the Council as soon as I know more."

Alloria shook her head and put the women out of her mind. "Does anyone have anything else that needs to be discussed? If not, we will end this meeting. Next time, I will expect reports on everything you are working on. We need to begin coordinating more fully. The time is upon us. We can't solely pursue our individual projects any longer."

The meeting itself was clearly not worth bringing all the Council members to headquarters, but the main gathering was not all. She had several discussions with individual Council members scheduled before they departed to their own locations. Some plans and conversations were best kept between two or three Council members.

Normally, she would have held the meeting using the meeting stones, a magical method for assembling the Council without physical travel. It was important for them to see and interact with each other in the same place occasionally, however. Her father had taught her that if all business was done through the stones, the Council members became aloof and apathetic, not seeing the other members as real people at all. He had been Vituma for decades and she took his counsel seriously.

It seemed the waited-for time had come, and it had done

so during her tenure. It was a privilege, truly, but also a heavy burden. The tools she had to work with seemed inadequate for the task, but she would make do. She would have to.

Three thousand years of planning had come down to the present. Succeed or fail, she and the other Council members would see the end of the world as they knew it.

14

"**M**ake sure you look for this symbol," Fahtin said, pointing toward the drawing of the shape she saw in her visions. "It appeared several times and I think it's the key to finding where we're supposed to go or what we're supposed to do."

Tere stared at the symbol as the others prepared. He wanted to have it memorized. There was no telling where it would be located or if it would be mixed in with other shapes.

It might appear as a stain on a vegetable in the marketplace, or in the bottom of a tankard after all but the foam or the wine dregs had been drunk.

He hated puzzles. Why couldn't they just find where they needed to go and charge in with arrows flying and knives flashing? Not that he was any good at that any longer without his magical sight to aid him.

"So it's going to be me, Lily, Raki, and Urun in one group and then Fahtin, Aeden, Khrazhti, and Marla in the other," he said. "We'll explore from Market Street to the east, and you'll take west of the street up to Craftsman Road. Whoever finds the symbol, come back here so we can bring the whole group and explore it together. Got it?"

"Aye, we've got it," Aeden said.

They had taken rooms at an inn in the southeastern part of the city. It wasn't bad. Tere had stayed in better, but then again, he'd also stayed in worse. The rooms were comfortable enough, though he kind of missed the one he'd gotten used to at the Academy, and their own private common room there. Gods, he was getting soft.

The innkeeper, a tall man with a large belly and thinning grey hair named Bernhard Lindner, had been very kind. To Fahtin, he'd been even more so, speaking to her more than Tere, even though the archer was the one who handed him the coin. Whenever he queried the party if they needed anything, it was always done while looking directly at Fahtin. He was well and truly smitten by the Gypta girl. Tere would have to figure out how to use that to their advantage.

"Try not to be too noticeable," he said. "If people pay as much attention to us as Master Bernhard does to Fahtin, they'll never forget us." The girl blushed and fiddled with a loose thread on her sleeve. "No telling what this whole thing's about. Fahtin said she sensed danger, but she doesn't know what kind. It could just as easily be an assassin's guild or something."

Lily scoffed at that. She would, a former Falxen assassin. Any guild with intelligence would bow down and kiss the feet of a Blade.

"'Try not to be noticeable,' says the man with white eyes," Aeden said. "I think the rest of us can blend in, but you and Lily, people will remember seeing you."

"What do you mean?" Lily asked. "Why would you think I won't blend in?"

Marla guffawed. "Please, woman. A tall, gorgeous red-haired woman with hardly a scrap of clothing on, showing nearly all her...charms. The men in the city won't forget seeing you for months."

It was Lily's turn to flush, then mumbled. "Look who's talking. Speaking of gorgeous redheads."

Marla winked at her. "Thank you, but I'm fully clothed. I don't stick out quite as much. Still, I'm going to wear my hood to cover my hair. You wouldn't know it looking at our group, but red hair is not all that common in Rhaltzheim. Blonds rule here."

"Too many clothes are restricting in battle," Lily said. "But maybe I can wear a cloak I can throw off if we need to fight."

Khrazhti nodded as she listened to Lily. She already wore a cloak covering her entirely. Tere could see wanting freedom of movement—had even known some male warriors who ran around with their chests and arms bare—but had always opted for loose clothing instead. Not that he was really complaining about the women's attire...

"Yeah, yeah," he said. "You make a good point. I'll cover my face with my hood, too. If I had taken that precaution in Praesturi, we would have saved ourselves a lot of trouble. All right, let's move out. Meet back here at fifth bell. Be careful. There's no telling what we'll come up against."

Tere took his group to their assigned area and they began to systematically walk down the streets, looking for anything unusual.

"Fahtin said there were tunnels, right?" Lily asked.

"Yep," Tere answered.

"Do you think there could be an opening somewhere up here in the city? I've heard of some cities having catacombs or larger ones with tunnels for the privies to drain. Maybe we can find an entrance."

"I'd just as soon not crawl down into a privy to find a tunnel underneath it, thank you very much. But yes, keep your eye out for something that looks like some kind of mine entrance or a deep basement. I think that symbol is the best lead we have, though."

Urun walked along beside them, swiveling his head to look around, but not saying anything. Tere had a thought.

"Urun, do you have any kind of spell that can search out tunnels? Dirt is part of the natural world, right? So that would make it part of Osulin's realm, wouldn't it?"

"No."

"No?"

"No. Osulin is the Goddess of Nature and Growing Things. Dirt doesn't grow; it's not alive. When we refer to nature, as respects hers and her mother Mellaine's realm, we're talking about things that are alive."

"Does that mean that the animaru wouldn't be included?" Lily asked.

The nature priest stopped walking and gave her a flat look. "They are definitely *not* part of nature. They're *un*natural."

"But death is a part of life, isn't it?"

Urun shook his head. "They're not dead, they're un-alive.

There's a big difference. Anyway, the answer to your question is no, I don't have a spell that can find tunnels, nor one to find gold or other metals, in case you were going to ask."

Tere considered his friend. "Are you okay, Urun? I didn't mean to offend you or make you angry."

The dark-haired young man ran his fingers through his hair and sighed. "Sorry. It's my fault. I think these weird episodes with magic going crazy are fraying my nerves. That and Osulin being occupied. I'm not sure what's going on, but it doesn't feel right. It all just has me on edge."

"I understand," the archer said. "I remember how it felt before I lost my magical senses, when the formivestu attacked us, and when all the magic of the world seemed to flip. I'm sure we'll figure out what's going on with Osulin, maybe even be able to help her. Hells, maybe if we find this prize Fahtin has us looking for, it'll do something for her. We'll all do what we can."

"I appreciate it," Urun said. "Come on, we have a lot of city to search, maybe even sewers to wade through. Let's get it over with."

Tere clapped the younger man on the back. "That's the spirit."

The area they searched held mainly homes on a few wider streets with lots of alleys in between. The places they went through weren't exactly rough-looking, but they weren't wealthy, either. They were normal homes for normal folk living their day-to-day lives.

It was as boring a day as Tere could remember, and he'd been locked in a prison cell recently.

They finished their area early and returned to the inn a full hour before they were supposed to meet the others. When the other group dragged in later, they shook their heads tiredly and said they didn't find anything.

It was a quiet dinner, with no one in the mood for conversation. They took a little time to determine where they'd search the next day and headed to their rooms to rest.

Tere woke the next morning feeling as if he had to push thoughts through a sieve clogged with swamp mud. He wasn't sure how to describe it other than that he felt stupid. Great. Now his mind was going, too. A thought occurred to him, something his mentor Arto Deniselo used to repeat often. *Your mind, it must do as you wish. In a beautiful duel, as well as in life, you must control it most of all.* The dueling master would be disappointed in him at the moment.

The archer managed to find his way down to the common room for breakfast with the others and sat down next to Aeden, who had probably already been up for hours.

"Another day of searching, huh?" Tere said. He got confused looks in response. *Did I say something wrong?* he wondered. Maybe it would be better to sit and listen to the others before he spoke again.

"Have you ever had one of those days where you wake up and panic because you don't know where you are?" Aeden asked. "It was like that this morning for me. At first I looked for the wagon, then I thought about it and realized I should be in the room at the Academy. It took more than five minutes to decide I was here in Ebenrau. Another five to remember why."

"I hate that," Marla said. "I'm not at my best today, either. I hope we're not coming down with some illness. Some types of sweating sicknesses do that to you."

"I feel a little better after doing some training," Aeden said, "but I'm still not feeling normal."

Tere ventured another comment. "We should pick up from where we left off yesterday, continuing with the plan."

"The plan?" Fahtin asked, putting a piece of fruit in her mouth.

"Yeah. You know, searching the city for that symbol that...

hey, can I look at the drawing you made of the symbol we're looking for? For some reason, I can't picture it."

"Drawing?" She scrunched her forehead in thought. "Oh, the drawing. Yes, of course." She pulled the paper from her belt pouch and handed it to him.

Tere studied the image for a long minute, then closed his eyes and fixed it in his mind, burning it there. Hadn't he done this already? It wasn't like him to lose an image he had purposely fixed into his memory. He shook his head at the effects of getting older and handed the paper back.

"So, where are we going to search today?" Marla asked.

Tere stared at her for a moment, though staring didn't mean the same thing for him. "Uh, we take up from where we left off yesterday. You know, the grids we made on the map of the city. We did the first couple of areas yesterday."

Marla cocked her head at him and blinked. "Yesss," she drawled. "I guess we did, huh? Remind me where we searched. All this stuffing in my head doesn't seem to remember."

Tere brought out his copy of the map and laid it on the table. He raised his finger to point out where they had spent their time the day before but then found that he couldn't recall. They *did* search the city the day before, didn't they?

Lily pointed toward a section on the east side of Ebenrau. "We went here and the other group went here. I think. At least, that was the plan. I think we finished, though I can't really remember if we found anything."

Tere noticed Khrazhti sitting silently, watching the humans closely. He couldn't see her face because of her hood, but her body position gave the impression she was holding her breath, keeping a close eye on everyone. What was that about?

Urun leaned over to scan the map. "Yes, that's right. We should do these two areas today. At this rate, it'll take us more than a week to get through all the sections of the city. Hopefully we'll find an opening to somewhere underground or something marked with the symbol before then."

"Yeah," Tere said. It was the most intelligent thing he could manage. He hoped his brain woke up before he walked in front of a charging team of horses and got trampled to death.

Though he wanted to discuss what they'd done the day before, he couldn't drag up any specific memories. So he ate in silence, hoping someone else would speak.

They didn't.

When they were finished, the two groups split up and headed toward their destinations.

"Good luck," he told them. "The areas today are a little larger—I think—so let's meet back here at sixth bell. We can eat wherever we're searching. No use in coming back here and wasting that time traipsing across the city to eat together."

The others replied sluggishly. Maybe they were all getting sick. That would explain the way he felt and the slowness of his thoughts. Tere shook his head and led Urun, Raki, and Lily toward their search area.

15

A eden wondered about how unfocused Tere seemed during breakfast. He sympathized; he wasn't having one of his best days either. As hard as he tried, he couldn't remember specifics about what they had spent the previous day doing. Today would be better, though. Even if they didn't find what they were looking for, he'd be able to give the others a detailed report of what his group did. He focused on his task for the day as he and the women walked toward where they'd start their search.

They were lucky that their area for the day included a market section. Lucky because it was more interesting than slogging through streets with nothing but residences along them. Maybe they could even find goods they wanted to purchase. They had a little of their own money, beyond what the headmaster had given them for trip expenses.

The morning consisted of checking along buildings for something that looked like it might lead underground and watching people to get a sense of the city. It was interesting enough, though the four travelers seemed to get their share of people looking at them as well. What did he expect?

People were bound to notice three beautiful women—even if Khrazhti was covered up completely so no one could see her face. No amount of cloak could hide the shape and the grace of the animaru, so between the three of them, Aeden noticed men's heads turning everywhere they went.

Marla seemed to have noticed also. "A lot of men are staring at these two," she told him.

"They're staring at *you three*," he said. "I don't understand why you never think people find you attractive. You're beautiful. I mean enough that I'm almost glad I didn't have to deal with it when you were growing up. I would have been in battles all the time, I think."

"Aww, thank you, Aeden. That's sweet, but I think you're being too kind. I did get in fights all the time, but that's because men are generally pigs." She patted his arm.

He laughed at that, but shook his head. "We really need to get you a good mirror, sister."

The group moved toward another section with homes, finally at the end of the market. A man came jogging up to them and Aeden's hand went to his sword hilt.

"Peace, friend," the man said, raising his own hands to show he wasn't a threat. He was a slight man, and several inches shorter than even Fahtin. His clothing was typical from what they'd seen in the city, trousers with a shirt tucked in and a coat over the top of it, all of it dark colors except the white shirt. His face was so common as to be forgettable, and though Aeden tried to fix the man's features in his mind, he couldn't make his brain do it.

He seemed to be focusing completely on Aeden, not even sparing a glance at the women with him. Aeden thought there was something strange about that, but couldn't finish the thought.

"I've noticed you and your friends the last two days walking around," the man said, smiling. "It seems like you might be looking for something. I can't stand to see folks in trouble like that. I'd like to offer my services. Whatever you're trying to find, old Lennard can help. I know this city like it's my own house. I'll help you, if you like."

"What's in it for you?" Marla asked.

"Well, not much, to be sure, miss. Mostly it'll do my heart good to help out. Course, my time is worth something. Isn't everyone's? How about I help you find what you're looking for and then you give me what you think is fair? What're you trying to find?"

Aeden was about to chase the man off when Fahtin blurted out, "We're trying to find a way into tunnels underneath the city." Aeden glared at his adopted sister, but she wasn't paying attention to him. She was looking hopefully at Lennard.

"Ah, the catacombs. You're in luck. I know just where to go. There's an entrance not too far from here, just over off King's Way. I can take you there now if you want."

Aeden traded looks with Marla. She furrowed her brow as if she was thinking it over but wasn't happy with the process. It was probably whatever sickness seemed to have grabbed hold of them. He tried to latch onto a thought, too, but it was as difficult as catching an eel with his bare hands.

"That's great," Fahtin said. "Aeden, let's go. It'll save us so much time."

Khrazhti kept quiet. She'd wedged herself into a shadowed area where two buildings met, perhaps trying to keep the man from noticing her.

Something still bothered Aeden about the man, but when Marla shrugged at him, he gave in. "Fine. We'll take your guidance, Master Lennard. Lead on."

"Yessir, I will. It's a good thing you ran into me, it surely is. Come along this way. We'll be there in no time."

The four followed the man as he started off. He took

them through several streets and a few alleys, keeping up a conversation as he did it.

"That over there is where the first chandler was in this half of the city. He did a good business, he did, until the trade guilds organized and spread throughout the whole place. Now his shop is a home. If you look to the right, over yonder, you'll see..."

He continued on without seeming to take a breath. It was all Aeden could do to keep track of where they were going. After so many turns, he wasn't sure how to get back to their inn any longer. He could find his way in the wilderness, but cities confounded his sense of direction.

"What do you do here in the city, Lennard?" Marla asked, cutting off an account of a feud that happened twenty years before in the area they were passing through.

"Oh, a little of this and a little of that. I spend a fair amount of time guiding folks in and around the city, telling them about historical places and events."

"You don't say," she said flatly.

"I do say. Why just the other day, a fellow was here all the way from Arania, and he came by land all the way around, not direct by boat. He was looking for..."

Aeden spotted a colorful blanket hanging over a rope outside a window, flapping in the breeze. Hadn't he seen one just like it earlier?

"How much farther, Lennard?" Aeden interrupted.

"Just a bit more. Two more streets over then we'll get you there, I guarantee."

True enough, he brought them up to a large building a few minutes later. It looked to be a storehouse of some kind. The man didn't take them to the large front doors, though. Instead he brought them around to the rear of the building, through a narrow alley, then stopped in front of a cellar door along the side. He swung one of the double doors up and motioned toward it.

Aeden leaned over the hole and looked into the darkness. "It's dark down there."

"Yessir," Lennard said. "Places underneath the ground usually are. Ha ha. Don't fret. I'm just having a little joke with you. There're lanterns down there. We just need a spark to—"

Marla elbowed the man aside with an arm holding a lit torch.

"How'd you..." the man said.

"I'm handy that way." Marla went down the steps. A clanking followed and then the light of her torch grew brighter. She handed up a lit lantern and Aeden accepted it from her.

"Good, good," Lennard said. "Keeps me from having to light one with flint and steel. After you, good sir, and fine ladies."

Aeden started to motion the man to go down first, but Fahtin pushed on Aeden's shoulder to start him moving as she reached for another lantern Marla was handing up. Khrazhti was already slinking down the stairs without waiting for another light source.

Shrugging, Aeden followed the animaru down, Fahtin at his heels. Lennard came down after them, closing the door above them.

"Don't want no one to know what we're doing now, do we?" the man said casually. Aeden supposed that made sense.

At the bottom of the stairs was a fair-sized room with two lit lanterns hanging from the walls on either side. Marla moved toward the other side to light the remaining ones. At the end of the room was a closed wooden door.

"Through that door," Lennard said. "There are a couple of rooms but then there's another door to the catacombs."

Sure enough, through the door was another hallway with a

door on each side and one opposite the one they came through.

Aeden moved toward one of the side doors, but Lennard put his hand on Aeden's shoulder.

"Those are storerooms for the person who owns the building above. It wouldn't be right to go snooping through their stuff, now would it?"

Aeden was going to argue, but Marla opened the door at the end of the hall and made a surprised sound. He hurried up to her to see what had caused the reaction.

The room the door emptied out into was huge. It must have been thirty feet to a side with a ceiling that seemed too high for the distance they traveled down the steps. It was too big to see the other side clearly, but as Marla moved along the sides and lit lamps on brackets on the wall, the whole picture gradually became clear.

There were no other doors in the room other than the one they came through.

Even in the state he was in, Aeden realized that wasn't a good thing. He whirled just in time to see one of the other doors in the hallway open and men empty out of it.

They were all armed, some with crossbows.

"*Ta te neach do cogheen doibh beathach!* Fahtin, get behind me."

"Now, now," Lennard said, accepting a sword from one of the other men. "Let's not make this harder than it needs to be. Just drop your weapons over there in front of you and no one will get hurt."

"What are you doing?" Fahtin asked from behind Aeden.

"Why, we're capturing you. Isn't it obvious? Don't worry, we don't want to hurt you. We'll sell you to good owners. Your man there will fetch a good price as a laborer, but you three, you'll make it worthwhile. Always a good market for beautiful women."

One of the other men leaned in and whispered something to Lennard.

"Oh, right," he said. "Two beautiful women. I haven't had a chance to see the third one there. Come on, honey, take down that hood and let us have a look at you."

Aeden scanned the men arrayed against them—at least twenty, half a dozen with crossbows. He looked toward Marla and Khrazhti and raised one eyebrow. Marla gave a slight nod and Khrazhti's hood dipped marginally.

"Stay behind me, Fahtin," he whispered.

"Okay," she whispered back.

"No," Aeden said loudly enough that all the men could hear him. "You won't be taking any slaves today. I'll give you one chance to turn around and leave."

Lennard looked at the men with him, then back to Aeden. He laughed. "*You'll* give *us* a chance?" He laughed again, and his men with him.

It was fine. Aeden used the time to perform a slight variation of the motions for a spell. He'd been practicing the form lately and even though he seemed to keep slipping with the movements, he felt the power growing in him. He whispered the words of power as the men continued to laugh. Just a little longer.

"*Chadu, nidar, kavach,*" he said firmly and felt the magic snap into place. The air in front of him glimmered for a moment. "Now."

Khrazhti threw off her cloak and stepped toward Aeden, motioning with her hand. A projectile that looked to be made of pure shadow shot out and punched through one of the crossbowmen. As he dropped to the ground, Marla finished a spell and a wash of flame shot out, scorching several men closest to her. The distance was too great for it to kill them, but as their eyebrows and hair shriveled from the heat, they were unable to attack in any way.

"Kill the man," Lennard yelled. "Try to keep from killing the women, or from scarring them too badly." His eyes went wide as he finally caught sight of Khrazhti. "You can kill the blue one."

Four of the remaining men with crossbows fired bolts at Aeden and Khrazhti. They slammed into the shield he had cast and bounced off of it, diverting to skip off the sides of the room.

Fahtin stepped beyond the shield just enough to throw one of her knives. It traveled end over end, sticking in the throat of the only man with a crossbow who hadn't either fired his bolt or been incapacitated. He gurgled as he dropped his weapon and brought his hands up to find the knife's hilt protruding from his neck.

"Before they reload," Aeden said, allowing the shield to drop as he drew his swords and rushed the group. Khrazhti was a step behind him. Marla took a breath to cast a spell and then raced after them, small spheres that looked like they were made of fire—or molten lava—spraying out ahead of her and blasting into some of the men.

Those who were struck with the fire missiles screamed as the projectiles embedded themselves in flesh or blasted through limbs. By the time Marla got to the first of the men, her sword and dagger were already out and carving a bloody path in front of her.

Three men rushed out to engage Aeden. They were the stupid ones. He danced through their blades like they were frozen in stone and cut into them. Aeden slashed one of their throats with his left sword while ramming the blade in his right hand straight through another's chest. The third man sliced downward toward the Croagh's head, but by the time the blade got there, Aeden had already sidestepped and passed the attacker.

He spun with the momentum of the sword that had just

torn out the throat of the man's fellow and slashed downward, cutting deeply into the attacker's arm and causing him to drop his blade. Khrazhti danced behind Aeden, adding a deep gash to the man's face with her swords as she advanced on two more men to Aeden's right.

The other attackers didn't last long. They weren't warriors, just street thugs and bandits who ambushed their prey and overwhelmed them with numbers. That approach didn't work here.

As if by some unspoken agreement, the three—and Fahtin occasionally throwing another knife now and again—cut down the enemies all around Lennard, but the man himself got only a slash on his forearm that made him drop his sword.

The crossbow wielders were all down, allowing Aeden to relax his worry for Fahtin a bit. She was still at the end of the room with all the attackers on the side where Aeden, Khrazhti, and Marla were fighting.

Abruptly, there were no men left on their feet except Aeden and Lennard, who was fleeing toward the stairs to the street.

Aeden took a step to run him down, but a flash of steel zipped by him and lodged in the man's right leg, just above the hollow behind the knee. He screamed and pitched headlong onto the floor, sliding for a few feet before coming to a stop. Whimpering, he attempted to drag himself along, but his injured arm buckled and he only made it a few inches. There was no way he'd escape.

"Check to make sure none of these others are going to be trouble," Marla said, stomping toward the man who had set up the ambush.

Less than a minute later, Aeden reported what he'd found. "There are five left alive, but they're injured. Two of them will probably die soon unless they get some help. None of them are in any condition to fight."

"Good," Marla said, dragging a squealing Lennard back toward his friends.

"What will you do with them?" Khrazhti asked.

Aeden wondered what she would do. He was pretty sure standard animaru procedure was to kill off any enemies that could be killed. He wasn't so sure that wasn't the right way to go. Of course, animaru couldn't really kill each other, so it wasn't the same situation.

"They all deserve to die," Aeden said, more for the men's sake than for his friends. "Their goal was to sell us into slavery, possibly kill us. They deserve nothing less."

Khrazhti accepted the statement with an expressionless face. She adjusted the grip on her swords.

"We may not need to kill them," Marla said, smacking Lennard's head hard to stop him from wailing and begging. "Hells, we could just leave them alone and most of them would bleed out and die down here before they got back to the street." She looked down into Lennard's wide eyes. "I seem to remember someone saying that we can pay you what we think you deserve. Is that right? Is my memory sound?"

"No, no," the pitiful man wailed. "Please. There's no need for that. Mercy."

"Oh, mercy," Marla said. "Like you were going to show us? Sell us to some master who would use us for his own pleasure and beat us whenever he felt like it? Mercy like that? I guess we could sell you, though I doubt you'd bring a decent price."

"What do you think he deserves to be paid?" Aeden asked as Fahtin walked up, making a point of not stepping in the rapidly expanding puddles of blood.

"I have a particular hatred for slavers," the Gypta girl said. "Too many times in our past have we been taken and sold to others." She gritted her teeth in anger, but turned after a moment as her expression turned to disgust. Aeden knew her well enough to know it wasn't over the blood so much as the act she was putting on. He had no doubt that if it were up to her, she would have him heal the attackers.

"Hmmm," Marla said. "You make a good point. We have searching still to do. We can't waste time with the likes of these." She raised her sword to cut into Lennard and he screamed like a child being spanked. Then, instead of slashing down at him, she raised her elbow and thrust the tip downward. Between his legs.

The man screamed louder, though this time in real pain and not anticipation of it.

"I guess I hit something," the red-haired woman said. She cleaned her sword on Lennard's shirt, then did the same with her dagger, and sheathed both of them. "Come on, let's get out of here. He should live, though his life will be different now. I hope he remembers what he tried to do today every time he needs to piss."

Fahtin walked by the screaming, squirming man, following Marla. Khrazhti glanced at Aeden, stepped over the corpse of one of the men, and walked toward the stairs, her cloak under her arm.

Aeden sighed. Should he help the men still alive, maybe heal them partially? He couldn't really find it in himself to do so. These were the type of men who would probably join the animaru against the humans, selfish and greedy.

"Those of you who can do it, you should probably go and get some help for your friends or they'll die. I hope you've learned a lesson. If I see you so much as giving a dirty look to anyone, I'll cut you down without a word. You can count on that." He cleaned his swords on the clothing of a nearby corpse and went after the women, who were already climbing up the stairs.

❧ 16 ❧

"How did we ever fall for that?" Aeden asked as they tried to find their way back to the inn.

"I don't know about you," Marla said, "but I think it would have been better to have stayed in the room and taken a nap today. I still can't think straight. It's good that I don't have to think much to fight street thugs like those."

Fahtin, walking next to Marla and in front of Aeden, stumbled and almost fell to the stone roadway. Marla grabbed the other woman and slipped an arm around her waist, pulling her close. Fahtin dangled from the arm like a doll made of rags.

"Are you all right, Fahtin?"

The Gypta woman put her hand to her head and swayed in Marla's support, trying to regain her feet. "Oh. I don't know. I'm sorry. I just got a little dizzy. There was a flash of light in my mind, like a little explosion. It made me lose my balance."

Aeden stepped up on the other side of Fahtin and put his

arm around her, just above Marla's. "Come on. Let's go back to the inn where you can rest. That was a lot of excitement."

"Yeah," she said. "I guess." Her face was anything but relieved, though.

"I'm sorry you had to witness that, and that you felt you needed to act tough toward injured people."

"I'm not a fragile little girl, Aeden," she said, raising her chin.

"I know. But I also know that you're the kindest person I've ever met, and that it can't be easy for you to walk away from wounded people, even if they attacked us."

Her eyes dropped. "I know they tried to hurt us, and I don't have a problem with defending myself or even killing if necessary, but it's hard to walk away. Some of them will die. Even if they are horrible people, it all makes me sad."

"I know, Fahtin. Like I said, I'm sorry you had to experience that."

"Uh huh."

"Are you *sure* you're okay?" Aeden asked, looking into her eyes. "Not just the situation, but what happened just now?"

"I'm okay. It was just that...well, it felt like it does when I have one of my visions, but I didn't see anything."

"It could be a precursor," Marla said. "That happens sometimes with someone who has natural magic. They get little warnings their power is going to do something."

Fahtin's lower lip trembled and she bit down to stop the movement.

"Aww, come on now, Fahtin." Aeden swept his other arm behind her knees to pick her up out of Marla's supporting arm and began walking. "We'll figure it all out. It'll be fine. There are strange things happening with magic. With all of us, really."

"I know," she said, leaning her head on him and settling into the cradle of his arms. "It's scary, though. You and Raki aren't having these kinds of effects. Why is this happening to me?"

Aeden didn't know how to answer that. Luckily, Marla did.

"Fahtin, it's different with each person. When I felt that spike of magic and cast Hurricane, it scared the hells out of me. I'd never seen that much damage from a single spell, let alone made it happen, and I've been at the Academy most of my life. I wasn't sure if it was going to rip me apart. As I was finishing the spell, the magic seemed to get away from me and take on life of its own. It was one of the scariest things that's ever happened to me."

"Really?" Fahtin asked, locking eyes with Marla.

"Absolutely. If it weren't for the fact that it was over in a few seconds, I'm not sure what I'd have done. As it was, I trembled for half an hour afterward, and I was very weak for several days."

"That's how I feel, too," Fahtin said. "I never would have thought you'd be scared like that. Or feel weak. I figured it was because I'm a coward."

Marla's mouth dropped open. "A coward? You? I've seen you act bravely a number of times since I've known you, and that hasn't been very long. The first time I saw you was in the middle of a battle with animaru surrounding you and your hands and feet bound with ropes. The bravery and fire in your eyes shocked me that day. It actually made me pause in the middle of my battle to wonder who that woman with the heart of a lion was. I wondered then if I'd ever be as brave as her. As you."

"No, you didn't," Fahtin said.

"I did. Fahtin, you have to realize that being brave doesn't mean that you're not afraid. In fact, to be brave you *have* to be afraid. Someone who is fearless is an idiot. Someone who knows fear but does what they need to anyway, that's a hero. Being frightened by what's happening doesn't mean you can't or won't do what needs to be done. Be afraid, but realize that you have people around you who love you and who will do everything they can to keep you from harm. Just like you'd do for us."

Fahtin's lip quivered a little more as the tears pooled in her eyes. She blinked them away, though, without releasing them. "Thank you," she whispered.

Marla leaned over and kissed the Gypta on the cheek. "We're family. We stick together."

The Gypta lifted her chin and took in a deep breath. "You're right, of course. As comfortable as this is, I'm not feeling as weak as before. Set me down so I can walk. Let's go back to the inn." She started walking again, not needing Aeden's support any longer.

Aeden glanced at his sister. She smiled and winked at him, then hurried to catch up to Fahtin. Turning, Aeden came face-to-face with Khrazhti, standing still and watching the three humans. He leaned over to see into her hood, their eyes meeting.

"Are you okay?" he asked her.

She nodded. "Yes. I am still learning about interactions between friends and what it means to be family. It is surprising to me. There is nothing like these things on Aruzhelim."

Aeden took one of Khrazhti's hands and started walking, pulling her along with him. "That is precisely why we can't let the animaru win."

He continued to hold her hand until they caught up to Marla and Fahtin, then he squeezed hers one last time and released it. They continued to walk in silence until they found a street they recognized and finally made it back to the inn.

Aeden was never as happy to see an inn as he was that day. Not that he remembered, anyway. There were still three hours until they were supposed to meet Tere's group for their evening meal, so he took the time to mend a few cuts in his clothing from the day's battle and to wash the blood from his clothes. Only a small bit of it was his, from two minor cuts. The women gathered in Fahtin's room to do the same. Marla had taken a few nicks, too, as did Khrazhti, but the animaru was already well on the way to healing and Marla told Aeden not to bother using his magic to heal hers.

"They'll teach me not to let anyone past my guard if they sting for a few days," she said. As if fighting that many men with only a couple of tiny slices were something to be ashamed of.

He shrugged and let it be. He was going to have to deal with his own cuts, so he guessed it was fair that she did, too. The thought of his tough twin sister made him smile as he cleaned his clothes.

After he'd already washed the blood off his body wherever he could find it, Aeden decided he had time for a bath. He soaked for a good long time, enjoying the warmth. He changed into his spare set of clothes while his others hung from a hook in the ceiling. Feeling refreshed, he went downstairs to await his friends.

Tere, Lily, Raki, and Urun came through the door to the common room a little before sixth bell. They spotted Aeden and joined him at his table.

"How was it?" the Croagh asked.

"Frustrating, is what it was," Tere said. "Didn't accomplish a damn thing except to realize that my mind is going. I'm definitely getting stupider."

Aeden smiled. Tere had apparently gotten more comfortable with everyone. Either that, or he really was getting more crotchety in his old age.

"I'm with you," Aeden said. "We had a hard time finding the inn again."

"The battle with all those men who ambushed us and tried to capture us for slaves didn't have anything to do with it?" Marla said as she entered the room with Fahtin and the cloaked and hooded Khrazhti.

"What?" Raki asked. "You were attacked?"

Tere put his hand up to stop anyone else from talking and swung his head back and forth to see if anyone else had been listening. "Hold on a second." He got up and crossed the room to talk to the innkeeper.

Aeden watched the two discuss something. The innkeeper nodded, glancing at Fahtin several times during the short conversation, and Tere handed him something that glittered in the lamplight. The archer came back to the group.

"Come on. I secured a private dining room for us. It's better not to have these kinds of conversations where everyone can hear."

"Thanks, Tere," Aeden said. "I was actually going to see if we could do that anyway so Khrazhti doesn't have to wear that cloak and hood all the time." He noticed her head snap to her left, toward him. "What? It's not fair that you have to hide all the time. I, for one, am good and tired of it. I might start wearing my hood up all the time in protest."

He wasn't sure, but he thought he saw a flash of white under that hood.

Once they were in the dining room—and Khrazhti had her face comfortably uncovered—Aeden and Marla told the others what had happened that day. Raki's eyes were wide and Lily nodded toward Fahtin. Tere's brow was wrinkled, though, as if he was trying to think through something.

"That's not good," the archer said. "Not only did someone notice we were searching for something after only one day, but you didn't figure out that they were setting you up for a trap."

"I know," Aeden said. "It's clear to me now, but for some reason, it seemed practical to go with them at the time."

"That's what concerns me." Tere looked around the room. "Who else feels like they're not thinking as clearly as normal?"

Everyone but Khrazhti raised their hands. Only after noticing everyone was looking at her did she raise her hand as well. Aeden figured it was a language or cultural thing. He couldn't really see animaru raising their hands in conversation. Not unless those hands were claws or bore weapons they'd use to attack the listeners.

"There is more," Khrazhti said, as if to make up for the confusion. "Fahtin felt magic again."

That began a whole new topic. By the end of it, Fahtin's cheeks were blazing red.

"I don't know about the rest of you," Aeden said to change the subject, "but as soon as I'm finished eating, I'm going to bed. I hope that when I wake up tomorrow morning, it'll be like this day never happened and I will think like normal. Either that, or I have a fever or something that I can point to as the cause. I hate to think I'm losing my mind. I don't have age to blame it on."

"Just wait," Tere said. "You will, and faster than you think. For what it's worth, though, I'm with you. Food, then sleep, maybe a bath in between if I can manage it."

One of the serving girls knocked on the door to bring food in. Khrazhti covered up and once everything was on the table, they all ate their fill, chatting about the parts of the city they'd seen. Aeden found his mind wandering. He rarely found cities interesting. Instead, he thought about his magic, and what he had begun learning at the Academy. He thought he might be getting closer to figuring out how to enhance another of the spells of the Raibrech. He wanted to try some things in the morning during his daily exercise.

After a seemingly short but very refreshing night's sleep, he woke early and started his day like he always did, with training.

They all met again at breakfast. When Fahtin walked into the common room, Aeden sat up straighter. She looked like she had a rough night.

"Are you all right?" he asked her.

"I'm fine," she said, but sat down heavily on her chair. "I had dreams and visions last night. I didn't sleep much."

"I'm sorry," Aeden said, sliding a cup of milk toward her. She nearly always had milk with breakfast. "Do you want to talk about it?"

"There's not much to talk about. Marla was right, I think. Maybe what I felt yesterday was a precursor like she told me. The worst part is that I didn't get much sleep, but I didn't really see anything that will help us, either. I saw that same symbol and I saw flashes of the other visions I had before. The only thing new wasn't even something I saw, but a feeling."

"A feeling?" Raki said.

"Yeah. We should take our packs with us when we go out searching today."

Aeden stared at her, trying to comprehend what she had just said. He wasn't feeling quite as stupid as the day before, but a heavy woolen blanket still lay over his brain.

Marla looked back and forth from Aeden to Fahtin. "I'm sorry, did you say we should take our packs with us to search today?"

"That's right. And before you ask why, I already told you I don't know. It's a feeling. I'm going to take mine. If the rest of you choose not to, that's fine."

"I'm not arguing with you," Marla said. "I'm confused about it."

"That makes both of us," Fahtin snapped.

That stopped all conversation for a few minutes. Surprisingly, it was Khrazhti who spoke first.

"I will take my pack when we go out searching. Fahtin's magic is unrefined now, but she will gain more control of it. I believe in her and in her abilities."

Fahtin reached over and put her hand on Khrazhti's, which was on the table in front of her. The animaru smiled at the Gypta. Yes, she was definitely getting better at showing expressions. Aeden found himself matching the expression, though whether it was in response to Khrazhti's or because of the tender moment between the two women, he wasn't sure. It was probably both.

Their meal was a quick affair and they spent a few minutes going over the map to be sure everyone knew where they were going. After that, the only thing to do was to get started. They headed out of the inn as a group, every one of them with their packs on, and made their way down the street to where they'd split up.

Before they got there, a large group of armed men, all wearing the same livery of red with black accents, and with an eagle's head crest on the chest of their tunics, formed ranks in front of them.

"You are required to accompany us to Lord Aeril Valmyar's estate. There, you will explain your activities and face the charges the lord makes against you."

❧ 17 ❧

"We can't let them take us, not Lord Valmyar," Marla whispered. "He's as crooked as a Vandal priest and is very powerful here. If we to go his estate, we'll disappear. We can't very well kill his soldiers, though."

"What's the meaning of this?" Tere said to the man who had spoken. "Why does the lord..."

Aeden whispered back to Marla. "Can you do something non-lethal that will distract them for a few seconds? I have a spell that I think will help, but I can't cast it instantly."

Marla nodded. "I have a few things I can try. Just be ready to do whatever you're going to do. We'll have to make a run for it. Make sure everyone knows and that we all head in the right way. I'm still not sure how we'll get away. They can run us down with horses."

"We'll head for the trees," Aeden said. "Lose them there. We can come back and get our horses later."

"It's as good a plan as any. Tell me when you're ready."

"...and if you can't tell me any more than that, I'm afraid we have to decline your lord's invitation," Tere finished.

The others whispered among themselves, passing the word that they'd make a run for it. When Lily whispered to Tere and he nodded, Aeden knew it was time.

"Now, Marla."

The man in charge of the soldiers had turned to give his men the command to take the group by force. Marla launched a single fire missile at the rear end of the man. It struck him and burned through his clothing at a gap in the armor there. He yowled and jumped, swatting at his own behind.

Aeden had already started casting, taking care to gesture precisely, humming the Song as he did so. He had found that with practice, he was able to hum the melody instead of singing the words of the song. He still had to pronounce the words of power, but he hoped as he became more practiced, he could invoke the magic without even pronouncing them aloud.

"*Fantim, lishant, stuta*," he said, timing the words perfectly with his movements.

A glimmering wave of force exploded out from Aeden. It expanded all around him, but especially toward the way he was facing. Toward the soldiers. It didn't disappoint.

The force of the spell blasted the men in the front rank, throwing them as if they weighed nothing. Their shields, already in place, took the brunt of the force, but it didn't stop the spell from tossing them back and over the second row, which itself was knocked down. The third row also lost their feet, slamming into the one behind them.

What had been orderly ranks of soldiers a moment before was now a pile of men squirming and trying to regain their feet. Their commander was nowhere to be seen when Aeden looked for him. He wondered if the man was tossed over the entire mass of men and was behind them now.

Aeden's knees buckled as weakness washed over him, but

he stayed upright. He turned and ran crookedly after his friends, already several seconds ahead of him. He hoped he could keep up with them. The spell had taken a lot out of him.

As he ran, the Croagh focused on one step at a time, thinking only of moving forward, of catching his friends. He pushed as if his life depended on it and kept them in sight. He even thought he might be gaining on them a little. Four turns and then a straightaway, they continued. Aeden was starting to wonder if they were lost when his friends slowed ahead of him. He caught up to them and then stopped alongside them.

The main gate was just ahead.

He cast his eyes back from where they had come, but didn't see the soldiers. It wouldn't be long until they showed up, though. It should be obvious which way they were going.

"Walk now," Tere said. "Just amble out of the gate like there's nothing wrong. We don't want to alarm the gate guards until we're already out or we may end up having to fight. That would be bad."

Fahtin's eyes were wide and darting about. Aeden put his hand out toward her, palm down, and pushed it downward, telling her to calm down and act normally. To her credit, she took a deep breath, then straightened her posture and walked calmly behind Tere as if she was just out for a morning stroll.

They had almost crossed the threshold of the gate when the fastest of the soldiers chasing them dashed around the corner into view.

"Stop those people," one of the soldiers screamed, but half of it was lost when he ran out of breath. Still, the damage was done.

The guards at the gate drew their swords and gathered to attack the group.

Khrazhti, walking slowly at the back of the group, raised a

hand as she reached the area just below the portcullis's spikes. Aeden could feel magic being called to that hand.

"Khrazhti, no. Don't—"

A blazing ball of darkness flew from the animaru's hand, the force of it throwing her arm backward.

It zipped through the air, a shadow casting a shadow as it raced along. It wasn't even near the gate guards and Aeden wondered how her aim was so far off.

Until he saw it land. Right on one of the massive pulleys for the gate portcullis. Another blast hit the other pulley a second later, tearing it apart and cutting that rope, too.

Khrazhti calmly stepped over the threshold as the portcullis crashed to the ground with the guards on the other side.

Aeden looked at the animaru's calm face and shook his head. She started jogging toward the trees along with the others. He looked back toward the men trying to lift the portcullis, shifted his eyes up to the archers who appeared on the battlements, and ran after his friends as Khrazhti passed him.

As Aeden ran, he began the motions of Saving Force. He obviously couldn't adopt a stable, wide stance as he sprinted away, but he turned his thoughts to convincing himself that though he was moving, he was still rooted to the ground's energy, strong and able to accept qozhel from the surface he was on. His hands circled out and up, then pushed down when they met in front of his chest. It was awkward to do while running, but he pronounced the words of power through his labored breaths.

The magic of the spell unified in completion, and the power sprung up behind him, a shield to protect them from the archers on the walls. At least, he hoped they would be protected.

Between running, trying to see where his friends were

going, and pushing his mind to keep the spell active, he couldn't look back to see if they would be attacked. He trusted in his magic and moved as fast as he could.

Aeden felt more than heard an arrow strike his shield and deflect off. It manifested as a small impact, as if someone had flicked a small stone at him and struck him in the back. Two other arrows stuck into the ground to his left, the archers who released them apparently not as accurate at the first bowman.

Several more shafts struck the ground around him or the shield itself. If they could just make it to the trees...

During his run, the thought occurred to him that maybe his shield wasn't tall enough or wide enough to protect his friends. He couldn't feel the extent of the bubble around him, nor could he consciously expand it, not without more concentration than he could spare. The magic seemed to know how to interpret his desire to protect others as well as himself, so he had no choice but to have faith in it.

The surroundings dimmed and Aeden wondered if a cloud had passed before the sun. It occurred to him just in time that he was running full tilt—or as fast as he could in his tired and distracted condition—into the shadow of the forest. His friends were ahead of him. All of them had turned to watch him.

His legs didn't seem to want to respond. He had forced them into motion, and now they didn't want to stop. He shouted in his mind at them. His limbs finally obeyed and slowed him before he collided with his friends. Lily stepped in front of Raki, leaned forward, and caught him before he barreled into the young Gypta.

It was like hitting a solid wall. A beautiful, cushioned solid wall, but still. Gods, the woman was strong. Her feet slid backwards slightly, but she kept her balance and they stopped, Aeden wrapped in the arms of the red-haired archer.

"Whew," he said. "Thanks, Lily. That could have been bad."

She smiled and released him. "No problem. You looked surprised to see us here. I didn't want you to trample poor Raki."

"Yeah," he said. "The spells tired me out and my body wasn't responding very quickly." He stumbled, but Lily reached out and steadied him.

"Rest for a minute, Aeden," Marla said. "They're still working on getting that portcullis up and the archers can't see us to shoot at us."

"I will, but let's move a little farther into the trees," he said. "No telling if there's one of those archers who might want to waste some arrows on the chance he might hit something."

They did as he asked and soon he was sitting on a rock, catching his breath.

"Aeden?" Khrazhti sat down next to him. "May I give you some of my energy? Like before?"

Oh, right. He had almost forgotten about that. She had done it once before, when they were hunting Izhrod Benzal. "That would be fantastic, Khrazhti. I really appreciate it."

"It is a little thing compared to the spells you cast to protect us, even though it was a foolish risk. If you had become too tired to run fast enough, you may have sacrificed yourself for no good reason."

He chuckled. "Not for no good reason. For all of you. Nice thinking with the portcullis, by the way. We never would have gotten away if you hadn't destroyed it like that."

She flashed him the smile she was getting so good at using. "I am a soldier. When I see weapons or defenses, I analyze their weaknesses and what I can do to defend myself from them. It was the logical thing to do."

"It was, and I thank you for it."

She nodded and cast her spell, flooding him with energy. He was suddenly able not only to stand, but he felt like he wanted to run some more.

"I'm not sure I'll ever get used to that. It feels amazing."

"I am glad to help."

"They're probably going to send people out through the sally port while they work on that portcullis," Marla said. "We should find a place to hide. Thanks for the shield, by the way. You're handy to have around."

"I do try," he said. "But yes, you're right. We should probably move." He glanced to his side, where Fahtin and Raki stood. "You know, it's a damn good thing we have our packs with us. It'll make hiding much easier with our supplies." Fahtin raised her chin, pride shining in her eyes.

❧ 18 ❧

The trees loomed around them, dense enough that it seemed like twilight within instead of morning. Tere knew the vegetation surrounded the city on two sides, except for where the road had been cut through it. The north and west sides of the city bordered the Lisinis Ocean and the Kanton Sea, so there wasn't much in the way of trees there on the cliffs overlooking the water.

"We're going to have to stay out here for at least a couple of days and then sneak back in to get the horses," Tere said. "Hopefully everything happened so quickly that they won't remember us. We should probably send two or three of the least memorable of us to get the horses. That means I'm out, and Lily definitely can't go..."

"Why not?" the red-haired woman said.

"Lily, dear," Tere said, not even bothering to turn toward her. "We've been through this before. You are tall, beautiful, and have red hair. I don't care if the whole city was on fire. Those men would definitely remember you."

The tall woman flushed, but looked oddly pleased.

"And that goes for you too, Marla," Aeden told his sister.

"Oh, stuff it in your nether regions," the Academy graduate delicately responded.

Aeden laughed.

"We can figure out who will go when it's time," Tere said. "For now, why don't we find a good place to hide. I'm sure soldiers will be looking for us, though maybe not too hard. I'd guess they'll barely enter the trees, loiter around, and then go back and report we've fled. No one in their right mind would chase troublemakers into thick trees like this."

"No one in their right mind would flee into trees like this," Marla retorted.

Tere shook his head. Why did he ever agree to be the de facto leader of this group? Just because the girl had seen him doing so in her dreams?

With no other options, he pushed ahead and blazed a trail through the underbrush. All they needed was to find a relatively sheltered area to use as a temporary camp and...

To his left, in a jumble of large rocks, Tere thought he spied a dark depression.

"Hold up," he said, raising his hand to get everyone's attention. "I need to check something out."

Tere took an arrow from his quiver and nocked it. Checking to make sure everyone else was staying put—except Lily, who had nocked an arrow of her own and was one step behind and to the side of him—he padded toward the rocks.

Sure enough, as he got closer, he confirmed that it was what he had thought. A cave opening, or at least a deep pocket in the rocks. He met Lily's eyes and she nodded, taking another step to the side so they couldn't be caught in one attack that affected both of them.

Together, they moved forward to check it out.

Tere's head swiveled as he looked for any enemies. He didn't find any. What he did find was that the opening did seem to be a cave. Lily followed him for several steps, but then he motioned her to stay put as he went in farther. He could see in complete dark, and though she seemed to have excellent night vision, she couldn't.

The archer went into the cave thirty feet before stopping in front of a small carving on the wall. He doubted anyone else would have noticed it, even if they were carrying a torch. Figuring he had gone far enough, he turned around and went back to the others.

"This looks like a good place," he told everyone as he and Lily returned to where the others had stayed. "We can make torches, or if any of you magic-type people can conjure up some light, that would be even better."

"I can make light," Marla said. "I'm pretty sure Khrazhti wouldn't have any spells like that. Aeden?"

"I have spells that make light, but mainly for attack or for identifying enemies," he told her. "I might be able to make them work, but I might blind half of us temporarily."

"Never mind," she said. "I'll do it."

She had Tere cut a few dead branches lying around and she cast a light spell onto each of them. The result was basically a few torches, though ones that didn't cause heat or smoke and didn't consume the wood. It was a pretty handy thing.

They were soon standing in front of what Tere had found on the wall. He had to point it out to them before—based on the sounds they made—they finally got the point. It was a shallow carving, or one that was weathered over time so it was faint at best.

"That's the symbol from my visions," Fahtin said, voicing what each of them had realized. "The place we were looking for was here all along."

"The first thing we need to do," Tere said, "is make sure it's safe. For the moment, we can set up guards until we can coordinate exploring a little more. I went down the cavern a bit and didn't find anything, so we should be good here for now. Don't make too much noise."

"You sound like you're not going to be here," Lily said.

"Smart girl. I'm going to go back to the front of the cave and see if I can't obscure or eliminate all the tracks that point to us like a flaming flash of sunlight in a dark room."

"Oh," she said. "Well, I can take a guard position until you get back."

"Thanks, Lily."

"Tere," Aeden said. "I have a spell that may work for our purposes. I've only really ever used it for hiding, but it can also eliminate tracks. I played around with it when we were in Satta Sarak and it erased the evidence of our passing through the underbrush."

"That sounds handy," the archer said. "Let's try it out. We have not only the path through the vegetation, but messy footprints in the dust on the cave floor."

Tere and Aeden went back to the cave mouth, letting the others figure out who would stand watch.

"It's called Darkness to the Hunters," Aeden said. "I used it to hide myself and Fahtin in that army camp we found. The basic spell can hide evidence of our passing, though."

The boy made gestures with his hands and whispered a few words. A ball of shadow appeared before him, a few inches off the ground. It swung left when he moved his hands left, and pivoting right brought it back to the other side. He used it on the doorstep of the cave, passing it over the mess all those feet had made in the dust and gravel deposited there.

Tere's eyebrows shot up. The dirt rearranged itself as the globe passed over each section. Once it passed, the floor looked like it hadn't been walked on in years.

"I like it," Tere said. "More thorough than sweeping it with a tree branch. Let's lay a false trail a couple hundred yards from here, traveling away from the cave, then we'll come back and erase any trace of our passing we find. We can work backward, erasing everything to the cave as we go and then taking care of the cavern itself up to where we stopped. That ought to throw them."

Aeden grunted his understanding.

"You all right?" Tere asked.

"Yeah. Have to focus."

"Oh, right. Well, I'll just talk then. Make a sound if you need me to do anything."

"Okay."

They did as Tere had explained, stomping through the grasses and ferns to simulate many people, winding off and away from the cave. When they'd gotten far enough for Tere's satisfaction, they walked backward to add a few more footprints until they reached where they'd started the false trail.

"Good," Tere said. "Now let's get rid of our original trail, working back toward the cave."

Aeden let Tere go first as he walked backward on the trail the group had made earlier. After a few minutes, Aeden mumbled to himself and turned to walk forward. Tere started to ask what he was doing, but waited, watching the boy. After thirty feet or so, Aeden turned and guided his shadowy globe to erase the whole section of trail between him and where he had turned around.

"Ah, good idea," the archer told him. "That ought to make it faster."

"I still don't think I'm thinking straight," Aeden said. Speaking seemed easier for him when he was standing still and not moving the shadows around. "It took me longer to figure that out than it should have."

"You're doing great."

They finished erasing the trail to the cave and repeated the same process for the cavern itself. When they got back to the group, Aeden let out a heavy breath and relaxed his muscles. He nearly fell over as the globe of shadow disappeared.

"Damn," the Croagh said. "I sure hope that with more practice, my spells don't drain as much of my energy. I'd be worthless in a fight right now, I'm so tired."

"It'll get better," Marla said, bringing him a water skin. "It gets easier with practice. A lot of it is that you aren't efficient with using the qozhel. You use too much of your own energy and not enough from the surroundings. You'll learn how to utilize it more efficiently as you continue to use it."

"That's a relief."

"Unfortunately," Marla said, "each person is different. The masters, and maybe even I, can give you tips and help you out, but you won't truly become efficient until you figure out how your body uses the magic and you experiment with it."

"Well, that's nothing new. I've been trying to figure out how to enhance the spells of the Raibrech since I first learned to use the magic. I'll get there eventually. Until then, I'll have to rely on my combat skills. It's fine."

"So." Fahtin seemed more cheery than she had in days. "Are we going to explore? We have half a day before it's night-time, and even when night does come, it won't really matter in here. It's not like it'll get darker."

"You're right," Tere said. "It's time to at least see who or what we're sharing this cave system with. Maybe we can find a more defensible place to rest tonight. I have a feeling it may take a while to find what we're looking for."

"Really?" Fahtin said. "Why do you say that?"

Tere fixed her with a level gaze. "Because nothing's ever easy."

❧ 19 ❧

The others fidgeted, anxious to get moving. Tere couldn't blame them. He had been outside with Aeden, walking around and breathing fresh air. The rest of his friends had been in this dark hole breathing stale air and not able to do much more than look at each other in the light cast by Marla's spell.

The archer looked around him and counted. "Hey, where's Raki?"

Marla jerked a thumb over her right shoulder. "He's down there a ways, on guard duty."

Tere glanced down the tunnel, but didn't see any light. "Without one of the light sticks?"

"Yeah, he says it ruins his night vision."

"Hmmm." Tere headed that way, wondering at the young Gypta. He didn't need light to find the young man; his sight worked as well in the dark as in the light.

As he approached, Raki's head snapped toward the archer and his eyes locked on Tere's.

"Anything interesting happen?" Tere asked him.

"No. It's been quiet."

"Can you actually see in this darkness?"

The boy nodded, probably assuming correctly that Tere could see him. "Yeah. My night vision has gotten a lot better lately. I don't know what it is. It seems like magic."

"It must be," Tere said. "It's not night vision, though. It's dark vision."

"What's the difference?"

Tere sat down on the floor, legs crossed and his back to the wall. "Well, night vision is what cats and other animals have. Their eyes are much better than human eyes at collecting any light available and using it to see when it's dark. But that's the point: they need some light to be able to see. In a place like this, with absolutely no ambient light, a cat is as blind as a person is.

"Dark vision, on the other hand, doesn't need any light. For example, my sight doesn't rely on light, but translates the images from the auras things project. Even inanimate objects have auras that let me see them. There are some spells and some creatures that can see heat, so that the hotter something is, the brighter it is to them.

"What you're doing is something else completely. Do you mean to tell me that you can see things just like it's daylight?"

Raki shrugged, then sat down next to the archer. "Not exactly. When it's as dark as this cave, I see things like it's twilight. Colors are muted and it's difficult to make out details more than thirty or forty feet, but otherwise, yeah, things look the same as when my surroundings are lit."

"Yep, magic."

"I really don't know what's happening, Tere. I'm not sure I like it. It all confuses me. Scares me."

The older man put his hand on Raki's shoulder. "That's understandable. So many things are changing, it's hard to keep up. Don't be too afraid, though. I think it's a good thing.

You're obviously manifesting some kind of magic, like Fahtin is, though I think you're further along than she is."

"But what is it? What will it do to me? What if it changes who I am?"

"Nah, don't worry about that. Magic doesn't change a person like that. It can make you more powerful, give you abilities, help you see things you never could before, but it doesn't change who you are inside. Only we can do that. Some people who develop magic become tyrants, but that's because it was in them the whole time."

"What if I'm already like that inside?" Raki said, frowning.

"You're not, kid. Believe me. I've seen how you act, how you think and feel. There aren't many others I'd feel as comfortable about getting magic as you. You'll use it to help Aeden and Fahtin and your other friends. You'll use it to do good and to help people. I have no doubt."

The boy looked at him, unblinking. "Thanks, Tere. That makes me feel better." He chuckled.

"What's funny?"

"I just got one of the best compliments of my life, and it was from the hero I have idolized since I could first listen to a story and know what it meant."

It was Tere's turn to frown. "I'm not that man anymore, Raki. Actually, the man in the stories never existed. People have a way of exaggerating things in stories. You'll see what I mean. Soon, there will be stories about Raki the Shadow. He's fourteen feet tall and his teeth are filed to points, which he uses to rip bad people apart on dark nights when they can't even see him coming."

Raki's chuckle was replaced with a full laugh. "You think so?"

"Just watch. All heroes are only people, Raki. Remember that. People grow old and worthless, then they die. Sometimes they die before they can grow old. People are not wholly good or bad. They're something in between. For what it's worth, I'm glad to know you before you become so famous I won't be able to talk with you alone like this for all the adoring fans wanting to be around you."

"Thanks, Tere. That helps ease my mind a little about the magic, though I still think there will never be stories about me that are as good as the ones about you. I mean, you fought a dreigan. A dreigan!"

"Yeah, yeah," the archer said, standing up. "That's one of the few stories I've heard about me that's accurate." He leaned toward Raki and put his hand up to his mouth. "To be honest, it's one of my favorites. I didn't mind it so much when you all told it around the fire that night when I first met you. Come on, now. Let's get the others and start exploring. The sooner we get out of this tomb, the better."

Tere and Raki took the lead, ranging out far enough ahead of the others that the light of Marla's light sticks couldn't be seen. It wouldn't do to announce to any dangers that the party was coming.

They traveled the twisting corridors for a time, and then Raki would wait while Tere went back to keep contact with the others. His vision wouldn't be ruined by going in and out of lighted places, but Raki's would.

It was fairly easy at first because the cavern didn't have any detours or corridors branching off. When they got to the first fork, Tere stopped Raki.

"Now it's going to get a little more confusing. I've got some chalk in my pack, but we'll need to make sure we don't pass by a place where something can come up on us from behind after we pass. That means before we let the group go by, we'll need to investigate every side passage."

"I understand," Raki said, "but that's going to make this take a lot longer."

"It will, but it'll be safer. There's no telling what we'll find in here. Besides, we could pass right by a tunnel that leads to where we actually want to go."

Both of them went back to the others this time.

They explained the problem to the group and had them wait where they were while the two scouts explored the offshoot passageway they had found. It ended up narrowing and getting shorter until it ended in a small space Raki could barely squeeze into crawling on his belly.

They backtracked and continued on in the main tunnel, repeating their actions each time they came upon another branch. Tere had his internal clock ticking out the time they spent exploring. At about fourth bell, he decided it was time to go back to the group.

"Just a little bit longer," Raki said. "I think I see a larger opening up there, off to the right. How about we check that out first and then we can go back?"

Tere shrugged. "Sure. That'll make the eighth branching passage we've seen. If it's a short one, we'll explore it, too. Otherwise, we'll stop and go to its end only after we've moved the others up."

They silently crept up to the opening. The boy had gotten so good at moving quietly and without a trace. Tere could rarely pick out tracks from him any longer. He had at least a little pride that he had started Raki on his way to becoming so accomplished, though the boy's natural ability—and his magic—deserved most of the credit.

It also seemed that Raki's vision was better than Tere's, or reached farther. When the boy mentioned the opening, Tere couldn't see it. He scratched his head. Hadn't Raki told him he could only see thirty or forty feet? The break in the wall of the cavern was at least fifty feet from where they had been. Was his dark vision getting better that quickly?

The opening was about twice the width of a door and a

bit taller. The two shadows flitted through it, one on each side and hugging the walls. It opened up into a chamber that was roughly triangular, with the point of the triangle being the part they came through.

The middle was littered with debris from what looked like rocks or stalactites falling from the ceiling and shattering, along with a few stalagmites. The walls were rough, though water trickled down in a few places, feeding puddles that seemed to drain through cracks alongside them.

It was a large cavern, twenty-five or thirty feet on each side. As the two explorers skimmed the walls, they finally made their way around to meet in the middle of the far wall, what would be the base of the triangle. There were no other large openings.

"Huh," Tere said as he scanned the ceiling, which ranged from about seven feet in height to twelve feet. "I don't see any openings that anything significant could get through."

"Me either," Raki said.

"It looks like we found a place to spend the night."

They made it back to the group quickly and found them sitting around looking bored. After a fast explanation of what they'd done and found, the party was on their feet and following after Raki to what would be their resting place for the night.

On the way to the chamber Tere and Raki had found, the archer hung back with the rest of the group and let Raki range ahead to make sure no dangers wandered into the area. As he walked along silently, the others chatted. If it could be called that.

"I'm tired of Erent Caahs this and Erent Caahs that," Marla said to Lily. "I know you're obsessed. Please, just spare us the stories."

"I'm sorry if I have respect for the greatest hero who ever

lived," Lily threw back. "You're just jealous because you're not half the hero he is. Not a quarter!"

"Come on, you two," Fahtin said. "I know it's dark and stuffy in here and we're not sure what will happen, but we need to stick together, not argue."

"Like you never argue," Aeden said. "You mostly figure people will do what you say because you're so adorable."

"You say that like it's something I should be ashamed of," Fahtin said.

"Well, now that you mention it—"

"What in Abyssum is going on?" Tere asked. He very nearly yelled it. "What has gotten into everyone?" He was met with silence. "Well?"

"They have been arguing like this for hours," Khrazhti said. "I am sorry, everyone, but you have been. I do not understand. We are all friends."

Aeden's eyes widened and then he turned them down. "I... I'm sorry, Fahtin. I don't know why I said that. For some reason, I just got angry. Maybe the tension from what happened in the last couple of days got to me."

"No," the Gypta girl said. "I'm sorry. It's not really like me to snap like that."

Everyone started speaking at the same time, then, apologizing to each other and trying to explain their actions. Tere shook his head and listened to it for a few minutes, then decided to put an end to it before he got a headache.

"Stop," he said. "Just stop. We're all tired and under a lot of pressure. Everyone's sorry for being angry. Let's just move on and forget whatever we've said to each other. It'll be better once we make camp and get some rest. Can we try to be civil and do that?"

A round of "yes" and "of course" came back at him.

"Good. We're almost there. Let's try to remember we're all friends, like Khrazhti said, and that shouting in a cavern is a good way to get the attention of things that may want to eat us. We don't know what lives in this cave system."

They entered the large chamber a few minutes later. Marla made more of the light sticks—she had been smart enough to bring extra sticks from outside the cave—and they set them up around the room.

"Too bad there's no wood in here other than those skinny sticks," Tere said. "I'd like to sit by the fire and relax for an hour or two."

Marla had been quiet since her comments to Lily, but she spoke now. "I can make a fire on the stone floor."

The archer looked at her. "You can? Don't you need fuel to burn?"

"Nope. Essentially, I'll lay a fireball down. I should be able to make it last for at least an hour if I make it less powerful than I'd use for an attack. It won't give off as much heat as a big fire, but it'll be something."

"That would be fantastic, Marla," Aeden said. "We would only need it for an hour or two. Once we go to bed, we wouldn't necessarily need to have it going."

"We would need light, though," Lily added. "Raki and Tere can see in the dark, but they can't keep watch the whole night."

"I'll watch for half the night," Raki said.

"No, Raki," Tere told him. "We'll need you rested for tomorrow. You and I can take a turn for three hours, but we'll need one more person, and a way to make sure they can see."

"It's easy enough," Marla said. "You two take the first and third watches and I'll take the middle. The lights will last about three hours. Wake me when it's my turn and I'll refresh the spell so I can see to keep watch. They'll go out when it's Raki's turn. When I get up, I'll start them all over again."

"Are you sure, Marla?" Aeden asked. "Won't it wear you

out casting so many spells like that, and missing a chunk of sleep in the middle of the night to boot?"

His sister laughed. "From weak spells like that? No way. I can cast those in my sleep. I've been using magic for more than a decade. Those simple spells are nothing. I'll be fine."

"It sounds like a good idea," Tere said. "Thank you for offering. The middle watch is horrible on its own, even without casting. As soon as we can figure out something else, we'll let you sleep all night. We have plenty of people for watches."

"It's no problem."

The fires Marla created were sufficient to cook over, but they didn't bother. They all ate a quick cold meal, and all but Tere settled in to sleep.

The night went quickly, with no sounds or movement interrupting the party's rest. In the morning, they continued their exploration, with Tere and Raki scouting ahead again.

❧ 20 ❧

Tere noticed some scrapes along the floor a few hours into the morning. They also encountered more side passages than the previous day. It was a long, laborious process to travel to the end of each of the passages to confirm that they didn't continue. The problem was that some of the side passages were beginning to spawn other caverns off of them.

"If this keeps up," Tere said, "we'll be in here for months. We're going to run out of food in eight days if we don't get more supplies."

"At least the guards will have stopped looking for us," Raki answered. "We could always backtrack and send someone into the city to get supplies."

"I suppose, but I'd rather finish what we need to do here and then leave."

With nothing else to do but risk something attacking them from behind, they continued what they had been doing. They hadn't seen or heard anything since they'd entered the caves, which seemed strange enough to Tere, but he had a feeling something would happen soon. He hoped he was imagining it.

Another side passage opened to their left and Tere steered Raki toward it. He smelled fresh air from that direction. At least, fresher than the stale air they'd been breathing. There was a touch of something else in it, too, but he couldn't place it.

The farther they went, the more familiar it seemed to Tere. He heard Raki sniffing.

"That smells like salt," the boy said. "Like from the sea."

"You're right. But there's something else. I've been trying to figure it out."

A few more twists in the cavern and it suddenly widened to twice as wide as Tere could have reached with his arms. The scent got stronger. Not just salt air, though that was definitely there. They must have traveled completely under the city and were nearing an opening near the Kanton Sea, or maybe the Lisinis Ocean to the north.

The passage widened again and looked as if it grew even larger up ahead. Tere slowed down. Raki took the cue and did so as well.

Tere took an arrow from his quiver and nocked it. There was something ahead. He couldn't see it or hear it, but he sensed something, as if a pair of hidden eyes were watching him. How he wished he still had his ability to see the magical matrix. He had never felt so blind.

The two crept around another turn and entered a massive cavern. It contained the opening to another passage off to the left, and one straight ahead. Both were as large as the one they had come through.

As they eased along the walls, part of the stone seemed to peel itself away from the other rock. It reared up, a massive body that looked to be made of the rock itself moving to block their path. As the two watched in horror, the creature opened its mouth wide and roared, warm air jetting out between teeth each large enough to impale a man.

The massive head, shaped like a gigantic snake's, reared back on its flexible neck, a precursor to striking. The creature's yellow eyes glowed slightly as it began its descent to eat the hapless humans.

In the middle of what Tere recognized as the creature's attack, its head suddenly stopped. It sniffed, air passing through its nostrils, only a dozen feet from Tere's face. Then, curiously, it tilted its head and narrowed its eyes.

Looking right at Tere Chizzit.

"Tere?" Raki said, his voice quivering with fear.

Tere ignored the boy and put his hand up as if such a simple act could stop the monster from eating him. The monster brought its head close to the archer, eyeing the bow in Tere's other hand warily.

It sniffed Tere's hand, then relaxed its stance, its whole body losing the tension it held only seconds before. It dipped its head, presenting the top of its snout to Tere.

"Ah, my friend," Tere said. "You remembered me." He stroked the creature's nose and stepped closer. "You look well. I had not thought I'd see you again."

"Tere?" Raki said again, slightly less frantically.

"Come on over here, Raki. Meet my friend from so many years ago. I'm sorry, but I don't know her name, but you'll no doubt recognize her from silly stories and such."

Raki slid closer to the mammoth beast, keeping Tere between himself and the monster.

"That's...it's..." Raki sputtered.

"Yes, this is my dreigan friend. Surely you remember the story. We just talked about it yesterday." Tere turned back to the dreigan. "This is my friend Raki. He's a big fan of yours."

The dreigan dipped its head, almost like a bow, and presented its forehead to the boy.

"Go on," Tere said. "Let her get your scent, and maybe give her a scratch on the nose. She seems to like it."

Raki did as directed, nervously chuckling while he did so. After a few strokes to the dreigan's scales, he seemed to relax a bit.

"Where is your young one?" Tere asked.

The dreigan moved its sinuous body—like a massive snake but with legs extending out from the sides like a lizard's—and stepped aside. Behind it was a smaller copy of itself, though not nearly as small as it had been the last time Tere had seen it.

Tere's face lit up with a smile for the younger wyrm, though it backed up toward the wall.

"I guess I shouldn't really expect you to remember me," the archer said. "You were young and not doing well at the time. Here, maybe this will remind you." He pulled an apple from his pack and held it out to the younger dreigan.

The creature, the size of a large wagon compared to its mother, which could be likened to an inn, looked at its parent. The larger dreigan motioned with her head and the smaller one timidly moved forward, half a step at a time. When it was close enough, it gingerly opened its mouth a few inches from Tere's hand. The human dropped the apple directly onto its tongue and the creature closed its mouth on the fruit.

"I didn't get to spend much time with them last time," Tere said, "so I'm still not really sure how they communicate with each other. They make sounds occasionally, but I think they talk mind-to-mind. All I know is that she understands me when I talk to her. Don't you?" That last part was said after he'd moved his head to face her.

The dreigan nodded.

Distracted, Tere was surprised when the younger dreigan nudged him, pushing on his shoulder with the flat forehead.

"You remember now?" he asked. "Or are you just hungry for more?"

The bigger dreigan rolled its eyes as if to say, *Children*!

"Raki, why don't you come over here and give our friend another apple?" Tere said, taking another one from his pack.

The boy excitedly stepped over, more quickly than maybe was prudent. The younger dreigan backed up a little, preparing for an attack.

"Slowly, Raki. He doesn't know you yet."

Raki faced the dreigan. "Sorry."

He successfully fed the other apple to the dreigan and soon was petting its nose and talking to it. Tere took his last two apples from his pack and tossed them to the mother dreigan.

"I'm glad to see that you're well and that you were able to escape that horrible place where we last met. I'm surprised to find you here, though. There are many people around."

The dreigan blinked at him, listening intently. Tere wished he could communicate better with her. That she could communicate with him.

"We're searching for something," he continued, "though we don't know what. We should probably get to it. Maybe after this whole mess is over, I can spend a little time with you and your young one. You know, just sit around and talk."

The dreigan nodded its head and glanced over at Raki, who seemed to have made a friend of the offspring.

They said their goodbyes and left, heading back to the others. It was getting late and there was still a lot of tunnel to search through.

Raki was quiet for the first few minutes, though he bounced with excitement. Finally, he let loose a flood of excited words.

"That was the best thing I've ever done," he said. "It was a dreigan. Two of them! The smaller one seemed to like me, too."

"Yep, seemed like it."

"How are you so calm? Dreigans! Who has ever seen one, let alone two?"

"I have."

"Oh, right. Well, who else, I mean?"

"Not many," Tere said. "It was nice to see them again. I'm glad the help I gave them had good results. So many things turned sour after I thought I had fixed them."

Raki deflated, shoulders drooping and his step turning to a slog.

"Sorry, boy. I'm a bit cynical in my old age. It was great to see them. When I first did, I was as excited as you are. I can remember that. Barely."

Raki's face lit up, regaining a little of his joy. "It was fantastic. Thank you for showing me that."

Tere laughed. "You're welcome, but it wasn't like I planned it. We kind of ran right into them, didn't we? Let's not mention this to the others, okay?"

They chatted about the dreigan as they made their way back to the group. Tere thought that would be it, but as soon as they made it to the large cavern, Raki burst out in excited babble.

"We saw the dreigan Tere saved all those years ago and there was the smaller one, and they were like *rowwr* but then Tere petted the mother and gave the little one an apple, and then I fed it and petted it and we talked, and it was the best thing that ever happened to me!" He had to suck in another breath after that, but opened his mouth to talk about it some more.

Tere put a hand on his shoulder and Raki looked up at him.

"Oh, sorry," Raki said, blushing.

The others didn't respond immediately, apparently processing what Raki had been saying.

After a minute of silence, Lily asked, "Are you saying you found a dreigan in the caverns? Like the one from the story with Raisor Tannoch and Toan Broos?"

Tere grimaced at the mention of Toan, the catalyst of Lela's death. He swallowed his bile, though, and answered. "Not *like* that one. That exact one. She remembered me, and after a few apples, so did her offspring."

"That story was true?" Marla asked. "I've heard it a few times, of course, but I thought it was made up. No one has seen a dreigan in a long time."

"I have," Tere said, "as did the villagers who were hunting it back then. Now Raki has seen one also. Two, actually."

All of them were clamoring to go see the creature. Tere sighed. He guessed he would be seeing his friend sooner than he thought. "Come on, then. Let's get this over with so she can have some peace and we can do some more exploring." He started off, but then stopped and turned to the excited people behind him. "You should probably get some apples out of your packs, too. They'll make our company more tolerable."

It was a quick trip to the dreigan's cave since Tere and Raki knew exactly where it was. Tere apologized for bothering the dreigan again and introduced his friends. The creature, and the smaller one, seemed interested to meet the other humans, especially when the apples came out of the packs. Raki spent most of his time talking at the smaller dreigan, as Tere had expected.

What he didn't expect was the reaction the mother had to Khrazhti.

At Aeden's prodding, the animaru stepped hesitantly up to the wyrm as Tere introduced the two. The dreigan got very still, its huge yellow eyes locking on Khrazhti. Tere wouldn't have been surprised to have heard a growl deep in its throat, but there was no obvious sign of aggression.

The reptile sniffed at Khrazhti and turned its head to regard Tere. The archer could have sworn there was confusion, or at least a question, in her eyes.

"Khrazhti is half human and half animaru," he told the dreigan. "The animaru are from the dark world of Aruzhelim. Khrazhti can cast spells and is an expert user of magic."

The dreigan nodded her head slowly, eyes going back to Khrazhti, as if her questions had been answered. The reptile moved its head closer to the animaru and sniffed again, this time more deeply.

"Put your hand out, Khrazhti," Tere told her.

She did so and the dreigan sniffed her hand. Then a long, serpent tongue flicked out and licked it. Aeden tensed and Tere held his breath.

Khrazhti smiled at the creature and released a sound that was half breath and half giggle. The dreigan put its head down, presenting the top of its snout and its forehead to the blue woman. Khrazhti didn't seem to need instruction after watching the others. She stroked the scaly head, causing the dreigan to close its eyes partway, seemingly in pleasure.

"Well, I'll be..." Tere said.

The others got their turn and soon everyone had met the dreigan and were satisfied. The pair seemed fascinated with Urun, too, though he barely spent any time with them. He was still in that funk, but it seemed the creatures recognized a nature priest when they saw one.

"Can we go now?" Tere asked. "We still have things to do, you know." No one disagreed, other than Raki saying, "Awww."

They all said their goodbyes and a few more apples were gifted to the creatures. Tere bid his friends farewell, telling them he would look forward to the next time they met, hopefully after the problem with the invaders was taken care of for good. Then the party went on their way to continue their exploration.

As he and Raki ranged out ahead, Tere glanced back toward the dreigan's cavern. He hoped his friends would be safe there, with no interference from people or any other creature. They deserved to be unmolested after all they'd been through. It would be something if he could convince the Academy to use some of its power and influence to make sure the majestic creatures never again had to worry about being hunted.

But that was a project for another time. The present belonged to finding whatever it was they were actually in the caverns for.

21

The good feelings Tere had gained from finding his dreigan friends again faded as he and Raki methodically searched the caverns. The archer's normally good sense of direction had been confused long ago, and he couldn't for the life of him picture where they might be in relation to the city above them. The dreigan's cave had smelled of sea air, and the passages there must have been large for the creatures to go in and out, but since the party didn't actually go to the opening, there was no telling if they were under the northern part of the city, the eastern part, or somewhere in between.

It irritated him to no end. He hated not knowing where he was.

On top of that, he felt...off. There was something boiling up in him, an unexplainable anger that he didn't like. It was irrational and he couldn't pin a reason on why he wanted to slap every person he had ever met.

He wondered what it was. The analytical part of his mind reached for some cause, but he couldn't find one. Instead, he did the next best thing.

"Raki," Tere said. "How are you feeling?"

"I'm fine. We haven't been searching all that long yet today."

Tere gritted his teeth. That *wasn't* the question he had asked the boy. He took a breath. There was no real reason to be mad at Raki. "I mean, what kind of mood are you in? For example, I'm feeling kind of irritated for some reason. There's nothing in particular, but even little things seem to be annoying me right now."

Raki flashed a look of disgust and anger at Tere, but then his eyes went wide before going onto the floor of the corridor. "Yeah. Me too. In fact, if you want the truth, what you just said irritated me for some reason."

"Thanks. I understand completely. I think something is affecting the way our minds are working. First, we had problems with thinking or remembering, then all the arguing and bickering. It's more than just being stuck in cramped places with each other. Let's go back and talk with the others. Maybe Marla, Khrazhti, or Urun can do something about it. I don't know if it's magic, but *some*thing is obviously happening."

A short time later, Tere explained what he thought was happening to the others.

"That makes a lot of sense," Marla told him. "I've been wondering why I've been feeling stupid or irritated or just plain separated from reality. If you're telling me you've been feeling the same things, maybe something is affecting us."

"I've noticed it, too," Aeden said. "Does anyone think they can do anything about it? If it's magic, can we fight it with other magic? I for one don't have any spells I think would work."

"Me either," Marla said.

The twins looked at Khrazhti. She frowned. "I have not been experiencing these effects you describe. Perhaps it does not work on animaru. My spells are largely for combat. I know of nothing I could do to help. I am sorry."

"Urun?" Tere said. "Urun!"

The nature priest was off in his own world again, staring straight ahead of him. At a wall. When Tere shouted at him, he blinked and shook his head, then looked at Tere. "What?"

"Did you hear any of what we were talking about?"

"Something about being angry at the stupid things everyone else is doing?"

"Uh, yeah. Kind of. Do you have any spells that can protect our minds from being affected by magic, or do you know of any creature or person who can do these things and make us feel emotions we don't want to feel?"

He stared blankly at Tere for a moment and then his eyes seemed to finally focus on the archer's face. "No. Sorry. The mind is a difficult thing. Though there is magic that can control it or attack it, my spells are more geared toward physical harm, not so much mental harm. That's not to say that Osulin won't grant me such spells in the future, though I guess she may not. I'm only saying I don't have anything that will help right now."

"Okay," Tere said. "I guess we'll have to try to combat whatever it is individually. For me, knowing something is going on helps me to keep it from affecting my actions too much. I still feel the effects in my thinking, but I will keep on guard and question everything and so try not to act out what I'm thinking or feeling. That might work for others, too."

Aeden chuckled. "That sounds like a good idea."

"Then why did you laugh?" Tere asked.

A guilty look crept onto Aeden's face. "I almost said something like, 'keep your stupid theories to yourself,' but then thought about it and realized that thought came from somewhere else, not my own mind. Using the technique you suggested, I kept myself from being rude to you. So I guess it worked for me, too."

Tere understood the humor in it, but he didn't feel like laughing. "Good. I'm glad it helped, and I'm glad you didn't say what you first thought. I suppose we should continue searching. The sooner we find whatever that symbol is leading us to, the sooner we can get out of here."

It took two more days before they encountered anything significant.

For an hour, Tere and Raki had been finding evidence of something else in the caverns. It seemed to Tere that the cavern floor was also slanting slightly upward. He wasn't sure how far they were under the city, but going up seemed to be a good thing. Maybe the tunnels would end and they could go back to ground level. Maybe it even emptied out into a basement in the city. It had been several days and he was afraid the inn would sell or simply take their horses. The amount they prepaid for their rooms and boarding of their horses would run out the next day.

Because of the debris scattered throughout the tunnel before them, the group had come back together and were proceeding down the main tunnel, not bothering to thoroughly explore the side tunnels. It was better that way, at least until they figured out who was making all the tracks and dropping things like peanut shells, bits of old clothing, and small amounts of twigs and leaves, almost as if someone was moving branches somewhere else to use as firewood.

When the party heard voices, they split up and moved up against the walls, some of them drawing their weapons.

Based on how the voices sounded, they were stationary, simply having conversations. Tere listened for a moment, but he couldn't make out what they were saying. It sounded like two, or maybe three, men, but that's all he could glean.

He pointed to Aeden, Marla, Raki, and Lily, then

motioned for them to follow him forward. They'd scout out what was going on while the others waited. The five of them should be able to handle any problem that came up, especially if there were only a few people ahead of them.

Tere snuck around the corner of the next twist in the passageway, which revealed the source of the voices. Three men stood in a bunch, apparently arguing. Beyond them were other people, some of them lying on scraps of cloth, others standing or sitting. A few of them were moaning quietly, and Tere saw flashes of red splotches on some of the cloth wrapped around them.

Fahtin came up behind Tere. The others were spread out against the wall on the other side of the corridor. The Gypta girl gasped.

The three men's heads snapped in their direction and spotted Tere and Fahtin, possibly some of the others. The archer growled in his throat at the girl's stupidity. Next time, he'd tie her up to make her stay put when there was sneaking to be done. With a sigh, Tere nocked an arrow and drew the bowstring back.

"There's more of them," one of the men shouted, sounding about as panicked as anyone Tere had ever heard. All three brandished what they apparently thought were weapons. Were those...tree branches?

22

"**H**arlen," another man said loudly, his voice shaking. "Harlen, there's more. Harlen!"

Tere relaxed his bowstring and glanced over his shoulder to make sure Lily did the same. She had nocked and drawn nearly as fast as he did, and he nodded approval that she hadn't loosed. She was a smart kid, knowing that there was no danger until the men closed the gap between them and Tere.

An older man rushed up, less a run than a fast walk. He looked healthy enough, but he plainly wasn't a warrior. He must be their leader.

"We don't want any trouble," Tere said. "We're lost in the tunnels and were searching for a way out."

The older man put his hands on two of the men's sticks and pushed them down. "Those will do you no good against an arrow, you two. Let's not aggravate the folks that have real weapons." He looked past Tere, and the archer sensed someone moving closer.

Tere could just see the colorful clothing out of the corner of his sight, probably Aeden. He would be an intimidating sight for the people in front of them, the warrior bristling weapons.

"Forgive us if we're a little less than trusting," the older man said. "We were recently attacked by armed men and women coming through our camp. I'm Harlen Sayla. Who are you?"

"Someone attacked you?" Fahtin asked. "For no reason?"

Tere closed his eyes and tried to focus on his breaths. He felt a headache coming on.

"Yes," Harlen said. "For no reason. We live in these caves because there's nowhere else for us to go. We mind our own business. It's hard enough trying to survive. We don't want to cause any trouble. They came through and one of them seemed maddened by something, maybe just that we were in their way. They started cutting people down. We lost three right away, before we could flee, and five more were injured but are still alive."

"That's horrible," Fahtin said.

"Yes. So pardon us if we're suspicious."

"That's understandable," Tere said. "We mean you no harm. In fact, we might be able to help. We have with us a nature priest. Urun?" He looked back to see the young priest walking toward Tere. "Urun here is a priest of Osulin. He has healing magic."

"I can heal their wounds," Urun said. "If you want, I can go and help while my companions wait here. We don't mean to frighten you, especially after being treated so poorly by other strangers."

Harlen glanced back over his shoulder at the couple dozen people all paying rapt attention to the conversation.

"Oh, stop being such an oaf, Harlen," a woman's voice said. "Let the priest through. If he can heal the others, that would be a great help. I don't have the supplies to do a proper job of it."

The woman pushed her way between a few people standing around and stepped out past Harlen and the other three men, nearer to Tere and Urun. She was older, perhaps in her early fifties, with greying brown hair and a creased, and careworn face that indicated she'd had a hard life. She looked the visitors up and down and sniffed.

"Tissa, come away from there," Harlen said. "You don't know what they'll do."

"I said not to be a fool, Harlen. If they wanted to harm us, they would have already. Look at them. They all have weapons. Even the girl there has knives strapped to her. Those archers, did you see how they moved? They could have put arrows into all four of us before we took two steps toward them." She turned to Urun. "Priest—Urun, he said?—we would welcome your help, and appreciate it. We don't have anything of value to pay for it, though."

"I don't need payment," Urun said. "It's my calling to aid those in need whenever I can. I just want to help."

"In that case, come on then. If these useless lumps would move out of the way, I'll show you to our injured."

Urun followed her deeper into the cavern, passing by the men standing there awkwardly.

"We'll stay here for the time being," Tere said, sitting down on the floor of the tunnel with his legs crossed. He nodded toward the men. "Don't take it too hard, fellas. A woman like that doesn't obey the same laws of nature we mortals do. You have my condolences."

A hand swung through the air and Tere casually snatched it before it struck his head in a playful slap. "None of that, Marla. Just stating facts. No offense to other women who are forces of nature."

The other members of the party came out from the shadows. When Raki appeared suddenly in the middle of the room, a few of the onlookers gasped. Marla stepped completely into the light and the eyes of every one of the men snapped to her, staring. Lily's full appearance from the shadow she had been standing in made their eyes bug out unnaturally. But when Khrazhti revealed herself, it was a whole different situation.

Because they'd been alone in the caves so long, her cloak was stuffed into her pack. All she was wearing was the skimpy outfit that barely covered all her female bits. That meant all that glorious blue skin was showing.

The sharp intake of breath of several of the men—and some of the women—in the cave tipped Tere off that they might have a problem on their hands if he didn't do something.

"Calm down," he said out loud. "Haven't you ever seen a beautiful blue woman before?"

Some of those gathered looked at him stupidly, while others shook their head. The leader, Harlen, spoke.

"I don't know about the others, but I never have. What... who is she?"

"Don't ask me," Tere said. "She's standing right there, man. Ask her yourself." As he said it, he noticed Aeden stepping up protectively near Khrazhti. Fahtin positioned herself on the animaru's other side, one of her hands on the hilt of a knife sheathed at her waist.

"Sorry, sorry," Harlen said. "We've never seen anyone with blue skin before, nor anyone who looks like you do." He tilted his head toward Tere as if asking whether Khrazhti understood him.

"Your apology is accepted," she said in her accented Ruthrin. "I am not of this place. I come from far away, but I mean you no harm."

"I...uh, okay. I'm glad." Harlen seemed to be at a loss for words.

The awkward situation irritated Tere. "While we're waiting, why don't you tell us about what happened, Harlen. You were attacked?"

"Yessir," the leader said, darting glances at Khrazhti as if he thought she'd lunge at him at any moment. "We're just people who have no other place to go. No homes and no money, you see. The city guards aren't too friendly to folks like us, so we found this cave to keep the rain off us and to stay close together—mostly to keep the danger level down. Not too many bandits would risk attacking so many people, especially since we don't have anything to steal."

"But not so with the ones who attacked you?" Tere prompted.

"No, not them. It was hard to tell because everything happened so fast, but there were eight or nine of them. Mostly men, but at least two women. They were dressed sort of like you folks, in sturdy clothing or armor, and all of them with weapons of some kind, even if just a staff, except it was all black. They looked like a band of thieves, but with the armor and weapons of warriors.

"They said they were searching for something and asked us about magic and power and something that would maybe glow in the dark. We didn't know anything about it.

"We told them we stay here in this area. Two chambers over is the opening to the outside. No one really wants to explore the caves. We're only using these few chambers—basically wide areas in the passageway—because it's shelter. There's no reason for us to risk danger by going deeper into the cave.

"They looked at us like we were lying to hide something. A few of them made comments about beating the information out of us, but the man who seemed to be their leader—a big man with a scar down his face—waved his hand at them and they quieted down. We thought they were going to leave, but then one of the men grabbed one of our women, saying he was going to take her with them for entertainment. Well, a couple of our men protested and pulled the woman back.

"The one who had tried to take her cursed at us and cut both of the men down with his sword. That started it off, and several of them attacked us, either with weapons or with fists. We're just regular people, not warriors. We fled, but not before a number of us were killed or injured.

"The leader got his people under control and they left to continue their search for whatever they were looking for. They could have killed us all if they wanted to."

"Damn shame," Tere said. "They also could have left you all alone. There was no reason to attack you at all."

"We're thankful that the rest of us survived, though three no longer have to deal with the requirements of this life. I hope the priest can save the others, or that number might grow."

Fahtin shook her head. "That's terrible. Tere, Aeden, we need to do something about them. We can't just allow a group to go around attacking innocent people."

"We can't forget our goal here, Fahtin," Tere said. "We—"

"Do you know what our goal is, Tere Chizzit? For all we know, it may be to hunt down these ruffians. What if one of them has that symbol on him or with him. Maybe a tattoo or a talisman or something?"

"Symbol?" Harlen said.

Fahtin turned to him. "Yes, we're looking for something as well, but all we know about what we're searching for is a symbol. Here." She took the paper out with the symbol's drawing on it. "This is what we think will help us find what we're after."

Harlen Sayla looked at the symbol but didn't react. "Nope, never saw that before. If they had something with that on it, we never saw it."

"Anyway," Tere said, his voice growing firmer. "What I was

saying was that we can't forget our goal. We'll help these people how we can. If we can find the ones who attacked them, then we'll try to make sure they will never do so again. But we need to remember we have a bigger goal, one that could mean the survival of all life on Dizhelim. Or the extinction of that life."

Fahtin cast her eyes to her hands, still holding the paper with the symbol on it. "I know."

Aeden put his hand on her shoulder. "Come on, now. No reason to argue. We'll do what we can. There's no reason we can't do both. Besides, the presence of a group of armed thugs searching for something in the same place we're in can't be a coincidence. I'm sure we'll run into them."

That seemed to mollify everyone. No one spoke for several minutes, until Urun returned, looking a bit ragged.

"All done," he said. Then, scanning the faces of his friends, he asked, "What's wrong? What happened?"

Tere quickly explained and Urun nodded. "Sounds like we better get moving," the nature priest said. Based on his apathy of late, the response surprised Tere. Urun was right, though. They'd done what they could to help the people here. Well, almost all they could do.

"Here," Tere said, pressing three gold coins into Harlen's hand. "It may not be much for such a large group, but maybe it can help."

The older man's face softened and his eyes went liquid. "This...this is more money than I've seen at one time in the last ten years, maybe longer. This will feed us for more than a month."

"Good," the archer said. "Use it wisely. We'll see what we can do about those people who attacked you."

The woman who had escorted Urun to the injured—Tissa —bowed to Tere. "That is very kind. What is your name? Are you some kind of hero or something?"

Lily opened her mouth, but Tere said, "I'm Tere Chizzit and no, I'm no hero. These two, though,"—he pointed to Aeden and Marla—"are. If, in the coming months, you hear about Marla Shrike and Aeden Tannoch, or you hear of the term Malatirsay, you'll know who they're talking about. We're all helping them to try to protect Dizhelim from monsters who have come to destroy us."

"Monsters?" one of the other men standing around said.

"Yes. If you see dark creatures, either human-shaped or on all fours, you run as fast as you can. Even warriors with weapons can't harm them. It takes magic. They haven't attacked big cities yet, but they will, eventually."

Harlen shook his head. "Monsters." He sighed. "Thank you for the warning. We'll remember it."

"One more thing," Marla said. "Which way did the people who attacked you go? We might as well start there."

Harlen and Tissa led the party to where their attackers had left. Tere picked out more than half a dozen different tracks in the tunnel. They didn't appear too old, though without wind or other natural forces affecting them, it was hard to tell.

The cave people thanked the party again and wished them luck. Aeden repeated Tere's warnings and said they'd try to find the attackers. With nothing left for them to say, Tere started down the passageway, following the tracks.

"You're no hero, huh?" Lily asked quietly a few minutes later.

"That's right," Tere said. For some reason, he wasn't as irritated with Lily as he had been with others that day.

"You will always be my hero," she said.

Yeah, the kid wasn't all that bad. Maybe he'd keep her around a while.

❧ 23 ❧

Even without his ability to see into the magical matrix, Tere easily followed the tracks of the thugs who attacked Harlen's group. There were at least a half dozen of them, as Harlen said, and there were few other tracks in these tunnels. The passageways were farther removed from the openings Harlen and Tissa had described.

It was strange to be traveling as one group. Tere had gotten used to scouting ahead with Raki, but everyone had decided it would be best to stick together. There was no telling how powerful those they tracked were or when the party might be attacked.

Following the trail, they ignored side passages, something that made Tere's eye socket twitch. He didn't like the thought of being surprised by people or creatures coming up behind them. There was nothing for it, though. They couldn't explore every tunnel and still catch up to the ones they followed. Tissa had told Urun the attacks had been two days before. That put the heroes' party quite a distance behind the ones they followed.

Evening fell, though there wasn't a noticeable change in

the cave. The party had come upon a widening of the passage, large enough to almost be considered a chamber.

"What do you say we stop here?" Tere asked. "We should probably eat something and get some sleep."

The others muttered their agreement or, like Urun, simply remained quiet. Tere took that as affirmation and dropped his pack. He sat down beside it and searched through the supplies he had left, frowning.

"Yeah," Aeden said, plopping down next to Tere. "I looked in my pack earlier. We only have a few more days until we run out of food. I'd say four if we're careful. If we don't find what —or who—we're looking for by then, we'll have to go to the city and get supplies."

"We'd better get finished by then," Tere said. "If we have to leave and then come back to pick up the search, the ones we're following will find whatever it is we're both looking for first. *If* we are looking for the same thing."

Aeden nodded. The young man seemed tired. Not the kind of tired that was from exertion or lack of sleep, but the weariness of constant pressure from pursuing something that seemed impossible to reach. Tere knew that type of fatigue well. He'd felt it many times when he was on one mission or another and uncertain what he needed to do.

"We'll figure it out," the archer told him. "I've been at this point before. We'll keep on and things will become clear in their own time."

Aeden's tired eyes flicked up to meet Tere's white orbs. "Thanks, Tere. I honestly don't know what we'd do without you and your experience. We all appreciate your help."

The Croagh got up and moved over to the fire Marla had cast in the center of the area, where the others gathered.

Tere selected some dried meat from his pack and chewed on it as his mind chewed on their situation. He hoped what he had told Aeden was true because at the moment, he felt as lost as anytime he could remember.

Morning came and the party started off again, Tere following the trail and everyone else following him. A few hours into the day's traveling, they came upon a cave feature they hadn't seen yet.

In front of them, the floor of the tunnel, stretching all the way to both walls, dropped off into darkness. Tere could see the other side, at least thirty feet away, but until Marla created one of her little balls of light and threw it, the others didn't know the chasm had an end. In the light of Marla's thrown globe, the tunnel stretched on from the other side.

"Well, that makes things difficult," Tere said.

The footprints they'd been following went right to the edge of the pit, almost like the people they were following stepped off into the gloom. Their strides were normal, not the long gait of someone running to leap an obstacle. Tere scratched his head.

"Where did they go?" Fahtin asked.

Lily kneeled to inspect the footprints by the light of a stick. "It looks like they just continued walking, right off the edge."

"What's down there?" the Gypta girl asked.

"It drops twenty feet or so," Raki answered. "There are some rocks and a few stalagmites but it doesn't look like a spike trap or anything like that."

Fahtin squinted toward the other side of the chasm, where Marla's ball of light sat. "That's kind of a long way, huh? Could you jump that, Aeden?"

"No. Even with a running start, that's a bit too far for me to clear."

"Then how did the ones we're following do it?" Lily asked. "That's quite a leap by itself, but carrying weapons and supplies, how could anyone make it?"

"Wait," Raki said. "Tere, is that an opening off to the left in the corner down there?"

Tere scanned the area and immediately saw what Raki was talking about. "It is. It looks like a tunnel goes off from there. Hold on." Tere lay down on the floor, head protruding beyond the edge. He focused on the area below him, the bottom of the pit. "I think I can see some dirt disturbed down there. Footprints, maybe. I don't think they crossed the pit at all. I think they went into it."

"Well, then," Aeden said. "It's an easy enough thing. We'll go down and follow them, right?"

Tere eyed the young warrior out of the corner of his vision. "I guess so. It seems like they know something we don't."

"Good. I have some rope." He unslung his pack and dug out a section of rope. Looking around, he frowned. "There's nothing to secure the rope to, though. We'll have to hold onto it and lower one person at a time. Tere, why don't you go first. Urun and I can hold the rope up here."

Tere didn't respond right away. He stared at Aeden for a moment. Why did the younger man want him to go first? Was he planning on dropping the rope, letting Tere fall and break his leg? "Why me?" he asked.

Aeden blinked at him. "Because you can handle yourself. If you're down there first to guard in case something comes through that opening while the others are going down there, you'll be able to hold them off. Plus, you can see in the dark."

Tere continued to stare at Aeden. He had to hand it to the boy, he didn't flinch when Tere's eyes were trained on him. Many people did. Still, that didn't mean he wasn't planning on sabotaging the archer.

"Tere?" It was Lily's voice. "Are you afraid we can't hold the rope while you're on it? I'll help Aeden. I'm strong. You won't fall."

Tere shook his head. Where had those thoughts come from? Aeden trying to injure or attack him? What was he thinking?

"Yes, you're right. I'll go first. But what about when there are only one or two left? What then?"

"It only looks to be about twenty feet or so to the bottom," Aeden said. "I can be last. I'll crawl out over the edge and hang from that part there, the one that's flatter than the others. I'll hang and then drop. I can land safely dropping the ten feet or so."

Tere didn't have any other arguments. In fact, he'd seen another highlander do the exact same thing many years ago. The plan was simple enough, and sound. Aeden took up the rope and wrapped it around his hand, then got into a strong stance. Lily did the same behind him. Marla stepped over and put herself in place behind Lily. Tere threw the rope down into the pit, making sure it hit the bottom and that there were a few feet of slack at the end. He faced Aeden and the others and pulled hard on the rope.

The Croagh didn't move an inch.

Satisfied, Tere took up the rope and backed up to the edge, feet to either side of the rope. His heart was beating overtime and he was hoping he hadn't made a mistake in trusting the others, but he made sure his face didn't show it. Instead, he merely glanced at Lily and then stepped off the edge, lowering himself hand over hand while he walked down the side of the pit's wall.

He was at the bottom in no time and he called up to let the others know. While they prepared to let someone else down, he examined the floor of the chasm and found that he had been correct. There were definitely footprints going off toward the opening on the other side of what, to him, was now a room with a very high ceiling.

Some scrabbling from above turned out to be Urun

awkwardly hanging and sliding down the rope until his feet slammed into the floor with more force than Tere thought wise. He actually flinched at seeing it.

"Ow," Urun said, then shuffled toward Tere, obscuring all the footprints that had been there.

The others came down with more grace than Urun. Even Fahtin, who had probably never held a rope in her life, did a better job of it. Khrazhti walked down the wall gracefully, hardly looking like she was exerting herself at all. Lily came down, then Marla, then Raki. Aeden threw the rope down and finally did as he said he would, hanging from the lip of the cliff for a moment before dropping. He bent his knees as he landed, absorbing most of the force of the fall. He quickly coiled up his rope and put it back in his pack.

"I don't know how we'll get back out," the Croagh said. "We can only hope there's another way around. Otherwise, we're going to be in trouble in a few days when our water and food run out."

Of course! Tere had been so busy worrying about his friends betraying him, he hadn't thought through what they were actually doing. He recalled his conversation with Raki a few days back about how something was affecting their minds. He needed to be careful and think. Their actions may have just doomed them. If he was going to lead—and the gods only knew how he had fallen into that role—he needed to do a better job.

🍃 24 🍃

Tere and Raki went back to scouting ahead of the party. The others stayed back twenty paces or so to keep their lights from affecting Raki's dark vision. Tere sighed at resuming the same old task of searching for hazards and things that may want to attack them. Gods, how he wished they could finish what they were doing and leave.

Tere was muttering to himself when he threw his arm up to stop Raki from continuing. He shook his head and narrowed his vision to what he thought he'd seen.

"Well, I'll be…" Tere bent down to get a closer look, pulling Raki down into a crouch with him. "Do you see that?"

"See what? I don't…oh."

Stretched in front of them, a few inches off the ground, was a tripwire. It was hair thin and strung tightly across the corridor, just waiting for passing feet to break it.

The two backed up, waiting for the party to catch up to them and stopping them from going further.

"Tere found a trap," Raki told them.

"Did you disable it?" Marla asked.

Tere shook his head. "Not yet. I was waiting for the rest

of you to catch up before I did anything. Don't know what it'll do. I was going to shoot the tripwire to activate it."

"Whoa. Hold on a second. If the one who laid it is smart, she would have put a visible tripwire there, enticing someone to activate it. Then she would have set the trap to affect the area far away from it. You know, an area like where we're standing. That way, when they activate the trap, thinking they're safe, they bring their own doom upon themselves. Let me see if I can figure out what it does."

Marla took her light stick and moved forward, scanning the ground as she did it. Raki called out to her when she got close. As she inspected the wire, Lily leaned over toward Tere.

"Do people do that, set up traps expecting them to be found and killing them *because* they found it?"

"I haven't run into any, but I could see someone doing that. Obviously, Marla has thought about it. It's kind of scary what they teach at the Academy."

"Yeah," the red-haired archer said.

"Okay," Marla said as she came back to them. "It's just a normal trap. When activated, it shoots a few crossbow bolts from up near the ceiling. They're hidden up in the shadows. Go ahead and break the tripwire."

Tere took an arrow out, nocked it, then drew his bow back.

"Wait until I get out of the area first," Marla griped. "Don't kill the Academy student. Sheesh."

Tere drew the string back again and held it for a moment, but then relaxed his bow and put the arrow back in his quiver. Instead, he grabbed one of the spare sticks Marla used as torches and tossed it down the corridor. It apparently broke the string because several quarrels zipped into the space where the wire had been and shattered on the stone floor and walls.

Marla raised an eyebrow at Tere.

The archer shrugged. "Why waste an arrow? We may end up needing every one of them."

She chuckled and shook her head.

Tere scooped up the stick and thrust it into his belt, then the party continued on their way.

Though following the trail was easy because the ones ahead of them kept to the main tunnel, not veering off into any of the side passages the party passed, the traps they set soon became irritating.

"That's three so far," Tere complained. "It's only a matter of time until we miss one and it gets us. Anyone have any ideas?"

It seemed no one did. They all stepped back as Marla used her Academy-taught skills to disable the newest trap. While she did, Lily edged closer to Tere.

"Do you think we should take one of the side passages? There may be more than one way to get to where the ones we follow are going. According to the homeless people, the group ahead doesn't know exactly what they're looking for either."

"I don't know," Tere said. "We could waste a lot of time going through different parts of the cave. Even if they don't know where they're going, we need to catch them and make sure they don't go killing innocents again."

"I'm glad to hear you say that, Tere," Fahtin said. "I agree. There is good we can do, so we should do it."

"Do your visions say that?" Raki asked.

"Well, no, not really. But being a hero and helping people is always the right thing to do. We'll be rewarded for it. Somehow."

Tere didn't point out that he himself had lost everything that meant anything in his life because of being a hero. The girl had a good heart. No reason for him to stomp on it. She'd eventually learn that acting like some kind of hero didn't protect you from anything and didn't have any tangible reward. Let life teach her that. He didn't want to crush her dreams, not right now.

With no resolution on another course of action, they continued on, Tere and Raki in front. Less than a half hour later, Marla called up to the two scouts, asking them to come back to look at something.

"What is it?" Tere asked.

Marla pointed toward the wall of the passageway. "I found something you might be interested in. A secret door."

"Really?" the archer said. "Where?" It pained him to ask the question. If he had his full magical sight, he probably would have seen the door as he passed.

"Right here." She put her hand on the rough stone surface. "I already tested it with magic, as best as I could anyway, and it doesn't seem to be trapped."

"How do we open it?"

"Uh, that's the problem. I'm not really sure."

"Too bad Shadeglide—I mean Jia—isn't here," Lily said. "She's really good with traps and secret doors and the like. Unfortunately, I'm not."

Tere scratched his head, considering the wall. "I can't even see any lines to describe the door. It's definitely beyond the skill of those we're following." As soon as the words came out of his mouth, Tere winced. "Damn, that was probably the stupidest thing I've said in twenty years. As if they'd decide on a whim to cut a hole in the wall, dig a tunnel beyond it, and then hide it. Gods, someone just kill me. I'm stupid."

Lily laughed a bit too loud at that, but she also put her hand on his shoulder and smiled at him. He grumbled under his breath and mentally tried to force someone else to speak.

"Can I try something?" Raki asked, suddenly there in front of the door.

"Go ahead," Marla said. "If we can't figure something else out, I can start casting destructive magic at it. I'd rather we have a more elegant solution to the problem, though."

Raki closed his eyes and ran his hand over the stone. He seemed like he was trying to feel for the edges of the door. After a few minutes, he shuffled to the side, repeating the hand waving and feeling at the stone. Several more minutes passed before he stopped on a spot he had checked out twice before. This time, he moved even more slowly, like he was memorizing all the little bumps on the wall.

"Ah," he said, then pushed his index finger into the wall. An audible click sounded and the door silently swung inward. "The trigger was hidden with darkness. Fake shadow."

Tere examined the place where the boy had pushed with his finger. It was just to the side of the door. He felt at it and part of his finger sank into the stone, but he couldn't see the depression. It was some kind of magic that defeated his sight. That made him all kinds of uncomfortable.

"Shall we?" Marla said, sweeping her arm out toward the new tunnel in front of them.

Tere sighed and stepped into the darkness, hoping there wasn't more of the magical shadow in there. Or something worse than the traps they'd been dodging.

❧ 25 ❧

Thalia Fendove frowned at the small stone in her hand. It emanated warmth and light, flashing slowly. Irritatingly. She knew what it meant, and she was really in no mood to deal with it.

She had to, though, for no other reason than her father, dead nearly ten years now, would be disappointed if she shirked her responsibility. It was something that transcended her own wishes, even the needs and desires of the family itself. Damn her for promising him what she did, and damn him for being the kind of man to whom promises meant something.

The pretty, dark-haired woman sat and set the stone in its holder on the table in front of her. She'd do it, answer the call, but she didn't have to like it. Then again, she also didn't want the others to know it mattered at all to her. Best to act calm, indifferent. That's what they would expect.

She took three long breaths, trying her hardest to blow out all residue of irritation and unwillingness. Aloof, that's what she needed to be. Give them what they expected and things would go more smoothly. Thalia tilted her head to one side, then the other, enjoying the satisfying crack of the joints in her neck. She rolled her shoulders, sat with perfect posture, then spoke the words that would bring the stone to life.

"*Aruna sirat vitosim.*"

Tendrils of light reached out and enveloped Thalia's head, snuffing out her sight, hearing, even the sensation of air on her skin for a moment. She gasped, cursing under her breath. She would never get used to that.

In a blink, she regained her senses. Instead of in the room where her physical body resided, she was in another place. A familiar place. She sat at a large table in the dimly lit Council meeting room. While she schooled her face to apathy, she counted the seats that were not yet filled. Of the thirteen, only two sat empty. Good, at least she wouldn't have to wait for long, assuming the other two would show up soon.

"Welcome, Thalia," Alloria Yurgen said in her dead voice.

"Vituma."

"We will begin as soon as Hane and Evindia arrive."

Thalia nodded and set herself to waiting. She considered each of the others sitting around the table. The meeting stones really were a marvel, even if they meant she had to attend Council meetings despite members scattered all across Dizhelim. Each person looked physically in the room with her, as if she could reach out and touch any one of them. As if she were actually in the room herself.

She couldn't touch them, of course, though she had tried when she first experienced the stones. In a brighter room, she might have noticed the difference between the real people and the images or whatever they were that sat around the table with her. Maybe that was why the room was never lit well.

Or it could be the whole ambiance Alloria was trying to portray. Infrequently, everyone had to travel to what could be considered the Council's headquarters—that is, Alloria's estate—and the real room was also poorly lit, with the edges so steeped in shadows, it was hard to tell how large the place was unless one actually paced out the walls.

Hane Bryce appeared in his seat and Thalia decided it was no matter. Dark room, light room, sitting in a forest glade, it mattered not. Sitting and planning with twelve other people was a waste of time as far as she was concerned.

Evindia popped into existence in her seat, meeting Thalia's eyes and pursing her lips as if to kiss her from afar. The beautiful blonde was wearing a very low-cut top, tight enough that Thalia could see every curve and ripple beneath. The darker-haired woman fixed her smoky gaze on the newcomer and put on her sly smile, the one she used as a default expression. She knew it made some uncomfortable, implying she knew something the other didn't and was amused by it. It wouldn't work that way on Evindia, of course, but on the others? Maybe.

"Good," Alloria said. "We are all here. My apologies for contacting you all when another meeting was not expected, but we got word from one of Ren's Academy spies. There are two things of note. The first is that the boy who eliminated Izhrod Benzal is believed by at least some of the masters to be the Malatirsay.

"If I may, Vituma," Ren Kenata said.

"Of course."

He bowed his head to her. "Thank you. This young man is the one who has caused so much trouble with the plans of the other Academy graduates. He and his friends were the ones who took down Izhrod Benzal. According to my spy, he is *one half* of the Malatirsay, the other half being his twin sister Marla Shrike."

A few of the Council members whispered between themselves. That was interesting, Thalia thought. She hadn't heard that part of the story before.

"Also according to the spy," Ren continued, "it is common knowledge at the Academy that the headmaster has committed himself to giving the two siblings aid, though there has been no formal declaration of commitment from the Academy as a whole."

"Malatirsay," the huge warrior Thritur Nyhus said. His beard fairly quivered with his apparent rage. "It's a thing made up by the so-called prophet. The false prophet who usurped the true genius of the time in which he lived."

"Yes, yes, Thritur," Isbal Deyne said. The grandmotherly woman's words carried enough steel to make the barbarian flinch. "We know of your extreme devotion to the memory of the one who gave the Council life. Let's just agree that there is such a label for the hero or heroes of the Academy and move on to more important things. Like why all this is worth us being called to discuss."

Ren looked to Alloria, who seemed to be ready to put her head in her hands. The Vituma did a fair job of hiding her irritation as she answered.

"Just this, Isbal: if the Academy were to unite behind a single person—or even two as close as brother and sister—it could cause us difficulties."

Ren added, "It is, after all, why Quentin Duzen killed Master Aeid. The master was about to announce his support for Marla as the Malatirsay, something that could have brought much or all of the Academy behind her."

"At this time," Alloria said, "we do not have the resources necessary to openly oppose the Academy or the animaru. Until we do, we must be intelligent and maneuver things to our benefit. If the kingdoms of the world stand behind the Academy, it will make things much harder for us. Don't forget our purpose.

"But enough of that," the Vituma continued. "The other thing we need to talk about is that the Academy spy said that a group of those who accompany the Malatirsay have headed to Ebenrau. It's unclear why, but they left suddenly and it seemed to be urgent."

Thalia could almost feel everyone's eyes turn to her.

"Thalia?" Alloria said. "You mentioned at our last meeting that you had information about something happening near Ebenrau, some magical anomaly or such. Have your agents found anything? I believe you said you sent some of them to investigate."

Thalia ran through several lies in her mind before finally answering with the truth. "The last I had contact with them, they had found caves under the city. They are investigating. We have no such thing as meeting stones, so short of trying to follow them—and they left several days ago—I can't do anything but wait for them to return."

She almost winced as she said it. Several choice curses flowed through her mind as she realized she had hinted that she was already nearby. It wouldn't take too much of a jump in supposition for them to understand she was actually in the city. She only hoped they would move onto another subject without asking.

Alloria stared at Thalia for a moment, a question forming on her mouth. The Vituma licked her lips. In her eyes, the darker-haired woman read that she had been given a favor. "Please let us know as soon as you get news. I don't like that there was some sort of disruption in magic and it coincides with where the Academy puppets are searching. Your agents, they are skilled?"

"They are."

"Skilled enough to be victorious in a battle against the star student of the so-called Hero Academy and her twin brother, who has proven to be extremely competent?"

"I...don't know. Ren has seen the girl in action; I have not."

"Well," Alloria said. "Let us hope they can evade her and her friends, or if they meet in combat, they can beat her.

"That is all we needed to discuss. I will expect you all at the regularly scheduled meeting next week. Do not hesitate to contact me if you have any other news. As the Dark Prophet said, knowledge is the key to victory."

Some of the Council Members faded from the room. Within seconds, Thalia felt the disorientation and the temporary loss of her senses once again, followed immediately by her coming back into recognition in the room she had started in.

"Gods damned magical meetings," she spat. She picked the meeting stone from its holder and put it into the bag in her belt pouch.

She wondered if there was a way to get another type of magical device like the stones that would allow her to communicate with her agents. Wasn't there some kind of magic book the Academy mages created that worked like that? She had many people working for her, spread throughout Dizhelim, just as the others had, no doubt. She would give much to know what was happening underneath the city in which she now waited.

❦ 26 ❦

Tere led the others, Raki by his side. The caverns had a different feel than the ones they had been ghosting through before. The tunnels felt both more civilized somehow—though he didn't even really understand what that meant when the word popped into his head —and also wilder, more primal. Was it another case of his magic-induced stupidity? Damn, he hated the place.

He tried to delve deeper into what he had been thinking about the passageways, opening his vision up to see the larger picture.

The stone did seem to be smoother than in other tunnels they had traveled, like they were either more expertly carved or that at least they were made by more precise means. Like magic. Or flowing liquid. His heart skipped a beat when he thought of being flooded out, drowned and washed to who knew where. He squashed that thought.

So, assuming the caves were created by magic, what did that mean? He couldn't think of any way that would be a good thing, not with the other effects they'd felt. The image of a huge, magical spider sitting in the middle of a series of tunnel "webs," waiting for its food, popped into his head.

Fortunately, before he went too much further down that line of thinking, they came to another fork in the tunnel. He stopped the party.

"Any thoughts?" he asked.

"I don't like it here," Fahtin said.

He forced a chuckle. It sounded hollow in the confined space. "That makes two of us, but we have to figure out what this place is. We don't have a way to go back, remember?"

The Gypta girl nodded at him.

"I have a feeling about the left tunnel," he said. "Why don't you wait here for a little while and I'll go check it out."

"*We'll* check it out," Raki said.

Tere smiled at the boy. "Sure. *We'll* check it out." His first thought was how much he looked at the young Gypta as a kind of apprentice, though with his natural talent, or magic, he'd outstripped Tere as far as moving stealthily a while ago. His second thought was that Raki wanted to isolate Tere from the others so he could slit his throat with one of those daggers he carried. *Where in Abyssum did that thought come from?*

Raki threw a concerned look at the archer. "Tere?"

"Sorry, boy. Bad thought crept in. Come on. Let's see what's down there." Despite the way it made a muscle in his neck twitch, he headed down the corridor, a few steps in front of the boy. He couldn't even hear if Raki had followed him.

It turned out to be a dead end. At least, it seemed so. They only went a few hundred yards until the corridor ended in a blank wall. He didn't feel like looking for hidden passages, at least not unless the other tunnel didn't pan out. "Let's head back and see what the other tunnel does."

Raki nodded. He hadn't said a word since they left the

others. He glanced around him as if he was looking for something.

"Tere?"

The archer's fingers twitched, as if they could think for themselves and wanted to wrap around the hilt of his knife.

"I'm getting weird thoughts. My brain is telling me that you brought me here, away from the others, to kill me."

Tere's head snapped around to stare at the boy. *He* was worried about *Tere* ambushing him?

The archer breathed out slowly, almost a sigh. "No, Raki. In fact, I was feeling like you were going to try to kill me. It's those damn mind tricks this place is playing on us. Thank you for saying something. I should have earlier."

"Well," Raki said. "You did tell us to say something if we started to feel strange or had weird thoughts."

"I did. Guess I'm not good at following my own instructions. Come on, let's go back. I'll try to do better."

The disappearance of the pressure hemming them in was palpable. Tere went over it in his mind as they slinked their way back to the intersection where the others waited, and he promised himself he'd be better at doing what was obviously good sense.

Once they all started off again, it was only a few twists of the corridor until their path widened out into an area five times the width of the previous tunnel. It wasn't a chamber so much as a bulge in the tunnel, forty feet or so across and maybe a little more than that long.

It ended in a door.

As Raki, just a step in front of Tere, crossed over some invisible line, the entire area lit up. There were no torches or flames of any kind. There was not even really a discernible magical light source. Instead, the walls and ceiling glowed with a soothing bluish light, allowing them to see as if it were morning in the fields above the rock encasing them. It grew in intensity, slowly enough that it didn't hurt the others' eyes. He sensed the light brightening, but it didn't mean much to his type of sight.

The door was simple enough, if sturdy looking. It looked to be made of stone and had no apparent hinges, knob, or latch. Between the party and the door were five poles made of stone, each with a ring on the end, and a small glowing ball suspended in the precise center of the circle.

Tere scanned the room for dangers, but didn't see anything other than the five poles and the door. Three of the poles were on his left, with the other two on his right, at varying heights above the floor.

"What is it?" Urun asked.

"I don't know," Tere answered.

Marla approached the first pole, scanning the floor as she went. She spent a moment inspecting the stone shape, even pushing on it and scraping it with her dagger. "Hmmm."

Tere was trying to figure out what the things meant when a thought occurred to him. Those poles, the circles, the little glowing thing in the center. They looked like—

"Targets," Lily said from beside him. "Those look like targets I saw one time at an archery competition."

Marla made the humming noise again and walked past the poles to the door, her eyes sweeping ahead of her, obviously looking for some kind of trap. She pushed on the door, then tried to jam her fingers into the cracks around it to pry the door open. She knocked with the pommel of her dagger, producing a solid thunk. It sounded like the door was stone all the way through.

On the way back, the Academy graduate poked at one of the little glowing balls within the rings at the end of one of the poles. Her dagger pierced the object and it winked out, only to appear again almost instantly. Marla carefully poked it again with her finger, and her digit sunk in about the distance of half her fingernail and stopped. She grunted, pressing harder, but the ball didn't give any more and didn't disappear.

"Strange," the red-haired woman said as she walked back to the others. "I guess what Lily said was right. Maybe we're supposed to attack the little glowing balls."

"And then what?" Raki asked.

Marla shrugged. "Who knows?"

"You want me to try?" the boy asked.

Marla nodded while Tere answered. "No. We don't know what they'll do."

"But Marla just poked one with her knife and it disappeared for a second."

"I saw it," Tere said, "but what happens if more than one is popped? Are there different things that occur or is there a certain order they need to be attacked? What if guessing wrong sets of some kind of trap?"

Marla said a few words under her breath and waved her hand outward, toward the poles and door. "I don't sense any magical trap. That's not to say there isn't a mundane trap, though."

Tere rubbed his chin, looking at the configuration of the poles.

"Everybody back," he said. "I want to try something."

The others backed into the narrow part of the corridor from where they came. Tere took an arrow out, nocked it, drew his bow, and released. The shaft flew through the first ring, puncturing the little ball. It disappeared and then winked back into place almost immediately.

Nothing else happened.

"Okay," Tere said. "Maybe they all need to be hit."

The archer took a breath, set his feet precisely to allow him the necessary movement, and started. He nocked an arrow, fired it, launched a second, then a third, fourth and fifth arrow all in such rapid succession that he was sure his arms were just a blur to the others. All of the arrows struck precisely where he had aimed them, and all five of the glowing balls blinked out.

By the time he had finished the last arrow and looked back at the first ring, the glowing target was sitting there, pulsing faintly, as if it had never been gone.

"The first ball came back as your third arrow hit its target," Lily said. "I was watching for it."

"I think they all have to be hit at the same time," Marla said, "or at least they all have to be out at the same time. Hitting them one at a time won't do it." She hummed again. "Let me try something."

She positioned herself so she faced the door. A few words of power, and when she threw her hands out, little fiery missiles shot out of them. They sped toward the targets, each unerringly bursting into one of the glowing balls.

The targets didn't even go out, but flared and seemed to absorb the magic.

"Well, damn," she said. "Apparently it has to be mundane, physical damage. Is there any way you have to hit all of them at the same time?"

"Raki and I could hit two of them with our knives or spikes," Fahtin said, "but I don't know how we'd coordinate doing it at the same time as Tere and Lily shoot arrows at it. The arrows travel much faster than we can throw things."

"Your special move?" Lily asked, raising her eyebrows at Tere.

"What? Oh, my spinning move? No. I can do three at a time. To do more, I'd need to nock and draw two more and fire those after. The first of the glowing targets would probably come back by then."

"What if I could do two while you do three?" the read-haired archer asked. "We should be able to coordinate it so we shoot at the same time."

"That would be good, but it's not so easy to make those kinds of shots," Tere said.

"I know. I have practiced them for years. I can do the first three with really good accuracy. It's the second and third draws that tend to fall apart because I can't do them fast enough with good enough accuracy to make it all work."

Tere spun to her. "What? You've practiced that move?"

"Of course. What did you not understand about me trying to be just like you? I've been trying my whole life to nail that move, or at least since I heard the first story in which you did it. Three arrows, then two arrows, then one arrow, with the bow being spun on the first two draws to hit six different targets altogether."

The old archer's face crinkled with a smile. "Girl, you are full of surprises."

She smiled back at him. "I do try. My hero always believed in surprises."

"Okay," he said. "Let's give it a try. I'll take the three on the left and you take the two on the right. I'll count it down from three. Go ahead and get into position and nock."

The woman placed two arrows on her bowstring and set her feet as Tere did the same with three arrows.

"Here we go," he said. "Draw on one and launch when I say loose. Three. Two. One. Loose."

Five arrows zipped through the air, the archers spinning their bows to give each a unique trajectory. Tere watched his missiles as they sailed through the loops and blasted the glowing targets out of existence. In his peripheral vision, he saw Lily's targets. One of them winked out, but the other only flickered as the arrow passed within a hair's breadth of the target, still inside the ring, but narrowly missing the glowing ball.

Lily cursed under her breath.

"It's no problem, girl," he told her, smiling. "That was

fantastic. I've never actually seen anyone else spin the bow like that other than me. The shot you just made would have been the difference between putting an arrow through the center of someone's eye to only punching it through the white. Very impressive."

A hesitant smile crept onto Lily's face.

"Now," Tere said. "Take a breath. Loosen up your arms. Then we'll do it again."

She did as he said, then nodded as she took two more arrows from her quiver. Tere nocked his three.

"This'll do it," he said. "Nock. Three. Two. One. Go."

Both archers released, spinning their bows at exactly the right time to cause the arrows to angle off in different directions. Tere watched the door so he could see all the targets in his peripheral vision at once. As if by magic, all five glowing balls suddenly ceased to exist.

The clatter of the arrows that had gone through their targets and continued on to bounce off the walls settled into silence. Nothing happened for several seconds. The empty stone circles remained empty.

A loud crack echoed in the corridor, and the door at the end of the space swung outward with a grinding sound.

Tere found himself with an armful of tall, red-haired woman, her firmness balanced perfectly with the softness pressing against his chest. He leaned his head back to focus on the beautiful archer doing her best to squeeze the breath out of him. He huffed, patting her on the back.

"Excellent job, girl," he wheezed. "With skills like that, we'll make a hero out of you yet."

27

The party slipped through the door, Tere in the lead. The corridor on the other side narrowed to the same five-foot width as before the target room.

"How many of these obstacles do you think we're going to have to get through?" Raki asked as he glided alongside the archer.

"I don't know. Not many, I hope. I don't want to lose several arrows each time we want to open a door. I'd almost rather fight my way through. What's the purpose in all of this?"

"I think it's testing our quality," Fahtin said. "It feels like a test, maybe to see if we're worthy of whatever lies at the end of all this?"

Tere turned around to face the Gypta girl. "Did you have another vision?"

She shook her head. "No. I do remember feeling like that, though, when I was having the visions I had earlier."

"Wonderful. Now we're in an old-fashioned hero story where the mad wizard tests the hero before he gives him the prize. I always hated those."

"Good thing we have an old-fashioned hero with us, huh?" Marla threw in.

Tere felt his irritation reaching unwarranted levels again. He clamped his mouth shut and strode a little faster to put some distance between him and the rest of the group.

They found three more branching tunnels, but they all dead-ended within a few hundred yards. If Tere didn't know better, he would have said that the cave was leading them down a specific path. He wondered if they should spend more time looking for secret walls and hidden passageways.

Just as he was going to mention it to the others, he detected light up ahead, around a bend in the tunnel. He threw his hand up to stop everyone else. They didn't reach him for a few steps, finally seeing his upraised hand in the light they carried.

"Back up a little bit," he whispered to them, "and be quiet. There's light up ahead. I'll go check it out." He took a step forward and found Raki's arm in front of him.

"Tere, let me do it. Even with light, I can become almost invisible. I'll go just around the corner and see what's there, then come back and tell you."

A stab of irritation jabbed at Tere. He swallowed, thinking it through. The boy was right. With whatever strange skills Raki had gained, he *could* become invisible. Much more so than the larger man.

"Yeah, you're right," he said. "Be careful, boy. Don't put yourself at risk. Just take a peek and then come right back. And don't forget to move silently. Being invisible isn't as good if you're making a racket."

Raki showed his teeth to Tere and started down the tunnel slowly. Even to Tere's sensitive ears, he made barely a sound. The boy was really getting good.

Tere noticed Fahtin's worried eyes searching the darkness in front of them, looking for Raki, no doubt. He put his finger up to his lips and she gave him a look that left him with no doubt what he could do with his finger.

A few minutes later, Raki came back, suddenly appearing in front of the others. His face was pale and his eyes huge.

"The Epra has hunted us down and found us. We're all doomed."

The Epra? Tere racked his brain until he realized where he had heard that word before.

"You mean, that creature that plucked you from the forest into his realm and said he was going to eat you?" Tere asked.

"Yes," Raki said softly. "The Epradotirum. He's ahead. Waiting for us."

Aeden put his hand on the boy's shoulder and spun him so they were face-to-face. He grabbed Raki's other shoulder with his other hand. "Are you sure, Raki? He told us he would find other prey, that he would allow us to do what we could with our mission. Why would he go back on his word?"

"I...I don't know," Raki said. "Maybe he changed his mind. Come on. Let's go back, get out of this place. I don't want to face him again. I don't want to be eaten."

Aeden frowned at the boy. "The monster scares me, too. We have to go forward, though."

Tere alternated observing Aeden and Raki. Why was the boy acting like this? He was no coward. The archer had seen the young Gypta face down scarier things than a supposed monster sitting and waiting for them.

Then he thought of it. Whatever spell was affecting them, it caused changes in their mind. It had sewn suspicion, irritation, stupidity...it could easily seed fear into their minds, as well.

"Raki," he said softly. "You don't scare that easily. Take a breath. Think about it. Is this place affecting your thoughts, maybe making the fear more than it really should be?"

Fahtin glared at Tere so hard, he felt her stare without looking.

Raki blinked. His eyes lost focus for a moment, deep in thought.

"I guess I might be overreacting a little bit," he said. "But the Epra..."

Aeden seemed to have had enough. "I'm going to see what this is about."

"No, Aeden," Fahtin said. "Don't. You know how powerful that creature is. We were like insects to him."

"That's exactly it. If he wants us, he can always pluck us from wherever we are and bring us to him. There's no use running. On the other hand, since he hasn't brought us to him, he must not be wanting to eat us. He's intelligent. I'll ask him what he's here for."

Before Fahtin could answer, Aeden strode down the corridor, not even bothering to take one of the light sticks. The glow from the other end of the corridor was enough to see where he needed to go. Tere jogged a few steps to catch up with him. No use letting the boy go alone.

They strode around the turn in the cavern and the light grew brighter as it widened again. There was another door at the end, and sitting right in front of it was the monster Raki had told them about.

It swiveled its head toward them and blinked. The rest of its body stayed motionless. It was nearly ten feet tall, roughly man-shaped, but with fine scales covering its body. Not fish scales, but ones that looked softer, like the ones on the belly of a snake. It trained its blue-grey eyes on the human in front of it.

Aeden stopped ten paces away from the beast, mouth open. Tere heard the others come to a stop as well. Apparently they decided to follow.

"Raki, that's not the Epra. It looks similar, but nowhere near as large."

"No, I am not," the creature said, its voice deep but not as cultured sounding as the Epradotirum's. "I am Tukra."

"What do you want from us?" Aeden asked.

"Want? I want nothing from you. I am happy to sit here, guarding my door, having no interaction with you or anyone else."

"Why are you guarding the door?" Tere asked.

"Because it is what I was put here to do."

"Put by whom?"

"It is not for you to ask questions of me, and it is not for me to answer ones such as you."

"Do we have to defeat you in battle?" Marla asked, ignoring what the monster had just said.

"No."

"Will you let us pass?" she asked.

"No."

Marla opened her mouth again, but the creature spoke first.

"Unless you solve my riddle. Then may you pass, but only then."

"With all the effects whatever magic is around here has on our minds, you want us to solve a riddle?" Tere asked.

The creature remained silent.

"*Vermi cuta tuu caernant,*" Aeden hissed.

Tukra answered without hesitation. "*Vermi supor di cuta meu hau eumant.*"

Khrazhti chuckled at the monster's response, but Aeden didn't appear to find it so funny.

"What is your riddle?" Marla asked with a sigh.

The monster turned its head toward Marla. "Listen well, humans:

. . .

A SHELL SO SOFT
> A solid core
> A whispered sound
> And then no more

PROJECTED OUT
> With ill intent
> Point to the globe
> With malice sent

LIGHT TO DARK
> The wind to still
> The end of one
> From other's skill

WHAT IS IT?"

Tere muttered under his breath. He hated riddles. Even so, he went through the creature's words in his head. If he weren't so frustrated, he would have laughed as he looked at his friends, each one seeming to be deep in thought, some mouthing words as he was.

"A snow storm?" Marla guessed. The creature continued looking straight ahead, not even acknowledging that she had spoken. After more than a minute of silently waiting, she huffed, "I guess that's a no."

The others mumbled to themselves, but no one else hazarded a guess.

More than ten minutes passed and Tere's cheek twitched. He considered the creature from the side of his vision. Maybe if he cut its throat, the door would open. Something kept him from attacking, though. Whether it was a feeling deep down that warned him he would not survive attacking or the ridiculous thought that killing the guardian would allow the door to open, he wasn't sure.

"I hate riddles," he said, not directing the comment to anyone in particular. "It's luck. You rack your brain for an answer and then when you're ready to give up, it strikes you like an arrow to the..."

He blinked. No, it couldn't be that. Tere went over the words again, sifting through them, testing them. He stood in front of the monster and gave it his answer loudly. "An arrow shot into the eye."

The beast raised its chin, its huge eyes focusing on Tere.

"Correct."

The door made a cracking sound and swung outward. Before it was completely open, its guardian faded and then disappeared entirely.

"Well," the archer said. "That was unexpected." He hitched up his pack and headed through the doorway, his dumbfounded friends following after a moment.

28

Jia Toun surveyed the forces gathered below the tree she was currently hiding in. The massive oak was on a hill above what looked like an army preparing for war. She was more than a quarter mile away from the outer ring of the sentry patrols.

"What do you think?" she asked her companions.

"I think this may be the same army Aeden saw," Aila Ven answered. "I'm not sure why they're here, though."

"Maybe it's not the same group," Evon added. "Aeden reported more like four hundred. Unless the army Aeden saw —who were heading east according to his story—has grown half again its own number, this is probably an additional force."

Jia shook her head. "That many people willing to sell out their entire race? I hope it's the same group, even if they've grown. Otherwise, it means there are close to a thousand human traitors."

Evon's eyes were sad as he looked at her. "I'm afraid there might be even more than that. Then again, it's also possible these belong to one of the lords and are merely the sign of some kind of civil war, even though I can't see any emblems or banners at all."

"What kind of world is it when the best situation is civil war?"

"Without knowing who they are and what they're doing here, it's all guesswork. I haven't seen any animaru in their camp, but we haven't gotten that close, either."

Jia narrowed her eyes, scanning the mass of bodies between the dozens of campfires. "I think I'll remedy that little problem. It'll be dark soon. I'll go down and scout around. I'll look for animaru and locate the officers' section of the camp."

Evon looked at her, mouth open. "Are you crazy? There have to be six or seven hundred soldiers down there. You're just going to stroll into camp?"

"I didn't say stroll, but yeah, you've got the idea. It's no problem. I do it all the time."

Evon shook his head as if he had misheard her.

"You heard right," she said. "It'll be fine. Don't worry. Worse comes to worst, I could always imitate a messenger. Armies often use boys for such tasks, and I'm small like that." She added the last part purely to make Evon feel better.

Aila put her hand on the Academy student's shoulder. "She's right. No one will see her if she doesn't want them to."

"She's that good?" Evon asked.

"Yeah, she is."

Jia smiled at her friend. Aila didn't know the half of it. She hadn't shown the extent of her abilities when they were working together in the thieves' guild, both of them under fake names. If she had, she would have called attention to herself. Doing that was the last thing an assassin wanted to do, especially during a mission.

"O-Okay," Evon said. "Be careful."

Jia flashed her friendliest smile to the young man. "I will."

"In the meantime," Aila said, "why don't you tell us what the situation is with Fahtin?"

Evon gave a little jump and almost fell out of the tree. "Fahtin?"

"Yeah. You know, dark-haired woman, taller than me, drop-dead gorgeous. Hazel eyes that would make a grown man weep knowing he had to stop staring into them. Any of this sound familiar?"

"I...she...that is, yes, I know who she is, of course." He ran one finger through his blond hair, scratched his scalp. "What was the question again?"

After almost two hours of what Jia suspected was very uncomfortable conversation for Evon, she headed off to scout the soldiers' camp. She nodded and waved away the admonitions to be careful and not put herself at risk.

It was one of the things she hadn't expected. She had gone from living with her grandfather—who had *trained* her to be as careful and safe as humanly possible, considering she was trained in deadly arts—to working odd theft and assassination jobs, to being one of the Falxen. None of those experiences included being *told* to be careful. Ever.

A smile slowly crept onto her face. She liked the idea that her friends were concerned with her welfare. The new experience brought a comforting warmth in her belly.

She turned her attention to the camp ahead. She had infiltrated everything from a king's throne room, as well as his private rooms, to campfires of barbarians. This task wasn't a great stretch for her skills. Still, it was going to be a long night.

First she'd have to get to the inner part of the camp. Then she had to locate the officers' section. It would probably be well marked with pennants or flags or something, but she'd have to cross a lot of ground to get there. Once there, she'd have to hide close enough to hear the conversations of the highest officers. All that, and there was no telling if the officers would say anything worthwhile or not.

Assassination was easier, definitely. If she needed to kill the highest commander, she'd slink her way into the officer area, kill the leader in her own time, and then disappear like she had never been there. Much better than waiting to see if someone mentioned anything important.

She sighed. Such was her burden. She hoped she'd hear something, but it was hit and miss.

As she dodged sentries and assorted men wandering around, without really thinking about it, she noticed something that might make her trip worth something after all. A man skulked out of the large clearing where most of the camp had set their tents and created their fires. His head swiveled, scanning the area around him.

What are you doing, and why do you look so guilty?

Whatever he was up to probably wasn't all that important. Or wouldn't be, she thought, if the insignia on his uniform didn't identify him as a major. He wouldn't be the highest ranked officer in the crowd, but he'd definitely be at a level where he knew what was going on.

She had an idea what he was about, so decided to follow him.

Just before the officer plunged into the trees, he looked around again, checking to make sure he wasn't being observed. He'd never see Jia, of course. She was too skilled for that to happen. After half a minute, she followed him.

The major went straight to a small clearing, not more than ten feet or so across. Sitting, waiting for him, was a woman. She rose when she caught sight of him and ran into his arms.

"Are you sure Hosvir doesn't have someone following you? He can't find out. He'll kill us both."

"It's fine, Jela," the major said. "He's in an important

meeting with one of those creatures. He'll be occupied for a while."

She breathed out a sigh of relief and then kissed him.

The man kissed her back, his hands roaming over her body. The pair made soft groaning noises as their kisses got more urgent and they started reaching hands under clothing.

I've seen about as much as I need to, Jia thought. She took out her small blowgun and two darts from a special container that kept the tips suspended in liquid. Taking aim, she puffed into the blowgun, sending a dart into the side of the woman's neck. A second later, the other dart flew through the air and lodged itself in the major's cheek. Both of them dropped to the ferns with twin dull thumps.

Jia checked to make sure both of her targets were still breathing. She used a strong dose of the poison on them, and one never knew if someone would have an adverse reaction. She chuckled. Adverse reaction to a poison. Was there any other kind?

She had about twenty minutes until the effects—the toxin only knocked targets unconscious—wore off. While she could carry the man, she would prefer not to have to do that while dodging sentries. Instead, she took off at a loping run to get her friends.

When she burst into view where Aila and Evon waited, both drew their weapons and spun to her.

"Damn you, Jia," Aila said. "You scared me half to death. Were you running? How in the world can you run that silently?"

"Sorry. I need you two to follow me right now. There's not much time. I'll explain when I can, but now is not the time for it."

She felt a little giddy when both of them nodded and followed after her without question. Just a simple thing like trust nearly made her tear up.

Jia led her companions to where the woman and the major were still lying unconscious. To Aila's wide eyes, the former assassin said, "They're just sleeping. We need to take the man back to well outside the sentry patrols. He'll probably come to in ten minutes or so." Thinking twice on it, she pulled out another dart, dipped it in the vial she had used earlier, and pricked his neck with it. "Maybe twenty or twenty-five minutes now."

Evon threw the man over his shoulder, huffing with the effort. The major was not a small man. Jia led them outside the patrol routes, far enough that they wouldn't be heard. She expected there were going to be screams in the officer's future.

After Evon dropped the man to the ground, he looked to Jia with one eyebrow raised.

"Okay," she said, "here's the situation. I saw this officer skulking around and decided to follow. He was meeting the woman we left for a tryst. She's apparently married to someone with power. I got the sense her husband may be the commanding officer for the army. I hit them with darts to knock them out, and here we are."

"But why?" Evon asked. "What good will a hostage do for us?"

Aila shared a look with Jia. At least the other woman understood what was happening. Evon was too innocent—or too kind—to even think of what they were about to do.

"Uh, you may want to head over toward that way, Evon," Jia said. "He'll wake in a little while, and when he does, I'm going to get information from him."

"Information?" Evon's eyes bugged out. "You're going to torture him?"

"Torture is such a dirty word," Jia said. "Let's just say that we'll have a talk and we'll share information. Mostly him, though."

"And when you're done?"

"Well, normal protocol is to cut off all loose ends. I suppose I could dose him with the poison again and leave him here to find his way back to the army. It won't matter that he saw us. We'll be long gone."

"At least you're not talking about killing him," Evon said. "Still, I think I have a better way."

"Better than torture?" Aila asked.

"Yes."

"Is it magic?"

Evon ran his fingers through his hair. "Not magic, exactly. One of the colleges at the Academy is the School of the Mind. It's also called the School of Psionics and Psychology sometimes. I should have the school mastered within a year. Anyway, psionics are kind of like magic, but for the mind."

"Oooh," Jia said. "I've heard the Academy graduates can control peoples' minds. If you do that, will you make him dance like a chicken? I've always wanted to see that."

Evon's brow furrowed. "I...can't really make him dance like a chicken, nor can I control him completely."

"Oh."

"What I can do, though, is make him think I'm someone else."

Aila frowned at the young man. "What good would that do? He doesn't know you. As far as he's concerned, you *are* someone else."

"I'm not being clear. I can prepare his mind so that when he opens his eyes, he won't see me, but someone he knows."

Jia nodded, but she was far from convinced. Torture still seemed the way to go. "Do you know someone well enough to impersonate them so he won't think anything is strange?"

Evon sighed. "It doesn't really work like that. I use my powers to make his mind receptive to a suggestion and then his imagination fills in the rest of it. I can suggest to him that

I'm someone important, with power over him. He'll see and hear me as that person and respond as he would if he was talking to that one. I think I can make him think I'm his commander. If I ask the right questions, we can get some information out of him."

"Oh," Jia said. "That sounds promising, and less messy than torture."

"I know. It is. There is another school in the Mental Studies lycad that deals with those things: the School of Interrogation and Coercion. I've studied a little bit there. I've learned some pretty gruesome techniques, but I would like to never have to use them. Anyway, you two should probably hide. I'll start preparing his mind and then, when he wakes up, I can try to get information out of him. When I raise my right hand like this, hit him with another dart."

Aila stared at Evon with what could only be respect. "What other stuff do you know?"

"A lot of things. I've been at the Academy for almost fifteen years."

"Hmmm."

Jia took Aila's arm. "Come on. We'll go over there so we can hear and see him but won't be within sight. I'll watch for your signal, Evon. Thanks."

"It's my pleasure. I'll prevent us from having to torture a man—even though he's selling out his entire species—and it'll give me a chance to use what I've been studying. I can't wait to tell Marla about it."

The man groaned and shifted.

"He's waking up," Evon said. "Hurry, go hide. I'll start working on his mind."

The two women did as instructed, slipping behind some thick bushes wedged in between two tall pines. Jia had a clear view and should have no problem hearing what they said.

Evon stared at the man, as if his eyes could pierce his skull and do the work he had promised Jia. She barely blinked, not wanting to miss a second of a type of magic she'd never seen before.

The major rolled and pushed his way into a sitting position. Evon stood silent, but his posture had changed. He was erect, almost imperious. Jia was familiar with the technique of using body language to communicate different things, but she hadn't expected Evon to be so skilled at it.

The officer squeezed his head with both hands, then rubbed his eyes. Why wasn't Evon saying anything?

The man finally noticed Evon. He jumped to his feet...or at least tried to. It was more like a drunken stumble. The aftereffects of the poison she used could last for several minutes.

Once the major had gotten to his feet and stood in a loose approximation of an attention stance—though still swaying slightly—he saluted. "Colonel Bramsson?"

"What's the meaning of this, major?" Evon said in a voice laced with command. Jia smiled. He was good.

"Uh, ah, I don't know, sir. I'm having trouble remembering. I think I might be getting sick."

"More likely you drank too much. You know how I feel about drinking on duty."

"Yessir."

Evon looked down his nose at the major, inspecting him.

"Umm, sir?" the major said. "Where are we?"

"How are your preparations for our mission?" Evon asked, ignoring the other man's question.

The officer straightened. "Everything is going according to schedule, sir."

"What exactly have you been doing, Major?"

"Exactly as ordered, sir. The men have been briefed and we're preparing to get underway to meet Kirraloth."

"Kirraloth?" Evon shouted. "What do you know of Kirraloth?"

The major winced as if struck. "Nothing, sir. That is, only what I heard in the meeting we had with the beast. I'm still not used to the idea of being around those monsters, sir, but I'll do my duty."

"And just what is your understanding of your duty, Major?"

"I...that is, we are to act as support, adding our troops to Kirraloth's. When we meet up in Kruzekstan, we will take Nanris and then move north to take care of the rest of the Crows. The dark things already killed most of them."

"Good. It's nice to see that you're not simply taking up space in command meetings."

"Yessir."

Evon cocked his head like something had occurred to him. "One more thing, Major. Have you seen my wife?" As he asked, he raised his arm in the signal they had agreed upon. Again, Jia was impressed. He made it seem to be a simple gesture as he spoke.

She put the blowgun to her lips and launched another dart. It struck true, sinking into the flesh of the major's right shoulder. He made to brush at it with his left hand, but he was already falling.

Jia and Aila rushed from their hiding.

"That was great, Evon," Aila said. "Who knew you could act so well?"

"I've studied it a little bit at the Academy."

"Of course you have," she said.

Jia retrieved her dart and hid it away in the holder she carried. "Well, that's about it. Our mission was not to stop the army—and we couldn't anyway with so many troops—but this information will be valuable. What do you say? Time to leave?"

"Definitely," Aila said. She considered the major. "Should we—?" she mimicked drawing a knife across her throat.

"No," Evon said. "Not that he doesn't probably deserve it, but no. We can't kill a man in cold blood while he's lying there unconscious."

"*I* could," Jia said. "I mean, I have. Uh, that is...you're right. We're the good guys."

"Good guys should still take advantage of situations that let them eliminate enemies who are trying to kill every human on Dizhelim," Aila spat.

"No. He's right, Aila," Jia said. "We don't want to become like them. This is important news. Let's get it back to the Academy so we can decide what we should do. Surus knows, we're going to need to act quickly."

❧ 29 ❧

Marla Shrike had just about had enough of the caverns they seemed to be trapped in. She wasn't fond of enclosed spaces, and the strange thoughts and feelings she'd been inflicted with since they got to Ebenrau made it all worse. She would scream, if it wouldn't show her companions that she was losing control. Some of them would no doubt use it as an excuse to attack her, taking advantage of her weakness.

"It's about time to renew the light sticks," Tere said to her.

Who had made him the boss, giving orders to the others? Sure, he was old, but that didn't mean he knew best. He probably wasn't even really Erent Caahs. She wouldn't be surprised if he'd cooked the whole thing up with that scantily clad, bow-toting, red-haired tramp, always flouncing about like she did. Marla had to work hard to keep the sneer off her face.

Part of her was shocked at the thoughts going through her head. Where did they come from? Maybe there was something to what Tere had said earlier, that a type of magic was affecting them. She shook her head, hoping it would break those thoughts into pieces, or at least rattle them loose.

The Academy graduate sighed and made the motions to cast the simple light spell onto the stick she was holding.

It didn't work.

What in the hells?

She cast the spell again, focusing on making her gesture correct and on keeping the appropriate thought in mind to bring the magic into being. It fought her, squirming like a worm newly uncovered from the soil, gyrating madly. Marla wrestled it under control and the little ball of light came into being. She held the stick out and Fahtin took it from her, smiling. Marla snatched the stick in the Gypta's other hand from her, only realizing how rude the action might seem after she'd done it. She forced out a smile so she didn't hurt Fahtin's feelings.

What was going on? Marla had a temper—that had been established—but it wasn't like her to think suspicious or mean thoughts about her friends. And her brother!

She darted her eyes to Aeden. He was watching her. What was he thinking?

"Are you all right, Marla?" He said it with such sincerity, she almost broke down in tears at what she had been thinking just a moment before.

"I'm tired," she said. "These damn caves are driving me crazy, making me think strange things. I want to get out of here." She hated how whiny it sounded, even to her own ears.

Aeden put a hand on her shoulder. "I know. Me, too. I keep feeling like we're going to tear each other apart, and the next second I feel like I've lost half my intelligence. I don't know what it is, but once we get to what we're looking for, I think we can make it stop."

She huffed a breath out. "I'm having trouble with my magic. It's not cooperating."

"I am having trouble remembering some words of power," Khrazhti said. Marla hadn't even realized the animaru was on the other side of Aeden. "It is...disturbing."

Marla wanted to snap at the blue woman for butting into the conversation, but she swallowed her anger. It was affecting Khrazhti, too? "Oh. I guess it's good to know it's not just me."

"Hang in there, sis. We'll get through this and figure out what we need to do. I don't know why, but it feels important. You know, hero stuff."

"Yeah. Hero stuff. Well, pass me those other sticks so I can heroically put little sticky balls of light on them."

Two and a half hours later, Tere and Raki came back to the group from scouting ahead.

"There's another door up there," Tere said.

"What kind of door?" Aeden asked.

"The door isn't anything special, but...well, let's go look at it together." He turned to lead them, but stopped. "Just out of curiosity, what was that bit with the Tukra? I've heard you use that curse before, but the monster responded and Khrazhti laughed. I didn't catch what it said."

Aeden's face colored. He worked his mouth to speak, but only a few squeaks came out.

"It was in Alaqotim," Marla answered for her brother. "Aeden's curse was in modern Alaqotim—'maggots eat your flesh'—but the answer was in that archaic dialect Khrazhti speaks. It said, 'Maggots would not like the taste of my flesh.' It thought Aeden was being literal and referring to it."

Khrazhti laughed again and Tere's mouth slanted into half a smile. "Oh," he said, and led them to what he'd found.

Marla approached the door with the others and saw Tere had been right. It was a normal-looking, heavy wooden door with iron bindings. She spotted a glow, no doubt because of her magical affinities, but that wasn't too uncommon. What *was* were the things surrounding the door.

Above it were two shapes etched into the stone. To either side of the door were cutouts from the stone, five feet long horizontally and only about a hand's width vertically. Within the open space were what looked like huge wheels side-by-side, only the edge of which they could see.

"Tumblers?" she asked.

"Looks like it," Tere said.

She stepped up to the wheel closest to the door on the left side. She could reach in and pull to make it spin. Engraved on the edge so that they were visible through the cutout were more symbols like the ones above the door, strange squiggles. All the wheels she hadn't moved yet showed blanks spaces. She pulled down on the wheel again and it spun easily, shapes flashing by as she did so.

"Twenty-four," Fahtin said from the right side of the door. "There are twenty-four of these symbols and the one blank, so twenty-five total positions on each wheel. The wheels must be big enough to go back into the wall for several feet."

Twenty-four. Marla racked her brain. The shapes looked familiar. Why couldn't she remember? Her mind was so foggy. She didn't like it.

"What are we supposed to do?" Raki asked.

Lily reached up and spun another of the wheels. "It's another puzzle. We need to line it up to the right combination. That's what it looks like."

Tere nodded. "There are ten wheels on each side, each with twenty-five combinations. What are the odds we could guess the right one?"

Marla snorted. "Uh, for only one side with ten of the wheels, it would be over ninety-five trillion combinations. Better not to even think about the chance of guessing for both sides."

Aeden gaped at his sister. "So much for some power making us stupid."

Marla shrugged. "I'm good with math."

Tere cursed. "We're not going to be going through them one at a time, then. It'll take forever."

Aeden pointed to the symbols above the door. "Maybe that's our clue."

Yes. Her brother was right. Whoever had created the puzzle wouldn't be looking for someone to simply try to randomly find the solution. There had to be a way to figure it out. She inspected the etchings. They were simple enough.

She should know the answer, was confident that if she could think clearly, she'd have come up with the answer already.

"Marla?" Aeden said. "You've studied at the Academy your whole life. Is there anything you can do to figure it out?"

A sudden flash of anger assailed her again, but she gritted her teeth and rode it out. After a few breaths that whistled into and out of her mouth, she was calm enough to speak. "Give me a couple of minutes. I'm feeling stupid again, math notwithstanding. My brain is grinding away slowly. We might as well put our packs down and sit. It may take a while."

Marla stared at the symbols. She cursed her sluggish mind again. They seemed familiar, but for the life of her, she couldn't remember where she had seen them. She tried closing her eyes and focusing her mind. Her fingers found her eye sockets and she began to rub them. They ached.

Nothing.

She sighed and went to one of the twenty wheels set in the wall, turning it slowly until she got to the blank part of its face again. The mechanism moved so easily. How long had it been there? There must be some kind of magic to keep bits of stone or dust from interfering with its motion. She flicked it with her finger, rolling it to the next symbol, then she moved it back to the one on the other side of the blank.

Ugh. She knew these symbols, but she couldn't pull the memories up. Instead she stared at them as she slowly moved the wheel through all twenty-four of the symbols.

"Hey," Aeden's voice said right next to her. "Why don't you rest a little bit? You haven't even eaten and you've been staring at those things for almost two hours."

"Really?" she asked. How had she lost track of things like that? "I guess I could use some food."

"It's almost time to go to sleep," he said. "Relax for a little while, get some sleep, don't think about the problem. Your mind will work on it in the background. Every time I do that, the answer always comes to me. It's like squeezing a wet seed too hard; it just slips out of your grasp. You'll figure it out. I have faith in you."

She chuckled. "You have to. As my brother, I think that's your job."

"Maybe, but you make it easy. Come on."

She followed him to where he had set up her bedroll for her and she gratefully sat down. Fahtin brought her a bowl of the stew one of them had made.

"Thank you."

"You're welcome," the Gypta said. "I'm glad you're taking a break to eat something."

Marla nodded and blew on the food in her bowl. A little time away *would* probably help her. It was also true that these effects had an ebb and flow, each person on their own individual schedules. Eventually, she'd feel less mud-brained and then the answer would come to her. She hated wasting everyone's time, but she'd figure it out eventually. It seemed she was the only one who could.

Lily took the first watch and everyone else settled down to sleep. Marla drifted off as soon as she lay down.

Some time later, she jerked into a sitting position. Aeden, a few paces away, had his swords out and was on his feet before she could even breathe. He scanned the area, noting Tere, who had apparently taken the watch from Lily.

"What is it?" he asked her.

Her face heated. "Sorry. I didn't mean to panic anyone. I think I figured it out. At least, part of it."

He slipped his swords back into their scabbards, both lying on the floor next to him. "That's great."

Marla was already on her feet and approaching the wheels on the left side of the doorway. "Cogiscro."

Aeden looked from her to the door. "Is that some kind of magic word?"

If she wasn't still so tired, she probably would have laughed, but instead she settled for a smile. "No. Cogiscro is an ancient alphabet. It's only really used for runic spells, where the runes are carved into items to channel magical power. There are twenty-four letters. The wheels have the characters so they can be chosen individually, but in the script form, the symbols are merged stylistically in a circular pattern to represent things."

"A magical alphabet?" Aeden said. "Okay, great. Any idea what we're supposed to spell out?"

"No, unfortunately." Marla frowned at the wheels and turned her eyes toward the symbols etched above the door. "That may help, though. Those letters spell *at*."

"At what?"

"No, listen to me. *At*, like we *ought* to be able to figure this out." She smirked

"Oh, sorry. So what does it mean?"

"It means up or top," Khrazhti said from behind them. "In Alaqotim."

"Exactly," Marla said. "I would expect for the language to be Alaqotim. It's obvious the puzzles in these tunnels were made long ago, most likely thousands of years ago."

"That's one step closer," Aeden said.

Tere had come over, and the others—all except Urun—had woken at the discussion.

"Did you say the script form of those symbols are arranged in a circular pattern?" Fahtin asked.

"Yes," Marla answered, "but the wheels and above the door are marked with the simple block symbols, so we don't need to worry about that."

"Umm," the girl said, "maybe we do." She held up the paper she had drawn the symbol from her vision on.

Marla blinked at the paper. "Oh! That does look like Cogiscro script. I'll take a look at it later, if you don't mind. I don't think it's going to help us with this problem. We need two words and that only looks like one."

"That's fine," Fahtin said. "I just thought it might help us overall. I'm sure it can wait until we open this door."

Marla considered the etchings above the door again. Up. "We might as well start somewhere." She moved over and began to spin the wheels, starting with the one farthest to the left of the door. Once she found what she was looking for, she spun the second wheel, then the third. Soon, she had seven of the symbols displayed. The other three wheels she left on the blank face. She stepped past the door to the wheels on the right side and spun the wheels to find the other symbols. This time, there were only five characters, with five blanks. She stepped back, proud of herself.

Nothing happened.

She pushed on the door, then tried to catch the iron banding with her fingertips to pull the door.

It didn't budge.

"Well, damn," she said.

"What did you try to do?" Aeden asked.

All the air left Marla's body. "I thought I had it figured out. I guess not, though."

"What did you dial into the wheels?"

"On this side," she said, pointing to the left set of wheels, "I spelled out the word for *left,* and on the other side, the word for *right.*"

"Oh. That was good thinking. With the ones carved above the door meaning up, it sounds logical."

"Yeah, but it wasn't good enough."

"I am sorry," Khrazhti said. She pointed toward the left side of the door. "But you made the word for *left* on those wheels?"

"Yes," Marla said.

"But you used seven of the symbols."

"Of course." Marla was started to get irritated. Who was this blue woman who thought she could second-guess her? "It wouldn't have been in Ruthrin. It says *siniste*. That's Alaqotim for left."

Khrazhti looked confused, her eyes switching back and forth between Aeden and Marla.

"What do you not understand?" Marla snapped at the blue woman.

"Marla, there's no need to get rude," Aeden said. "She's just trying to help."

She let a long breath out. "I'm sorry, Khrazhti. This place is getting to me. I didn't mean to be rude to you. Are you confused about something?" Marla tried to say it in the kindest way she could.

Aeden nodded to the animaru. "Go ahead, Khrazhti. What's the problem?"

"It is only that if these tunnels and these puzzles are thousands of years old, as you have said, your word may be incorrect. In my language—ancient Alaqotim—the word for the left side is *sonistre*."

Marla slammed her palm into her forehead. "Surus damn it all!"

Khrazhti whispered to Aeden, though Marla heard it just fine. "Why does she strike herself? Have I angered her?"

Aeden laughed. "No. She's embarrassed that she didn't think of that. And I think she wants to apologize to you." He raised his eyebrows at Marla.

"I do," Marla said. "I'm sorry for being rude. You are completely right. I mean, correct. I put the wheels so they spelled *verus* on the right side. Is that correct?"

"It is *vira*."

Marla quickly changed the wheels so they spelled out the words in ancient Alaqotim. As soon as she put the last one in place, something clicked and the door popped open enough to grab it and move it the rest of the way. She turned and smiled at Khrazhti.

"Thank you. I'm sorry about being such a bitch, I really am. I wish we could do what we need to do and get out of here. I think you've seen the worst of me since we first met."

"Does being a female of a canine species have some significance?" Khrazhti asked.

"It's just an expression," Aeden said. "It means she acted poorly."

"I see. I accept your apology. It has been difficult traversing these caverns. I desire to be finished with this task as well."

❧ 30 ❧

"The Dark Prophet damn it all to the abyss," Ronan Sinson said. "I think we're at a dead end. Any ideas?" He was regretting taking command of their mission.

Lachlan searched the wall for any sign of a hidden door. He was the group's sniffer, adept at such tasks. If there was a door or other opening, he would find it.

"Nothing," he said. "I've been checking as we go along and I don't think I've missed anything. Maybe another passage back near the beginning, where the pit was?"

Ronan spat. Thalia would not be happy. "I wish we knew if someone was actually coming up behind us."

"I told you we should have set magical traps," Liam said. "If we had, I could tell you if they had been tripped."

"We've talked about this," the scout said. "If the traps were magical, they would be easier to detect, if any of those trying to find the end of this maze can use magic. I'm betting they can; otherwise, how do they know to be here?"

"They could have gotten orders from someone else, just like we did."

Ronan clenched his fists. "Enough. There's nothing we can do now but to backtrack." He looked toward the mages and the fighters he brought. "Do us all a favor and try not to trip the traps we set on the way here."

Ronan followed Lachlan back through the passages they'd already explored, the other seven members of their team a few steps behind. Two of the others—fighters with some experience in scouting—scanned for secret passageways they might have missed when they passed the first time. It was aggravating, much like this entire mission. Why couldn't Thalia just send them to kill someone? He hated searching for treasure. So many times, it ended up being a dusty old book or something equally worthless.

It was getting close to evening, he thought, though he couldn't be sure because there was not really day and night underground. They'd need to stop soon to rest. Maybe if they were lucky, they'd find whatever it was they were looking for tomorrow and they could leave these damn caverns.

Their casters, Liam and Amira, hadn't been much help up to this point. They were supposed to guide the group to whatever magic they'd been sent here for, but with all the twists and turns in the tunnels, the mages' ability to sense that magic was worthless. Instead, they were just two more bodies shuffling through the subterranean maze.

At least they could make light so the others didn't have to keep lighting torches and breathe in sooty air the entire time.

A few hours later, the leader finally called a halt. They'd have to continue after getting some sleep. The wish that they'd be done the next day seemed further out of reach than it had when he thought of it earlier. He set the watch schedule and curled up to sleep. One more day.

In the morning, the group prepared to set off. One of those who had taken watch the night before, a tall swordsman named Haris, approached.

"I heard some things last night," he said. "I was on second watch and some kind of scrabbling noise came from up the tunnel, from where we're headed. I'm not sure where it was, or even if it was above or below us, but something is moving around in these caves."

"Keep your eyes open. Tell the others. It's probably just more of those peasants we saw up above. They're no threat to us."

Haris nodded and went off to inform the others of his orders.

Later in the morning their scout, Lachlan, held his hand up for the group to halt. He paced around the area, squatted down to inspect something, then returned to Ronan with several small objects in his hands. They looked like he had found junk lying on the cave floor.

"What is it?" the leader asked.

"It's one of the traps I set as we went along. It's been dismantled."

"Tripped?"

"No, taken apart, made inactive. Whoever did it, they were skilled."

Ronan rubbed his forehead. "So, a trap was tinkered with here, then they left this tunnel somewhere after this point. Behind us."

"Exactly."

"Well then, we better start searching more carefully. There has to be a secret door somewhere, because they certainly didn't take the same path we did and I don't remember passing them in the tunnel."

"CAN YOU LOOK AT THE SYMBOL NOW?" FAHTIN ASKED Marla when they stopped again to rest. "I'd really like to know if it's that writing you were talking about, the one on the wheels. Maybe it means something and knowing it will help us."

"Cogiscro," Marla said. "Yeah, I can take a look at it." She put her hand out toward Fahtin, palm up. The Gypta woman would continue to pester her about it until she tried to decipher the picture, so she might as well do it now.

Fahtin's eyes brightened as she handed the paper to Marla.

The Academy graduate didn't think the chances were good that she'd be able to make any sense of the design Fahtin had seen in her visions. It might not be Cogiscro at all, and even if it was, it didn't seem probable that the Gypta would have been able to draw it accurately.

She stared at the design on the paper. Starting at the top, she looked for the individual symbols entangled within other symbols, gradually working her way to the right and around the circle. It was like a compass: north, east, south, west.

Marla cocked her head. She picked out a symbol, then another just to the side and below it. A third followed. Huh. Maybe there was something there after all.

By the time she got all the way around the circle of the design, the others were gathered around her and Fahtin. When Marla looked up, she gave a little jump. Seven faces were all around her, all focused on what she'd say next.

"*Valcordinae*," she pronounced. "It says Valcordinae."

Fahtin clapped her hands and hopped excitedly. "Great. What does it mean?"

Marla was afraid the other woman was going to ask her that. "I...uh..."

"It means 'strong minds.'" Khrazhti said. "It derives from the original terms in my language: *valere*, meaning strong, and *cordis*, meaning mind. I believe the words meaning the same thing in the Alaqotim spoken now would be different."

Marla nodded toward the blue woman and handed the paper back to Fahtin.

"Strong minds, eh?" Aeden said. "What is that supposed to mean?"

Tere grunted. "It means that what I've been saying this whole time is true. Something is messing with our minds, playing with our emotions and intelligence. Maybe testing us."

"But what?" Fahtin asked. "In my visions, I only saw blackness and Tere standing against it.

"Just Tere?" Marla asked.

Fahtin bit her bottom lip as she did when she was nervous. "I only saw Tere. I'm sure the rest of us were doing our part in the vision, but it only showed him for some reason."

"Probably because I'm the one who dies," the archer grumbled. "Even visions don't go my way."

Lily patted him on the shoulder.

"I don't think so, Tere Chizzit," Fahtin said, "and don't you go and get all gloomy on us. You're important in this mission, I know it. I just don't know why. Maybe it's because you have more hero experience, because you're the leader."

"Fine, fine," he said. "Let's get on with it. If I'm to die— oh, don't look at me like that. If we're to see this to the end, then we should get moving. Delaying will only see us starved or ambushed by whoever attacked the homeless people."

"I agree with that," Aeden said. "Maybe now that we have a confirmation that we need our minds to be strong, we'll have an edge against whatever we run into."

The group gathered their packs and continued, Tere and Raki out front scouting for danger. The caverns grew smoother and the turns more erratic. They gave the sense of being carved by water, perhaps a full underground river, though there was no other sign of moisture.

It wasn't long until the twisting corridors brought them to another widened area. As before, it ended with a stone door.

"Another door," Marla said. "Wonderful. What will it be now?"

Tere approached the door as Marla scanned it with some kind of magic, moving her hand across the stone a few inches away, not touching it.

"Huh," Marla said. "It doesn't seem to have any kind of trap or magical lock or anything. I'm not sure how we're supposed to open it."

Tere reached out and pulled on the latch. The door swung open. "I don't know. Maybe like a normal door?"

If fire was green, it would look like Marla's eyes. "That was stupid. What if there was some kind of trigger or trap I hadn't found?"

"Then we'd probably be in trouble," he said. "But there wasn't."

The archer squeezed by her and stood in the doorway, head moving, alert for anything that might be dangerous. Marla stepped up next to him and peeked into the room.

The chamber beyond looked as non-threatening as could be. It made Marla immediately more wary.

The space wasn't too much different than many of the other widened areas or chambers they'd found so far in their exploration of the tunnels. Thirty feet wide, maybe forty or fifty long, smooth stone walls like the caverns they'd been most recently traveling in. It looked innocuous enough. A glow that came from somewhere—or nowhere—illuminated the space so the walls on either side could be seen. It didn't seem to have a source, almost like every surface of the rock was lambent. It was obviously magical. There was another door at the end of the chamber, exactly opposite the entrance. It stood open.

There were no other features. No stalactites, stalagmites,

or anything else where someone—or something—could be hiding.

"Maybe we finally caught a small piece of luck," Aeden said, poking his head between Marla and Tere to get a view of the room.

"Yeah, maybe," Tere said. "Just in case, let me walk the room before anyone comes in." He turned to Marla who was standing next to him. On the other side of the threshold. "Anyone *else* comes in."

There was some grumbling behind them, but Tere didn't react to it. With his attention fully on the room ahead, he stepped over the threshold.

He half expected the light to go out as soon as he entered, but it didn't. Nor did anything materialize to attack him.

"Don't go too close to the door," Aeden told them. "If there's something beyond, it would be better for us to be together when it attacks us."

"Yeah, yeah," Tere muttered.

Aeden made sense, though. Marla went toward the right and Tere toward the left, hugging the walls as they inspected the room. When their circuit took them to within ten feet of the other door, they stopped.

Marla could see at an angle through the doorway and she was sure Tere could see as much. They were not in the direct line of vision of the hallway beyond. The tunnel continued beyond the door, darkening after a dozen feet. Whatever lit the room, it didn't continue into the corridor on the other side.

Something about the situation still tickled Marla's wariness, but she couldn't for the life of her spot the danger. She sighed and shrugged at Tere.

He had a similarly disagreeable expression on his face, but in a moment motioned the others to enter the chamber with them. As they filed in, he jerked his hand up, palm facing the party, like he'd just figured something out.

"Don't everyone enter. Prop the door—"

Before he could finish his sentence, Urun crossed the threshold, the last one to do so. No sooner had he stepped both feet into the chamber than both doors slammed shut with a solid thud and a few cracking sounds as if the force of the heavy doors had damaged the walls.

Urun turned and slammed his shoulder into the door. It didn't budge. Tere tried the same thing with the door near him and Marla. It might as well have been the solid stone wall itself. They were trapped, victims of another of the cave's snares.

"At least the light didn't go out," Aeden said. The glow winked out, followed by each of the light sticks being snuffed as if they were candles in a high wind.

"*Aruna recipia dui!*"

❧ 31 ❧

In an instant, Tere had an arrow out of his quiver and nocked. His vision swept the room, expecting something to attack them, but nothing did. For nearly a minute, he remained on guard.

"Can you see anything, Tere?" Aeden asked. The boy's mind seemed to be working well, remembering that few things could render Tere sightless.

"Nothing but the room and us," he said. Lily had moved closer to him when he spoke, her shoulder now touching his back on the left side, the perfect place to keep from hindering his movements. "I don't know what—"

A flash lit up the room. The light focused on Marla like a spotlight Tere had seen sometimes used in stage plays. The Academy graduate started, as surprised as any of the others.

Then she dropped to the ground like her legs were wet noodles.

"Marla," Aeden shouted. He moved toward where she had fallen, but in the dark, he misjudged and slammed into Urun, knocking the priest down.

"Ouch," Urun said. "That was me, Aeden."

"Sorry. Where's Marla? Is she all right?"

Tere shuffled a few steps to the side, reaching the downed woman before Aeden did. He reached out and touched the Croagh's shoulder. "Here, Aeden."

Marla didn't move. She looked dead, though as Aeden moved her to straighten her limbs, Tere thought he noticed her chest moving in and out.

Aeden started making motions with his arms and mumbling words of power. Tere recognized the way he was moving. The young man was going to heal her of whatever had afflicted her. It was a good choice.

Before Aeden had finished his spell, the light flashed again. This time, the Croagh was lit up. Like Marla, he collapsed immediately, landing on top of his sister.

"What the..." Tere said. "Urun, can you do anything?"

The nature priest crawled toward the two collapsed companions. As soon as he felt them, he moved his hand over Aeden, but whether it was to heal or simply to find out what was wrong, Tere didn't know.

"They're dying," the priest said. "It...feels like poison. Magical poison. I'll see if I can counteract it and keep them alive. I'm not sure if—"

The light flashed again and Urun collapsed in mid-sentence.

The remaining four all started talking at the same time. Tere blocked them out. They were panicking. He needed to think clearly. He hadn't seen anything other than the light in each of the attacks. No weapon, no enemies, nothing. What could he do? There didn't seem to be any kind of defense against the light. Each time it flared, someone went down.

Almost before he finished the thought, it flared again, this time on Raki. The boy's eyes went wide and he tried to run, but a fraction of a second later, he too dropped to the ground.

Tere's heart thumped in his chest. His friends were dying,

one by one. He might be next, or he might have to watch another one fall. Neither was a good option. He pounded on his head, trying to start up his brain, get it thinking of a solution. He was in charge of the mission; the safety of his friends was his responsibility.

Think, you idiot. Think.

Khrazhti went next, dashing Tere's hope that the animaru was immune to whatever weapon was being used against them.

In his entire life, Tere had never felt so helpless as he had the last few months, especially since he had lost his ability to track movement in the magical field. What good were his experience and his desire to help when faced with something that could so easily and quickly cause death?

The light flared again, illuminating Fahtin's horrified expression. She too tumbled to the floor.

"Tere?" Lily called out.

He didn't know what to do, what to say to her. She was casting about in the darkness, searching for him. He stepped over to her and took her hand. "I'm here."

The woman swallowed and breathed out intentionally. She was terrified, but was trying to control her panic. He knew the feeling well. His own heart was thundering, his head throbbing from the increased blood flow, but also from his attempts to force thoughts through it.

Why hadn't the power taken him yet? Why was it forcing him to relive his failure with each attack? Another of the cruel ways life displayed his worthlessness.

Lily's words came back to mind. *You're not worn out and useless. You'll always be my hero.* Right on top of those memories came another one, the words of a younger Lili, his sister. *A hero's greatest weapon is his mind.*

His mind.

A flare erupted, so close that Tere thought it had finally

targeted him. In the brief flash, Lily's face turned toward him. Strangely, it wasn't panicked. It seemed...resolved. She fell, pulling his arm down as he guided her gently to the floor.

It was only him now. The only one left of all his companions.

His mind.

The symbol they'd been chasing depicted the word Valcordinae. *Strong minds.* It was plain that no physical effort would stop the attacks and save his life. Many of the challenges they had faced had been mental, not physical. Whatever was testing them, it seemed to want to determine how strong their minds were.

But why?

Wrong question. For the moment, the more important question was *how?*

Tere searched his memory, thoughts racing for fear the attack on him would occur any second. Did he feel anything when the flashes came for the others? Something akin to detecting magic?

No.

The others, though, had panicked when the light flashed on them. What had caused the fear? Anticipation, since they had seen others fall to it? Lily had mastered her fear, squeezing Tere's hand just before she fell, as if she took refuge in him, in his strength. She believed in him.

And he had let her down. Just like he had let everyone else down.

Focus. He needed to focus. The enemy was looking for strong minds. The attacks seemed too efficient, though maybe not meant to kill right away. Urun said Marla was dying, not that she was dead. There was still a chance they were alive.

A light flared around Tere. It had finally come for him, the last one standing. He was responsible for his friends, possibly for the safety of the world if Aeden and Marla fell here. How disappointed would the Lilys be?

An irrational panic flooded into his thoughts, an intense fear of dying. It was too powerful to fight, and he was tempted to let it sweep him away. But something was wrong with those thoughts. He'd never been afraid of dying before, only of failing.

"No!" he screamed. "You're not real. It's all a fabrication. You'll have to do better than that. Face me, if you exist. I'll not go easily."

A great wave of force slammed into Tere's mind. His knees buckled and he dropped to the floor, right knee slamming hard against the stone. He didn't even notice the pain. His entire existence was that power pushing at his brain, threatening to crush it to pulp.

The archer rallied, pushing back against the assault. He gritted his teeth and flexed his mind, digging into stores of energy he didn't know he had. He wasn't dead yet, and he wouldn't give up until he was.

A low, keening hiss escaped through his teeth as he pushed so hard he thought his entire head would explode. In a way, it would probably be less painful than what he was feeling at the moment.

Still, he persevered. Every part of his head throbbed, his brain pushing and being pushed, enduring forces that no soft human tissue should be able to bear, all the while wondering if it was real or all imagined.

A small part of Tere's mind ran through his life in an instant. His small family, his sister and her belief in him, his mentors Toras Geint and Arto Deniselo, his friend Raisor, the long years on the road searching for evil men and protecting good people, and his time in the Grundenwald. It all flashed through him, images of friends and loved ones and him at the center, always trying to do what was right but often failing. In his own eyes. As the images flew by, he noticed something he hadn't before.

He wasn't a failure to others. They looked to him for strength, for protection, as an example. What was he missing? How had he never seen it? Maybe he had, long ago. Maybe he'd forgotten.

Maybe it was time to remember.

The purpose of his life was to protect others. A self-appointed responsibility, but an important one. Whatever it took, whatever he had to do, any sacrifice he had to make, he would be a guardian for those who could not fight for themselves.

"Enough!" he shouted at the power bombarding his mind. "Enough."

With a reserve of energy that had been hidden from him, he strained, his entire body tense, his brain pressurizing like it was expanding to twice its size within his skull. He grunted as he forced...something from his mind toward whatever it was that assaulted him.

A silent explosion rocked his entire world. He fell, his body lacking even enough energy to hold himself upright.

❦ 32 ❧

Tere collapsed to the stone floor of the chamber as if in slow motion. He bounced slightly, then lay still for a moment. Was he dead, or would he be in the next few seconds? His mind was fuzzy and nothing seemed to make sense.

Light flared, but not the type that assailed him before. This was the softer glow that had been present in the room when they entered. He tilted his head from where he lay and saw not only had the ambient illumination come back, but the light sticks they had been carrying also flickered into being like they had always been there, casting their own light.

A soft crack pulled Tere's eyes to the side of the chamber. The door swung open, stopping on its own before it struck the wall. Tere wasn't even sure if the portal he was considering was the door they had come through or the one at the other end.

The archer laid his head back, resting it on the floor. He thought he was alive. At least, the dull pain of muscles that had tensed to almost tearing, and then run out of energy, told him he wasn't dead yet. He lay there, breathing slowly in and out, until he forced himself into a sitting position. Even that took everything he had in him.

It was another several minutes before he could force himself to scan the floor of the cavern, noting where each of his friends had fallen. Lily was closest, so he dragged his body toward her.

He felt at her neck, fingers unwieldy. There was a thrum of a pulse there, thank the gods. He let out a sigh.

The red-haired woman's eyes fluttered and then slowly opened, catching sight of Tere, whose hand was still on her neck. Strangely, she didn't panic as he thought he would if he woke with someone's hand on his neck. She narrowed her eyes to focus on him. A smile slipped onto her face that made his heart ache.

"You saved us," she said.

"No, girl. We just got lucky, I think. Are you all right?"

She nodded as best she could with her head resting on the floor. "I feel like someone hit me in the back of the head with a club, but I seem to be alive. I'll take it."

The built-up tension made a laugh explode from him. "Yeah." He realized his hand was still on her, though it had moved up to her cheek. He pulled it away quickly. "I better check on the others."

Lily being alive seemed to energize him. He crawled to the next closest person, Aeden. The Croagh was already stirring, as were several of the others. A warm wave of relief washed over Tere. Maybe they had all escaped without serious harm. If they did, it would be a miracle, but he wasn't above accepting miracles.

By the time Tere got around to each of his friends, they were all sitting up and shaking off the effects of whatever it was that had happened to them. Maybe Lili—his sister—had been right. As long as he drew breath, there was something he could do. If his luck held, it would be enough.

He told the others of his realization and how he fought against the power.

"That actually sounds logical," Marla said. "We don't seem to have any lasting effects from it, other than some bruises from falling to the floor. It's possible that a magical attack to the mind could simulate what we felt. The lights were probably on the entire time, but our minds registered the room as being dark. Kind of scary."

"It's a good thing your mind was strong enough to resist it," Lily told Tere.

"I don't think it was like that," he said. "I pieced it together as each of you were attacked. I only figured it out as the last of you fell." He nodded at Lily as he said that last part. "You would have done likewise if you were the last one standing."

"I don't think so," she said.

Tere noticed Fahtin staring blankly toward the door. She seemed pale as well.

"Are you okay, Fahtin?" he asked.

"Huh? Oh, yes, I'm fine. It's just that I had a vision as I lay there, thinking I was dying."

Raki sat up straighter. "You did? What did it tell you? Do you know what we need to do now?"

She rubbed her eyes and shook her head. "It wasn't very long, more like a flash of understanding. I can't even really remember what I saw, only what I felt and how it affected me."

"Tell us," Aeden said.

"I...I don't know how to explain it. Whatever it was I saw, it made me understand that the final puzzle in the caverns promises great reward. Not only to our little group alone, but to an extended collection of people, maybe even the entire world. I don't know what the reward is, but it's accompanied by great danger."

"So what we just experienced wasn't the last test?" Aeden asked.

"No."

"Great."

"Don't forget," Tere said, "that the group who attacked the homeless is still out there." He cocked his head when a thought came into his mind.

"What just occurred to you?" Marla asked him.

He chewed on the thought for a moment before answering. "I wonder if the attackers are ahead of us. Do you think the cave's magic resets each of these tests each time? They may already be at the final test."

"Have you seen any sign of them being ahead of us?" Marla said. "Tracks or anything like that?"

"No. I had assumed the route they took might get them to the end first. There's no telling, though. Theirs may be longer, or ours might. It seems that not only do we have a great challenge up ahead, one that can bring great reward, but we also have to get there first."

"Aye," Aeden said. "That tells me we should probably get moving. They could be anywhere."

"My thoughts exactly," Tere said.

The party was slow in getting to their feet. They grunted and grimaced. Marla rocked up onto her knees and put her hand on Aeden to push herself to a standing position. Fahtin waited until Lily had regained her feet and then put a hand out to help the Gypta up.

Tere pushed himself up, unsure if his knees would buckle and throw him back to the floor. His body ached like he'd been flogged with saplings and left out in the sun to bake. It was all he could do to move.

"Ugh," Aeden said. "Whatever that attack did, it feels like it stole all my energy. I wonder if it would be better to rest for a little while."

"I don't think we have a lot of time," Fahtin said. "I can't be sure, but it seems like we're almost finished. I would like nothing better than to lie down and sleep right now, but we should probably keep moving."

Raki groaned, but moved up toward the front of the group to scout with Tere. The archer considered his friends. They all looked to be in poor condition, like he was. He wondered if it would be better to rest rather than to go ahead. If they stopped, the others in the tunnels might get to whatever the prize was ahead of them. If they didn't, Tere had serious doubts they'd be able to meet further challenges. The thought that the next challenge might be another one of the mind and not something physical decided him.

With one final look around and to the doorway they had come in—which was also now open—Tere clapped Raki on the shoulder and went through the door ahead of them.

Tere settled into his role as scout, Raki ghosting along the wall opposite him. Something had changed during his battle with that magic attacking his mind. He couldn't quite point to what specifically, but the difference lay in the way he perceived the things around him. But was the change for the better, or did it make things worse?

It was almost like he had been blind—or stupid—for his entire life and now some sort of obstruction was taken away from his thoughts, allowing him to understand things he never could have. What things? He wasn't sure.

The fact was, he *really* didn't like this place he was in. Caverns were no place for a man who preferred the forest and open plains, and that was without considering the magic involved in the tunnels. He wanted to be done with their task and to get out from underground. Once he could breathe fresh air and see the sun again, he'd figure out how his mind had changed and if it was for better or worse.

As Tere thought, he scouted the area ahead by habit, not focusing on it as much as he should.

Which didn't matter since the attack came from behind them.

A shout from Aeden echoed in the tunnels. The young man was too smart to make such a noise unless the party was being attacked. Tere wished he had memorized some of the young Croagh's curses so he could use them now. He traded concerned looks with Raki and both took off in a lumbering run toward the party several hundred yards from the two scouts.

❦ 33 ❧

hen Tere got within sight of his friends, it took
him a moment to make sense of what he saw: a
full battle, his six friends against a greater
number of attackers dressed all in black. They had similar
warrior builds—other than the two women—and all had dark
hair and tan skin. These were the ones who attacked the
homeless encampment.

As Tere arrived, he caught sight of Lily firing arrows at
one of the figures who was standing toward the back of the
group, waving his hands and saying something. The old archer
couldn't hear exactly what, but it was no surprise when Lily's
arrows bounced off an invisible obstruction in front of
the man.

A mage. Wonderful.

What looked like a flying, elongated pyramid made from
shadow zoomed toward Urun, racing an arrow and a bolt fired
from a crossbow. All three attacks were deflected, but the
nature priest stumbled against the onslaught despite his
shield.

"The casters," Tere shouted as he let loose three arrows one after another with blazing speed. One went toward the man Lily had targeted and two went toward a gesturing woman, dressed similarly in black robes. Tere cursed as the arrows all bounced off whatever shield was in place.

A second later, a gout of flame flared up around Urun. Through the flickering flame, Tere could see the outline of the priest's shield. It looked like it was about to go down.

A flash of dark energy zipped across the space between the groups, punched a hole through the female caster's shield —though it was deflected a bit from its trajectory—and blasted through the woman's arm. Her hand immediately dropped. Tere nodded to Khrazhti, who sneered at the woman she had just injured.

Marla was speaking softly and gesturing, her eyes focused on the man who had cast the fire spell.

"Lily, leave the casters. Let's take out the archer and crossbow."

The red-haired archer nodded and fired off two arrows in a heartbeat as Tere did the same. The mages' shields didn't extend to the enemies Tere and Lily targeted. Her arrows took the man in either eye, and Tere's struck one on top of the other in the crossbow-wielding woman's right eye.

The fire mage was beginning to glow, bits of flame dancing across his body. Tere couldn't tell where he was targeting, but he had a feeling it would be Urun. The enemies no doubt noted that Khrazhti could cast as well, but the nature priest's shield was flickering, obviously about to drop. Tere couldn't let them take down Urun's protective magic. Without the priest's shield, being caught on fire would most likely kill him.

Before he could draw back his bow to shoot the mage, though, Marla finished her spell. Water appeared from thin air, splashing upward from the floor as if the fire mage was standing on a geyser. It nearly lifted him off his feet, and would have if the man hadn't twisted to partially avoid it.

The spell served its purpose. The jet of water drenched the fire mage and not only interrupted whatever spell he had been casting but also doused the fire he had stoked from within. He no longer glowed and instead of flame, small tendrils of smoke wafted up from him.

Tere released the arrow he had trained on the mage, but it bounced off something. He quirked an eyebrow. Maybe it was only a shield for physical attacks and not magic. Strange.

Four fighters had reached Aeden and were cooperating in trying to take the Croagh down. They were all so mixed together, with Khrazhti stepping in to help take some of the pressure off Aeden, Tere didn't dare risk shooting. He might have done so if he could still track the movements in the magical field, but without it, he wouldn't take the chance. One could never know when a combatant would move unexpectedly into the line of fire, even tripping and being suddenly in the way of an arrow already loosed.

One of the men, large and sporting a scar down the right side of his face, shouted. "Logan, Haris, Seth! With me. Liam…" He barked out a few other words, but Tere couldn't understand them. He did recognize the accent, though. The leader, at least, was from the Great Enclave. By the looks of the others, they probably were too. He wasn't sure what significance that held, but he didn't have time to ponder it at the moment.

While the leader was commanding his fighters, he smoothly launched attack after attack at Aeden. With the biggest of the fighters wielding a two-handed sword on one side, and another man with a sword and shield on his other, Aeden had his hands full.

A flicker of dark motion caught Tere's attention. When

he looked to where he had seen it, another man suddenly appeared, a throwing spike in his left shoulder. Raki's form materialized behind the man, striking at him with his knife. The black-clothed man blocked the strike and counterattacked, but Raki had vanished again and the attacker's short sword struck nothing but air.

Before the man disappeared as well, a flash of silver transformed itself into one of Fahtin's knives, landing in the man's forearm. He looked up at the Gypta girl, taking one step forward. Marla kicked him in the face as she waved her hands to cast another spell.

It seemed the battle was well in hand. Tere shot two arrows at the assassin Fahtin and Raki had been fighting, but he had apparently learned his lesson and ducked into the shadows to disappear. Tere wished he still had his magical sight. It would make skewering the shade much easier.

The leader of the attackers went at Aeden with his sword. He took a step toward the Croagh and then blurred, moving too quickly to be seen clearly. Aeden's eyes widened and he moved faster than Tere had ever seen him do so before. He did an admirable job in defending himself, though the super-fast assailant did land two minor cuts.

Aeden blocked several more strikes and spun away as the other man slowed to a more normal—but still very rapid—pace, continuing his attack. Tere noticed that as the scar-faced man settled back into normal speed, there was a brief moment when his motion paused, almost as if his body was trying to recalibrate from the faster-than-normal attacks he performed before. Had Aeden noticed it?

The man with the sword and shield took up the attack, trying to hem Aeden in with his shield by ramming him. The Croagh shifted his body, mitigating the shield's momentum, and redirected it so the shield bearer stumbled forward.

Aeden slashed at him, but the man brought his sword up to parry the strike.

But Aeden hadn't only redirected the shield's force. He used the momentum from being shoved by the shield and spun a half circle to slice with his other sword at the man with the two-handed blade. He followed up with the sword that had been deflected by the shield bearer and continued battering the bigger man with strike after strike.

The attacker somehow got his huge sword up to block Aeden's blows, but he backstepped away from the Croagh's whirling blades. After the man had taken three steps back, Aeden dodged away to gain some space from the two men attacking him. He warily circled them, his eyes darting to the others to see how they were faring.

Khrazhti lunged at the man with the shield, distracting him from trying to go after Aeden again. Instead, he whirled his blade toward his right, barely deflecting the blue woman's weapon, then turned his shield to face her. Now the animaru had the shield bearer and an attacker with a bastard sword focused on her.

The latter man had a smooth, sinuous style of fighting. His sword was meant to be used with two hands, but he would often start a maneuver with both hands on the hilt, then release his left hand to complete the attack with only his right hand, allowing him more reach than if he kept both hands on the weapon. Tere respected his skill. It wouldn't keep him from killing the man if he had an opening, but the archer appreciated good swordsmanship when he saw it.

The sneaky one was still hidden somewhere in the outlying darkness. Tere kept an eye out for him. If he were that man, he would...

There. A ripple of shadow near Fahtin. She was concentrating on the men fighting with Aeden, holding her knives up and jerking her arm occasionally as if she thought she saw an opening to throw, but then decided against it.

The darkness behind her seemed to become solid.

Tere launched two arrows in the blink of an eye. Both struck their intended target before the assassin could make it to the Gypta girl. The man fell on his face just behind her, an arrow in his eye and another in his throat. Fahtin spun toward the sound and brought her knives up into a guard position. She studied the dead man for a moment, then glanced at Tere and crossed her knives in salute. He nodded back, looking for more opportunities to help.

Marla threw her arm toward the fire mage and a long, solidified, piece of light zipped to punch a hole high in the mage's chest, knocking him backward. She sprinted the few steps to him and opened up his belly with her sword. He looked down at his ruined abdomen then back up at her. The enemy mage raised his hand as if to object to something, then fell backward, his eyes already starting to glaze over.

"*Kanim*," Aeden shouted—the word meant mage in ancient Alaqotim—and both Tere and Khrazhti snapped their heads around toward the mage who had cast the dark magic. The blue woman nodded, slipped one of her blades into the scabbard, blocked a strike from the bastard sword wielder, and flicked her open hand toward the enemy mage.

The woman in black robes screamed and put her arms up to feel around her, her eyes unfocused. Tere wasn't sure what spell the animaru had cast, but it looked to have affected her vision. While Aeden charged the shield bearer, taking the man's attention back from Khrazhti, the blue woman slipped aside to attack her other swordsman foe.

The mage had not been forgotten, though. Raki appeared behind the woman and sliced one knife across her throat while he thrust the other into the attacker's lower back. The woman slid off Raki's knife to the ground in a heap.

The attacking force was down to four men. The leader was still trying to get through Aeden's guard while the shield man was up to his old tricks of trying to put the Croagh into harm's way by pushing with his shield. To add to the confusion, the large man with the two-handed sword took every opportunity to slash wildly at Aeden when he could do so without hitting his comrades.

The attacker with the bastard sword attacked Khrazhti, who was still distracted by having cast her blinding spell on the mage. The sword came down in an overhead, diagonal strike, but Khrazhti smoothly flicked her sword to deflect it as if it was already part of her movement.

Marla was heading toward the action when the leader blurred into motion again. Aeden spun, shuffled, and came up behind the wielder of the huge sword, keeping the man between him and the leader. He caught the man's sword near the hilt and twisted it with his own swords in a way that caused the attacker to torque his body and go where Aeden directed him.

Right into the path of the leader.

The scar-faced man grunted and adjusted his strike, shouldering his fellow but redirecting the blade he was trying to cut Aeden with so as not to strike his companion. When the leader tried to get around the other man, Aeden kept circling the larger man, refusing to engage while his opponent moved at blurring speed.

Was he...

Tere's mouth curved into a smile. Aeden's mouth moved, but it wasn't to use his magic.

He was counting.

The super-fast leader dropped back to a normal speed. No —not quite normal, but that awkward moment Tere had seen earlier when the man's body faltered in adjusting to the slower speed again.

Aeden twisted out of the way of the two-handed sword and landed a savage slash on the leader's sword arm, opening it up down half its length. The man dropped his sword, his hand trembling as the tissue became saturated with blood that then began to pour from the wound. He looked up into Aeden's eyes. Aeden met them and, rotating, slashed with his other sword.

The cut tore through the man's face, exactly where the other scar had been, but deeper. Much deeper. His head split open, brain matter and fluids splattering out.

Aeden had already moved back to the man with the two-handed sword, attacking relentlessly with both his swords, forcing the big man back. By the time the leader's body had settled on the floor, Aeden and his opponent were already several feet away.

The other man's sword was too big and heavy to maneuver fast enough to block all Aeden's strikes for long, and so the Croagh nipped at the foe for a few strikes, taking chunks of skin and bleeding him. After a particularly complex combination of five slashes and a thrust, the man dropped his weapon and then slid off Aeden's sword.

While Aeden had been busy with the leader, Khrazhti had slipped to the side of the shield bearer and cut at his lower legs, lacerating his right calf so severely, the man was hopping on one foot. She kicked his shield, forcing him back and off-balance, then she lunged in low with her sword angled upward and thrust her blade deep into his belly. It stunned the man for a moment, time the animaru took to kick his shield aside and slice his throat.

The remaining man, the one with the bastard sword, turned and sprinted down the corridor.

Tere tsked as he casually nocked an arrow, drew it, and loosed. It struck in the hollow behind the man's right knee. He fell onto his face and slid for several feet. He didn't get back up. Not because of Tere's arrow, but because of Lily's, the fletching of which still quivered as it stood out from the back of his head.

The archers nodded at each other.

"That was it?" Marla asked, kicking at the corpse of the fire mage at her feet.

"It wasn't enough for you?" Tere said.

"I didn't mean it that way. It's just that...well, it didn't seem like much after all that anticipation."

"I don't think they were sent here for us," Aeden said. "They were looking for whatever we're looking for. I'm sure whoever sent them thought they'd get in, get whatever is at the end of these tunnels, and get out before they found any real competition. Maybe they thought slaughtering homeless people was the hardest thing they'd do down here."

"Hmmm," Marla said. "Anyway, I don't think we have to worry any longer about them being in front of us and getting to the prize before us. I guess there's only one way to get to it. This way."

"I still wonder," Tere said, "if they had to go through all the puzzles and hazards we did or if they just walked through all the ones we already finished."

"We'll probably find out if we have to go out the same way we came in," Aeden said. "I sure hope we don't have to do them over again. Getting to the end is bad enough without having to do everything twice.

"I agree," Tere said. "Anyone hurt enough to require healing from Urun?"

No one spoke up, so while retrieving arrows and thrown weapons, they checked through the corpses' pockets and purses before continuing on.

Only one thing of note was found among the dead, in the leader's pocket: a letter apparently written by their boss.

. . .

Ronan,

Find whatever it is that is causing the magical disturbance and bring it to me. Liam or Amira should be able to sense it and lead you to it. This is Council business. Eliminate anyone who interferes with your mission. I'll be waiting at the meeting location.

T

After Marla read the note out loud, she folded it up and put it in her belt pouch. None of the others commented on it. After everyone nearly dying in the trap room and then having to fight, no one seemed to be in much of a mood for conversation. Tere and Raki took the lead and the others followed them, all of them so tired they simply put one foot in front of the other and moved as if in a daze.

The party stopped two hours down the tunnel from where they had killed the black-clothed attackers.

"One final night's rest and then we push on until we're done?" Tere asked.

Lily cocked her head at him. "How do you know we're close enough to the end to say something like that?"

"I don't really know. Maybe it's only a feeling. It seems to me we're approaching something...something...I don't know. It's like I feel we're drawing closer to some kind of power. I can't explain it."

"I think you're right, Tere," Fahtin said. "I sense something, too. I haven't had any visions, but something is prickling the back of my neck. If we're not at the end of all this by this time tomorrow, I will be very surprised."

Tere nodded, then swallowed hard. The end. One way or another, they'd be finished with this mysterious quest. He hoped they all survived it.

❦ 34 ❧

It was a tired group that dragged themselves down the corridor. Tere was nearly dragging his feet, something he couldn't remember himself ever doing. They had slept, but it didn't seem to make them feel any better, so they decided to push through to the end rather than to spend more time resting. It wasn't just him and Fahtin any longer; the others felt the sensation, the anticipation of something just up the tunnel.

After slogging across the stone floor of the tunnels for an hour, the cavern began to widen again. They knew by now that meant a larger room up ahead, probably the next—and hopefully last—trial they would need to face.

They weren't disappointed.

The tunnel widened from ten feet across to more than a hundred. Again, as with several of the other caverns, an ambient light source that could not be traced to one location. It didn't light up the space like daylight, but it was bright enough that the others could see as well as Tere.

The sight stopped them in their tracks to stare.

In the center of the room were tiles that looked like the stone itself was changed or dyed in some way to make perfect squares, three feet on each side. They alternated, black and white. There were six rows of the squares, five in each row.

Across the rows of squares was an ornate door, though it was difficult to tell with the distance and the lighting whether it was wood or stone. Relief carvings of leaves, vines, and fanciful creatures filled every inch of the surface.

Off to the side of the squares was a stone cube, two feet by two feet on each face. Each side held a number in the center and six symbols around the edges. Lined up in two rows of five on either side were smaller cubes, less than a foot on each edge. Ten black cubes on one side of the larger cube and ten white on the other. Those, too, had symbols etched into them, but only one on each face.

Tere had never seen anything like it.

"Uh," he said.

Marla stared at the squares and cubes, a thoughtful look on her face. No one else said anything for more than a minute, until she tsked. "Exulmucri."

"What was that?" Tere asked.

"Exulmucri. It means, roughly, Crusaders. It's an ancient game. Some think it was the first game invented in Dizhelim, the precursor to Stones and King's Gambit."

"So, it's a strategy game?" Aeden asked.

"It's *the* strategy game. It was last popular thousands of years ago. At least, that's what I learned about it in the Academy. I studied it for the School of History but I never actually played it or saw any of the cubes, just pictures. Well, other than the die, the big one. We've all seen those, or simple versions of them. By the way, the word for the cube originally came from the Alaqotim word *daeren*, meaning 'something played.'"

"Oh, good," Tere said. "Since you know so much, you can take the lead. It's obvious that the challenge is to play the game, though I don't know how we'll do it or who the opponent is."

"No," Fahtin said with more force than Tere had heard her use before. "My visions were very clear that you had to take the lead, Tere. I didn't see specifically what would happen if you didn't, but I got the sense that we would not survive it. You have to be the one to take charge."

"Surus's hairy balls," Tere said, making Fahtin gasp. Tere shrugged at the Gypta girl. "Sorry. Okay, if I have to do it, then I guess I'll have to do it. Marla, can you explain to me generally how it works? Then, I'll rely on your guidance during the match."

Marla glanced at Fahtin, then at Aeden, neither of which made any kind of motion to tell her what they thought. She sighed. "That sounds like our best option."

She stepped up to the squares, then turned and considered the cubes lined up on the side of the room. The longest look was reserved for the large cube with the numbers and symbols etched into it, the die.

"All right, here are the basics. As with Stones, which everyone knows, this game was based on military strategy. The goal, of course, is to kill the opposing army. There are two players, distinguished by the white and black pieces, or tokens." She waved at the smaller cubes.

"Each player gets ten soldiers, signified by the tokens. The die, the first in history, by the way, is rolled by the players to actually play the game.

"There are six types of soldiers. The player can use as many of each type as she wishes, with one exception, which I'll talk about in a minute. The smaller cubes have the symbols for each of the six types, and when the player chooses them at the beginning of the game, the symbol for that type of soldier will be arranged facing up. The cubes themselves are used as tokens on the game board to signify where each soldier is arranged at any moment."

Marla picked up one of the white cubes, turning it until the symbol she was looking for was facing up. "These are the different types. This one is the commander. There must be one commander for each player and there can only be one commander. As the name implies, this is the leader of the army."

She turned the cube to another symbol. "This is a healer. The job of this piece is to heal." The Academy graduate formed a wry smile at that and turned the cube again.

She went through the others, showing everyone the symbols on each face of the cubes. "This is a mage, a type of soldier that does magical damage. Archer, which does damage from afar. Assassin, which can do a lot of damage through stealth and trickery. Finally, there is the foot soldier, which can either use a shield to block and protect, or can attack with a spear."

Tere nodded. So far, it was fairly simple. The symbols didn't look like any kind of language, but simple pictures that indicated—to him, at least—what type of soldier they were depicting. For example, the archer had a little bow with an arrow in it and the foot soldier had a shield with a spear crossing it.

"The tokens are arranged on the game board. Each player has three rows. The far back row holds only the commander, and the other two rows hold the rest of the tokens in which-ever configuration the player chooses. Generally, ranged types like mages and archers are placed in the second row, but they don't have to be arranged like that.

"The arrangement can be important because while any

token can be targeted by any other, if it's farther than two rows for ranged or one row for other attacks, it will take multiple turns to get to the target and in the meantime the attacking token can be attacked by closer enemy tokens.

"Each token will be killed if it sustains two damage, except for the commander, which will be destroyed when it sustains one damage.

"To start, the two players roll the die and the one who gets the highest roll can go first. After that, they alternate turns by rolling the die and choosing an attack symbolized on the upward face of the die. The little symbols on each face—there are six of them, corresponding to the types of tokens—show what actions can be taken.

"For example, if I were playing and it was my turn and I rolled a three, I would have the following choices: Advanced Intimidate for the commander, Multi Mire for the mage, Double Heal for the healer, Basic Attack for the archer, Stealth Attack for the assassin, or Shield Bash for the foot soldier. Don't worry about what all those mean right now. I can tell you as the rolls come up.

"The player would choose whichever action you want and designate an opponent or group of opponents if it's a mass action. Depending on the distance, the actions may be taken immediately—if the target is within range—or may be delayed by a turn or two because of how far away the target is. Even if an action takes multiple turns, the player can start new actions with another token each turn.

"That's the gist of the game. There are strategies and finer points in the rules, but we'll have to cover those as they come up. If I remember. It's rumored that there were complete game sets and books on strategy when the Academy was built, but they were all lost in the great fire that destroyed most of the library more than two thousand years ago." Marla eyed the board. "I'm not sure how the magic of the caves will make this happen, or if something will come through the door up ahead to be the opposing player."

Tere blew out a breath. "Okay. The game seems straight-forward enough." He turned his head, scanning the chamber's corners in case he had missed something. "What should we do?"

"Win," Raki said.

Tere gave him a flat look. "Thank you for that magnificent strategy." The boy smiled at him, and after a few seconds, Tere's neutral mouth turned upward slightly.

"I'm not really sure," Marla said. "This is an accurate depiction of a game board, but your guess is as good as mine for how it works. Typically, it's the roll to see who goes first, but that die looks pretty heavy. Maybe two of us are supposed to cooperate and lift it to roll."

Tere eyed the huge cube. It looked to be made of stone. Something that size would, if it were granite, weigh almost fourteen hundred pounds. After thinking for a moment, he stepped past the cube and approached the ornate door. He reached out and tried the handle. It wouldn't budge.

Tere shrugged and turned back toward his friends. Marla stood in front of them, her mouth open.

"It was worth a try, right?" he said.

The archer didn't have any other ideas on how to initiate the game, though, so he walked around the large cube, kicked at it softly—it seemed to be solid and not hollow—and crossed his arms over his chest, considering the die. He finally spit on his hands, rubbed them together, and prepared to shoulder the thing into motion.

When he put his hand out to feel the smooth face of the die closest to him, it flared with light from within. Without warning, it jumped away from him, bouncing twice along the floor, spinning, and coming to rest. The number five, etched into the center of the face, was on the top, the symbols for the tokens' actions glittering in the strange light of the room.

The die remained in place for two seconds, then disappeared and reappeared instantly where it had started. Another two seconds and it jumped again, this time without Tere's prompting, and rolled along the wall, this time bouncing three times. When it came to rest, the number on top was a three.

"Huh," he said. "Well, that's handy."

The white cubes glowed brightly in front of him. He had no sooner turned his attention to them than one of them disappeared.

"Wha—?"

"Tere," Marla said, pointing above him.

Tere tilted his head up and saw a glowing symbol above his head. It was a stylized star. The symbol of the commander.

"I guess that means it recognizes you as the player," Aeden said. "We're on the right track."

One of the black cubes flipped so that the commander symbol was on the upward face, then floated over to the farthest row from where the party was standing.

Nothing else happened. Tere waited, as did the others, swinging their heads back and forth. Waiting.

"It's your turn to pick a type of token," Marla said.

"How do I do that?" Tere asked.

"Maybe you only have to think of what token you want and where you want to place it," Urun suggested.

Tere did so, thinking about how Urun helped them out as a healer. He wasn't sure how the game actions would take place, but thought that the healer should be placed in the second row, protected by the first. Maybe after he selected the different jobs, each of his friends would control the corresponding cube during the game.

One of the white cubes disappeared and the healer symbol appeared over Urun's head. With a flash, the priest was suddenly standing in the second row on Tere's side, in the center column.

"Okay, that seemed to work," Tere said, and thought ahead to who he would assign to which job and location. Flashes and pops issued one after another, as if someone was slamming a lantern's shield open and closed repeatedly. He blinked and found that all his friends were standing on the game board with symbols over their heads. Two generic foot soldiers, represented by two of the white cubes with the foot soldier symbol on top were there to fill out the ten spaces in Tere's army. The enemy player side of the board was also filled with pieces.

"That seemed to work," Tere said. "I'm assuming that I need to step into my space to start the game, then take my first roll. Are you ready to guide me, Marla?"

Silence greeted his question.

"Marla?"

Nothing.

"Abyssum! Can any of you hear me or talk to me?" He scanned the immobile forms of his friends standing on the squares he had assigned them.

There was still no response.

The archer sighed. "Figures. I guess I'm on my own, as unfair as it is. I don't even know what actions are depicted by the symbols." He shrugged, then stepped onto the row closest to him. As he did, the generic tokens transformed to people, on his side and on the side with the black tokens. The rest of Tere's party were there, though now they were dressed in clothing depicting their type, all in white. His two foot soldiers were burly men, shield in one hand and spear in the other. Across the board, foot soldiers, a mage, an archer, a healer, and an assassin were standing ready, all easily recognizable as what their type was by the style of their black clothing. At the rear, an older man, still vibrant, nodded to him and touched the back of his sword to his forehead in salute.

The game was well and truly started.

$\mathbb{R}$ 35 $\mathbb{R}$

Tere Chizzit, commander of the Army for the Protection of Dizhelim, looked out over his troops from the third row of the battlefield. In the front rank was a generic foot soldier, foot soldier Fahtin, foot soldier Aeden, and another generic foot soldier, all four with shield and spear. Next to one of the foot soldiers, at the edge of the board, was archer Lily, her bow and red hair standing out from the shining metal of the shields nearby. The second rank contained assassin Raki, healer Urun, mage Khrazhti, and mage Marla.

Across the field stood the enemies. The front enemy rank —which was in the row directly in front of his own front ranks—consisted of five foot-soldiers, nearly identical to his own generic foot soldiers except they were black copies to his white forces. The second rank included a mage, a healer, an archer, and an assassin, with the dark commander in the farthest back rank, directing his forces.

You have won the roll. Start the combat? a voice said directly into his mind.

"Yes," he said.

Nothing happened.

"I guess you don't reply to verbal commands," Tere mused. *Strong minds.* The symbol of this place meant strong minds, not strong voice.

Tere reached out with his mind, imagining himself nudging the large die since it was too far for him to reach. He assumed the game wouldn't like him running off his square to push on the die to roll.

He was right. With his mental prodding, the die jumped into action.

I still don't know what the attack symbols mean, he thought as the huge cube bounced and then finally came to rest with the number two facing upward.

You have rolled a two, the voice said. *Your possible attacks are:*

Commander – Morale Boost (doubles speed for one ally target)

Mage – Freeze (stops movement or action on target for one round)

Healer –Heal (heals one damage on one target immediately)

Archer – Blind (makes target unable to attack or defend for one turn)

Assassin – Disable (attacks vital area, making target unable to act for two rounds)

Foot soldier – Spear Attack (does one damage to one target)

Tere chose to have one of his generic foot soldiers attack an enemy foot soldier with Spear Attack. His soldier thrusted with his spear, slipping in past the target's shield and sticking the point into the enemy foot soldier. The dark figure grunted and winced.

The die had transported itself back to the starting location while Tere was deciding on his attack. It went into motion and, after a few bounces, settled on five.

Opposing player chooses to perform archer Double Attack. This attack does one damage to two targets in one turn.

Fahtin and the foot soldier next to her both flinched and

cried out, indicating that they were the targets chosen by the opponent.

Tere muttered under his breath. He didn't like to see his friends hurt. He couldn't care less about the generic foot soldier; the man wasn't real. Fahtin, though...Tere felt a phantom pain when he heard her cry. There was nothing he could do but continue the game.

He rolled the die again.

You have rolled a one, the voice said. *Your options are:*

Commander – Intimidate (target backs up one square next turn)

Mage – Mire (slows target to half speed)

Healer – Simple Heal (heals one damage, takes two turns to cast)

Archer – Injure (slows movement by half)

Assassin – Blend (prepares for non-blockable attack)

Foot soldier – Block (negates up to level three attack on the foot soldier)

Tere chose to have Urun perform Simple Heal to take off the point of damage Fahtin had suffered. The weak spell would take two turns to heal her, though.

The game continued. *Opposing player has rolled a six and chooses to perform Firestorm.*

"Percipius damned, sons of—" Tere started, but cut off as flame whooshed from the enemy mage and washed over Fahtin and the foot soldier next to her. They screamed as their bodies burned to ash. While it was horrifying to hear the generic foot soldier's screams, a sound a thousand times worse tore from Fahtin's throat. The beautiful young woman, one of the kindest people Tere had ever known, collapsed as she shrieked, her body being consumed by the second until there was nothing left but a scorch mark and a small pile of ash on the square where she had stood only seconds before.

"Nooooo!" Tere screamed. His mind felt like it was exploding and pain lanced through every part of his body, almost as if he had received the attack himself. He dropped to his knees. "Gods no."

Player must continue the game, the voice told him. *Your roll. If you do not take action within twenty seconds, your turn will be forfeited and opposing player will take a turn.*

Tere roared and nocked, drew, and fired three arrows in the blink of an eye, all at the enemy commander. The man stood there, a knowing look on his face, as the shafts went through his body as if he were made of smoke.

Calm yourself, Tere scolded himself in his mind. *Take a turn, or the damn game will take it for you, killing someone else.* He clenched his teeth together, tried to straighten his thoughts, and promised to grieve—and to get vengeance—later. He still felt like he would lose his mind and his control over it, something he had only ever done once before in his adult life. When Lela Ganeva was killed.

With a mental flick, Tere sent the die into motion. It rebounded from the wall, bounced off the floor, and finally came to rest.

A number six was on its upward face.

You have rolled a six, the voice spoke directly into his head. *Your choices are:*

Commander – Destruction (a spinning attack that does double damage to up to three tokens standing side by side)

Mage – Firestorm (burns two targets to death, even if at full health)

Healer –Massive Heal (heals up to four targets for one damage each)

Archer – Volley (does one damage each turn to up to three targets in close proximity for two turns)

Assassin – Counterattack (stands ready and can counterattack up to two times when attacked, doing double damage to kill the one attacking the assassin)

Foot soldier – Savior (protects up to three fellow soldiers for a total of three damage)

Tere chose to have Lily, who was in the front row, perform the Volley attack on the second row of the opponent's army. Arrows feathered the healer, mage, and archer, applying one point of damage to each.

While Tere was inspecting the board, the other player—which at this point Tere figured was whatever magical creature or entity that was controlling the cave system all along—started the die in motion.

Opposing player has rolled a two and chooses to perform Heal, which mitigates one damage. Effect applied immediately. Healer is now at full health.

The die returned to the starting position and Tere used it again. As soon as it settled to the floor, before he even chose his option, the second round of damage from Lily's Volley took effect, killing the mage and archer. Unfortunately, the healer, though struck with an arrow that took off one damage, was still alive due to being healed the turn before.

You have rolled a three. Your choices of actions are:

Commander – Advanced Intimidate (makes two targets back up one row)

Mage – Multi Mire (slows movement to half for two targets)

Healer –Double Heal (heals one target for one damage each turn for two turns)

Archer – Basic Attack (does one damage to one target)

Assassin – Stealth Attack (does two damage to one target)

Foot soldier – Shield Bash (stuns two targets who are side by side for one turn each)

Tere chose to have Raki perform Stealth Attack in the enemy's second row. It would take two turns for him to travel there, but the effect would be worth it. It was a guaranteed kill. The die reset and then went into motion again.

Opposing player has rolled a six...

At seeing the number and hearing it announced, he cursed under his breath. "Damn game is probably rigged. Another bleeding six!"

...and chooses the action Savior, which allows the foot soldier to protect up to three tokens next to each other for a total of three damage combined over two turns. Tokens protected: healer and assassin.

Tere was satisfied, at least, that the types that could do massive damage with sixth-level actions were dead and that the commander was too far to take advantage of his high-level attack.

Tere activated the die.

You have rolled a three.

This time, he chose to have Lily perform Basic Attack. The arrow zipped across the short space to punch through the injured foot soldier's chest, taking off its last point of damage. The soldier grunted, then dropped to the game board.

Opposing player has rolled a four and chooses assassin action Infiltrate, which allows the token to become untargetable for one turn as it moves within range to strike the opponent's second row.

Tere surveyed the board. The enemy had its healer, assassin, commander, and four foot soldiers still alive, with the healer having taken one point of damage. On his side, he had Aeden, Lily, Urun, Marla, Khrazhti, Raki, and one foot soldier, besides himself. He felt better about his chances, though Fahtin's death still threatened to overwhelm him if he got caught up in thinking about it.

You have rolled a five. Your choice of actions are:

Commander – Mass Motivate (speeds all remaining troops, doubling their movement/actions for two turns)

Mage – Massive Freeze (stops all movement on three targets for two turns)

Healer –Advanced MultiHeal (heals three targets for one damage each)

Archer – Double Attack (does one damage each to two targets in one turn)

Assassin – Dark Wind (stealth attacks two targets, doing three damage total)

Foot soldier – Swinging Spear (does one damage to each of three targets standing side by side or a combination of single and double damage if there are only two together. If there is only one, instantly kills that one, even if protected)

Before Tere could choose, Raki materialized next to the opposing assassin and slashed out twice with his knives. *Player assassin strikes enemy assassin for two damage, but foot soldier skill Savior mitigates two points of damage.*

Cursing under his breath, Tere chose to have Aeden perform Swinging Spear, slashing at three foot soldiers standing next to each other. Each received one point of damage.

The opponent took its turn.

Opposing player has rolled a one. Tere fought off the urge to whoop at the low roll. *Chooses to have the healer perform Simple Heal.*

Tere blew on his hands, an old habit whenever he had played dice games in his past. With a mental shove, he sent the die spinning.

You have rolled a six.

The old archer thought about his options for a moment. This move could put him on the path to victory. He didn't want to screw it up. After a moment—he couldn't wait too long or the game would warn him again—he chose Volley. Lily fired off three arrows rapidly, and the healer and two of the injured foot soldiers dropped.

Opposing player has rolled a six and chooses the commander action Destruction. It will take two turns to arrive within range to attack.

Tere blinked. He had two rounds before half his remaining forces were annihilated.

"Damn it," he spat.

You have rolled a three.

Tere directed Raki to perform Stealth Attack on the uninjured foot soldier, killing him outright. *That's four foot soldiers dead, the remaining one injured. The healer, mage, and archer are also dead, leaving only the one injured foot soldier, the assassin, and the commander, who is in the process of attacking with his most powerful move,* Tere thought. *I have one uninjured foot soldier, myself, Marla, Khrazhti, Aeden, Urun, Lily, and Raki.*

The sound of the die bouncing across the stone floor interrupted Tere's musings. Now was no time to lose focus.

Opposing player has rolled a five and chooses assassin action Dark Wind.

Tere groaned. The enemy assassin stepped from the shadows and slashed at Marla and Khrazhti. The blade unerringly slashed out Khrazhti's throat and just barely missed Marla's, slicing into her shoulder and chest and doing one point of damage. The blue woman slumped to the ground in a spray of dull red and Marla stumbled. Before Tere could do more than prepare to scream, the commander's Destruction attack landed, killing Lily and the foot soldier instantly and finishing off Marla.

"Noooo!" finally ripped itself from Tere's throat. "No." The entire room seemed to dim, then blackness pushed in from the edges of his vision. That had never happened with his magical sight, not like it did back when he had working eyes. He found himself breathing rapidly, gasping for air.

You're going to hyperventilate, a voice said in his mind. *Calm yourself. Breathe. Protect those who live. Vengeance will come later.*

You must take your turn in a reasonable amount of time, the game voice pushed on top of Tere's other thoughts. *If you do not, your turn will be forfeit and the opposing player will take a turn.*

Tere controlled his breathing, trying to think. He activated the die as he struggled to get his mind straight.

You have rolled a three.

Tere couldn't believe his luck. Something inside him refused to believe he would end the game with his current turn. There had to be some trick. He shook his head and made his move, directing Raki to perform his skill Stealth Attack.

The young Gypta stepped out of the shadows with his knives bared. He drove one into the lower back and the other across the throat of his victim. The enemy commander fell to the game board, dead.

That was it. Tere had won. Now all he had to do was...

The huge die jumped to life and rolled across the floor, landing on a five.

"But I killed your commander," the archer said absently.

The objective of the game is to destroy the enemy army, the voice told him. *Defeating the commander does not end the match. It only concludes when all of the opponent's tokens are destroyed.*

The opposing player chooses the action Swinging Spear.

The last enemy foot soldier spun and slashed Raki with his spear, cutting the boy down.

Tere froze for a moment. He had counted on the death of the commander ending the game. Could he have chosen another attack, done something else that would have resulted in Raki still being alive? He put his hands to his head, wanting to tear out any hair he found.

He could not handle the game threatening him with losing his turn again, so he regretfully activated the die.

You have rolled a two.

Tere directed Aeden with a thought, commanding him to use his Spear Attack on the last foot soldier. Aeden's spear punched through the already-wounded soldier and destroyed it.

Opposing player has rolled a three and chooses the assassin action Stealth Attack.

Tere watched in horror as the enemy assassin materialized behind Urun and savagely tore his throat out. There was only one enemy token left, the assassin. Of his army, there was only himself and Aeden. They could win, but at what cost? He had watched as all his friends but Aeden had been cut down. He had to end it now. The die spun at his direction.

You have rolled a four. Your choice of actions are:

Commander – Power Slash (cuts into two targets standing side by side, dealing one damage to each)

Mage – Multi Freeze (stops movement completely on two targets for one turn)

Healer – Multi Heal (heals two targets for one damage each immediately)

Archer – Strong Attack (does two damage to one target)

Assassin – Infiltrate (in one turn, moves behind enemy lines, within range of back row and become invisible to attack for one turn)

Foot soldier – Protect Ally (uses shield to negate one attack to a fellow soldier)

He had a choice of either Protect Ally or Power Slash. If he had Aeden protect himself or Tere, the assassin could attack the other. On the other hand, he could damage the assassin with Power Slash. Even if he couldn't kill the enemy, he'd be one step closer to ending him.

Tere chose Power Slash and his sword cut into the assassin, taking off one point of damage. He only hoped he didn't make a mistake in choosing the attack.

Opposing player has rolled a six.

"Damn!" Tere spat.

...and has chosen Counterattack, which causes the assassin to

stand ready and counterattack up to two times when attacked, doing double damage to kill the attacker.

Tere rolled the die.

You have rolled a four.

The irony was not lost on Tere that he'd faced the same choice a few minutes earlier. If he had Aeden protect himself, the assassin could attack either him or Tere. It wasn't clear if Counterattack would still be in force. If so, the assassin could conceivably kill both Tere and Aeden. There was only one choice.

"I choose Power Slash," Tere said aloud as the magic of the game forced his body into motion, slashing at the assassin and doing the last point of damage. Before falling, however, the assassin—almost as if by reflex—lashed out with his daggers, cutting deeply into Tere's throat.

It was something Tere had never felt before, the tension of the skin and the cartilage in his neck easing as his flesh parted. Blood splashed out from him, spraying down his chest and into the assassin's face. He tried to pull in a breath, but something wasn't working. A bubbling sound rose up, coming from his own ruined throat.

As he dropped to the floor, the assassin did the same. At least Aeden was safe. He was the important one any—

🐿 36 🐿

Tere Chizzit sucked in a breath as light exploded around him. It seemed like it exploded, anyway, compared with the darkness he was in after he had been killed. He was standing in front of the game board, his friends around him. The illumination was the same as it had been before the game; the dim, barely adequate glow from an unknown light source.

What in the hells was going on? He had distinctly felt being killed. Even more strange, he was sure that all his companions but Aeden had been dead as well. Seeing Fahtin and Marla, Raki and Urun, Khrazhti and...and Lily, all of them alive; it was almost too much. The game hadn't been real.

But it had all felt so genuine. He had no doubt that if he hadn't won, they would have been dead for real.

Something was still wrong, though. The others weren't moving. It was as if they were frozen in place, their eyes open and staring ahead of them. At nothing. Apparently, he wasn't finished yet with whatever the cave had in store for him.

Another test? He clenched and unclenched his hands, then moved his feet. He wasn't frozen.

A luminescent globe, about the size of a man's head, lowered from the ceiling. It hadn't been resting there. It seemed to materialize as it descended. The closer it got to his head level, the brighter it shone. It stopped moving at eye level and hovered.

Tere reached out and grasped it with both hands. He pulled it toward himself, met with a slight resistance, almost like he was picking it from a branch like a huge, glowing piece of fruit. When he had it cradled in both hands, a door at the left end of the room, twenty feet from the door he had assumed they needed to open, lit up with a pale, orange light. He hadn't even known a door was there.

Tere cocked his head, then walked toward the orange door. If whatever lived in the cave wanted him to go through that entry way, he might as well do it. He hoped it wasn't another test. He was good and tired of silly games that could mean his death, and that of his friends.

The door opened ahead of him without him having to do anything. The globe in his hands pulsed in time with the door's light and he walked through into the dark chamber beyond.

As soon as the globe crossed the threshold, the massive room lit up with a pale orange light. It was bigger even than the room with the game board.

In the center was a well, at least fifteen feet across and surrounded by a small wall made of perfectly fitted stones. The light from within the well—a yellow-orange glow brighter than the room or the globe he held—flickered on the inside of the wall like the blaze from a large and ferocious fire, though without menace.

In the part of the wall facing Tere was an indentation, exactly the size of the globe he carried.

"Why not?" he said as he knelt and fitted the sphere into the space. It slid in easily and clicked as it made contact.

From deep in the well, the light exploded upward, painting the ceiling two dozen feet above with the colors of a sunset. It shrank in on itself, condensing into a cloud of light, then twisted and took humanoid form. Its head turned toward Tere and though there were no eyes, Tere had no doubt it was looking straight into his.

As if hurricane force winds were driving it, the creature flew toward Tere, and then through him. He didn't have time to do anything other than gasp as a strange warmth radiated through his chest where the thing had made contact. It flew out of Tere's back, swirled around the cavern, then slammed through the ceiling, splitting into millions of tiny shards of light as it did so, though strangely, one larger chunk fell to the cave floor.

Steps thundered and Tere caught motion from his companions as they rushed into the room, but he didn't look toward them. Instead, he watched the magic pass through the rock toward the outside world, then spread even thinner to cloak the sky in a fine mist. But how did he know that?

He tracked it, observed it, felt it. Through the magical matrix of the world.

His magical sight was back.

Tere Chizzit dropped to his knees and broke down, weeping like a small child.

"TERE?" MARLA SAID AS SHE SKIDDED TO A HALT IN FRONT of him. "Tere, what did you do?"

It was strange, weeping like he was. Not so much because he was a grown man and probably shouldn't be losing composure completely, but because his ruined eyes leaked no tears as he did so. Instead, there were dry, hacking sobs from the archer.

Not the most dignified of actions.

"I..." he said.

"You didn't see?" Aeden asked Marla. "You didn't experience the entire game. I did."

The Croagh's red-haired sister shivered visibly. "I did. I... felt myself die."

"Me too," Fahtin said.

"What I meant," Marla continued, "was what did you do just now? Not only were we released, but the sheer amount of magic flooding this cavern was something I have never experienced, even in the strange magical shifts we've been feeling lately."

Urun stepped up to Tere and waved his hands over him. "I felt it, too." As the priest's hands moved, Tere could see magic spreading out in fine tendrils, probing the older man for injury.

"I'm fine, Urun. No need to check me over."

Urun started.

"I got my powers back," Tere said. "Whatever was within that well, I think I freed it when I put the globe into the wall there." He pointed toward the indentation with the globe in it. He jerked his head back when he realized it had turned to stone, becoming part of the wall itself.

"Things feel different," Aeden said. Khrazhti, standing next to him, nodded. "Not only do I not feel the effects restricting my thoughts, I actually feel smarter than before, and more powerful."

"That's right," Marla said. "It does seem that whatever was slowing our thoughts and weighing our minds down is gone."

"Valcordinae," Tere said. "Strong minds. I think that magic has to do with thinking and it was trapped somehow. It used its powers to affect us, to bring us to it. Now that it's free, we're no longer under its effects. At least, not the negative effects."

"So, the game?" Marla asked. "It was to, what, determine your ability?"

"Our worthiness, I think," Tere said.

Raki had his hand to his forehead. "It all seemed so real."

"You all experienced what happened?" Tere asked.

"Everything," Aeden said, "though I didn't experience death like the others."

Tere's companions stared at the floor, or ceiling, or their own hands. Anything but having to meet anyone else's eyes. They had a haunted look. Tere had felt death, like they had. He understood that look completely.

"You sacrificed yourself for me, at the end there," Aeden said.

"Nah. How was I to know the damn assassin could counterattack even after receiving a fatal blow?"

Aeden's eyes drilled into Tere's dead orbs. "You knew."

Tere's face heated of its own accord. Blushing now? What had he become? "Guessed. At the most. There was a chance I wouldn't get hit."

"Come on, Tere. You knew there was a good chance you'd die and that if you had me do my action, there was a chance the assassin would have killed you or me in the next turn or two."

Tere put his hands up to ward off the argument. "Okay, okay. It was a calculated move. You're the important one, Aeden, not me. If there is one person who can't die, it's you. Or Marla, actually, but she was already dead. How was I to know it wasn't permanent?"

Aeden opened his mouth, but nothing came out. He closed it and, of all things, dropped his eyes to his feet.

Lily stepped up to Tere, her green eyes wide and liquid,

inspecting his white orbs. He couldn't help it, he put his hand to her cheek and cupped it. "I'm glad it wasn't," he whispered. He cleared his throat and said, a little louder, "I'm sorry, kid. I've been a bastard the last few weeks. I've been under a little bit of pressure. It's just that—"

Lily put her hand behind his head and pulled him toward her, then kissed him, deep and full of passion. It lasted for several seconds, during which Tere all but froze, enjoying the sensation, but not reacting as he should have. The beautiful, red-haired archer broke off and smiled at him.

"You're forgiven."

An hour later, when Tere finally took a breath, his cheeks burned even hotter than they had before.

"Uh. Okay, then. I...I'm glad we got that straight. Where's my bow, anyway?"

The others suddenly found that they needed to search the well or to adjust their scabbards or anything else that would keep them from meeting Tere's gaze.

"You can't hide your smiles from me," he said to them with a sigh. "I have my powers back, and they seem even stronger than before."

❦ 37 ❦

Qydus Okvius, headmaster of the Sitor-Kanda Academy, glanced at the clock displayed on one of his bookshelves. It wouldn't be long now.

The headmaster's assistant spoke to someone on the other side of his closed door. He had closed it himself, not more than four minutes ago. When he had felt *it*. He ran through the probability in his mind and wasn't surprised in the least when Yxna Hagenai opened the door and rushed into his office, closing it behind her.

Yxna rarely showed emotion, not anything more than a smile or a frown. She had learned long ago to school her face into an unreadable mask. The Edged Weapons Master wore that stone face now, but Qydus had known her for decades, and the light dancing in her eyes could not be hidden from him.

She was shaken, as much as the master *could* be shaken.

"Did you—"

"Yes, Yxna," he said before she finished her question. "Please, sit. I will have Aletris bring some tea."

"What in Abyssum was it?" she asked, lowering herself gracefully to the chair in front of the headmaster's desk so their eyes were level with one another. "My talents lie more in the physical arts than in the magical, but even I felt the phenomenon. It seemed that the entire world lurched."

Qydus rose from his seat, patting her arm as he passed her to open his office door. "Aletris, would you be so kind as to bring us in a pot of tea?"

"Yes, Headmaster. Right away."

He reclaimed his chair and looked into Yxna's hazel eyes. They almost seemed to move, like a sunlit storm at sea, a bubbling, boiling tempest. "Do not undervalue your magical ability. You are potent with the magical arts, and sensitive to the magical currents in Dizhelim.

"Yes, I did feel the anomaly. No, I do not know what it was. We will gather the rest of the masters to discuss it in a little while. To be truthful, I expected you, but not quite so soon. It happened only—" He narrowed his eyes at the clock again. "Five, no, six minutes ago."

"I was already on the way to see you and was nearby."

"Ah. Well, I do have some ideas on what happened, though I would beg your indulgence in holding my tongue until we are all gathered. Repetition seems unnecessary and I would like to avoid such."

The tea arrived. Aletris poured for the masters and left. Yxna stared at her cup for a moment, then sipped it. Her hand was steady, as would be expected, but Qydus found his shaking slightly. Was it fear, anticipation, or the part of his body that was humming with magic? He frowned at his cup. He didn't like any of those options.

"I can wait a few moments to hear your thoughts," Yxna finally said. Qydus had to replay the conversation in his head before he recalled what he had last said to her.

"Thank you, Yxna. Let us finish our tea, and then we will head to the large auditorium."

They sat in silence, sipping their tea as if they had all the time in the world. It was important to stop and contemplate, especially in these momentous times. Surus knew they might not have the opportunity again soon.

As he emerged from the office, the headmaster considered the three masters sitting in chairs, obviously waiting for him.

"Aletris, please tell any of the masters who come that we will be meeting in the large auditorium in the administration building." He turned to the waiting masters as a fourth arrived. "Thank you for your patience, masters. Please come with me. We will discuss the issue with as many in attendance as we can manage."

One of the masters, Isegrith Palus, nodded. "Headmaster, if I may?"

"Of course, Isegrith. I appreciate it."

The master of Fundamental Magic waved her hands and whispered words of power. Light blossomed from her hands, shot through the door of the building, and flared to life outside, throwing its light brightly enough that it illuminated half the room through the windows.

"The signal has been sent," she said. "The others will know to come here, if they're not already on the way."

Within half an hour, all but a few of the masters of the Academy were seated in the auditorium.

"Most," the headmaster said, "if not all, of you felt the magical disturbance less than an hour ago. I would speak of it. First, let me explain the little I know. I felt the...surge, but did not recognize its signature. I know not exactly from whence it came, but it seemed to come from the east and north.

"From the direction of Ebenrau, if I am not mistaken."

There seemed to be no dissenting opinions, judging by the nods and confident looks of the masters.

"I have ideas on the type of magic, but I will hold those for now, allowing others who may be more sensitive to the particular type of power to speak. I would have you know, however, that we sent a group on a mission to Rhaltzheim, to Ebenrau specifically, nearly two weeks ago. I believe the anomaly may be related to that mission."

Conversation burst out among the masters, groups of two or three huddling together to speak about what he had just said.

"What was this mission, and to whom did you assign it?" Master Nasir Kelqen, the Master of the School of Research and Investigation, asked.

Qydus glanced at Yxna, whose shoulders shrugged minimally.

"A seer had a vision, and I sent a group to investigate it. The group included Marla Shrike and her brother, Aeden, among others. They were to investigate the seer's vision."

Some of the masters seemed to accept that as explanation enough. Others, however...

"And was this group sanctioned by the Council of Masters? Why is a student—albeit one who has mastered several schools—leading a team instead of those in the employ of the Academy for such things?" It was Vaeril Faequin, the Master of the School of Alchemy, asking.

Qydus sighed. "I have spoken to some of you, but not all. It is convenient to have most of the masters gathered in one place, so I will address the situation now. I, and several of the other masters, have determined that Aeden Tannoch and his twin sister, Marla Shrike, together are the Malatirsay."

Sound burst forth. The headmaster understood the emotion driving the conversation, but it did not mitigate the impropriety.

"Enough," he shouted, using magic to amplify his voice. The room quieted immediately. "Must I remind you that you are the masters of Sitor-Kanda? It does not become you to chatter like first year students. You will conduct yourself with proper decorum.

"I apologize if I have delayed in presenting the information to you all. Circumstances have been changing rapidly, and I felt it better to discuss the subject in smaller groups before addressing it to the entire body of masters at once. What I have just witnessed justifies that decision. We will discuss it more fully, and I will present the evidence for our official determination later. For now, please set aside this issue.

"The topic at hand is the strong magical surge. There have been others—weaker, I admit—over the last months. These are, we believe, signs that the time of darkness is at hand. Whether the phenomenon is for good or ill, I cannot say. Perhaps it is neither, but only a byproduct of these times. It is my hope that the team will return soon and explain what happened. I ask that you be patient for that report."

"Mental energy," one of the masters called out. "Mind magic."

Qydus squinted into the audience as Master Jusha Terlix stood up. "I beg your pardon, Jusha."

"The surge," he said, "it was mental in nature. Specifically magic of the mind, not just generic magical energy. I sensed it clearly—as if a great accumulation of it was released into the world. I...I don't know anything that could have done that. It feels like that aspect of my magic is now stronger."

The headmaster scanned the audience. Several of them nodded as Master Jusha spoke and one or two sat back smugly as if their suspicions had been confirmed.

"Interesting," Qydus said. It aligned with what he had felt, though he had difficulty explaining it. Jusha had said it simply and succinctly. "Thank you for your insight. Does anyone else have information or opinions to add to this?"

None did. The headmaster waited for several minutes, but it seemed the meeting had accomplished all that it would.

"I appreciate your time," he said to them all. "I will continue to prepare my presentation of the other information I mentioned and, when our team returns, I will present that information as well. I ask again that you be patient. The world is in flux, and we can but try to keep up. If you remember or discover anything related to today's...excitement, please see me. Until then, masters, we have students that might need consoling or explanations, or both. Please do not mention the issue of the Malatirsay. That will come in time. Thank you."

Qydus stepped down from the speaker's dais and headed out a side door toward his office. Yxna followed him, along with a few others with whom he had been discussing his plans. That was good. They had a lot of work to do, even before Marla and Aeden returned.

If they returned.

EPILOGUE

The small stone vibrated and flashed.

Another summons for a meeting, Thalia Fendove thought. *Well, I expected it, after that strange sensation earlier. I guess I'll have to report on what happened sooner than I had anticipated.*

The dark-haired woman sighed. Sometimes she wasn't sure she should ever have accepted the invitation to join the Dark Council. As if she could have refused her dying father. He was on the Council, as was her grandfather, but some had declined the invitation before, though those seemed to have had runs of bad luck afterward. Fatal doses of bad luck. Best not to tempt fate.

She decided not to change clothes. The soft silk robe she wore, open at the front to reveal most of her breasts, would have to do. If it distracted the men—and probably at least one of the women—that was fine. She didn't have anything to hide, proud of the body she'd sculpted with all that battle training. Well, that and the strenuous activity of her favorite pastime. Most people didn't realize how much exercise it was to torture others.

She placed the meeting stone into its holder, and activated it with a thought and the words of command, "*Aruna sirat vitosim*." She appeared in the meeting room where Alloria's actual body sat, the details of not only that room, but the others who had already activated their stones filling in around her. Thomlyn Byrch's eyes popped when he saw how she was dressed. She leaned forward for him, and she could have sworn his fluffy white beard bristled.

The meeting stones were not really stone. At least, she didn't think so. They seemed more like gems, but not quite. Maybe they were a mix between rock and gemstone. There were only thirteen of them, and they had been used since the founding of the Dark Council. Some stories said they were created by the Dark Prophet himself.

Whatever. They made meeting together much more convenient than being physically in the same place. The Council members didn't even know where the others were. A good thing, in her mind.

"Thalia," Alloria said, nodding her skinny, pale head.

"Vituma," Thalia said, bowing her own head slightly. No harm in being polite. Alloria was their leader, after all, a direct descendant of the Dark Prophet himself. It was funny, that, considering her coloring.

The others greeted each other while biding the time until everyone was present. When they finally were, Alloria started the meeting.

"This emergency meeting is due to the recent disruption in the world's magic," the leader said.

Thalia knew what Alloria was talking about. Her own magic was a bit unorthodox. She had overheard others of the Council debating whether or not she actually had any magic at all. Her sensitivity to power wasn't as refined as some of the others, but she had felt that strange jolt earlier. She had some information related to it, but still didn't understand what happened.

"For those who are without magical sensitivity," Ren Kenata said, "there was a surge of power no more than two hours ago. Even at the Academy, I never felt anything like it. The makeup of the world's magic seemed to shift, increasing but in a very specific way."

"Thank you, Ren," Alloria said. "I would ask if any others have information on this occurrence."

Thalia waited patiently, hoping someone else would say something. After half a minute of silence, she resigned herself to speaking. She opened her mouth, but Amatia spoke first.

"I have had a vision," she said. Amatia was a gorgeous woman with brown skin, long black hair, and eyes so dark one would think her pupils were shaded from light at all times. She had magic of her own, the most important of which was her ability to see things, past, future, and present. She didn't always have visions, but when she did, they were always worth listening to.

"Regarding this power surge?" Alloria asked.

"I believe so," the seer said. "I saw a dark pit, one that flared to life and light. The circumstances that caused it are murky, but once it was activated, the light flooded the world, dispersing over all things."

The Council waited, silent, for Amatia to continue.

She did not.

"Is that all of it?" Gareth Briggs asked. Thalia didn't usually like older men, but she could stare at Gareth for hours on end. His looks and his charm were his deadliest weapons, but it didn't hurt to look at him.

"That is all," Amatia said. "That, and the distinct impression there are more such pits with their own stores of power. I know nothing of where they are or what their nature is, but I am sure this was not the only one."

Alloria stroked her pointed chin, looking contemplative. "I see. Thank you Amatia. Is there anything else?"

Thalia caught Evindia Elkien staring at her and she winked at the beautiful blonde woman. Her coloring was similar to Alloria's, but her figure was fuller than the leader's slender frame. She threw those thoughts out of her head. No distractions.

"I have something," Thalia said. "The team I sent to Ebenrau, they were killed."

"And?" Alloria said.

"It wasn't too long after they were killed that the power surge happened. I think maybe they're related. My men were chasing down that source of magical power I mentioned last time. Apparently, someone else was investigating it, too. Someone better equipped for combat, if the results were to be believed. Not too much could have overpowered that group. Maybe Ren's rumor from our last meeting was correct and the twins found them."

"I asked you before why you had not gone, and you told me it was beneath you."

"I told you I had other things to do," Thalia said. "If someone or something killed the team I sent, I wouldn't have lasted long against them, so it is fortunate I didn't go or you would have to invoke the procedures to add another Council member."

"A valid point," Alloria said.

"But what do we do about it all?" Ren Kenata asked.

Yoniko Takesi answered. "We find the other sources of power and we make sure the next time there is a conflict over one, we destroy those looking for it and take it for ourselves."

"Yes," Alloria Yurgen said. "Amatia, we need more information. The rest of you, we must step up our activities. We will break for ten minutes. Prepare food or drink and make yourselves comfortable. We have planning to do, and it cannot wait for our adversaries to make their next move."

🕉

THE ANIMARU HIGH LORD KIRRALOTH STEPPED OUT ONTO the balcony of the building, squinting against the bright light of the S'ru forsaken world he had been transported to. He had disliked the place immediately, and not only because of the accursed light. Even the air around him seemed abrasive, containing particles of the power that had been described to him but that he had not believed existed. Life.

The animaru lord had recently come over to this world, this Dizhelim, to take command of the troops here. They had been plagued with faulty leadership and lax discipline. That, and plain bad luck. The Gneisprumay was here, in this world, as prophesied.

It was good that Kirraloth was something of a trouble-shooter. Generals and priests had their place, but what their efforts needed was someone smarter, cleverer. Someone like him.

He stood taller than the officers and lords on the balcony with him. Slender, like a colechna, but with thick, dark skin rather than scales, and hairless like most of the semhominus, though without their features and limitations. He was not one of the common types of animaru. He was unique, his own type, as befitted his station.

While the rest of S'ru's subjects had constantly squabbled and warred, Kirraloth remained in the background, account-able to no one but their god. Well, their god and his shadow. He hadn't specifically held a position over the military and religious factions, but rather to the side, of equal level. He made sure things ran smoothly and when they didn't, he nudged them back into line. Sometimes forcefully.

Now, though, he had been given command over all the animaru in this new place. Procedures would change, as soon as he got his bearings and decided what to do.

Kirraloth glanced aside at the two ranking generals. Sastiroz and Jarnorun appeared similar, just two high-ranking semhominus. For Jarnorun, it was true. For Sastiroz, though, it couldn't be further from the truth. He was erfinchen, something known only to a scant few on this side of whatever magical tunnel had been used to bring them all here. Like all his kind, Sastiroz could take any form, shift his substance to appear like anything he had learned to replicate. There were limits, of course. He couldn't shrink himself too small or grow to the size of a dozen-foot-tall coga. Still, his talents were useful, and would be more so in this world.

Both the generals were capable, but he wanted more.

"How many are there?" Kirraloth asked, shifting his attention to the mass of dark bodies on the field below the balcony.

"Nine thousand, three hundred, ninety-four," Jarnorun said, bowing.

"What of the fessanum, the one who opens the portal to our world to bring the animaru here?"

"He is in this building, on a lower floor," Sastiroz said.

"When can he next open a portal? I understand that they can only be opened at certain times?"

"It is so, High Lord," Jarnorun answered. "The next opportune time is several weeks from now."

"Bring him to see me in my office. We will become more selective in choosing which animaru we will bring over. I need more capable leaders, such as yourselves. We are finished coddling this world. We will add to our numbers, plan, and crush these life-infested creatures. Before we are finished, we will kill them all and let S'ru sort them out. After speaking with the fessanum, I will expect the two of you in my office to begin the planning."

"Yes, High Lord," both of them said. "I will fetch the fessanum," Jarnorun added, and quickly stepped from the balcony into the building.

"What of you, Sastiroz? Have you anything to say about this place?"

The erfinchen considered for a moment, his eyes meeting the high lord's. "It cannot be darkened and made ready for S'ru soon enough. The constant light and life irritate me, and I would see them gone."

"They will be gone, and soon. Khrazhti and Suuksis were competent enough commanders, but they were conditioned by their many centuries of military service. I will bring a fresh approach to the conquest. We will make this world comfortably dark, and soon. All we need do is crush any and all we find here. The time for mercy is at an end. We go to destroy."

"But what of the Gneisprumay?"

"I am not concerned about this one. If we destroy every particle of life in this world, we will get to him eventually. I care little if he suffers or not, but he will cease to exist. It is what we animaru do best, and it is time to show the fessani the truth of it."

❦

"WHAT DOES IT ALL MEAN?" AEDEN ASKED.

Tere shook his head. "I'm not really sure. I think what we just witnessed was important. Extremely important. We should get back to the Academy and report what we found to the masters. Maybe they can figure it out." An idea struck him and he turned toward Aeden's sister. "Unless you know, Marla. You're the most educated of all of us in this kind of stuff."

The Academy graduate shook her head, red hair tossing about her. "I have no idea. I think we need to talk to the masters about it. I wonder again if there were books on all this in the Academy library before it was all destroyed."

"And this?" Tere said. He held up the small stone, easily held in the palm. It had small glowing marks on it. The symbol that Fahtin had seen in her vision, the one they found etched into the wall of the cave.

"Valcordinae," Marla said. "You saw it fall from that glowing thing you told us about, when it went up through the ceiling and broke into all those pieces?"

"Yep. It was brighter then, but the little symbols, the..."

"Cogiscro," Marla said.

"Yeah," Tere agreed. "The Cogiscro symbols—they're still making light. I can see magic inside it, though it seems pretty weak."

"I wonder what it's for," Aeden asked. "That's another thing we should probably ask the masters about when we get back to the Academy."

"Which brings us to our current predicament," Tere said. "There is nowhere to go but back the way we came. We'll have to figure out how to climb out of the pit we dropped into and hope all the traps didn't reset."

Marla looked at the well, now dark and empty. "Why would they? We passed all the tests, made it to the end, and freed whatever magic was in there. I'm guessing that thing powered all the traps. We should be okay. Devising a way to climb a pit's walls sounds like an easy challenge after all we've gone through."

Tere laughed. "True, it does. I'm not sure about the rest of you, but even though I'm tired, I'd rather start now. No telling how long it'll take us."

With groans and mutters, the others agreed. Tere led them out of habit, leaving the chamber back into the room with the gameboard. He reached the squares and turned to look back at his friends.

He smacked his palm to his forehead.

"Uh, guys. Maybe we don't have to backtrack at all."

Aeden scratched his head. "What? Why not?"

Tere pointed to his right. Aeden followed Tere's finger to his left and his eyes lit up.

The door they had originally thought was their destination stood there. Tere hoped it led to another way into and—more importantly—out of the maze of tunnels.

"Worth a try, right?" he said. He stepped up to the door and pushed down the latch. The door swung inward. Before even looking beyond it, Tere's face crinkled into a smile.

Marla handed him one of her light sticks and Tere poked it through the threshold. As soon as it passed, the light and the part of the stick it was attached to disappeared.

The archer groaned, but when he pulled the stick back, the light appeared again. He pushed and pulled the implement a few more times, making it disappear and come back again. It was like he was dipping the stick into a silo of pitch that didn't adhere when he pulled it back out.

"Any ideas?" he asked.

Aeden stepped up beside Tere and slowly pushed his finger toward the darkness of the doorway.

Tere batted the finger away. "Are you out of your mind? What if it eats your finger or kills you with some kind of magical poison?"

"I can't sense any magic," Aeden said. "Can you?"

Oh, right. Tere had forgotten his magical sight was back. He peered at the darkness and though he could see the glow of magic, it was faint. It didn't seem dangerous, but he wasn't sure that meant anything.

"I can't tell. It's too foreign, unlike any other magic I've seen."

Aeden pushed his finger out again, this time breaking the plane of darkness across the doorway. He paused a moment, then pushed farther until his whole hand had disappeared.

"I don't feel anything." The Croagh stepped forward and made his arm disappear up to the shoulder, then drew it back out, unharmed.

"Hmmm," Marla said.

"Oh, for Surus's sake," Lily said, pushing the men aside and lunging for the doorway. Tere snatched at her, but the woman twisted to evade his grasp. She plunged into the darkness and disappeared completely.

Tere stared at where Lily had gone. Aeden's mouth had dropped open and his arm was still raised, frozen in place.

"Lily?" Tere said, an edge of panic creeping into his voice.

A head of red hair poked out of the darkness, suspended in the air. "You couldn't hear me from the other side?" she asked.

"Uh. No."

"Well, you can hear me now. Come on. It's fine." Her head went back into the darkness, but a moment later, one of her hands thrust out of the black, grabbing at the air in Tere's direction.

He numbly took the hand and clamped his around it. She pulled, surprisingly strong, and he stumbled forward. Into a small room with a door at the other end. His breath caught when he saw that the wall he'd entered through was solid stone.

"Some kind of illusion," Lily said, pushing her hand through it. "I don't know if it's unsolid all the time or if it's especially for us right now, but we should probably get everyone else through there before it decides to be stone again."

A quick explanation by Tere's disembodied head to the others and soon everyone was cramped in the little room.

"I hope that door leads somewhere," Marla said, "or we may be trapped here if the wall goes solid again."

"Good point," Aeden said. He unlatched the door and opened it. Fresh air flooded the little room.

Tere passed by Aeden, through the doorway. The darkness was no obstacle for his sight, so he saw clearly what was outside. A brick wall several feet ahead and a narrow alley crossing his path. On the right, it ended in another brick wall with a door set in it. To the left the small path led out into a street.

"We're back in Ebenrau," he said, shaking his head. "I'm not sure where, but it's definitely the city. That fake wall must have been a magical gateway, bypassing all that rock and all those tunnels."

"Too bad we couldn't have used it to get down there in the first place," Marla said.

The little group cautiously entered the street, closing the door to that small room.

"Huh." Lily said, drawing Tere's attention. She flushed when everyone looked at her questioningly. "I checked the wall before I left the room. It had become solid again. Now, the door seems locked or barred in some way."

Aeden nodded. "It makes sense. It's a one-way gate. Even if the well doesn't have the power in it anymore, whoever made it probably didn't want others mucking about down there."

"That begs the question, though," Marla said. "Who made the gate, and when? I had assumed it was ancient, by the looks of it. How would someone make that back door if there wasn't a city here when the well was made?"

"Stop," Fahtin said. "I started feeling less stupid after the well released its magic, but thinking on things like that are making me feel dumb again."

Tere smiled. The conversation had an easy, teasing quality. It had been too long since they had shared that.

It didn't take long for the group to get their bearings. They were in one of the areas they had explored when they had first come to the city. Once Raki recognized a building and the surrounding area, they were able to go straight to the inn where they had rented rooms.

"We've been gone for at least a week," Urun said. "Not to mention the last time we were in the city, we were being chased by every guard within earshot, and then some."

"He's right," Marla said. "I wonder what happened to our horses. Do you think the guards knew who we were and confiscated everything?"

"No," Tere said. "It's a big city. They wouldn't have been able to trace where we were staying. The horses, on the other hand, it depends on how long it's been exactly. The innkeeper may have decided we weren't coming back after a few days and sold our horses to pay the rest of our bill. It may be a long walk home."

Luckily, that had not happened. They arrived safely at the inn—it seemed that they were no longer being looked for—and the innkeeper, surprised at their return, calmed their fears.

"Ahh, Mistress Fahtin, you and your friends have returned. I was afraid something untoward had happened to you. Are you well?"

Tere met Fahtin's eyes and shrugged slightly to her.

"We are well, Master Bernhard. I am so sorry we were delayed. Have you...kept our horses in the stables?"

"Of course, Mistress, of course. I knew you would return. They are safe and well in the stables."

Sighs of relief exploded from several of Tere's companions.

"Wonderful," Fahtin said. "How much do we owe you for

your services?"

"A gold mark and three silvers should cover it all."

Tere slapped two gold marks on the counter. "For your troubles, Master Bernhard. We appreciate your faith in our return."

"Of course, of course. Will you be leaving, then? I have rooms available yet."

Tere eyed his friends. All of them looked back at him with the same excitement he felt. A night of sleep in a real bed instead of on the ground in a cave or a clearing near a road.

"In that case, Master Bernhard, we will gladly take rooms and partake of some of your fine food in the dining area."

"And a bath," Fahtin said.

"Yes," Tere agreed, "and baths."

"Very well," the innkeeper said. "What you gave me easily covers those costs and leaves a bit left over for my troubles. No, no, please don't give me more. It is my desire to serve. What you gave me is plenty."

Tere gave a slight bow to the man. "You are very kind, Master Bernhard. Thank you."

After their baths, food, and a good night sleeping in beds, the party took an early breakfast and made their way back to the Academy. It took almost a full week to get there, and the trip was delightfully uneventful. When they arrived back at their rooms in the dormitory, they were greeted by Jia, Aila, and Evon.

Fahtin rushed over to hug Aila and Jia. Marla and Evon hugged awkwardly, almost like they were going to simply shake hands but decided to follow Fahtin's lead. The others stood around, mostly looking at the ground. Tere found the entire thing uncomfortable but humorous.

"The masters wanted to meet as soon as you returned," Jia said. "Are you in a condition to do so now, or would you like to rest first?"

Tere, figuring his stint at leading the group was now over, looked toward Aeden and Marla. The red-haired Academy graduate spoke when Aeden nodded to her.

"We can meet with them now. We have news, and I'm sure you do, too. Let's all hear about everything together."

"I see," Headmaster Qydus said after Marla, Aeden, and Tere explained what they had experienced. *That was it?* Marla thought. *I see?*

Jia had explained what they had discovered, the human army and animaru cooperating. That wasn't welcome news, but not unexpected, either.

It has truly begun, then. The time of darkness is firmly established. Gods help us.

Master Isegrith raised her hand and the headmaster nodded to her. "This well, you have told us everything you remember about it?"

"Yes, Master," Marla said.

"It's odd, isn't it?" the master said. "I can recall nothing in the histories or even in the prophecies about concentrated power in a hole in the ground, let alone that it gave the distinct impression that it was mental magical energy."

"Not an impression, Master Isegrith," Fahtin said. Marla's eyes widened at so firmly correcting a master of the Academy. "Begging your pardon, but it *was* mental energy. I felt a strong connection to it, a sensitivity that identified it somehow. I can't really explain it, but Tere also can confirm the type of magic it was."

The master turned her head to Tere.

"She's right. Not only did it erase the mental effects we'd been fighting during our search, but I could see it clearly in the magical matrix. It took some thinking, but I understand now that I can see not only the use and power of magic, but also the different types. My magical sight has not only returned but improved. Expanded. There's no doubt. It was magic of the mind."

"Very well," Master Isegrith said. "I worded my statement poorly. Is there any indication there are other sources of magical power like the one you found?"

"We don't know anything further. We were hoping the masters could figure it out. We're sorry. Fahtin's powers proved invaluable in finding this one, though. Maybe she'll see something else."

The headmaster had been silently watching the conversation. He now turned his eyes to the Gypta woman. "Have you seen anything else, Fahtin? Anything to indicate what we should do next?"

She shook her head. "No, Headmaster. I'm afraid I haven't had any visions, feelings, or sensations of abnormal magic since the ones involving the well we found. Unfortunately, I can't force them to come, not yet."

"It is not your fault, child. Do not worry yourself over it. Doing so will only restrict your mind from accepting the visions that come of their own accord. With training, perhaps you will be able to control your emerging powers, but allow that to develop in time. You have been a great help already."

Fahtin smiled at the headmaster and dipped her head. Marla had always found Master Qydus to be kind and fair, having the correct thing to say in all circumstances. She thanked whatever powers had put him in charge over the Academy.

"So," Master Yxna said, "what are we to do? Surely you're not suggesting we merely wait until the next problem develops, Headmaster."

"No, Yxna, I am not. It appears to me that we have two important things to work on. One is the possibility of more concentrated sources of magic, in wells or any other form. If we can find them, perhaps we can harness them, or at least release the power into the world for our use. I'm sure we all agree that the overall level of magic in Dizhelim has increased, though maybe only slightly. We must remember, too, that this Council Ren Kenata's letters mention is also concerned with these sources, as evidenced by the group trying to find the one under Ebenrau.

"The second issue is that of human armies joining the animaru. Sitor-Kanda was never meant to field an army. We train others, primarily the Malatirsay, but do not have the numbers to fight battles against thousands of enemies."

"Are you saying the Academy won't fight?" Aeden asked.

"No, no, nothing of the kind, young Aeden. I am merely saying that despite the magic and the combat prowess of many of the Academy students and masters, we do not have sufficient numbers to wage a large-scale war."

"The nations," Marla said, tapping her chin with her finger. "We need to recruit others to build an army."

"Just so," the headmaster said. "We must approach the nations and kingdoms of the world and try to bring them to our cause. In reality, it is already their cause, since we are talking about the survival of all humans, encali, pouran, demid, astridae, and all other races, anything living on Dizhelim."

Aeden blew out a breath. "Only two things, but they might as well be two million. Gather an army from all the kingdoms of the world and find other sources of hidden magic, using them if possible or at least keeping them out of the hands of the enemies."

"The task of the Malatirsay was never said to be easy," Qydus Okvius said. "Alas, it is our burden, our responsibility, and our privilege to do what is needed. Rest, for you must be weary from your travels. We will meet tomorrow and begin laying plans to accomplish our two goals. On the morrow, we will start the defense of our world in earnest."

HERO'S MIND GLOSSARY

Following is a list of unfamiliar terms. Included are brief descriptions of the words as well as pronunciation. For the most part, pronunciation is depicted using common words or sounds in English, not IPA phonetic characters. Please note that the diphthong *ai* has the sound like the English word *Aye*. The *zh* sound, very common in the language Alaqotim, is listed as being equivalent to *sh*, but in reality, it is spoken with more of a buzz, such as *szh*. Other pronunciations should be intuitive.

Abyssum (*a·BIS·um*) – the world of the dead, Percipius's realm.

Acolyte – a current Hero Academy student who has mastered at least one school, but not three or more.

Adept – a Hero Academy student who has mastered at least three schools and continues to study at the Academy.

Aeden Tannoch (AY·*den* TAN·*ahkh*) – a man born to and trained by a highland clan, raised by the Gypta, and able to utilize the magic of the ancient Song of Prophecy.

Aeid Hesson (*AY·id*) – former Master of the School of

prophecy at the Hero Academy. He was murdered in his office at the Academy.

Aesculus (*AY·skyoo·lus*) – the god of water and the seas.

Agypten (*a·GIP·ten*) – an ancient nation, no longer in existence. It was from this nation the Gypta originated.

Ahred Chimlain (*AH·red CHIM·lane*) – noted scholar of the first century of the third age

Aila Ven (*AI·la ven*) – a woman of small stature who joins the party and lends her skills in stealth and combat to their cause.

Ailgid (*ILE·jid*) – one of the five highland clans of the Cridheargla, the clan Greimich Tannoch's wife came from.

Ailred Kelzumin (*ILE·red kel·ZOO min*) – the Master of the School of Water Magic at the Hero Academy.

Ailuin Lufina (*EYE·loo·in loo·FEEN·ah*) – one of the adepts at the Hero Academy who volunteered to aid in the investigation of Master Aeid's murder.

Alain (*a·LAYN*) – the god of language. The ancient language of magic, Alaqotim, is named after him.

Alaqotim (*ah·la·KOTE·eem*) – the ancient language of magic. It is not spoken currently by any but those who practice magic.

Alaric Permaris (*AL·are·ic per·MAHR·iss*) – the thug who hired the guys who attacked Marla in Dartford.

Aletris Meslar (*ah·LET·ris MES·lar*) – the personal clerk and assistant to Headmaster Qydus Okvius, of the Hero Academy.

Aliten (*AL·it·ten*) – a type of animaru that is humanoid but has wings and can fly.

Alloria Yurgen (*ah·LORE·ee·ah YURE·gen*) – the leader (Vituma) of the Dark Council. She is the 102nd leader since the Council's creation.

Alvaspirtu (*al·vah·SPEER·too*) – a large river that runs from the Heaven's Teeth mountains to the Kanton Sea. The

Gwenore River splits from it and travels al the way down to the Aesculun Ocean.

Amatia (*ah·MAH·tee·ah*) – a member of the Dark Council, a seeress.

Animaru (*ah·nee·MAR·oo*) – dark creatures from the world Aruzhelim. The name means "dark creatures" or "dark animals."

Arania (*ah·RAH·nee·ah*) – a kingdom in the western part of the continent of Promistala, south and east of Shinyan.

Arcus (*ARK·us*) – the god of blacksmithing and devices.

Arcusheim (*AHR·coo·shime*) – a large city on the southern shore of the Kanton Sea, the capital of the nation of Sutania and the home of Erent Caahs before he left to travel the world.

Arto Deniselo (*AHR·toe day·NEE·say·low*) – a dueling master in the Aranian city of Vis Bena who taught Erent Caahs how to drastically improve his combat abilities.

Aruna (pl. Arunai) (*ah·ROON·ah; ah·roo·NIE*) – a citizen of the tribal nation of Campastra. Originally, the name was pejorative, referring to the color of their skin, but they embraced it and it became the legitimate name for the people in Campastra.

Asfrid Finndottir (*ASS·frid fin·DOT·teer*) – the Master of the School of Cryptology at the Hero Academy.

Aruzhelim (*ah·ROO·shel·eem*) – the world from which the animaru come. The name means "dark world," "dark universe," or "dark dimension." Aruzhelim is a planet physically removed from Dizhelim.

Atwyn Iaphor (*AT·win EE·ah·fore*) – a student at the Hero Academy, a companion of Quentin Duzen when he was still on campus.

Assector Pruma (*ah·SEC·tor PROO·mah*) – roughly "first student" in Alaqotim. This is the student aid to a master in one of the schools at the Hero Academy. There can be only one per school and this person conducts research, helps to teach classes, and assists the master in any other necessary task.

Aubron Benevise (*AW·brun ben·uh·VEES*) – the Master of History and Literature at the Hero Academy.

Auxein (*awk·ZAY·in*) – an aide to the master and the First Student (Assector Pruma) at the Hero Academy. For larger schools, there may be more than one. In some schools there may not be any.

Awresea (*aw·reh·SAY·uh*) – a kingdom that no longer exists, the home of Tazi Ermenko who taunted the god Fyorio and was destroyed. The fiery, desolate location where the kingdom was is now known as Fyrefall.

Ayize Fudu (*aye·EEZ FOO·doo*) – a Hero Academy adept, one of Quentin Duzen's associates.

Barda Sirusel (*BAR·duh seer·oo·SELL*) – the boy who tried to bully Marla when she was a child.

Beldroth Zinrora (*BEL·droth zin·ROR uh*) – the Master of the School of Dark Magic at the Hero Academy.

Bernhard Lindner – the owner of the inn in Ebenrau where the party stays. He was smitten with Fahtin.

Bhagant (*bog·AHNT*) – the shortened form of the name for the Song of Prophecy, in the language Dantogyptain.

Bhavisyaganant (*bah·VIS·ya·gahn·ahnt*) – The full name for the Song of Prophecy in Dantogyptain. It means "the song of foretelling of the end," loosely translated.

Biuri (*bee·OOR·ee*) – small, quick animaru that recall the appearance and movements of rodents. They are useful as spies because of their small size and quickness.

Boltshadow – one of the Falxen sent to kill Khrazhti and her companions. A former student at Sitor-Kanda, he is skilled at wielding lightning magic.

Brace – the term used by the Falxen for a group of assassins ("blades").

Braitharlan (*brah·EE·thar·lan*) – the buddy assigned in the clan training to become a warrior. It means "blade brother" in Chorain.

Brausprech (*BROW·sprekh*) – a small town on the northwest edge of the Grundenwald forest, in the nation of Rhaltzheim. It is the hometown of Urun Chinowa.

Brenain Kanda (*bren·AY·in KAHN·duh*) – a mythological heroine who stole magic from the god Migae.

Bridgeguard – the small community, barely more than a guardpost, on the mainland end of the northern bridge to Munsahtiz

Broken Reach – a rugged, unforgiving land to the southeast of the Grundenwald. There are ruins of old fortifications there.

Calarel Kelhorn (*CAL·ar·el KEL·horn*) – one of the adepts at the Hero Academy who volunteered to aid in the investigation of Master Aeid's murder.

Campastra (cam·PAHS·trah) – a tribal nation in the southwestern portion of the continent of Promistala

Catriona (Ailgid) Tannoch (CAT·ree·own·ah ILE·jid) – the wife of Greimich Tannoch. She is originally from the Ailgid clan, but now has taken the last name Tannoch.

Ceti (*SET·ee*) – a higher level animaru, appearing aquatic with small tentacles, even though there is no water in Aruzhelim. They are very intelligent and have magical aptitude. Some of them are accomplished with weapons as well.

Chorain (*KHAW·rin*) – the ancestral language of the highland clans of the Cridheargla.

Clavian Knights (*CLAY·vee·en*) – the fighting force of the Grand Enclave, the finest heavy cavalry in Dizhelim.

Codaghan (*COD·ah·ghan*) – the god of war.

Cogiscro (*coe·JEE·scroe*) – an ancient system of runic writing that was used in magic spells. The symbols phonetic and are arranged in a circular pattern.

Colechna (*co·LECK·nah*) – one of the higher levels of animaru. Theyappear to be at least part snake, typically highly intelligent as well as skilled with weapons. They are usually in the upper ranks of the command structure. Their agility and flexibility makes them dangerous enemies in combat. A few can use magic, but most are strictly melee fighters.

Cridheargla (*cree·ARG·la*) – the lands of the highland clans. The word is a contraction of Crionna Crodhearg Fiacla in Chorain.

Crionna Crodhearg Fiacla (*cree·OWN·na CROW·arg FEE·cla*)) – the land of the highland clans. It means "old blood-red teeth" in Chorain, referring to the hills and mountains that abound in the area and the warlike nature of its people. The term is typically shortened to Cridheargla.

Croagh Aet Brech (*CROWGH ET BREKH*) – the name of the highland clans in Chorain. It means, roughly, "blood warriors." The clans sometimes refer to themselves simply as Croagh, from which their nickname "crows" sprang, foreigners not pronouncing their language correctly.

Dannel Powfrey – a self-proclaimed scholar from the Hero Academy who meets Aeden on his journey.

Danta (*DAHN·ta*) – the goddess of music and song. The language Dantogyptain is named after her.

Dantogyptain (*DAHN·toe·gip·TAY·in*) – the ancestral language of the Gypta people.

Daodh Gnath (*DOWGH GHRAY*) – the Croagh Ritual of Death, the cutting off of someone from the clans. The name means simply "death ceremony."

Daphne – one of the tavern maids at the Wolfen's Rest inn in Dartford.

Dared Moran (*DAR·ed·mo·RAN*) – the "Mayor" of Praesturi. Essentially, he's a crime boss who controls the town.

Darkcaller – one of the Falxen sent to kill Khrazhti and her companions. A former student at Sitor-Kanda, her specialty is dark magic.

Dark Council – a mysterious group of thirteen people who are trying to manipulate events in Dizhelim.

Dartford – a small town on the mainland near the north bridge to the island of Munsahtiz.

Darun Achaya (*dah·ROON ah·CHAI·ah*) – father of Fahtin, head of the family of Gypta that adopts Aeden.

Denore Felas (*den·OR FEHL·ahss*) – a great mage in the Age of Magic, the best friend of Tsosin Ruus.

Desid (*DAY·sid*) – a type of animaru. They're nearly mindless, only able to follow simple commands, but they are fairly strong and tireless. They are about five feet tall with thick, clawed fingers useful for digging. They have the mentality of a young child.

Dizhelim (*DEESH·ay·leem*) – the world in which the story happens. The name means "center universe" in the ancient magical language Alaqotim.

Dmirgan – a town in Kruzekstan, where a young Erent Caahs killed a man he thought was a murderer

Drachvorden (*drakh·VOOR·den*) – a city in existence during the Age of Magic. Two rogue mages, called the Power Twins, attacked the city and were killed by the hero Zejo Troufal.

Dreigan (*DRAY·gun*) – a mythical beast, a reptile that resembles a monstrous snake with four legs attached to its sides like a lizard. The slightly smaller cousin to the mythical dragons.

Drugancairn (*DROO·gan·cayrn*) – a small town on the southwest edge of the Grundenwald Forest.

Ebenrau (*EBB·en·ra·oo*) – the capital city of Rhaltzheim, one of the seven great cities in Dizhelim

Edge – one of the Falxen sent to kill Khrazhti and her companions. A former assassin and bodyguard in Teroshi, he is skilled in the use of the Teroshi long sword and short sword.

Encalo (pl. encali) (*en·CAW·lo*) – four-armed, squat, powerful humanoids. There are few in Dizhelim, mostly in the western portion of the continent Promistala.

Epradotirum (*EP·rah·doe·TEER um*) – an extremely powerful entity who lives in another plane of existence, touching the mortal plane when, every few centuries, he is hungry. Aeden and some of his friends met the Epra while running from assassins near Satta Sarak.

Erent Caahs (*AIR·ent CAWS*) – the most famous of the contemporary heroes. He disappeared twenty years before the story takes place, and is suspected to be dead, though his body was never found.

Erfinchen (*air·FEEN·chen*) – animaru that are shapeshifters. Though not intelligent and powerful enough to be leaders among the animaru, they are often at higher levels, though not in command of others. They typically perform special missions and are truly the closest thing to assassins the animaru have. A very few can use some magic.

Erlan Brymis (*ER·lan BRAI·miss*) – one of the adepts at the Hero Academy who volunteered to aid in the investigation of Master Aeid's murder.

Esiyae Yellynn (*ess·SEE·yay YELL·in*) – the Master of the School of Air Magic at the Hero Academy.

Espirion (*es·PEER·ee·on*) – the god of plans and schemes. From his name comes the terms espionage and spy.

Eutychus Naevius (*YOO·tik·us NAY·vee us*) – a renowned mathematician in ancient times. One of his principles, the third theorem of alternating magical series, was the key Marla used to decrypt Ren Kenata's letters.

Evindia Elkien (*eh·VIN·dee ah EL·kee·en*) – a member of the Dark Council.

Evon Desconse – a graduate of the famed Hero Academy and best friend to Marla Shrike.

Exulmucri (*EX·ool·MOO·cree*) – an ancient game of strategy, thought to be the first of its kind. It was also the first game to use dice.

Fahtin Achaya (*FAH·teen ah·CHAI·ah*) – a young Gypta girl in the family that adopted Aeden. She and Aeden grew as close as brother and sister in the four years he spent with the family.

Falxen (*FAL·ksen*) – an assassin organization, twelve of whom go after Aeden and his friends. The members are commonly referred to as "Blades."

Featherblade – one of the Falxen sent to kill Khrazhti and her companions. He is the leader of the brace and his skill with a sword is supreme.

Fireshard – one of the Falxen sent to kill Khrazhti and her companions. She wields fire magic.

Forgren (*FORE·gren*) – a type of animaru that is tireless and single-minded. They are able to memorize long messages and repeat them exactly, so they make good messengers. They have no common sense and almost no problem-solving skills

Formivestu (*form·ee·VES·too*) – the insect creatures that attacked Tere's group when they were on their way to Sitor-Kanda. They look like giant ants with human faces and were thought to be extinct.

Fyorio (*fee·YORE·ee·oh*) – the god of fire and light, from whose name comes the word *fyre*, spelled *fire* in modern times.

Fyrefall – a desolate and dangerous land in the south central part of Promistala, full of hot pools, geysers, and other signs of volcanic activity.

Gamore Nabavian (*gah·MORE nah·BAHV·ee en*) – one of the Power Twins, rogue mages killed by the hero Zejo Troufal in the city of Drachvorden just after the War of Magic ended.

Gareth Briggs – a member of the Dark Council.

Gentason (*jen·TAY·sun*) – an ancient nation, enemy of Salamus. It no longer exists.

Gneisprumay (*gNAYS·proo·may*) – first (or most important) enemy. The name for the Malatirsay in the animaru dialect of Alaqotim.

Godan Chul (*GO·dahn CHOOL*) – an ancient mythological race of spirit beings, created accidentally from the magic of the God of Magic, Migae. The name means, roughly "spirit's whisper."

Goren Adnan – the Master of the School of Military Strategy at the Hero Academy.

Graduate (at the Hero Academy) – a student of the Hero Academy who is either an adept or a viro/vira. That is, anyone who has mastered at least three schools at the Academy and is either still studying there or has left the school.

Great Enclave – a nation to the west of the Kanton Sea and the Hero Academy.

Greimich Tannoch (*GREY·mikh TAN·ahkh*) – Aeden's close friend, his braitharlan, during his training with the clans.

Grundenwald Forest (*GROON·den·vahld*) – the enormous forest in the northeastern part of the main continent of Promistala. It is said to be the home of magic and beasts beyond belief.

Gulra (pl. gulrae) (*GUL·rah; GUL·ray*) – an animaru that walks on four legs and resembles a large, twisted dog. These are used for tracking, using their keen sense of smell like a hound.

Gwenore River – a large river that splits off from the Alvaspirtu and travels south, through Satta Sarak and all the way to the Aesculun Ocean

Gypta (*GIP·tah*) – the traveling people, a nomadic group that lives in wagons, homes on wheels, and move about, never settling down into towns or villages.

Hamrath – a small town on the coast of the eastern part of the Kanton Sea, just north of the bridge from the mainland to Munsahtiz Island.

Hane Bryce – a member of the Dark Council.

Harlen Sayla (*HAR·len SAY·lah*) – the leader of the homeless group of people living in the caves under the city of Ebenrau.

Heaven's Teeth – the range of mountains to the east of the Kanton sea, in between that body of water and the Grundenwald Forest.

Ianthra (*ee·ANTH·rah*) – the Goddess of Love and Beauty.

Ianthra's Breasts (*ee·ANTH·rah*) – a mountain range between Arcusheim in Sutania and Satta Sarak. Even though there are three peaks, the two that dominate were named for the physical attributes of the Goddess of Love and Beauty, Ianthra.

Inna Moroz (*EEN·ah MOE·roze*) – a Hero Academy adept, one of Quentin Duzen's associates.

Iowyn Selen (*EE·o·win SELL·en*) – a great mage in the Age of Magic, the love of Tsosin Ruus's life.

Iryna Vorona (*ee·REEN·ah voe·rone·ah*) – Master of the School of Interrogation and Coercion at the Hero Academy.

Isbal Deyne (*ISS·bahl DANE*) – a member of the Dark Council.

Iscopsuru (*ee·SCOP·soo·roo*) – the name of Benzal's fortress outside of Nanris in Kruzekstan; it's over eight hundred years old. The name means Rock of Surus in Alaqotim.

Isegrith Palas (*ISS·eh·grith PAL·us*) – the Master of Fundamental Magic at the Hero Academy.

Izhrod Benzal (*EESH·rod ben·ZAHL*) – a powerful

magic-user, one who has learned to make portals between Aruzhelim and Dizhelim. The dark god S'ru has an agreement with him so he is second to none in authority over the animaru on Dizhelim.

Jarnorun (*jar·NOR·un*) – an animaru lord, one of Kirraloth's two main commanders.

Jehira Sinde (*jay·HEER·ah SINDH*) – Raki's grandmother (nani) and soothsayer for the family of Gypta that adopts Aeden.

Jhanda Dalavi (*JON·dah dah·LAHV·ee*) – the Head Scrivener at the Hero Academy. He is in charge of the small army of scribes who make copies of books and who create many of the records necessary for the functioning of the school.

Jia Toun (*JEE·ah TOON*) – an expert thief and assassin who was formerly the Falxen named Shadeglide. She uses her real name now that she has joined Aeden's group of friends and allies.

Jintu Devexo (*JEEN·too day·VEX·oh*) – the high chieftain of the Arunai during the time of the false Malatirsay.

Josef – the owner of the Wolfen's Rest inn in Dartford, a friend of Marla Shrike.

Jusha Terlix (*JOO·shah TER·liks*) – the Master of the School of Mental Magic at the Hero Academy.

Kanton Sea (*KAN·tahn*) – an inland sea in which the island of Munsahtiz, home of the Hero Academy, sits.

Kebahn Faitar (Kebahn the Wise) (*kay·BAWN FYE·tahr*) – the advisor and friend to Thomasinus; the one who actually came up with the idea to gather all the scattered people and make a stand at the site of what is now the Great Enclave.

Keenseeker – one of the Falxen sent to kill Khrazhti and her companions. He is a huge, strong warrior who wields a massive battle axe.

Khrazhti *(KHRASH·tee)* – the former High Priestess to the dark god S'ru and former leader of the animaru forces on Dizhelim. At the discovery that her god was untrue, she has become an ally and friend to Aeden.

Kirraloth *(KEER·uh·loth)* – an animaru high lord, given the command of all animaru on Dizhelim after Suuksis failed to turn or destroy Khrazhti.

Kruzekstan *(KROO·zek·stahn)* – a small nation due south of the highland clan lands of Cridheargla.

Leafburrow – a village in Rhaltzheim, north of Arcusheim off the River Road, the location of a bandit ambush where Erent Caahs demonstrated his special spinning arrow technique.

Lela Ganeva *(LEE·lah·gahn·AY·vah)* – the woman Erent Caahs fell in love with.

Lesnum *(LESS·num)* – large, hairy, beastlike animaru. These sometimes walk around on two feet, but more commonly use all four limbs. They are strong and fast and intelligent enough to be used as sergeants, commanding groups of seren and other low-level animaru.

Leul Abrete *(LOOL ah·BREET)* – a traveling merchant for whom Skril Tossin searches to get information in the murder investigation of Master Aeid.

Lilianor (Lili) **Caahs** *(LI·lee·ah·nore CAWS)* – Erent Cahhs's little sister; she was murdered when she was eleven years old.

Liluth Olaxidor *(LIL·uth oh·LAX·ih·door)* – the Master of the School of Firearms at the Hero Academy.

Lily Fisher – an archer of supreme skill who was formerly the Falxen assassin named Phoenixarrow. She uses her real name now that she has joined Aeden's group of friends and allies.

Lis *(LEES)* – a minor deity who battled the sun, nearly killing it, and causing so much damage that to this day, it is weakened in the wintertime.

Lucas Steward – a young student at the Hero Academy. He's often used by the masters as a messenger because of his strong work ethic and reliability.

Lusnauqua (*loos·NOW·kwah*) – the rugged land surrounding Broken Reach, in the center of the eastern section of the continent of Promistala.

Malatirsay (*Mahl·ah·TEER·say*) – the hero who will defeat the animaru and save Dizhelim from the darkness, according to prophecy. The name means "chosen warrior" or "special warrior" in Alaqotim.

Manandantan (*mahn·ahn·DAHN·tahn*) – the festival to celebrate the goddess Danta, goddess of song.

Marla Shrike – a graduate of the famed Hero Academy, an experienced combatant in both martial and magical disciplines.

Marn Tiscomb – the new Master of Prophecy at the Hero Academy. He replaced Master Aeid, who was murdered.

Mellafond (*MEH·la·fond*) – a large swamp on the main-land to the east of Munsahtiz Island. The name *means pit of Mellaine*.

Mellaine (*meh·LAYN*) – goddess of nature and growing things.

Miera Tannoch (*MEERA TAN·ahkh*) – Aeden's mother, wife of Sartan.

Migae (*MEE·jay*) – the God of magic. The word "magic" comes from his name.

Moroshi Katai (*mor·ROE·shee kah·TAI*) – a mythological hero who battled the Dragon of Eternity to found the nation of Teroshi.

Moschephis (*mose·CHE·feess*) – the trickster god, from whose name comes the word mischief.

Mudertis (*moo·DARE·teez*) – the god of thievery and assassination.

Munsahtiz (*moon·SAW·teez*) – the island in the Kanton sea on which the Hero Academy Sitor-Kanda resides.

Nanris – the unofficial capital of Kruzekstan, more important than the actual capital of Kruzeks because most of the wealth of the nation is centered in Nanris.

Nasir Kelqen (*nah·SEER KEL·ken*) – the Master of the School of Research and Investigation at the Hero Academy.

Osulin (*AWE·soo·lin*) – goddess of nature. She is the daughter of Mellaine and the human hero Trikus Phen.

Pach (*PAHKH*) – in Dantogyptain, it means five. As a proper noun, it refers to the festival of Manandantan that occurs every fifth year, a special celebration in which the Song of Prophecy is sung in full.

Pedras Shrike – Marla Shrike's adoptive father, the groundskeeper for the administrative area of the Hero Academy.

Percipius (*pare·CHIP·ee·us*) – god of the dead and of the underworld.

Phoenixarrow – one of the Falxen sent to kill Khrazhti and her companions. A statuesque red-haired archer who had a penchant for using fire arrows.

Pilae (*PEEL·lay*) – a type of animaru that looks like a ball of shadow.

Pofel Dessin (*POE·fell DESS·in*) – a traveling scholar who meets Marla and Evon on their journeys.

Pouran (*PORE·an*) – roundish, heavy humanoids with piggish faces and tusks like a boar

Praesturi (*prayz·TURE·ee*) – the town and former military outpost on the southeastern tip of the island of Munsahtiz. The south bridge from the mainland to the island ends within Praesturi.

Preshim (*PRAY·sheem*) – title of the leader of a family of Gypta

Promistala (*prome·ees·TAHL·ah*) – the main continent in Dizhelim. In Alaqotim, the name means "first (or most important) land."

Qozhel (*KOE·shell*) – the energy that pervades the universe and that is usable as magic.

Quentin Duzen – a Hero Academy graduate, the antagonist against Marla and Evon.

Qydus Okvius (*KIE·duss OCK·vee·us*) – the headmaster of the Hero Academy, Sitor-Kanda.

Raibrech (*RAI·brekh*) – the clan magic of the highland clans. In Chorain, it means "bloodfire."

Raisor Tannoch (*RAI·sore TAN·ahkh*) – a famous warrior of Clan Tannoch, companion of the hero Erent Caahs.

Raki Sinde (*ROCK·ee SINDH*) – grandson of Jehira Sinde, friend and training partner of Aeden.

Ren Kenata (*REN ke·NAH·tah*) – a Hero Academy adept who was is not only one of Quentin Duzen's associates, but also a member of the Dark Council.

Rhaltzheim (*RALTZ·haim*) – the nation to the northeast of the Grundenwald Forest. The people of the land are called Rhaltzen or sometimes Rhaltza. The term Rhaltzheim is often used to refer to the rugged land within the national borders (e.g., "traverse the Rhaltzheim")

Ritma Achaya (*REET·mah ah·CHAI·ah*) – Fahtin's mother, wife of the Gypta family leader Darun.

Roneus Lomos (*ROE·nee·us LOE·mose*) – the Master of the School of Stealth at the Hero Academy.

Ruthrin (*ROOTH·rin*) – the common tongue of Dizhelim, the language virtually everyone in the world speaks in addition to their own national languages.

S'ru (*SROO*) – the dark god of the animaru, supreme power in Aruzhelim.

Saelihn Valdove (*SAY·lin VAHL·doe·vay*) – the Master of the School of Life Magic at the Hero Academy.

Salamus (*sah·lah·MOOS*) – an ancient nation in which the legendary hero Trikus Phen resided. It no longer exists. Things of Salamus were called Salaman.

Sartan Tannoch (*SAR·tan TAN·ahkh*) – Aeden's father, clan chief of the Tannoch clan of Craogh.

Sastiroz (*SASS·teer·oz*) – an animaru lord, one of Kirraloth's two main commanders.

Satta Sarak (*SAH·tah SARE·ack*) – a city in the south-eastern part of the continent of Promistala, part of the Saraki Principality.

Semhominus (*sem·HOM·in·us*) – one of the highest level of animaru. They are humanoid, larger than a typical human, and use weapons. Many of them can also use magic. Most animaru lords are of this type.

Senna Shrike – Marla Shrike's adoptive mother.

Seren (*SARE·en*) – the most common type of animaru, with sharp teeth and claws. They are similar in shape and size to humans.

Shadeglide – one of the Falxen sent to kill Khrazhti and her companions. She is small of stature but extremely skilled as a thief and assassin.

Shadowed Pinnacles – the long mountain range essentially splitting the western part of Promistala into two parts. It was formerly known as the Wall of Salamus because it separated that kingdom from Gentason.

Shaku (*SHOCK·oo*) – a class of Teroshimi assassins.

Shanaera Eilren (*shah·NARE·ah ALE·ren*) – the Master of Unarmed Combat at the Hero Academy.

Shinyan (*SHEEN·yahn*) – a nation on the northern tip of the western part of Promistala, bordering the Kanton Sea and the Cattilan Sea. Things of Shinyan (such as people) are referred to as Shinyin.

Shu root/Shu's Bite (*SHOO*) – a root that only grows in Shinyan, the key ingredient to the poison Shu's Bite.

Sike (*SEEK·ay*) – a class of Shinyin assassins

Sintrovis (*seen·TROE·vees*) – an area of high magical power on which the Great Enclave was built. In Alaqotim, it means *center of strength*.

Sirak Isayu (*SEER·ack ee·SAI·yoo*) – a member of the Dark Council. He comes from the southern part of the continent of Promistala, near the Sittingham Desert.

Sitor-Kanda (*SEE·tor KAN·dah*) – the Hero Academy, the institution created by the great prophet Tsosin Ruus to train the Malatirsay. The name means roughly "home of magic" in Alaqotim.

Sittingham Desert – a large desert in the southwestern part of Promistala.

Skril Tossin – best friend of Marla Shrike and Evon Desconce, a Hero Academy adept.

Snowmane – the horse the Academy lent to Aeden, a chestnut stallion with a white mane

Solon (*SEW·lahn*) – one of the masters in Clan Tannoch, responsible for training young warriors how to use the clan magic, the Raibrech.

Srantorna (*sran·TORN·ah*) – the abode of the gods, a place where humans cannot go.

Surefoot – Marla Shrike's horse.

Surus (*SOO·roos*) – king of the gods.

Sutania (*soo·TAN·ee·ah*) – the nation south of the Kanton Sea, the capital of which is the city of Arcusheim.

Suuksis (*SOOK·sis*) – an animaru lord; Khrazhti's father.

Taron Gennelis (*TARE·un jeh·NELL·iss*) – one of the adepts at the Hero Academy who volunteered to aid in the investigation of Master Aeid's murder.

Tarshuk (*TAR·shuk*) – a semi-desert-like area to the

southwest of the Heaven's Teeth range that has stunted trees and scrub.

Tazi Ermengo (*TAH·zee air·MANE·go*) – the king of the doomed kingdom of Awresea. He taunted the god Fyorio and was destroyed along with his entire kingdom, which was renamed Fyrefall.

Tere Chizzit (*TEER CHIZ·it*) – a blind archer and tracker with the ability to see despite having no working eyes. He is Aeden's companion in the story.

Teroshi (*tare·OH·shee*) – an island nation in the northern part of Dizhelim. Things of Teroshi, including people, are referred to as Teroshimi.

Thalia Fendove (*THA·lee·uh FEN·doe·vay*) – a member of the Dark Council.

Thomasinus, son of Daven (*toe·mah·SINE·us*) – the hero who banded the remnants of the troops of Gentason together to create the Great Enclave. Once they elected him king, he changed his last name to Davenson.

Thomlin Byrch (*TOM·lin BIRCH*) – a member of the Dark Council.

Thritur Nyhus (*THRY·tur NY·hus*) – a member of the Dark Council.

Tildus Uworn (*TIL·duss YOO·worn*) – a Hero Academy adept, one of Quentin Duzen's associates.

Toan Broos (*TOE·aan*) – traveling companion of Erent Caahs and Raisor Tannoch.

Toras Geint (*TOR·ahs GAYNT*) – an old tracker and scout who befriended Erent Caahs when he was a boy and who mentored the young hero, training him to track and hunt, among other things.

Trikus Phen (*TRY·kus FEN*) – a legendary hero who battled Codaghan, the god of war, himself, and sired Osulin by the goddess Mellaine.

Tsosin Ruus (*TSO·sin ROOS*) – the Prophet, the seer and archmage who penned the Song of Prophecy and founded Sitor-Kanda, the Hero Academy.

Tuach (*TOO·akh*) – one of the masters in Clan Tannoch, responsible for teaching the young warriors the art of physical combat.

Tufa Shao (*TOO·fah SHA·oh*) – the Master of the School of Body Mechanics and Movement at the Hero Academy.

Tukra (*TOOK·rah*) – an ancient magical being whose responsibility was to guard a door in the tunnels of Valcordinae.

Ulfaris Triban (*ool·FARE·iss TRY·ban*) – a Hero Academy graduate, companion to Izhrod Benzal

Urtumbrus (*oor·TOOM·brus*) – a type of animaru that are essentially living shadows.

Urun Chinowa (*OO·run CHIN·oh·wah*) – the High Priest of the goddess Osulin, a nature priest.

Vaeril Faequin (*VARE·ill FAY·kwin*) – the Master of the School of Mechanista Artifice at the Hero Academy.

Valcordinae (*val·COR·di·nay*) – a series of extremely ancient tunnels with a well of magical power at its core. The word is ancient Alaqotim for *strong minds*.

Vanda (*VAHN·dah*) – a modern god, claimed by his followers to be the only true god. It is said he is many gods in one, having different manifestations. The Church of Vanda is very large and very powerful in Dizhelim.

Vatheca (*VATH·ay·kuh*) – the headquarters and training center of the Falxen. It is a mixture of two Alaqotim words, both meaning "sheath."

Vincus (pl. vinci) (*VEEN·cuss; VEEN·chee*) – Aila's chain blade weapons.

Viro/Vira (pl viri) (*VEER·oh / VEER·ah / VEER·ee*) – a former Hero Academy student who has graduated with a mastery in at least three schools and no longer lives at the Academy or participates in its function.

Vituma (*vi·TOO·mah*) – the leader of the Dark Council. The name derives from the ancient Alaqotim term for *prophet's shadow*.

Voordim (*VOOR·deem*) – the pantheon of gods in Dizhelim. It does not include the modern god Vanda.

Vulmer Liadin (*VUL·mer LEE·uh·din*) – the first headmaster of the Hero Academy, appointed by Tsosin Ruus himself to run the school for the Prophet.

Wolfen – large intelligent wolves that roam desolate areas in the Rhaltzheim.

Wolfen's Rest – the inn in Dartford, on the mainlaind not too far east from the bridge to the island of Munsahtiz.

Xadorn Deleer (*ZAH·dorn de·LEER*) – one of the Power Twins, rogue mages killed by the hero Zejo Troufal in the city of Drachvorden just after the War of Magic ended.

Yoniko Takesi (*YOE·nee·koe tah·KAY·see*) – a member of the Dark Council.

Yxna Hagenai (*IX·nah HAG·en·eye*) – the Master of Edged Weapons at the Hero Academy.

Zejo Troufal (*ZAY·joe TROO·fahl*) – a hero who lived at the end of the Age of Magic. He was Erent Cahhs's idol when he was a boy, before he himself became a hero.

LETTER TO THE READER

Dear Reader,

The Hero Academy series is off to a rousing start. If you were with me from the beginning of the stories in Dizhelim (Wanderer's Song, the first book of the Song of Prophecy series), this is likely the sixth book you've read in that world. Still, this is just the start. I've already got two other books in the series finished as I write this and a third is well under way. There's a lot of story still to tell.

Are you enjoying the different flavor of the Hero Academy books compared to the Song of Prophecy series? I tried something different with this series, as befits a very high book count for the total series. I hope you like it.

Thank you for reading this story. I have a lot of books out, some of which are free to my PEP Talk newsletter subscribers. If you'd like news about what might be coming up next and want to try out some of the books to see if you like the stories and the worlds they're in, you can join by going to my website at https://pepadilla.com.

Happy reading. I hope you join me in future books and series.

P.E. Padilla

AUTHOR NOTES

The Song of Prophecy and Hero Academy series were part of an experiment of sorts. From the summer of 2020 through to January 2021, I planned to launch seven books in seven months. Granted, some authors do that consistently, month after month, for long periods of time.

Seven months was enough for me. Actually, I can't really speak of it in the past tense because at this point, I have two more books yet to complete. By "complete," I mean that I need to get them edited and get the cover art for them. They're both written already.

As I was saying, launching a book a month for seven months is quite a chore. With cover art, self-editing, editing by a professional editor, formatting, glossaries, maps, and a myriad of other tasks, any little thing that goes wrong can immediately mess up the schedule. I'm glad to be coming to the last couple of books for the seven-month period.

While I still plan on releasing books regularly, I probably won't do one per month long-term. I think that's good anyway because many of my readers are behind even with the seven books. Since the series is epic fantasy, the books usually weigh in at a heftier page count than many other genres, so it takes more people a while to read them (though some blast their way through them so quickly it simply amazes me).

I'm looking forward to launching several more Hero Academy books in the coming year, but I'll also probably release some books in at least one other series. I will not let the other series stop me from launching in the HA series, however. There are few things that irritate me more than when an author has a good series going and then they stop launching in the series to start another one. There are at least four authors I'm waiting on right now to put more books out in a series I love, yet they started new series and the other one simply lies stagnant.

I will not do that. I already know what will happen in the HA series start to finish, so there's no need for me to delay. Even working on other projects, this series will be the priority. That's good because with the number of books in the Hero Academy series, it'll take several years to finish, even writing at full speed and expending most of my effort on these books.

I recently discovered the X-Ray function of the Kindle and have been working on incorporating the glossaries I always include with my epic fantasy books into it. It's slow going, but once I bake it into my normal launch process (instead of trying to catch up on earlier books), I should get to the point where I've got it all done before launch. I'm not sure how many people use X-Ray, but it's there in case they do. It's a handy feature I've appreciated in some of the books I've read.

That's about all I have to say for now. I've not quite hit my stride with the books I released this year, but soon, things will hum along smoothly and before anyone knows it, the Hero Academy series will be finished and I'll be writing in a different one. It's exciting to think about and I can't wait to make it happen.

ABOUT THE AUTHOR

A chemical engineer by degree and at various times an air quality engineer, a process control engineer, and a regulatory specialist by vocation, USA Today bestselling author P.E. Padilla learned long ago that crunching numbers and designing solutions was not enough to satisfy his creative urges. Weaned on classic science fiction and fantasy stories from authors as diverse as Heinlein, Tolkien, and Jordan, and affected by his love of role playing games such as Dungeons and Dragons (analog) and Final Fantasy (digital), he sometimes has trouble distinguishing reality from fantasy. While not ideal for a person who needs to function in modern society, it's the perfect state of mind for a writer. He is a recent transplant from Southern California to Northern Washington, where he lives surrounded by trees.

pepadilla.com/
pep@pepadilla.com

ALSO BY P.E. PADILLA

Adventures in Gythe:

Vibrations: Harmonic Magic Book 1 (audiobook also)

Harmonics: Harmonic Magic Book 2 (audiobook also)

Resonance: Harmonic Magic Book 3

Tales of Gythe: Gray Man Rising (audiobook also available)

Harmonic Magic Series Boxed Set

The Unlikely Hero Series (under pen name Eric Padilla):

Unfurled: Heroing is a Tough Gig (Unlikely Hero Series Book 1) (also available as an audiobook)

Unmasked (Unlikely Hero Series Book 2)

Undaunted (Unlikely Hero Series Book 3)

The Shadowling Chronicles (under pen name Eric Padilla):

Shadowling (Book 1)

Witches of the Elements Series :

Water & Flame (Book 1)

Song of Prophecy Series :

Wanderer's Song

Warrior's Song (this book)

Heroes' Song

Hero Academy Series :

Hero Dawning

Hero's Mind (this book)

Hero's Nature

Tales of Dizhelim (companion stories to the SoP and HA Series):

Arrow's Flight

Song's Prophet

Order of the Fire Series:

Call of Fire

Hero of Fire

Legacy of Fire

Order of the Fire Boxed Set

Made in the USA
Las Vegas, NV
08 June 2021

24383678R00215